STRIKEOUT

Baseball, Broadway and the
Brotherhood in the 19th Century

STRIKEOUT

Baseball, Broadway and the
Brotherhood in the 19th Century

James Hawking

SUNSTONE
PRESS

SANTA FE

Sunstone books may be purchased for educational, business, or sales promotional use.
For information please write: Special Markets Department, Sunstone Press,
P.O. Box 2321, Santa Fe, New Mexico 87504-2321.

Book and Cover design ›Vicki Ahl
Body typeface › Constantia
Printed on acid-free paper

Library of Congress Cataloging-in-Publication Data

Hawking, James, 1946-
  Strikeout : baseball, Broadway and the brotherhood in the 19th century / by
James Hawking.
       p. cm.
  ISBN 978-0-86534-864-6 (softcover : alk. paper)
  1. Baseball--United States--History--19th century--Fiction. 2. Baseball
stories. I. Title.
  PS3608.A8925S77 2012
  813'.6--dc23
                              2012001095

WWW.SUNSTONEPRESS.COM
SUNSTONE PRESS / POST OFFICE BOX 2321 / SANTA FE, NM 87504-2321 /USA
(505) 988-4418 / ORDERS ONLY (800) 243-5644 / FAX (505) 988-1025

To Judy and Pat

Each of whom drove me to Cooperstown

CONTENTS

Preface

This book is divided into threes: three "parts" and then into groups of three chapters. The first of each group of three chapters takes place on the field and in the stands of a baseball game played long ago. The second chapter in each group concerns the personal lives of some of the players. The third chapter in each group relates to the business of baseball and the players' union. The cycle is then repeated. Thus this book is organized like a well-adjusted American life—one third baseball, one third family, and one-third earning a living.

For those wanting to know more about the players or other baseball figures featured in each chapter, there is a section of biographies at the end of the book, numbered 1-54 corresponding to the chapters and the character featured in each chapter. Likewise, for those who are interested in a comparison between baseball at the period of the book and baseball now, there is a section called Baseball Then and Now, also numbered 1-54 and corresponding to points raised in each chapter. These sections may be read after each chapter or as a whole at the end of the books.

Acknowledgments

I would like to thank John Thorn and Gary Mitchem for their encouragement in the early stages of this project, David Nemec for his helpful suggestions and insights, and David Stevens for sharing his expertise on John Ward and Tim Keefe. Peter Mancuso, chairman of the 19th Century Committee of SABR shared his knowledge of 19th Century baseball, and Don Jensen shared his considerable knowledge of Helen Dauvray and the theater world of her time. J. Thomas Hetrick gave me some helpful suggestions, and Tim Wiles and Freddy Berkowski of the A. Bartlett Giamatti Research Center of the National Baseball Hall of Fame assisted my research by maintaining a superb collection of baseball history. Drucilla Ronchen shared her expertise on American Sign Language and the deaf community throughout history. A special thanks to Sarah Johnson of *Historical Novels Review* for her knowledge and support. My son Spike Hawking listened to me patiently through all phases of the writing and research.

Part One
Baseball's Greatest Tour

The Championship
Sportsman's Park, St. Louis
October 25, 1888

John Montgomery Ward stood tapping his foot on first base, confident that the six run rally in the top half of the ninth inning had assured the New York Giants of winning the World's Championship Series and the Dauvray Cup that went to the victor. Immediately after the deciding game, Ward would collect his wife and catch up with Albert Spalding's Australian tour. Now, with the score 11-3 and the victory safely in hand, Ward had one last chance to talk to players on the American Association St. Louis Browns about solidarity with the Brotherhood of Professional Base Ball Players in the event that the National League forced the players into a strike. Most particularly, Ward wanted to talk to the Browns' first baseman-captain, Charles Comiskey. Ward got his chance when Orator Jim O'Rourke fouled the first pitch into the stands. A small red-headed boy darted into the specially priced $1.50 seats to pilfer the ball, and Owner Chris Von der Ahe's security force set out after him.

"I sure wish you were heading out West with me, Charlie. My All-Americas could use you at first base."

"With the money I'm dropping on this series, I'll need a good offseason barnstorming to cover my losses. Maybe your boys won't try so hard in the next two games, now that you've won your *Dauvray* Cup."

"Will Chris share his series money with you boys?" Ward asked, shifting from his role as base runner into his job as a union president eager to expand his membership. Technically many of the American Association players were members, but they did not participate beyond paying their dues, if that. If there was ever going to be a strike, the National League would go looking for players in the affectionately named "Beer and Whiskey League." Ward thought he would need American Association solidarity, and there was no more important figure in the Association than Comiskey.

"Chris treats us well enough. He spent $20,000 on our train to New York, everything first class. Lobsters, champagne, caviar, reserved Pullman cars."

"Wouldn't you like to move back to Chicago, Charlie?"

"I'd never want to work for Spalding and Anson. You'll have had enough of them by the end of your tour."

"Maybe something will work out for you to get back to Chicago, Charlie."

The boy managed to elude the security guards and blend into the crowd of ball-goers leaving the park. On his way out, he tripped over a character who will appear whenever there is a ball game. Ken Courtney, hereafter to be referred to as K.C. which also stands for Knowledgeable Crank, is always there to share his stock of information about the doings of the baseballists of the day, ranging from the latest rumors to solid statistical reports. Many might regret that such a keen intellect should be applied to the meager matter of a boy's game, but that would not be fair. In all probability, K.C. would not have learned to read if not for the daily sports page, and he certainly took no interest in decimals until Henry Chadwick promoted the idea of batting average. The only use K.C. had ever found for trigonometry was to calculate the distance of the throw to second base.

"One hundred twenty-seven feet and Buck Ewing throws it straight to where the base runner will arrive. It was Buck who beat these Browns, not just today with his home run in the first and his triple-bagger in . . . (A brief glance at the scorecard confirmed his memory) the third with the bases loaded. But mostly the way he kept the Browns from running."

On this day K.C. was accompanied by his wife who has indulged his baseball mania in exchange for a promise that after they followed the ballplayers to Australia, they would leave from there to Paris. They were both enjoying the idleness and the affluence that came from selling his gas lamp business.

"The newspapers say that Mr. Ward and his wife are also planning to go to Paris after the tour finishes in Australia."

K. C. went on as if he had not heard her.

"St. Louis stole the game yesterday because Buck's hands were too sore to catch. But now Buck sits back there with his fancy new mitt that has more and more padding sewn into it every time I see him. Nothing gets past him, and if they try to steal, he throws them out. Sometimes he lets the ball get past him a little on purpose to trick them into trying. For this series, Ewing's the best catcher, the best player, and much as I hate to admit it, maybe even the best captain. Johnny Ward's still my favorite, though."

"I prefer Mr. Ward, dear. He's so handsome with his sandy hair, trim little moustache and those pale blue eyes. Not to mention that he's refined and Columbia-educated and married to the best actress on Broadway. You've always told me that Mr. Ward was your favorite."

"He still is, but this series belongs to Buck. Look, they're giving up on catching the kid with the ball, and they're finally taking a brand new Spalding out of its red box."

With the first pitch after the resumption of play, Ward decided to set out for second base. In spite of his having read the pitcher well, the throw beat him to the bag, but Ward executed a perfect slide, bending his left leg away from the tag while his right leg reached around the baseman to allow him to touch the cushion with his big toe. Comiskey unleashed all his stored rage and suppressed vocabulary in a five minute tirade at the umpire. Ward used the time to introduce himself to second baseman Yank Robinson, widely known to be discontented with management and a natural member for the union.

"Do you think Chris is going to share any of the money he's taking in on this series?" Ward began, hoping to find a sore spot.

"Ain't so much the money as the dignity. Now me, I can't stand sleeping in no Pullman car, so I stay up all night when we're on the train, or I sleep in a chair. Old Chris comes by and fines me. And he always yells that my uniform is too dirty. I have to buy four because my weight goes up and down, and the dry cleaning eats up most of my salary with the fines taking whatever's left. Chris says I'm a drunk, but it's all I can do to buy the cheapest rotgut. They're paying Comiskey big money for saying that he uses Merrell's Penetrating Oil and putting his picture on the bottle. Did you ever hear of such a thing? And the fines! For everything. Smoking. Spitting. Swearing. Showing up drunk. Any little thing. I miss Curt Welch. He used to keep a barrel of beer on ice in centerfield, and we could have a cold draft during a holiday doubleheader. Look at Charlie go. He's gonna keep yellin' until he forgets how much money he's losin.'"

"Mr. Comiskey seems unusually enraged at the umpires today," observed K.C.'s wife.

"Charlie just knows the series is over even though they still have two games to play. And we can head out to Denver. I've been looking at train schedules, and I think we can catch up with the Spalding tour there."

"Fine, but from now on, you can just go to the games alone. I know you can't understand this, but I've had enough of baseball for a while."

After Comiskey had yelled himself hoarse, Ward took advantage of a passed ball to take third where he encountered Arlie Latham, known to the newspapers as "the freshest man on earth."

"Yank tells me Chris hasn't been fair with you boys."

"Vat for should I be paying the shtupid ballplayers."

At the mention of the owner's name, Latham automatically launched into his well-practiced imitation of the German brewer who owned the team. The Browns third baseman would have liked to put on his fake moustache and derby hat to complete the impression, but that would come after the game when he was entertaining the boys in the pool hall.

"Yank says he doesn't give you dignity."

"He can keep his dignity. The cheapskate doesn't give us money. Look at this place. Tickets for fifty cents, some of 'em for $1.50, and all the watered beer he can sell at downtown prices. Johnny, the Association boys will be 100% with the Brotherhood. Let me organize them, and we'll strike whenever you give us the word. I'll get you every player on this team, and the rest of the Association will follow behind us, just like they do in the standings."

"Maybe you could put together a list of sympathetic players to give to Tim Keefe. He's the secretary-treasurer. I'll be out of the country most of the winter."

"So it's true that you won't be here tomorrow, and that young fastball pitcher Cannonball Crane is going with you? Maybe there's still money to be made betting this series."

The inning ended and Ward walked out to his shortstop position, but there wasn't much to do. Tim Keefe continued to pitch with his uncanny ability to mix speeds without giving any tips to the batter and his baffling assortment of curves, including one of his own invention that didn't seem to spin at all but just dropped to the batter's feet. The last striker of the day lifted an easy fly to O'Rourke who trotted into the infield with the ball.

"Now I must fulfill my obligation to the trophy's eponym and deliver her husband to her in time to join the tourists for their trip across the Pacific."

Keefe agreed.

"We can't have him pulling a Johnny Ward."

In the private language of the New York Giants, tardiness was referred to as a "Johnny Ward," owing to the unpunctual habits the shortstop had developed while rushing between Columbia University and the Polo Grounds. That was why O'Rourke was entrusted with the mission of delivering Ward to his wife in time for the departure of their train.

The Trophy
Planter's Hotel, St, Louis
October 25, 1888

For Helen Dauvray the final stage of packing for any trip was brushing her hair. As she sat across from a dressing table mirror, she assessed herself as a theatrical producer might do when looking over an actress, which she was well-qualified to do, being both.

"Dark brown hair which the stage lights pick up as black. Black eyes, expressive and easily made up to be visible beyond the first few rows. Tiny white hands which show up best against dark clothing. Upturned nose and round cheeks. Round everywhere. Spherical bosoms and below those, rounded hips. Just like the girl next door or the minister's mischievous daughter."

She sighed as she recognized her strengths and her weaknesses. Although she made a perfect star as Kate Shipley in "One of Our Girls," she would never be able to waste away from tuberculosis as Camille, nor would she age into Phèdre. But what had made Helen an accomplished actress was not her looks so much as her voice, and not even her voice so much as her ear. After a few hours of listening to the music of a new accent or dialect or even a foreign language, she was able to imitate the tones and express a full range of emotions, whether in Mexican Spanish, Australian English or Parisian French. Today she and John would probably be leaving on a tour that would take her back to places she remembered. The first stop would be Denver where she had made plans to buy some downtown property and to see a performance at the Tabor Grand Opera House. Then the tour would head to San Francisco where the theater community was almost as interesting and lively as New York's. After that, she was looking forward to Australia where as banjo-playing Little Nell, the California Diamond, she had touched the hearts of a whole continent, earning enough money to provide the foundation for her multi-million dollar fortune and her consequent independence. Then the other baseballists would sail back to the states while she and John would keep going west to Paris. Her friends there would meet her elegant and handsome husband who spoke perfect grammatical French, albeit with an unapologetic American accent. Then they would go to Paris where the city was preparing for *l'Exposition Universelle* (The Universal Exposition) celebrating the centennial of the fall of the Bastille. They would finally have the *lune de miel* (honeymoon) that she had been too ill to enjoy the year before when they had married. Johnny would be free from baseball until April.

A knock on the door made her think her husband was back, but it was her sister, Mrs. Clara Helms, wearing bloomers and a characteristic scowl. Very few women could remain beautiful with such a twisted face, but Clara was one of those few. High cheekbones, large green eyes and a womanly figure that showed through her tomboy clothing gave her a kind of beauty that was impossible to conceal. As a sculptress working all day in a studio, she gave much less thought to her appearance than Helen did. Clara kept her hair short and easy to manage and selected her clothing for comfort. Back in New York, she was usually covered with a layer of marble dust and yet, on first seeing Clara, Helen's friends and acquaintances almost universally commented on her striking appearance, some even making explicit what others merely implied.

"Considering that you're the actress, it's quite a surprise to see how much prettier your sister is."

In spite of this, Helen had always loved and nurtured her younger sister. The gap in years between them had been considerable at first, but Helen had started lying her age downward when she was eight and performing as a five year old and had continued to make adjustments until Clara and she were about the same age. Helen had secretly subsidized Clara's career as a sculptress by buying paintings from gallery owners who agreed to use some of the proceeds to buy Clara's statues. Helen had even managed to do this without losing money by reselling several of the paintings at a profit when the time was right. In this and many other areas, Helen had a sense of fashion and the ability to sense imminent shifts in taste before the rest of the market.

Things had started to be confused when Clara had invested some of her earnings in Helen's theatrical company, Dauvray Productions. Helen used this stock to subsidize her sister, whimsically declaring dividends whenever she saw that Clara needed money. But Helen had not opened a new play in over a year, one of the many things for which Clara blamed Ward.

Clara's impending divorce was endangering Helen's investments. A double mansion on Park Avenue and an extensive jewelry collection belonged to Dauvray Productions, a fact that Clara's loathsome estranged husband might use if he obtained Clara's share of the company, which he would be able to do if he won a divorce in New York where adultery was the only grounds recognized, and the property laws all favored the husband if the wife was at fault. Helen wanted some guarantee to protect her assets from Mr. Helms and his lawyers.

"Just remember, Clara, your husband has probably hired Pinkertons who would like nothing better than to catch you in a compromising position. People are quick to believe the worst of artists and their bohemian friends, so just be as careful as possible until your divorce is final."

"Don't worry about my divorce, sister. You should be working on divorcing your philandering husband."

"Johnny is no such thing."

"Then why did an angry husband chase him around the Polo Grounds?"

"It was all a misunderstanding."

"And that's not the worst of it. He claims he's a suffragist, but he resents that his wife is a successful businesswoman. And he makes snide comments about my bloomers. And I think he tells stories about me to the other baseball players."

"I'm sure he does no such thing. And please remember that he is my husband, and we are about to embark on our long-awaited *lune de miel*."

"Some honeymoon. You'll be running halfway around the world with a bunch of drunken baseball players, just like last year in New Orleans."

Clara was alluding to the year before when Ward and King Kelly had been barnstorming in New Orleans. Helen's plans for a romantic evening speaking only French in the French Quarter had been ruined when an inebriated Kelly had climbed into a carriage with John and Helen.

"According to the newspapers, Mr. Kelly has yet to join the tour, so that should make them all a little more sober."

After a few more minutes of similar exchanges, there was another knock on the hotel suite door. This time it was Jim O'Rourke in his muddy Giants uniform.

"Mrs. Ward, I return your husband intact, triumphant and uncharacteristically punctual. When he finishes accepting the maledictions of the cabman who lost his ill-considered wager on the Browns, Johnny will be here to complete his ablutions and begin your circumnavigation."

"So the Giants have won the Dauvray Cup?" asked Clara, who had never understood why the corporation had wasted $500 on sponsoring such a thing.

"Eleven times did a Giant foot touch home plate, while the gallant Sir Timothy limited the dejected Browns to three sorry consolation tallies. Captain Ewing's hard throws retired all potential base embezzlers, and Johnny's play would have resulted in a chorus of appreciative song had we been playing at home."

Ward entered the room, dustier than O'Rourke but somewhat less muddy.

"I'll be glad to get out of this thing until April. For the next few months I'll be wearing the fashionable All-America uniforms designed by my loving wife."

Clara had not been impressed with Helen's design, and she liked the current Giant uniforms even less.

"You men need some uniforms that show that you really are men, not those loose baggy things that hang off you. The Giants should have something that shows off their Giant muscles, not you so much, Johnny, but the others."

Comiskey and Von der Ahe had graciously arranged a ceremony to award the Dauvray Cup to this year's World's Champion New York Giants. Buck Ewing accepted the trophy for the Giants, and Clara said a few words on behalf of her sister and Dauvray Productions. After she had finished talking, she was surprised to be approached by Tim Keefe. Ordinarily Sir Timothy would have been too shy to initiate a conversation with a woman he barely knew, but he was accidentally encouraged by something Ward had said. Keefe had remarked, as everyone did, on how strikingly beautiful Clara was, and Ward had responded with an attempt to be discouraging.

"I think she has her eye on you. Don't be fooled by how sweet she looks. Just remember that my sister-in-law is malevolent and spiteful. Besides, for all the talk of divorce, she is still married, and I sincerely hope that someday she moves back in with her unfortunate husband."

Ward's remarks had the opposite of the intended effect.

"If she has her eye on me maybe I should talk to her," Keefe decided. He was trying to work up the nerve to approach her when she addressed him.

"Why did you not accompany my brother-in-law and the tourists to Australia, Mr. Keefe?" she asked to begin the conversation.

"Business with the Brotherhood will keep me in New York part of the winter, especially with Johnny out of the country, Mrs. Helms."

"Please don't call me that. I wish now that I had followed Lucy Stone's example and kept my own name when I married. I hope that doesn't shock you. Are you a suffragist, Mr. Keefe?"

Because she felt herself attracted to this tall, muscular athlete, she decided to ask him the question she eventually asked every man, until now always eliciting a disappointing response. Most said that they supported the idea of women's voting, but they usually qualified it with some remark about gradualism or requiring a husband's permission or limiting the franchise to female heads of households. Keefe only laughed.

"My two sisters are both for Cleveland's re-election, which means that I have to vote for him. The three of us agreed that if the two of them both favored a candidate, I'd cast our vote for him. I only get to choose if there's a disagreement between my sisters. It usually works out all right because they both know a lot more about who should be in the legislature or who should be mayor. So I'll be busy keeping an eye on the baseball owners when they try to cheat the Brotherhood, not to mention negotiating my own contract. Other than going back to Cambridge to vote, I suppose I'll be in New York most of the winter."

"What an original man," Clara thought to herself, "and how handsome!"

She pulled a calling card out of her purse and handed it to Keefe.

"As long as you are going to be in New York for most of the winter, Mr. Keefe, you might come by my studio and be my model for a statue. And please call me Clara."

The Travel
Rocky Mountains
October 26, 1888

Albert Goodwill Spalding was using the diner on the CB & Q train to serve as a makeshift counting room, enabling him to total his sacks of dollars, half-dollars, quarters and small change just before the train began its ascent into the mountains. Spalding was preparing to make a substantial deposit when they reached Denver, and, better still, he had held down expenses on the U.S. leg of the tour. Opening in Chicago had been a success because the cranks came out to watch Spalding pitch for the first time in eleven years. In St. Paul a crowd turned out after seeing Mike Kelly's picture on placards advertising the game. Kelly, the only player Spalding had agreed to pay, had never showed up. The substitute catcher had struck out five times, and the cranks gradually noticed they had been cheated. In Iowa Anson's family alone had sold enough tickets to cover travel expenses. In Nebraska the White Stockings had reunited with last season's mascot Clarence Duval, a diminutive African-American whose plantation dances added to the pre-game excitement. Best of all, Duval was not costing Spalding anything because the White Stockings players had voted to pay the little fellow's expenses. Anson claimed that he had never forgiven the "little Zulu" for deserting the team, but the two had taken to spending time together and Duval could be seen swimming in the six foot Anson's hand-me-down sweaters.

By keeping expenses low and gate receipts from within the United States high, Spalding just might be able to realize his secret plan, known to no one else on the tour. He wanted to keep going west from Australia and play baseball in Asia, then Africa, then Europe, then the British Isles. Fourteen years before he had been part of a tour of England in a largely unsuccessful effort to promote baseball in Britain, but Spalding was confident that he could sell a new and improved brand of the sport to the previously reluctant British. Spalding's dream was nothing less than for baseball to conquer the world. Just as Alexander had taken Greek culture from West to East, Spalding was going to spread the virile values of baseball in the opposite direction. Some claimed that he was just trying to expand the markets for his sporting good company, partly true but not enough to justify the investment. Later it was suggested that he had hit upon a clever ruse to keep Johnny Ward out of the country while the owners imposed new restrictions on the players, also partly true, but again, only a secondary reason for the long trip.

Adrian Anson, the captain of the White Stockings, entered the dining car and dropped into the seat next to Spalding. Anson had put $3000 of his own money into the tour, but he was less concerned about the balance sheet than the behavior of his players.

"Yesterday they were up on top of the cars playing freight train baseball."

"What's that?"

"A game of catch on top of the cars until you lose all the balls you start with."

"And were they doing this drunk?"

"I'd hate to think a sober man would do such a thing. But the worst came when the All-Americas heard some wolves on the prairie and decided they could howl louder. They call themselves the Order of the Howling Wolves. Jimmy Fogarty is the ringleader. When they're not howling, they're painting each other black like in a nigger minstrel show. I'm tired of dealing with ballplayers that are even worse drunks than the micks I have on my team."

"Think how much drunker they'd be if Mike Kelly were here leading them. We all loved Kel, but he was inebriated more often than not, and he loved to spread his enthusiasm for drink. That's the reason I had to sell him."

"There were 10,000 other reasons you sold him, and if you want to be such a prohibitionist, why did we even invite him on the tour?"

"Why do we play this game, Adrian? To sell tickets. And no name sells more tickets than Mike Kelly's. Anyway, Ward has joined us now, so he should be able to get his All-Americas under control. And Cannonball Crane, the young pitcher he's bringing with him, is a boy Carrie Nation would be proud of. Never touched a drop. And Ward himself only drinks wine with meals."

"Wine with meals, you say. Won't the boys like to see that in the hotel dining room!"

"He won't be staying at the same hotel as the team. Mrs. Ward wants to visit some of her old friends, and they plan to see an opera while they're in Denver."

Spalding said this in a neutral tone, but he was trying to provoke Anson. He enjoyed his captain's hostility to Ward.

"Too good for a hotel with the boys, and going to the opera too! He's an aristocrat and a communist and an anarchist. The Brotherhood is nothing but a labor union like the bomb throwers from Haymarket. Why would you have him on the tour?"

"Isn't it better to keep an eye on him?"

Anson didn't seem to hear him, and he went on enumerating Ward's faults.

"And he speaks French in public. A singles hitter. And not many singles. He hit .251 this last year. And he's a lawyer—a lawyer! He tried to sneak in colored players like George Stovey and that Fleetwood Walker. He probably wants the league to get rid of all its principles. Admit Africans. Play ball on Sunday. Sell beer. Charge a quarter."

Spalding himself had no particular objection to colored players, had often wished for Sunday ball and sighed with envy over the profits American Association owners made by selling cheap beer at inflated prices, but charging any admission less than fifty cents would be an inexcusable retreat.

Anson went on.

"And why are Ward and his bunch called the All-Americas? We're all Americans, too."

"Do you want to wear the silk scarves and flag patterns that Mrs. Ward designed? We could switch names."

Anson pretended not to hear this.

"I never liked Ward, Al. Not when he was a sneaky kid with Janesville pitching for a local team and shutting us out in an exhibition game."

"Actually we scored three runs in the first two innings, but then he shut us out the rest of the way. He was seventeen."

"You have a good memory, Al."

"Not really. Ward reminded me of it, and I had Chadwick look up the box score. Ward was right."

"I remember. Sneaky pitching with his back turned and running up. They don't allow that kind of unmanly tossing any more, and that's a good thing."

Earlier in the day, John Tener had complained about sharing a berth with Fogarty and his endless chain of cigarettes. Tener was a White Stocking, but because of the odd number of players on the tour, one of them had to room with an All-America, and Tener was the lowest ranking White Stocking, both in terms of experience and value to the team.

"Have you been able to do anything about my berth, Mr. Spalding?"

"Yes, I have. You may share a berth with Mr. Ward, but for the most part, he will be sharing quarters with his wife. She took her own Pullman berth on the Galesburg car, and they will also be staying at a different hotel, so you will usually have the room to yourself. And if you do have to share a room, you will find that he is a sober, educated man. And as a personal favor, if you hear anything about the

Brotherhood, I'd appreciate it if you shared it with me. The more I know of their plans, the more we can make sure all the players are happy."

"The Brotherhood is a secret organization, Mr. Spalding."

"We know who belongs, but we just need to get an idea of what their complaints, if any, might be."

"Well, some of the boys are saying that if the league doesn't treat them right, they might go out on strike."

"No worries, then. The League always treats the boys right, not like in the old days. It frightens me how much money we're paying out to the players—$3000 a year or even more. The contracts are clearer and fairer today, thankfully. Let me know what you hear. I want you to be part of the team. And by the way, I'd like you to serve as treasurer for the tour. When we start going to other countries, we'll need to exchange our money and find out how to do the banking. It should give you good practical business experience."

Tener did not enjoy being put in the position of being a spy, but he did like that he would have his own room some of the time, and he knew enough about Ward to know that he would be a better roommate than Fogarty with his practical jokes. As Spalding had suggested, Ward was not sleeping in his assigned bed, so Tener had the room to himself until Ward came in shortly before midnight.

"Helen couldn't sleep with the train chugging uphill, so she remembered that Spalding had given me a berth too. I thought I'd be alone or at least with one of the boys from my team. I was hoping to talk over how the games were going, what the weaknesses of the Chicago team might be, things like that. But I couldn't ask you to be a spy."

"Spalding did."

"What do you mean?"

"He asked me to spy on the Brotherhood."

Ward thought for a second, then laughed.

"It means that Al is taking us seriously. What is it that he wants to know?"

"If the players are united and strong, or are they just weak blowhards."

"I wish I knew that too. So from what you're saying, I take it you're on our side in this."

"Is a Ballplayer a Chattel?"

Tener was quoting the title from Ward's article in *Lippincott's* the year before, the one in which he had challenged the owners' right to reserve players for life.

"So you're with us. Good. Tell Spalding the truth—the players are united and strong and if there's any funny business on the part of the owners, they'll see a strike. All the players are agreed."

"Is that the truth?"

"It will be."

"Is it true that Day is trying to sell you to Washington?"

"Not if I don't let him, and I doubt if I'll let him. I'll decide where I play next year myself."

"I wish I could play anywhere I like. I'd go home to Pittsburg."

"We all have our dreams. Comiskey wants to go to Chicago, but not with Spalding. Jim White wants to start his own minor league team in Buffalo. But for or now, I have to get ready for Denver. I won't be joining the boys for the Saturday game. I have some real estate business to finish and then I'll be ready for Sunday."

The Catch
River Front Park, Denver
October 28, 1888

"**C**ongratulations on beating Charlie Comiskey and winning that cup your wife designed."

"Why thank you, Adrian. I was just glad to help the National League win the World's Championship."

It was the top of the third inning, and Ward was the first base coacher. Because he had unsurprisingly arrived at the park late, this was his first chance to talk with his counterpart as team captain. Anson was the Brotherhood's fiercest opponent, but Ward always went out of his way to be pleasant to him. Ward hoped that someday even Anson would join the union and make their victory complete. Anson continued with his characteristic heavy-handed sarcasm.

" I'll bet the trophy is as pretty as your uniforms."

Ward was just getting used to wearing the uniform Helen had designed with a silk American flag scarf serving as a belt. He couldn't help feeling that his pants could fall down at any minute, revealing his jock strap and protective cup, which would be embarrassing for many reasons. Ward's own uniform and that of his pitcher Cannonball Crane were still fresh and cream-colored, but the rest of the All Americas were already showing a dingy gray.

"And your uniforms look pretty too, Adrian, with Chicago written across your chest in case you get lost overseas."

"Are we going to bet anything on the series, Johnny? A suit of clothes on each game, perhaps. I won't count the games that we've won already."

As a rule, Ward tried to avoid gambling, but he kidded his counterpart along.

"Not a fair bet, Adrian. I've seen those cheap checkered gabardine monstrosities you use to 'reward' your players for an especially good performance. And think how much material each of your suits takes while one of mine uses no more than one of your pocket handkerchiefs."

Shortstop Ed Williamson made two sparkling defensive plays in a row, one to his left that required a spinning throw and the next one deep in the hole to his right. In the bottom of the third, Anson lifted a sky ball that kept traveling to the right field fence until it bounced against the outfield wall. Anson gasped and wheezed all the way to third base where he collapsed in a heap. Before the inning was over, Chicago had a 3-0 lead.

Between innings, the celebrated equestrienne Myrtle Peek entertained the crowd with a performance that included progressively more difficult tricks at increasing speeds, followed by slowly and perfectly executed paces resembling a ballet performance. The western crowd appreciated her horsemanship more than anything that had happened on the field thus far.

K.C. had struck up a conversation with a wild-haired man who could have been anywhere from sixty to eighty, so he regretted his next remark as soon as he uttered it.

"The players look better today. Yesterday they were just horrible. They looked like a bunch of useless old men. Sorry for what that implies."

"That's all right. I know my playing days are over."

"They all look like they're a hundred years old."

"That's not just old age that makes Anson breathe hard. There's a scientific explanation. It's reduced atmospheric pressure and thinner air. It makes the ball go faster and the players go slower."

"Are you some kind of scientist?"

"A mining engineer, but back home in New York I studied physics and meteorology as well as geology. It's a fact that atmospheric pressure is less up here."

"Anson's hit was a corker. It traveled farther than I thought it would."

"That's what I've been telling you. And it's harder to breathe up here. That's why the game yesterday was so bad. Now the players are getting used to it. They had a lot of trouble yesterday."

"The *Rocky Mountain News* called it the worst game ever They had a cartoon of Anson feeding his players Chicago air. Now I understand why I got so out of breath climbing up to my seat. Look at that home run Tom Brown just hit to tie the game for the All Americas. It's the farthest I've ever seen, and he's famous for weak hits."

Down on the field, the game went back and forth as the players learned to adjust to their deoxygenated blood and the unnaturally rapid air currents. Cannonball Crane gave up his attempts to throw a curve ball in the thin atmosphere and eventually retired from the game completely. Ward consulted with Hanlon who had been managing in his absence. They brought in the reserve catcher to pitch which left them with an inexperienced man behind the plate.

"I'll be glad when Mike Kelly shows up," Ward said to Anson as the change was being made.

"You can forget about that, Johnnie. We've been leaving messages at every saloon in New York, and we can't find him."

"But Spalding has Kelly's picture all over the programs on the tour, even the ones he just printed for California."

"That's Spalding. Anyway, the cranks like to come out to shout 'Slide, Kelly, Slide.' But King Kelly won't be on the trip. We've been checking all the taverns in Boston too, but no one's seen him."

"So that leaves me without a first rate catcher and my best hitter. No wonder you wanted to bet."

By the sixth, the All-Americas had an 8-3 lead, but Chicago scored two in the bottom of that inning. In the Chicago seventh, Anson hit another long triple with two men on. This time he reached third base in slightly better condition. A base hit brought him home and tied the score at 8-8. In the eighth inning it seemed that the All-Americas were going to take the lead on a deep fly to center that looked like a sure four-bagger. Jimmy Ryan took off the moment the ball was hit and ran as fast as he could through the sandy footing. Keeping his eye on the ball all the way, he ran deep into right center field to catch the ball in the bare fingers that stuck out from his outstretched fielder's glove.

"Best catch I've ever seen," said the old mining engineer. "Ryan must have learned how to read the air currents here quickly. Yes, that was the best catch I've ever seen in nearly fifty years of playing and watching baseball. I was one of the boys who invented the game back home in Cooperstown. I still have the first ball we played with to prove it."

K.C. had talked about baseball with a lot of old timers, and some of them claimed memories that stretched back farther than fifty years ago, but his mother had always taught him to be polite. Besides, the old fellow had the kind of wild eyes and potentially violent manner that invited caution. In no way did K.C. want to get into a discussion of the origins of baseball. He would leave that to Ward who had written about it in his book, or Chadwick who had his own theories about rounders, or Spalding who wanted to prove that the game was completely American. K.C. was interested in what was happening in front of him.

"It was as good a catch as I've seen, and I've been coming to games a long time too."

Now with two out in the bottom of the ninth and a man on first, a Chicago batsman sent a long fly ball over the head of center fielder Ned Hanlon. It looked a sure bet to end the game, but Hanlon was as quick as Ryan had been to judge the path of the ball and immediately turned and ran with his back to home plate, never looking back. As he neared the ball, he had to run through a hill of sand kept in the deep outfield where it was thought no one would ever hit a ball. Hanlon seemed to lose his footing as he ran past the edge of the artificial hill, but like a dolphin coasting above the sea, he sailed forward parallel to the ground and reached out his ungloved right hand to secure the horsehide. The umpire had run far enough into the outfield to have a clear view, and he bellowed "out" emphatically. The game would continue into extra innings.

"And that catch was even better," the old mining engineer managed to say with what was left of his voice.

"Hanlon ran back to where he thought the ball would be without even looking at it. He uses every new trick."

In the tenth inning, Anson had a conference with his pitcher who then proceeded to throw five pitches wide of the plate as the catcher stepped out for each one.

"What's he doing?" asked the old engineer.

"It looks like he's walking him on purpose. He's afraid Brown will hit another home run."

"That seems cowardly."

K. C. agreed with this sentiment, but he knew that Ward had ordered batters walked on purpose when he was captain of the Giants.

"Ward only did it to set up double plays, not to avoid strong strikers."

In the eleventh inning, Ward came up with a man on third base and one out. On the first pitch, he seemed to attempt a bunt down the first base line, so Anson crept up closer. Ever since Ward had begun to hit left handed, bunting and fake bunting were his favorite tactics to bring home a run from third with less than two out, but he knew that he had to be unpredictable. With Anson drawn in, Ward brought the run home by slapping an easy ground ball past him. By the time the second baseman picked it up in short right field, Ward was racing past Anson who was stumbling back to first base. Ward was unable to score, but when he led his team back onto the field for the bottom of the eleventh, his leadership had been established. Without admitting it even to himself, he had missed being captain of the Giants ever since he had given the job back to Ewing, but it was probably just as well that he would be a captain only for the tour. He would have enough to do in the upcoming year. The one run lead held up through the bottom of the eleventh, and the All-Americas had won the first game with Ward in charge.

Denver's Monday newspapers paid tribute to what they called the greatest game ever played in the mountains, but the Sunday edition had denounced Spalding's travelers as frauds, and that was the story that was going to precede them heading west.

The Pre-Game
Colorado Springs and points west
October 29, 1888

The only favorable reports in the Sunday newspapers had been about Myrtle Peek, so Spalding decided to publicize their Colorado Springs game with a horseback excursion through the Garden of the Gods to Pike's Peak, assuming they would be back in time to play the game. Helen declined to go on the trip because she couldn't see how they could go there and back without hurrying everything, and she knew Johnny was not much good at hurrying except between bases.

"Come on, Helen. You won't even have to ride a horse. Aside from Myrtle Peek, the women will go in carriages, and only the men will ride," he had said to encourage her to come.

Growing up in the West, Helen had owned her first pony before she was five, and she had always spent part of her child star earnings on horses. In Paris, she had paid for equestrian lessons from the best masters, and the first improvement she had made to her double mansion was to add stables so that she could ride in Central Park.

Ward had ridden with her a dozen times, but he was still perfectly unaware of how much better she rode than he did. Helen, on the other hand, saw all too well how poorly Ward sat in the saddle.

"I think I'd rather stay in the hotel and meet you when you get back to the town."

"You should come with us. You've been spending too much time indoors."

"What could be more outdoors than a train ride through the mountains, especially on this narrow single gauge track. Out on the observation deck you can see herds of buffalo and flocks of geese."

"I didn't see any buffalo, and the geese just seemed to be taunting me for not having my gun with me. Besides, we were indoors all the time in Denver between the opera house and the real estate offices."

Helen stayed in the hotel while her husband galloped off with the ballplayers. How could he have seen Myrtle Peek ride a horse and still have stated that women were better off in carriages and men on horseback? That he had never realized how much better Helen rode could be taken as a tribute to her feminine skills, an ability never to make the man feel inferior. Being underestimated had often served her well in her business dealings in the male world. When she was Little Nell, the California Diamond, thirteen years old and passing for ten, she had learned to buy land in mining territory. By the time she was fifteen passing for eleven, she had figured out how to buy stock in mining technology companies, and soon after that she was rich enough to go off to Europe where she changed her name from Ida Gibson to Helen Dauvray. She learned to pass as French, to the point where she performed on the French stage to favorable notices.

The one central deception in her life had been to create the illusion that she was rich because she was an actress. The reality was that she was an actress because she was rich, and her stage triumphs had only been possible because she was willing to put up the necessary francs or dollars to guarantee production. When the public began to love her performances in Bronson Howard's plays, she bought the mansion and continued to collect jewelry, letting the world think that she had done this with theater earnings. When "One of Our Girls" became a long-running box office smash, she commissioned Howard to write more plays with her in mind. Happily, she had been able to pay generously for actors, stage hands and even playwrights while still showing a substantial profit.

After a late breakfast, Helen rode out to the depot where the ballplayers were to assemble for the last stage of their ride into the ballpark. She was not surprised that they were an hour late because Helen knew her husband well enough not to expect any operation of which he was a part to proceed punctually, but she had not been prepared to see him with a bandaged head and a badly torn uniform with a missing belt.

"Chéri, qu'est-ce que t'est arrivé?" (Darling, what happened to you?)

"Mon cheval m'a désobeis, mais je me suis sauvé, et le cheval va bien aussi. Ne te déranges pas." (My horse disobeyed me, but I saved myself, and the horse is doing well too. Don't let it bother you.)

Helen wrapped her husband in her arms, making a cursory check for broken bones. Spalding's mother, who had seen both Ward's accident and Helen's greeting, observed to her son.

"I don't understand French, but I suppose he must have said 'I rode into a post, and so did my horse because we're both stupid.'"

Ward's injuries were not serious, but they were just another proof that he was not much of a horseman. Although he was somewhat battered, he played in the abbreviated game in Colorado Springs, another game which set off a round of telegrams warning the next town not to expect quality baseball from the tourists and that King Kelly wouldn't be there.

Once they were on the train headed out of Colorado, Helen had to nurse Ward on a narrow slab that took the place of a Pullman on the westernmost leg of the trip.

"With the profit Mr. Spalding is making on this trip, he could afford better."

"Al says that we'll be lucky to break even. What makes you think he's lying?"

"For one thing, I can look around and count a house. And I know how to multiply by 50 cents even if I never had any formal schooling."

Helen took pride in being an autodidact which was not entirely justified because when she was growing up, she had always had excellent private tutors.

"When we get to San Francisco, we'll stay at the Baldwin Hotel. You'll like it there."

"Between this train and whatever kind of ocean liner Spalding arranges to Australia, I'll need some rest. And I have friends to see in San Francisco. Did you know that they have a theater that puts on racy plays in French?"

Ward's eyebrows met, so Helen knew he was about to become tiresome. Ward was giving every sign of becoming a jealous man, and that meant he would have one more reason to control her life and she would have one more reason to seek another divorce. Buying land in Colorado had given her another set of state courts should this step become necessary again, and she still owned land in California. If it happened, it would really be her third divorce. The first was from the unspeakable Mr. Tracy who had just started to comprehend her financial assets when she was fortunate enough to discover his extramarital affair, enabling her to divorce him under favorable terms. Her sister's divorce, which was still in progress, was really her second because Clara was too irresponsible to consider the importance of finalizing her divorce under Colorado law and keeping Dauvray Productions out of a New York settlement. Should it be necessary to divorce Ward some day, Helen wanted to protect her assets. Should he try to divorce her, the only grounds New York would permit would be her adultery, and she had neither the energy nor the inclination to allow that to happen. So she ignored his glare and switched to her most affectionate tone. She wasn't ready for the end of her marriage yet. Maybe it was just beginning.

"And we'll go to Paris for our *lune de miel*."

"First, we have to play ball all over Utah, California, Hawaii, New Zealand and Australia. Then we'll figure out the best way to get across Australia and then on to Malta and Paris."

"I've looked into that already. You seem to forget that I spent quite a bit of time in Australia when I was Little Nell playing my banjo. They remember me there. I could probably perform there now and have a following. But there is no need to be jealous of me then because I was eleven years old the last time I was down under."

That figure was thrown out quickly without regard to what her publicity had been saying or either the real or stated age she was at the time. Helen's age shifted so much that only Clara remembered how old Helen turned every Valentine's Day. The only limit on Helen's rejuvenation was Clara's refusal to become the older sister.

"I'm not jealous. And I want you to enjoy yourself on this trip. You need something to take your mind off your sister's divorce. And you need to let me take care of business and travel arrangements. I used to do that when I was a manager."

A few years before, Ward had been the emergency manager of the Giants for a month after the regular manager had been caught embezzling and before Jim Mutrie was hired. It was true that he had made the travel arrangements, but there was no choice because all National League teams had agreed to use the New York Central or one of the roads it owned, so all Ward had done was book a specific time. Helen, on the other hand, had years of experience moving a sizable theater company through the United States and doing so at minimal cost. She had been traveling around the world since she was a girl. John had been going from New York to Chicago to Philadelphia to Boston to Indianapolis to Pittsburg to Cleveland to Washington, but he failed to see why the husband should defer to the wife on business arrangements. Helen resigned herself to be content with whatever accommodations Spalding provided to Australia and then she and Johnny would proceed to Paris.

6

Alcohol
On a train through Nevada
November, 1888

The Order of the Howling Wolves had failed to stock up on liquor before entering Utah, so there was nothing to drink until the train crossed the border into Nevada and the bar car re-opened. After spending some time there, a few of the players dangled Clarence Duval over the edge of the platform until they were stopped by Anson who preferred verbal abuse when dealing with the mascot. Even when the players were sent back to their respective sleeping quarters, there were sporadic cries from berth to berth, like prisoners calling from cell to cell to plan a jailbreak. Anson demanded some action, so he again went to Spalding's berth and shook him awake.

"Can you hear that? The women can't sleep. My wife, your wife, Williamson's wife, your mother, Ward's actress. It's not respectable. I almost wish Kelly had come. He'd have gotten everybody drunk quicker, and they'd be passed out by now."

"Ward should be getting them under control. He's the captain of half of them."

"That's another thing. While we were in Denver, my Mrs. bought a copy of *Cosmopolitan* which we just got around to reading. There was an article by Ward in it, and what do you think it said?"

"I have no idea," Spalding said, having wondered when Anson would finally get around to hearing about the article, specifically the reference to "Baby" Anson.

"He writes about how I cheat by kicking at the umpires, and he says that they call me 'Baby' because of that."

Everybody on the White Stockings called Anson baby because of the way he could generate tears of anger when discussing the slightest difference of opinion as to whether the ball had reached his hand before the runner had tagged first base. For the most part, they meant it as a compliment to a leader who defended their rights. Not many men could attain the shade of fire engine red which he reached during such discussions.

"He's just jealous, Adrian. Your ability to reason with umpires is one of your many talents. If I could kick the way you kick, I'd be managing myself."

"Ward's one to talk. At least I never punched an umpire in a hotel lobby the way he did to Honest John Gaffney a few years back. And some of the players think he should be their leader! Bah!"

Spalding used this opportunity to change the subject.

"Have the players heard anything about a possible salary limit?"

"I don't know. Isn't Tener supposed to keep us informed?"

"He says he hasn't heard anything. Let's say hypothetically that the league was going to impose a maximum salary, say $2500 for the best players provided that they're sober. Not that I've heard anything, but just suppose."

"No ball player is worth more than two thousand a year," said Anson, momentarily forgetting that he was talking with the man who paid him eight thousand. "Unless he's the manager too and leads the league in hitting."

"We both know that if it weren't for baseball somebody like Kelly would be lucky to make ten dollars a week carrying the hod. Clarkson might make a little more in the family jewelry business. But Ward says salaries are too low because ballplayers are entertainers and should get paid the same as artists like Adelina Patti."

"Who?"

"The opera singer. The soprano."

"Does she make a lot of money? Maybe that's why they're doing all that howling. Maybe they think they're going to be opera singers."

"And Ward thinks ballplayers should be paid thousands, even when they're injured, drunk or otherwise useless."

"I always said he was a communist. Say, would that $2500 limit apply to me?"

"Of course not. You're my captain. You're management, not labor."

The next morning in the dining car, Ward was trying to spread the Brotherhood gospel to the players. Most were members, but none had yet taken an active role in the union. Pfeffer, Tener, and Williamson of the White Stockings joined Ward, Hanlon and Fogarty of the All Americas for an impromptu meeting of the Brotherhood members. Ward began by reading from a prepared statement.

"There was a time when the League stood for integrity and fair dealing; to-day it stands for dollars and cents. Once it looked to the elevation of the game and honest exhibition of the sport; to-day . . ."

Hanlon interrupted.

"We've all read the manifesto. What we need is a grievance meeting."

Pfeffer spoke slowly as he always did when he was trying to minimize his Chicago German accent.

"It's the fines. It doesn't matter what they say they will pay us if they can take back whatever they want before we see it. Anson fines me for not covering first base when he can't get his fat ass over there to take the throw. If I thought he could read, I'd give him a copy of my new book *Scientific Baseball*. And a few years ago he fined me $100 for dropping a ball. More than a week's pay. And I'm the best second baseman in the league. Think what the muffins have to pay out."

Ward remembered that this was the same complaint Yank Robinson from St. Louis had been making. The popular Ed Williamson spoke up next, even though he had always been reluctant to be identified with the union for fear of offending Anson and Spalding.

"If he fines us for every drink we take, he'll have our salaries for a year before Opening Day. I can see fining you for taking something stronger than beer during a game, but Spalding wants us to sign a Carrie Nation pledge. Fining us for what we do in the game is one thing, but we should be free to do what we want on our own time."

Cannonball Crane disagreed.

"A temperance pledge seems reasonable to me. I think management has a right to expect us to be sober, at least during the season."

Fogarty was lighting a new cigarette from the old.

"Have you ever taken a drink?" Fogarty asked the young pitcher.

"Never, I'm proud to say."

"Then you don't know what you're talking about. I'd never be able to play ball without the relaxing effects of drink. You'll have to give me a chance to see what I mean when we get to California."

"The important issue is that we should be free to choose where we work," said Tener. "I sure would be more comfortable if I could play in Pittsburg. I think a ballplayer should be able to live where he wants just like anyone else. We can't play forever, and we should be able to develop the connections to make a living after our playing days are finished."

Hanlon was a member of the Detroit team that had gone out of business. Their players were being assigned to other teams without being consulted.

"I hear that they're making me play for Pittsburg next year. I wish I could trade you my trade. I agree that we should play where we want to play. And I think the players should make their own rules on the field too. The game belongs to the players. Let's take it back. If we want to count walks as hits, it should be our decision. If they sell us, we should get a share of the price. I hear they're going to sell you to Washington, Johnny. Is that true?"

"They'll have to do a lot of convincing if they want me to play at Swampoodle Grounds."

Jimmy Fogarty had as many grievances as the others, but he had a more practical suggestion.

"If they're going to withhold our salaries for drinking, we should do all the drinking we can now while we aren't getting paid anything but our room and part of our board. So gentlemen, let me be your native tour guide as we visit the Bear Republic. You'll see taverns in the Tenderloin where the music flows and astonishing women serve you drinks. I'll show you brothels so respectable one minute you expect somebody's mother to serve you tea and so shocking the next minute that you expect the madam to come out and tell the girls they've gone too far. And that's just in the Anglo section. After you see Chinatown, you'll beg Spalding to continue the tour on to Cathay. I'm going to make entertaining young Crane my special project. Will you be joining us, Captain Ward?"

"I'm afraid that I will be confining myself to a glass of champagne in the Baldwin Hotel where my wife and I have reserved a suite. I trust that no one will blame me for deserting."

The Shame
Haight Street Grounds, San Francisco
November 4, 1888

Umpire Jack Sheridan was insisting on starting the game promptly at 2:00 even though the late-arriving California crowd was still coming in. Over 18,000 had bought tickets, taking advantage of a rare chance to see what they thought would be top quality baseball on a sunny autumn day. After a late evening of champagne and speaking only French, Ward had overslept and missed the carriage procession from the Baldwin Hotel to the park, arriving barely in time to hand in the starting lineup.

Leadoff man Ned Hanlon, for whom a night of heavy drinking was a rare experience, backed away from an inside pitch and was slow to notice that the ball had hit his bat and was rolling out to the shortstop. It would have been an infield single had he run immediately, but he hesitated because his head was still suffering the residual effects of a night at Pigeon-Toed Sal's where Fogarty had been correct in his assurances that the drinks were unwatered. Only after shortstop Williamson had fumbled the ball once or twice, did Hanlon start his belated dash to first. The throw beat him by five feet, but Sheridan had also been out late the night before so he called Hanlon safe anyway. The pattern for the game had been laid out.

George Van Haltern came up and received loud applause because he was a Californian himself. After he dodged two wild pitches, he hit a cloud scraper that should have been caught but landed right next to the sun-blinded right fielder for a triple bagger. Ward was clear-headed enough to take advantage of the opportunity to drive in the run by hitting a soft grounder to the shortstop. The next batter lifted another easy fly towards center fielder Ryan, who ran in when he should have stayed where he was. The ball went over his head for another triple. Fogarty, whose self-appointed role as tour guide had obligated him to stay out with the last revelers, struck out swinging at the wrong ball of the two that seemed to be heading toward the plate. Another run scored on an error by the third baseman, followed by a single that left men on first and third. This brought up Egyptian Healy, named so because he came from a town called Cairo in the part of Illinois known as Little Egypt. Captain Ward gave the sign that the runner on first should attempt to steal third and get caught in a rundown enabling the runner from third to score. However, second baseman Pfeffer, a scholar of the game himself, had read about this play in Ward's book and had devised a counter which he himself had described in his recent tome *Scientific Baseball*. Pfeffer stepped in front of the shortstop who was covering, took the throw and immediately sent it back to the catcher who tagged the surprised runner for the third out. Ryan led off the bottom of the first with a double and came home on two sacrifices before Anson hit a towering pop fly gathered in by Ward.

K. C. found himself sitting next to an African-American gentleman who sported a red white and blue button with the names Harrison and Morton printed over something suggesting an American flag. When Ward caught Anson's pop-up to end the first, the man had jumped to his feet applauding. K. C. was glad to see that they were cheering for the same team, which in his mind always entitled him to begin a conversation.

"I see you're for the All-Americas too," K.C. began.

"I'm more against Mr. Anson. Last year he refused to play when Fleetwood Walker was on the other team and referred to our race in the most opprobrious terms. How can we ever come together as a people with an attitude like that? It's 1888, not still slave times. It's just the kind of backsliding I feared when the Democrats stole the last presidential election. But the Harrison rally last night inspired me. I hope I'm not offending you, but I feel very strongly that Afro-Americans should have a chance to play major league baseball."

K. C. never thought much about politics, but he agreed with the general idea his new friend was putting forth. *The Sporting News* had recently written an editorial saying Negroes should be allowed to play in the major leagues, and K. C. was in agreement. To him the issue seemed to be promoting the highest quality baseball with fairness merely incidental, but it worked out to the same thing, so he agreed with his companion and added his store of inside baseball knowledge to the discussion.

"Ward wanted to sign George Stovey and Frank Grant for the Giants, but the league wouldn't let him do it."

That does Mr. Ward *some* credit, even if he did fail to go through with it. How do you feel about Negro players?"

"I think the best nine players should take the field, be they Negroes, Whites, Indians, Mexicans, Chinese, Jews, females, sodomites or drunkards."

Tension disappeared. The Black gentleman chuckled.

"Well, they certainly seem to be allowing drunkards."

The game proceeded slowly and painfully into the third inning. Williamson had dropped another pop fly. Ward advanced the runner, and the next batter lifted a fly to short center field. The center fielder had been asleep on his feet and did not notice the ball until he heard it land. Anson chose this moment to explode at Williamson, who had not ventured out to catch the ball, nor had he covered second base, thereby allowing the batsman a double. From this point on, the game blurred to the point where it was no longer clear to the cranks which team was ahead. There was no scoreboard, and the most distant were losing interest in the competition. A catcher tripped over his own mask and dropped a foul pop fly. A bounding ball hit off the padding of a second baseman's glove and carried out to right field. As if to prove that the equipment was not to blame, a bare-handed left fielder juggled an easy fly ball before dropping it. Anson, who still refused to wear a glove, dropped a hard throw from Pfeffer who may have done it on purpose to embarrass his captain. Ward had a comment as he stood safe at first.

"Is Spalding keeping you at first base to promote the sale of gloves? Wouldn't it be better if you started wearing one and then you could do testimonials?"

Anson, who was not without his own brand of wit, responded.

"The only testimonial I'll give will be for Louisville sluggers. I'll say they're good for bashing in the heads of smart alecks."

The errors continued. A perfect throw from a center fielder hit the runner and skipped past the third baseman. A pitcher attempted to pick off a runner at first, but the first baseman had momentarily turned his head, and the ball struck him in the ribs and rolled free. The catcher dropped a third strike, but the runner would have been retired had the first baseman managed to catch the throw. The ball that bounced off the right fielder's head struck only a glancing blow, so he suffered more embarrassment than pain. The third baseman ducked to avoid being hit by a line drive.

The only thing that kept the game moving was the fifteen strikeouts recorded by the two teams combined. Players struck out on wild swings at pitches that barely had the velocity to reach home plate. Neither pitcher had much control, but the batters kept fanning the air. When the batters didn't swing, Umpire Sheridan, eager to finish the game before November's early sunset, called them out on any pitch within his field of vision.

A sense of being cheated ran through the male spectators in the overflow crowd, each of whom had paid fifty cents for a product that was clearly inferior to that of twenty-five cent games in the California League. The female spectators were even more offended because most of them had understood the advertisements for Ladies' Day to imply free admission and were surprised to be asked to pay half price. Nor had it helped when Mike Kelly's many female admirers figured out that the only way they would see him would be as a picture on the scorecard.

"I guess the parade from the hotel was what drew the people in. They seem to be tired of the game," K.C. suggested in an attempt to explain the overflow crowd.

"That parade was led by a degraded dwarf doing what he called a plantation dance. That made me want to turn around and go back to the hotel."

"That's Clarence Duval. He used to be the Chicago mascot," commented K. C. who knew the name of the hoodoo for every team in the National League but could not keep straight the first names of his wife's brothers or the married names of her sisters.

"Whatever he is, it's disgusting to think that he will be the only Afro-American going around the world representing America."

The game continued with the All-Americas staying ahead and scoring four in the eighth and three in the ninth to finish with a 14 to 4 victory. Ward knew that even though his team had won, they had played very poorly. As to the White Stockings, Anson was the only one of them that seemed to know where he was, and he didn't like being there. The California sporting press was preparing articles calling it the worst baseball game ever played.

"The boys just need time to get used to stronger whisky, just like in Colorado we had to get used to weaker air," was the excuse Ward offered, but fortunately no one had quoted him.

As K.C. left the Haight Street Grounds with his new friend, by way of parting he said , "I hope and expect that we will see Negro players in the major leagues soon."

"After what I saw today, I think we Negroes should start our own leagues and bar the Caucasians from participating."

8

California
San Francisco and elsewhere
November, 1888

With a suite in the Baldwin Hotel, Helen was beginning to find the tour more comfortable. She was pleased that some of the theater owners remembered Little Nell. The more Ward heard Helen's old colleagues talk of Little Nell, the older Helen seemed. Ward was not too happy when Helen renewed her acquaintance with an actor who was now appearing in a less than respectable theater giving off-color plays in French and Spanish. Some of their conversations were in rapid colloquial French which Ward tried to follow, but he found he could only understand a few words here and there, mostly when Helen herself spoke. After a few days in the hotel, Ward had to leave to lead his All-Americas against local teams around the state.

"Does your contract require it?" asked Helen who understood that it was desirable not to be sued.

"I don't know. I suppose so."

For someone with a law degree to be unable to remember what he had signed shocked the self-educated Helen. What had they taught Johnny at Columbia? When she finally found a copy of the contract, it seemed to obligate Ward to do whatever Spalding wanted for as long as he wanted, at least until the next baseball season started. Resigned to having her husband barnstorm through California, she stayed in the hotel having tea with Mrs. Anson and Mrs. Williamson. When newspapers arrived from other towns in the Bear Republic, she noticed Ward's name did not appear in some of the box scores and correctly deduced that he had taken time off to go hunting.

The All Americas had been resenting their leader's absence until Ward returned with a bag full of pheasant. Spalding was not paying for food when the teams were not together, so for most of the players this was their first decent meal since San Francisco.

Anson umpired one of the games when the All-Americas facing a local team. Anson challenged Ward when he came to bat.

"I'll bet you five dollars you don't get a hit."

Ward didn't normally bet, but the pitcher looked so soft, he felt he had to accept the challenge. The next pitch came in over his head and a foot outside.

"Strike one," Anson called, barely containing his laughter. The pitcher caught on right away, and the next two pitches were equally impossible to hit. Anson called them both strikes. Ward returned to the bench red-faced and cursing. In fairness to Anson, he did refuse the $5 when offered.

After a few more exhibitions, they headed back to San Francisco and the final banquet that would send them off to Australia. Between Ward's overly optimistic planning and the rough California trails, the All Americas did not reach the hotel until nearly eleven at night. Ward went to his suite to change and was surprised to see no trace of Helen, not even her trunks.

The ballplayers stuffed themselves into formal wear, some more successfully than others. Anson's broad shoulders pushed against the fabric of his evening dress, and his sunburned face and neck seemed to be fighting a choking collar and losing. The more slender Ward, as comfortable in evening clothes as in a baseball uniform, was seated at a table with Spalding, Anson, Williamson and their wives as well as Spalding's mother. The dinner was being served in nine courses, each representing an inning.

One of Helen's servants had telegraphed her that Clara was entertaining a tall mustachioed gentleman overnight. The maid threatened to tell Mr. Helms if the situation continued. With such information, Helms could obtain a New York divorce, creating a scandal for Clara and a financial problem for Dauvray Productions. Helen had to leave, and she couldn't tell anyone why without damaging her sister's reputation.

Ward, still wondering what had become of Helen, ordered "petit paté à la Spalding." In the spirit of amity, Spalding ordered the "stewed terrapin à la Ward." Anson skipped over the menu and asked the waiter to bring him something with as much beef as possible.

"I hope Mrs. Ward will have a safe trip," began Mrs. Williamson. "She received a telegram two days ago and had to go back to New York on family business. She seemed quite upset."

"She can seem anything she wants. She's an actress," Ward said without thinking. Then he corrected himself. "I just mean that I hope her business goes well."

When Ward returned to his suite for the night, he found a telegram from Helen that had been slid under the door. She had sent it from Omaha.

Had to return to New York. Help Clara finalize divorce. Will meet you in Paris. At the Ritz by January 1. Then proceed from Paris to Malta as planned. Sorry. It could not be avoided.

Ward looked around the room. A piece of paper in the waste basket had the name Ludovic Halévy, 22 Rue de Douai. Was this an old lover of Helen's from Paris? Was that where she was going? All this speculation ruined Ward's last night on land. He tried to console himself, as he often did, by imagining his beautiful wife giving herself to him, but somehow his thoughts were distracted and it was another man in whose arms he was imagining her, someone with the unlikely name of Ludovic.

There was someone in Helen's arms, but Ward would have been relieved to know it was a woman. (He lacked the imagination to envision sapphic adultery.) There was nothing sexual nor even sensual in the hugs. The woman in the next Pullman compartment on the train to New York had been sick ever since they had left St. Louis. Between vomiting and sudden sprints to the water closet, the young sufferer was ready to jump off the train if that meant she could avoid further mortification. Helen helped her on her trips, surveying the corridor to make sure she could move from the sleeper without her modesty being offended by curious male eyes. The woman's outer garments were soiled beyond redemption, so Helen lent her a dress. Helen persuaded the dining car staff to prepare some chicken soup, and she brought it back to her new friend.

"Mrs. Ward, you are treating the way I imagine my mother would have done if she had been at all maternal. You must have children of your own."

"I used to take care of my younger sister. And my brother. My mother wasn't very maternal either, so I stepped in."

"You will make a wonderful mother should it ever come."

"I don't think my health will ever permit me to have a child, but my husband wants a son."

"They all do. May I ask what your husband does?"

"He's an attorney. And also a baseballist. Maybe you've heard his name. John Montgomery Ward."

"Is he related to the mail house owner?"

"Only distantly. He plays for the New York Giants, and they just won the baseball championship."

"Isn't one of them married to Helen Dauvray?"

"Yes. That would be Mr. Ward."

The young lady was starting to recover, but her reasoning process was still slow.

"If Mr. Ward is married to Helen Dauvray and you're Mrs. Ward, then you must be Helen Dauvray. I saw you in 'One of Our Girls.' How could I not recognize you? My husband always buys such cheap seats. I suppose that's why. You're Kate Shipley."

After the woman fell asleep, Helen returned to her gas lamp and the pile of plays she was reading. She was reading popular French plays with an eye to what might succeed in the United States, and she was reviewing some American plays to see what might be popular in France. Reading on the train tired her quickly, so she went back to sleep.

In the morning her new friend had recovered enough that they had a real conversation. Trying not to tarnish her sister's reputation too much, even to a stranger, Helen explained why she was going back.

"I just want her to be divorced before my nasty brother-in-law can create a scandal to steal our property."

"Why don't you take her with you to France? That would keep her out of trouble. Would she like Paris?"

"She's a sculptress. I'll take her to see the Rodins. Maybe that will work."

At first Clara denied that she was receiving visits from Keefe. Then she said it was just business because she was designing next year's Giant uniforms for Keefe and Becannon. Then she denied that they were having sex. Then she denied that they were having sex in any way that her husband could discover. Helen offered a bribe.

"Come to France with me. We'll watch them finish La Tour à Trois Cent Mètres (The Three Hundred Meter Tower) and go to the museums. I have friends who will be glad to introduce you in art circles. One of them is the widow of the man who wrote the music to Carmen, and you can't get more bohemian than that. Her cousin wrote the words. They just moved into a double mansion like ours. I'll pay your way. Then, when my husband arrives, you can quietly go back home and resume whatever it was that you were doing with Mr. Keefe, provided that your divorce is finalized by then."

"So I'm to stay away from my love long enough to guard our business interests. You can't fool me when you try to make it seem bohemian. But I'll be glad to go to Paris. Timothy is staying in New York because he says the owners are up to some new ideas, like reducing what it takes for a walk to four balls and limiting the salaries of players by classifying them."

"It seems rather deceptive of the owners to be discussing salary limitations while Johnny is out of the country."

9

The Mascot
The Pacific and elsewhere
November, 1888

Just before boarding the *Alameda* for what was ostensibly a trip to Australia, Spalding made a final stop at the telegraph office. He sent the following message to the National League office.

> Ward now at sea. Will not receive news until February. Make necessary arrangements. Will proceed with reverse Phileas Fogg plan.

In New York, steps were being taken to control the growth of players' salaries and to ensure the owners that there would be a chance to make a comfortable profit. Spalding feared that some of the owners would want to overplay their hand which might provoke the players and bring about a strike, but without Ward's leadership there was not much chance of anything like that happening in the off-season. When April came, the players would not have been paid since September and would be too broke to strike.

Of more immediate importance, the balance sheet for the tour was robust. Strong attendance in California had guaranteed that Spalding would have enough money to take the tour around the world. As long as he had been in the game, people had been giving baseball players free dinners, and Al knew how to take advantage and keep expenses low. Not having to pay Mike Kelly's salary was another blessing. Spalding smiled as he looked at the scorecard with Kelly's mug smiling out at the fans, drawing them in. Having the attraction of the most popular athlete in America without having to pay him or put up with his shenanigans seemed to Spalding a perfect outcome.

To Spalding what the balance sheet showed was capital for a larger venture— his baseball tour around the world. Johnny Ward had noticed that it was just as easy to get home by going west by way of Europe as it would be to go back across the Pacific, and he was planning to go from Australia to Paris to reunite with his recently disappeared wife. Spalding hoped that Ward would be an ally if the plan to keep heading west was put to a vote. Spalding was smart enough not to mention any of this the first few days out while the players were vomiting over the side of the boat.

Ward squeezed into the tiny airless cabin and consoled himself by thinking of Helen. He still resented that she had left the tour, but he had to admit that she would not have been comfortable crammed into this room, and he was just as glad that she had not seen his seasickness. When he did imagine himself with Helen just before he went to sleep, it was in a soft bed in a hotel with a solid floor and room service.

A few days out to sea, rumors began to spread that they might continue west from Australia and expand the tour around the world. Players began to think that they had come up with the idea themselves. Everything was contributing to what Spalding was calling his "reverse Phileas Fogg plan," going around the world heading toward the setting sun. Without fully understanding what was entailed, the players agreed to extend the tour, including some games back in the United States at the end. Unlike Alexander's troops, Spalding's men did not hesitate to go into the unknown.

In Hawaii the players were honored with a feast hosted by King Kala Kaua, complete with hula dancers and a pig roast. As eager as the American colony in the islands was for a game of baseball, the missionaries had banned Sunday recreation in a land where the concept of the Sabbath was unknown to most of the islanders. Ward had wanted to meet Alexander Cartwright in order to ask him about the early days of the New York Knickerbockers, but Cartwright lived on Maui, which was too far for a quick visit.

"Just as well," said Spalding. "I don't like the idea of baseball starting in New York City. I can't see that as good for business."

"The facts are what counts, Al."

"The facts are what we make them, Johnny. Neither of us likes Henry Chadwick's saying that baseball is just a game from his youth in England."

"I agree. No rounders. But you keep him on your payroll writing the *Spalding Guide*."

From Hawaii, the long trip to New Zealand gave Anson a chance to practice his cricket using Duval as his bowler. Anson was a skilled cricketeer, but there was something about Duval's delivery that fooled him consistently. Anson still blamed the little fellow for deserting the season before, occasionally threatening to throw him to the sharks, but Anson spent more time on the tour with Duval than he did with his wife. Mrs. Williamson made it her mission to teach Duval to read, and he in turn taught the ship's largely British crew how to shoot craps. When they arrived in New Zealand, the crowds were small, and Duval was the most popular attraction, even more than Professor Bartholomew, the aerialist. The New Zealanders were gracious enough to treat the plantation dance with respect, just as they had learned not to scorn Maori rituals.

"When will we see the profits?" Anson asked Spalding, a legitimate question since Anson had invested some of his own money in the tour. In his heart of hearts, Spalding was hoping to break even or at least keep the losses low. The tour to England fourteen years before had failed to export the game, but Spalding felt that things might be different now that the game was developing so well. The only threat that remained came from the outrageously high salaries for players, and he was on his way to taking care of that.

"The profits will be there when we get to England, Adrian. We're going to play in front of Queen Victoria. Now, tell me what have you heard about the Brotherhood? Are they still complaining?"

"What have they got to complain about?"

Tim Keefe was still stranded in New York doing a job he really did not care to be doing. The National League owners had just announced a player classification plan which divided the players into five categories with Category A salaries set at $2500 down to Category E at $1500 with Class E players required to perform additional duties such as taking tickets and cleaning the ball park. With Ward not only out of the country but out of touch with the mainland, Keefe was left alone to deal with the press, the owners, and the complaints of the players. Mike Kelly had turned up in New York as mysteriously as he had disappeared. He stopped by Keefe's hotel to complain about the sobriety clause that would "downgrade a man for quenching an ordinary thirst." Mickey Welch expressed similar sentiments when he met Keefe at Nick Engel's Home Plate Saloon. Keefe drank only moderately, but the bar was the informal headquarters of the Brotherhood and the New York Giants. Even O'Rourke, a physical fitness enthusiast who neither drank nor smoked, stopped by to sip lemonade. When he did, Keefe asked him for a professional opinion.

"You're a lawyer, Jim. They seem to be saying that they're going to cut salaries. Can they do that?"

"In my particular case, it is unlikely that they could effect any such reduction, because I have a firm contract, and I demanded that they withdraw that clause that bound me in perpetuity. Have you settled your contract yet? After your superb performance last season, you should be able to demand unprecedented compensation."

"It's true that the Giants will need me pitching next year. Brouthers and some of the others from Detroit are going to be joining Kelly and Clarkson in Boston. I've never liked that arrogant Orangeman Clarkson, even when Tommy Bond was teaching both of us how to pitch back in Cambridge. But it's not just about me. It's the whole league. Maybe this will be what it takes to make Ward see that we would be better off starting our own league. I wish he were back in New York, but I see from the newspapers that they're planning to go all the way around the world now and might not be back until April. That's what Spalding was planning all along. Now that leaves me in charge. I just wish I could get out of New York and head back home with my sisters and our aunt."

Keefe and Clara had agreed to stop seeing each other until after her divorce was final in order to avoid compromising situations. To make this easier, Clara went to Paris with Helen. When Keefe went home to Cambridge to vote for Cleveland, he told his confessor about the affair with a married woman. Having never even mentioned fornication, he was nervous about starting right in with adultery, but the priest assured him that Clara's Protestant marriage was not something with which he should concern himself. In fact, the path was open to making an honest woman of her after the divorce. This made Keefe even more determined to sign a good contract for the next season.

The newspapers carried the story of how the Spalding tourists were now going around the world, meaning that Ward would be out of touch indefinitely. In theory, Dan Brouthers was in charge as the vice-president of the Brotherhood, but he was busy moving from Detroit to Boston and settling in on his new team. Like most of the veteran players, he did not believe that the classification plan had any possibility of succeeding, but he too saw it as something that would unify the players. He did make one trip to New York to visit Keefe and discuss the situation.

"It ain't just the money, Tim, as important as that is. There's something wrong with the way they're treating the players. When my Detroit team folded, nobody asked me nothin'. They told me that I'd be going to Boston. The Beaneaters are a good team in a fine city, but some of us got treated even worse. They stuck Ned Hanlon down in Pittsburg and they won't let Deacon White go back to start a minor league team in Buffalo, which is a bad ball town, but he wants to go there and build a new ball park."

"We have to teach them that a ballplayer is not a chattel, to quote our friend Ward," Keefe said, using what was becoming the Brotherhood's informal motto.

"Is it true that Day is thinking about trading Ward to us? We could still use a shortstop," Brouthers said hopefully.

"Now that Day sees how strong Boston is, he won't be doing anything to make you stronger. He still talks about trading Ward to Washington."

"The only way Ward would go to Washington would be if Benjamin Harrison stepped aside and allowed Ward to be inaugurated next March 4th."

"Well, as Brotherhood members, Ward is our president. At least he will be when he gets back in the country."

10

The Relative
Oval Cricket Grounds, Adelaide, Australia
December 27, 1888

Australians had no idea how to build a pitcher's mound, so Ward had to put one together wherever they stopped. At one time, Ward had claimed that he had invented the pitcher's mound while a student at Penn State, but he later found that the idea to elevate the pitcher had been discovered independently many times before. He still deserved credit, just as either Leibniz or Newton could legitimately claim to have invented the calculus. Cannonball Crane, who had taken to drink enthusiastically, had been unable to take his turn pitching due to his discovery of still stronger and smoother forms of brandy at a morning visit to a local winery. Captain Ward had to find a substitute pitcher, and he decided to do it himself.

Ward had not pitched for over four years, but his arm was recovering from the sliding injury which had ended his pitching career, and he decided to take a nostalgic turn between the points. For the first two innings he had been enjoying himself, but when Baby Anson came to bat in the third, he stepped out of the batter's box after the first pitch and began to complain to Tener, who was acting as umpire.

"Ward is pitching illegally. He's turning his back to the batter. And he's taking a running start. That makes two rules he's violating."

K.C. had found it easy to talk to everyone in this matey country. While the players all gathered around the umpire voicing various complaints and interpretations, K. C. saw an opportunity to begin a conversation. The man sitting next to him was studying "Palmer's Guide to Baseball" which had been included as a supplement in the local newspaper.

"How do you like our American national game?"

"Would you like to improve the equation?"

"Pardon."

"Place a little wager."

"Oh no, I never bet."

"I'm really more of a cricket supporter, but I am curious to see how you Yanks play the game."

K.C. let this pass and even tried to build on it.

"Today is a special treat. Johnny Ward has returned as a pitcher. It's what you call a bowler."

"And is Mr. Ward a distinguished bowler?"

"He used to be. He led the league in wins with 47 a few years ago."

"Don't they all win or lose as a team?'

"Not like a pitcher. And he led the league in earned run average or he would have if they had been calculating it back then."

"And what would earned run average mean?"

"You take the number of earned runs and then divide by the number of games pitched."

"I see."

"But you mustn't count unearned runs."

"What's an unearned run?"

"One that scores because a player has made an error, like muffing the ball or making a bad throw. Any run that scores because of an error doesn't count."

"So if you make a run because the other team fields poorly, it doesn't count. That's rather sporting."

"They count against the team, just not in the pitcher's record. Anyway, Ward used to be a great pitcher. He once pitched a game where he retired all 27 batters without so much as a hit, a walk or an error."

That sounded like an improbable American exaggeration, but the Australian let it go, so K.C. continued with his educational mission.

"And he pitched one game that lasted eighteen innings and ended 1-0 and he won it. The game took four hours."

"With so little scoring, it's no wonder that it was that quick."

"Anyway, after Ward hurt his arm, he became an outfielder and then a shortstop."

The Australian consulted the diagram on his sheet, proud to have retained something from his morning's reading.

"I see this diagram. First baseman, second baseman, shortstop, third baseman. I understand that the basemen attend to their respective bases, but what does this shortstop do?"

"He catches the balls hit to him on a fly, or if they bounce, he throws them to the first baseman."

"Is that all? It seems the catcher does more."

"It's the catcher's job to prevent steals. Ward led the league in steals the year before last."

"That doesn't sound very honorable. Why would they use that kind of name?"

"I don't know. It was probably the sportswriter Henry Chadwick's idea. He's on the tour."

"I think I read about him. Isn't he the English chap who invented baseball?"

"No, he just thinks he did. But he did invent how we talk about it. Box scores and batting averages."

"We've had cricket box scores since my gramps was a pup."

"And once Ward scored 114 runs."

"I'd wager his team won that game."

"That was for a whole season."

The argument over Ward's pitching style raged on, involving more and more players. In a voice loud enough for most of the spectators to hear, Anson was complaining.

"Playing under the old rules is unsportsmanlike."

Normally Ward was in better control of his emotions, but Anson's remark reminded him of the time in California when Anson had been umpiring. To hear Anson invoke sportsmanship infuriated Ward. To make matters worse for Ward, the Australians in the crowd seemed to agree with Anson.

"Poor sports you All Americas. And your outfits make you look like bloomer girls."

Spalding came out to mediate, and Ward addressed him as an equal, former pitcher to former pitcher.

"Al, when you pitched in Chicago, you used the old rules. And you know that the old rules restrict the pitcher even more. Nowadays you can't throw overhand, and I'm willing to give up overhand pitching if I can use my old delivery. That's what you did in Chicago."

"Chicago was different, Johnny. The cranks there knew that I was doing something old-fashioned, but here we're trying to spread the modern game. And today's rules say that you can't turn your back to the batter and you can't take little steps forward while you're getting ready to launch."

"But those aren't the rules I pitched under. And I'm pitching underhand like in the old rules. I'm not getting any advantage. And how can you apply normal rules to a game that's being played two days after Christmas?"

By this time, the spectators were shouting that Ward should stop complaining and be a sport. Anson took up their chant.

"Let's not waste all of our time yelling at Tener, Johnny. He's just trying to enforce the rules. Just forget the running start."

Ward adjusted to the new style of pitching, and he had to admit that the running start had done nothing to add to his velocity or his control. The outfielders chased down enough of his mistakes to enable the All-Americas to hold on to their early lead.

"Is Ward really being unsportsmanlike?" asked K.C.'s new Australian friend.

Even the most knowledgeable of cranks had trouble keeping up with changes in the pitching rules, especially since some of them had come more from baseball precedent rather than black letter law. When Ward had been a pitcher, there had been no overhand deliveries allowed according to the rules, but the arm angles had been climbing upwards with the tacit consent of the umpires. K.C. had observed the process with a keen eye.

"Ward was pitching the way they did ten years ago, but they changed the rules. If anything, Ward was following rules that make it harder on the pitcher. Whenever they change the rules, it's to make it easier on the batter."

"But he's making up his own rules. That hardly seems sporting. We don't let our bowlers make their own rules."

K.C. eventually saw the comparison between bowlers and pitchers as fruitless, so he turned to the details of the tour, trying to impress his companion with the grandeur of the American game in the eyes of the world.

"The tourists were sent off by the president of the United States," K.C. offered, exaggerating slightly because President Cleveland had really only met briefly with the White Stockings and had in no way endorsed the tour.

"You mean that fellow you just turned out of his job?"

"And they crossed the United States by rail."

"With all those Pullmans we hear about, that must have been easy. Crossing Australia by rail takes a good deal more courage and stamina."

"You're right there. In Hawaii the ballplayers met King Kala Kaua. He held a dinner for the two teams."

"We have a lot of native kings on the various islands around here, too. We try not to let them get too full of themselves."

"Then we're going to meet the Khedive of Egypt."

"Some kind of imperial civil servant, isn't he?"

"Then King Umberto of Italy."

"We have Italians here too. We can't keep them out, but no one is encouraging them to come."

"Then we'll meet the Prince of Monaco."

"Don't go to the casinos there. Full of snobs and robbers. The ones here are more fun."

"Then we plan to meet the Prince of Wales."

"I should think so. Everybody meets Bertie sooner or later. If meeting the Prince of Wales raised your prestige, half of England's ladies of the night would be ennobled."

K.C. had heard that too. The only card left to play was the Queen.

"And Queen Victoria. Spalding is arranging for the tourists to meet Her Majesty."

Frustration had driven K.C. to bend the truth because Victoria had not yet consented to be amused, but all his other attempts to impress had failed. Her royal name elicited another yawn, but K.C. went on.

"She's supposed to come when the tourists play at the Marleybone Cricket Club where we will meet Dr. W. G. Grace."

"W. G. Grace, you say! Will you shake his hand?"

"I assume the customary politenesses between gentlemen will be exchanged."

"In that case, mate, let me shake your hand now."

The game ended with the All-Americas ahead 12-9 and with everyone angry with everyone else.

The Uniform
Paris and elsewhere
January 1889

Helen and Clara were unpacking for an extended stay at the Ritz in Paris while Clara's divorce was being finalized. Helen had arranged for a quick legal action in Colorado keeping their assets safe from Clara's soon to be ex-husband.

Clara showed Helen a sketch of the uniform she had devised for the 1889 Giants. It was less elaborate than Helen's All-America uniform. Clara's costume had a conventional belt and a modest script announcing that the wearer represented New York. The pants clung to the player's form with a sort of codpiece in front to relieve discomfort and allow room for the new-fangled protective devices.

"So this is what Johnny and Timothy will be wearing next year. Are you sure?"

"Oh yes. As soon as Keefe and Becannon Sporting Goods got the contract, Timothy asked me to come up with something original. You can see that it highlights all their best features. My Timothy looked wonderful when he changed into it."

"For now, you'll have to stop saying 'my Timothy,' and there'll be no watching men change their clothes. Not until your divorce is final. I'll be so happy when that happens."

"Me too. I wish there were a divorce bouquet that I could throw and have you catch it. Then you could be the next one to get a divorce."

Around the time of his marriage, Ward had been pursued by George McDermott, his former landlord who claimed to have discovered Ward and his conspicuously beautiful eighteen-year old wife Jessie in a compromising position. Helen had accepted Ward's explanations, but Clara would neither forget nor forgive.

"We don't need to involve Dauvray Productions in still another divorce, Clara And besides, I love my husband."

"You should think about it. Your husband should understand that he has three strikes and then he's out. We all know that he's already had strike one with Mrs. McDermott."

"We don't know anything of the sort."

"And if he doesn't show up in Paris, that will be strike two."

"He'll show up in Paris. The whole Spalding tour will be coming here according to what I've been reading in *New York Herald's* new Paris edition."

For reasons she could not understand, Clara's art career had not been going well. She was hoping that the exhibits being planned for the Exposition would give her a chance to reverse the trend. It had been more than a year since anyone had bought any of her work, so she had lugged a few of her best small pieces across the ocean. She soon realized that the jury that picked the American art favored the American expatriate sculptors residing in Paris and looked down on anyone living in New York. To make matters worse, the American works were being moved out to make space for statues made by Europeans from the many countries which were not exhibiting. Clara was told that some of the most advanced painters such as Degas, Pissarro, Monet and others were exhibiting in unofficial galleries not approved by *L'Exposition Universelle*. Some were even exhibiting their work in cafés. When she visited some shabby galleries, most refused even to look at anything done by a woman. She did receive several offers to be a model for statues or paintings, but most of the offers seemed suspiciously like invitations for her to remove her clothing, something she saw as an affront. In New York, men ran most of the galleries and she was accustomed to barriers to female artists, but Paris was proving to be decidedly worse. Clara was so discouraged that she considered giving up sculpting completely, or maybe after she had made one last great statue. This made her think of Timothy in and out of the new Giants uniform.

While Clara was spending her days in the art world and her evenings in the hotel, Helen was spending her days in the museums and most of her nights in a genuine Paris salon thanks to her former colleague, M. Ludovic Halévy. When she had arrived in Paris many years before, he had discouraged her ambition to perform on the French stage, but he eventually became a collaborator with her, and he had been forced to admit that Helen enunciated her French better than most native actresses. He would have been glad to work with her again, provided that she was willing to finance his latest project. Helen declined, and he moved on to another backer without great distress, but he was still glad to receive Helen at his new home on the Boulevard Haussmann. His cousin, the widow of the composer Georges Bizet, lived in the other half of the mansion with her second husband and her son Jacques. Ludovic's son Daniel was constantly in the company of his second cousin Jacques and their friend from the Lycée Condorcet, petit Marcel, whom they referred to as the "porcelain psychologist," porcelain because of his complexion and his mother's family's business and psychologist because of his interest in what motivated people.

Halévy was a gracious host, presenting Helen as a highly successful protegée when he introduced her to his cousin, Mme. Straus. Helen was invited to soirées where she was asked to recite, perhaps for the novelty of an American actress who could speak flawless French, perhaps for her skill in interpreting Racine. Everyone was talking about General Boulanger and the possibility of a coup against the republic. M. Halévy's son Daniel explained all the threads of support for the general Boulanger. (legitimiste, orleaniste, bonapartiste, republicain) He amused her by explaining why an attempt at a coup was doomed to failure.

"Boulanger is more interested in his mistress than politics."

During political discussions, Helen was able to participate intelligently thanks to Daniel. Jacques made her aware of all the varieties of music that were to be heard in Paris. Helen's favorite was little Marcel, who had been effusive in his compliments on her recitation from Phèdre.

"Never before have I heard Racine's poetry so sublimely felt, not even when Sarah Bernhardt herself recited in this same room. You make every hemistitch balance the one before, keep the rhyme delicate and subtle and still deliver it all clearly and with intense emotion."

It would have taken a stronger person than Helen to resist such flattery. Yet there was nothing of the sexual in the boy's approach. He was too young, too sensitive and too androgynous to be a likely lover. Rather, he was a listener, something much harder to find. Helen found herself talking to Marcel about her husband, the good, the bad and even about how he had been chased by a jealous husband. When Marcel had asked what Johnny looked like, she took out a cigarette card she had brought with her.

"How handsome your husband is. When you walk together on the Champs Elysée, you will be the most beautiful couple in Paris."

Once Marcel had accompanied her to the theater, and she surprised herself with how frankly she had opened herself to him. Most of the time, he showed himself to be an adolescent boy like any other, but occasionally he seemed to have insights far beyond his years. When she remarked on it, he had given his own explanation for his apparent wisdom.

"What I know of love so far is only from literature and imagination, but I learn more when I talk with you. I hope to meet M. Ward when he comes to join you in Paris.

On the other side of the world, Ward lay alone in what Spalding had called a stateroom. Tener was staying in Spalding's stateroom to be in a better position to keep track of the books. The ship was just landing at Ceylon where there had been no communication with the States and no American newspapers, and now they were sailing for Egypt. Ward had the tiny room to himself and was unable to read or write because he had run out of candles. His thoughts turned to Helen and jealousy was turning into fear. Why would she bolt suddenly and who was this Halévy she was joining?

If she was having an affair was it forgivable because it was in France? Ward had not considered Helen's youthful love affairs in Europe with the same nervousness as if they had been in New York and the fellows were showing up at Delmonico's. Helen's intense and passionate face appeared in his imagination. He recalled the graceful gestures as her tiny hands stroked him, her actress's ability to undress herself instantly, the soft warm body underneath. Nothing would make him divorce her, even infidelity.

But could she divorce him? His thoughts changed direction and he became his own defense lawyer as he lay there in the dark. Could she charge him with adultery on the basis of the misunderstanding that had happened about two months after they had secretly married, shortly before their public marriage. George McDermott had accused him of wrestling with his wife, but there was no evidence against him. He vaguely remembered seeing Jessie's bared breast and taking it in his mouth, but a momentary, almost accidental, impulse could not stand up as adultery, not without better witnesses. He might just as easily be accused of adultery for the way he had looked at those Hawaiian dancing girls with grass skirts and no tops. From there his thoughts drifted back to some of the best memories he had of watching Helen undress. It was just as if she were there with him, except that if she had really been with him, it would have been too dark to see her. His thoughts drifted away from defending himself, and he concentrated more on the facts of the case than on the law. After a minute or two, he was sound asleep.

12

The Journalist
Indian Ocean and elsewhere
January, 1889

"**Y**ou mean to tell me there is no place in Ceylon where I can send a telegram to Europe or the United States."

"I'm afraid not, Johnny," said Spalding, feigning sympathy. He had arranged for the American newspapers to be waiting for him at the post office along with a report from his Pinkertons in New York. Had he chosen to do so, he could have told Ward that Helen and her sister had left for Paris. The report also included some salacious details about Tim Keefe staying all night with Clara before Helen had returned, but Spalding found this embarrassing. He didn't want his own life opened to such scrutiny. In his letter back to New York, he ordered his detectives to confine their inquiries to meetings between players, especially those around Nick Engel's Home Plate Saloon.

Just before leaving Australia, the aerialist had been severely injured in a crash, so Spalding had shipped him home. This set Ward to thinking about what would happen if any of the players on the tour suffered a severe or even a career-ending injury. When he brought this up, Spalding was ready with an answer.

"I know my White Stockings are protected. Our club has always paid players when they are injured, even though the contracts do not require us to do so. Did you ask that question of the other clubs when you took their players?"

This put Ward on the defensive. As a lawyer, he should have at least read the contract with Spalding and asked for some assurance for injured players, himself included, but he had been too busy at the end of the season to give it more than a cursory glance.

As they sailed out from Colombo, Ward and Spalding were enjoying the weather from plush deck chairs which were in short supply on the *Alameda*. Spalding reserved the two comfortable chairs for himself and one of his guests. They were soon joined by a bearded, ink-stained Englishman, Henry Chadwick. Ward gave his chair to the older man and moved to a stool.

"I was just telling Johnny that we're on this tour as baseball missionaries, converting the world, at least the English-speaking world, to baseball," Spalding told Chadwick by way of catching up.

"Which is why we have to present baseball at its very best, Al," Chadwick added. "No more games with scores like 25-20. We're in the business of promoting healthy exercise. But in England, there will be cricket to compete with. In France, the boys do nothing but sit around tea rooms and even the country boys don't know what to do with a ball and a bat. What do you think, Mr. Ward? Now that you're a baseball author, you and Mr. Pfeffer."

"I hope that France falls in love with baseball just the same as America. Mrs. Ward loves to spend time in France. But I don't know if we want to call ourselves missionaries. Look how they treat the Hawaiians, telling them they have to honor the Sabbath. Don't tell me that you want to convert the world to not playing ball on Sunday, Al."

"I just follow the laws. If they want to put me in jail for playing on Sunday, we don't play on Sunday, and we might as well make the best of it by saying how holy we are, not like those heathens in the Association.

"How do you like being in charge of a team again, Mr. Ward?" Chadwick asked. "It must be difficult to take orders from an intellectual inferior like Mr. Ewing."

"You're forgetting that Jim Mutrie is the manager, not me or Buck.

"Ah yes, Truthful James. Surely you can't expect me to believe that Mr. Mutrie has become a master of strategy."

Reminding himself that every word he said could appear in print, Ward spoke cautiously.

"I don't know why you gave Mutrie that nickname. He's no worse a liar than anyone else running a ball club."

Ward looked pointedly at Spalding, who seemed not to notice. Chadwick took up the challenge.

"I've known Mutrie since he was a cricket player. If all who hear the sobriquet I have assigned him assume it to be sarcastic, that's not my fault. In any case, I have a story to file as soon as we reach Cairo. I must excuse myself and return to my cabin."

Chadwick picked up his writing pad, and wandered off. Spalding commented as he left.

"There's the man who invented baseball as we know it, Johnny."

"Baseball had been played long before he came along, you know that, Al. He invented things like keeping the scorecard and batting averages and box scores, but not baseball."

"That's where you're wrong, Johnny. Chadwick invented baseball in the newspapers, and we wouldn't have crowds of 10,000 cranks ready to pay a half dollar without the newspapers. And the newspapers love the box score, the batting average, the assignment of credit and blame. I know that Anson thinks more about his batting average than winning the game, but I applaud him for that. People come to see the best, and Henry has given us a way to show that Anson is the best. Actually, I think someone else invented the batting average and the box score is just something he brought over from cricket. For almost forty years now, Henry has been inventing the game of baseball as we know it today. Clean and free from hippodroming with clear rules and detailed records. But now that he's gone, you and I can agree that he is deluded when he continues to insist that baseball is descended from rounders or other English games. We both know that can't be true."

"You've read my book, Al. You know I agree with you that baseball originated in America, through town ball and other things. Although Mrs. Ward did show me a passage in Jane Austen that referred to base ball, but it seemed to be a thing that girls played. But I could never think that baseball came from cricket."

"Duval could never have made Anson look as big a fool by pitching him a baseball as he did bowling a cricket ball. "

Ward and Spalding shared a brief laugh at Anson's expense, but neither would have brought up the subject in front of him, not after the rage he had shown the last time it had been mentioned.

"Australia was fertile baseball ground, but I think England will be better. When I was there fourteen years ago we did not have as good a product as we have now, thanks to my White Stockings and the fine team you assembled."

"When you talk about expanding overseas, you should see how well they play ball in Cuba, Al. I might go back there next winter. They have their own league in Havana, and more than a few players that could make the Giants."

"But they're probably too dark to be playing in the National League. I know you wanted to sign Stovey and Grant, but Anson and the boys wouldn't stand for it. Same with St. Louis. They told their owner that they wouldn't play against Negroes. The first time Anson refused to play against Fleet Walker, I wrote a letter telling him I didn't agree, but he isn't the only one. And you can't change human nature. And there can't be that many players on such a little island. Although I do remember Steve Bellán was pretty good."

"Besides Cuba, I saw enough talented colored players in South Florida to make a major league team that could win in the Association or even the League."

"Forget about the darkies, Johnny. England is the future. Maybe we'll find some players there. Or in Ireland. You can't beat the Irish for baseball, no matter how much Anson complains about them. But if we can plant some seeds in France and Italy too, that would be fine. For now, our next stop is Suez."

"Japan might have been ready for a tour, too."

"Again, too dark-skinned and small. I wouldn't mind selling them tiny sporting equipment, though. We'll bring the game to the shadow of the pyramids, then play in the Colosseum, then to Paris to see the new tower they're building. It's by the same fellow who engineered the Statue of Liberty. Then England and Ireland and back home."

"I might only go as far as Paris."

"Whatever you want, Johnny. Mrs. Ward can show my wife and mother and the other ladies all the smart shops in Paris. Then you can stay behind, and I won't even invoke the clause in the contract that requires you to play all the way through the tour, provided you rejoin us when we return to the states, as stipulated."

Ward had never thought that he was obligated to go around the world by surprise, but he once again regretted not having read his contract more thoroughly. Helen had noticed this clause, but he had not paid attention to her when she pointed it out.

"But wouldn't your wife like to come with us? She would be able to meet the Queen."

Johnny knew that Helen was a francophile republican, not about to be impressed by a British queen, especially one as dowdy and dull as Victoria. Ward had once heard Helen say that jewels were the only thing interesting about royalty, and Victoria was completely uninteresting because she almost never wore hers.

"I'll have to see what Helen wants. I suppose I'll meet her in Paris, then I'll rejoin you in New York."

"We're going to come home as heroes, Johnny. We'll be honored for bringing baseball around the world and establishing it as America's National Game, no matter what nonsense Chadwick has to say about rounders. And 1889 will be baseball's greatest season yet."

"For the players or the owners?"

"Johnny, it's talk like that which makes my friends think you follow Karl Marx. Next thing, you'll be saying 'Ballplayers of the world, unite. You have nothing to lose but your chains.' Wait, you've already said that in your magazine article. 'Is a Ballplayer a Chattel?'"

"A fair question, Al, especially for someone who has to worry if he's being sold to Washington. We just want a fair contract and for you to honor it after you sign it."

"Then we can all agree. Jim White has been saying 'No one is going to sell my carcass unless I get a share.' Now some of us might say that a player deserves a share of the money when he's sold, say a third. If Washington bought a player manager for $15,000, that would mean $5000 for the player over and above his salary."

This was beginning to look like a bribe attempt. Did Spalding think that slipping him $5000 on his way to Washington would make him keep quiet about the reserve clause?

"The players have a lot more complaints, Al. Like fines. And those contracts that we sign for life and that let you release us any time you want."

"Some day you might be an owner, Johnny, and you won't want to listen to the complaints that the players make. You pay some lummox $3000 a year to hit .250 and he does nothing but whine because the muffin next to him in the outfield makes $3500 when either of them would be lucky to get two dollars a day as farm hands in harvest season. Wouldn't you like to be a part owner like Anson and have your future set up?"

"I don't want to be anything like Anson, but I do think that the players should be the owners. Maybe all of us could have a big cooperative. You could join us, Al. The boys tell me you still looked good pitching in Chicago, and you're no older than O'Rourke."

"You can't mean that, Johnny. Not about me being able to play, but about players owning clubs. That's what we had in the old days in the NAPBB, and there was hippodroming and revolving from team to team. You can talk to Chadwick about it. Or Bob Ferguson. We had to start the National League to take the game away from the fixers and to bring stability."

"That was when you jumped from Boston to Chicago in the new league."

"Because I knew it would be run in a businesslike manner. Not all ballplayers can function as businessmen like you and me, Johnny. You speak French, I speak Italian. You're a member of the bar, and I'm a sporting goods business owner. Most of these mugs couldn't manage a barber shop in Rockford much less a million dollar baseball league across the country."

Ward returned below to his cabin, concerned about how isolated he was from what was going on in the rest of the world. He knew he was supposed to meet Helen in Paris, but he had no idea how to inform her when he would arrive. Something must have been decided when the baseball owners met, but he had not seen a newspaper, nor had he heard from Keefe. The important thing was for him to get to Paris and see Helen, and, if necessary, to win her back from this Halévy, whoever he was. Then they would speak French, have their *lune de miel*, with no drunken ballplayers this time. And then he could find out what was happening back in New York. Under the circumstances, Ward was forced to give up the illusion that he could control events and just drifted along with the ship toward the Suez Canal.

13

Scorecards
The Great Pyramid, Egypt
February 9, 1889

Spalding had arranged for a ball game to be played against the most grandiose backdrop the world could provide, the pyramids of Egypt. The players stepped off from the Hotel Orient led by baton-twirling Clarence Duval. Then the All-Americas mounted donkeys while the White Stockings looked down from camels. This made Ward's team feel cheated, so they insisted on switching mounts halfway through the long ride. By that time, the Chicagos were glad to exchange the foul-smelling, green-spitting, evil-tempered beasts for docile donkeys. This time it was a camel that threw Ward to the ground, and from an even greater height than before, but he was thankful for the soft landing the sand had provided.

Shortly before the game was supposed to start, Pfeffer called him over. The second baseman was smoking one of his customary four pre-game cigars while waving an American newspaper in the air.

"Have you seen the New York papers? The owners have a classification scheme that makes sure that none of us makes more than $2500."

"We should have a meeting back at the hotel," Ward answered, "but for now, let's just enjoy where we are. Look at the size of those things. I'll bet none of us could even throw a ball over one."

In the first inning, Ward foolishly attempted to steal a base, but as soon as he hit the ground for his slide, he found himself flat on his back, stuck in the sand. He could do nothing but await the tag from Williamson who was pushing through from second base to the point where Ward had come to a halt. Ward had planned to glide over the loose-packed sand on the top, but he landed with enough force to carry him down into a more sluggish layer. Williamson finally completed the formality of applying the tag.

Ward shook the sand from his scarf/belt and went back out on the field which Spalding had laid out. Home plate was set in front of the great pyramid of Cheops. Down past third base, the umpire could orient himself on fair/foul calls by drawing an imaginary line through the nose of the Great Sphinx. The infield and outfield were constructed over the flat underground tombs of the Fifth Dynasty pharaohs. It had been easy to build a mound, but it tended to sink, and the pitcher could not find solid ground for his back foot to push off. The batsmen were disadvantaged by frequent gusts of wind containing a mixture of sand and small pebbles as well as the occasional flying insect. Balls struck on the ground were fielded by the catcher springing out from behind the plate, and fly balls to the outfield landed a few feet from fielders unable to struggle through the sand. Curve balls that would have skipped away from the catcher spun into the sand, permitting the runners to steal while the ball was being dug up.

Chicago scored twice in the bottom of the first. The inning would have been more successful except that a temporarily blinded Anson wandered off first base and got picked off while stuck in the sand. To make matters worse for the Chicagos, the All-Americas scored seven runs in the second, mostly because of balls propelled by a wind to left field which died as abruptly as it had started.

Healy was striking out more batters than his counterpart. Spalding had insisted that Ward pitch Healy in Egypt because he thought that would attract more of the natives to the game if the pitcher was called Egyptian, even if it only meant he was from an Illinois town called Cairo which was not pronounced anything like its Egyptian namesake.

The seven run inning had made K.C. squeeze the second time through the batting order into an impossibly small space. Pfeffer's scorecard was even less spacious than the standard ones. Worse yet, K.C. had not seen the final out, and there was no one to ask. True to her vow, his wife was staying in the hotel, and no one else had noticed whether it was the shortstop or center fielder who had run over the pharaohs' tombs to catch the ball. He just guessed it had been the shortstop Williamson.

K. C. was seated on a raised sand dune next to an English-speaking native who considered himself a guide, but to K. C. he was another crank or potential crank. There were only a few hundred spectators present, mostly Americans from the embassy and a few curious Egyptians who had followed Clarence Duval, intrigued by his plantation dances and his gaudy outfit. Spalding had been unable to charge admission, so this game was being played mostly for the benefit of the photographer. The most conspicuous spectator was a rifle-carrying sheik who was observing from horseback, but he soon lost interest and rode off.

"Some idea Spalding had, playing here in the middle of all these monuments," K.C. began.

"Who is Spalding?"

"The leader of the tour."

"The short Nubian with the baton?"

"No. That was Clarence Duval and his plantation dance."

"What about the man with the monkey?"

"That's Cannonball Crane. The monkey is a hoodoo."

Alcohol was making Crane increasingly eccentric. He had adopted a pet monkey which he insisted on smuggling through customs. The guide had no idea what a hoodoo was, so he tried to treat K.C. as he would any other tourist.

"Are you glad to be out here among all these ancient works? We can tour them later. I have many stories about the pharaohs and the treasures they hid."

"Awesome. Looking at all these gigantic tombs is almost better than the game itself. But you have to wonder why anyone would build a grave so big. I hope I'm not offending your religion."

The guide's religion was officially that of his Muslim parents, but he had pretended to be an Anglican to learn English and a Catholic to learn French, so he was flexible. Usually he told the tourists he was Coptic Christian because most of them seemed to like that. Lately he had been escorting pyramidologists, and at first he had taken K.C. to be one of them. He was writing a string of numbers and symbols on a sheet of paper in a way that reminded him of those other kaffirs, but now he wasn't sure. It was hard to judge this American's religion, unless it was concerned with these things he called bats and balls.

"What's that down the third base line?" K. C asked. "Looks like a lion."

"What's a third base line?"

Shocked by his companion's ignorance, K. C. was reduced to pointing.

"That is the Great Sphinx."

"The one with the riddle?"

"I suppose so."

"Did you see Daly hit that one?"

K.C. recorded the home run that brought the score to 10-3. It was the only scorecard Pfeffer had managed to sell that day. The scorecard concession was not proving profitable, all the more reason for Fred to worry about next year's paychecks and the fines that would be deducted from them.

Daly's drive had gone over the right fielder's head, and then skipped a few times over the surface. It took so long to retrieve the ball that Daly managed to fight his way through the sand all the way home. When Chicago began to bunt, Ward ordered his third baseman to play dangerously close to the batter, which he did until a line drive nearly took his head off before it curved foul. After that he played back and allowed a few more runs to score on bunts, but eventually enough Chicago batters struck out to end the inning. The All-Americas led 10-6 going into the bottom of the fifth, and even Anson agreed that would be their last at-bat.

Spalding was already planning even better pictures when they would be playing in the Colosseum in Rome.

K. C. watched as the fifth and final inning drew to a close.

"It looks like Egyptian Healy is going to win the game."

"Is he the one who tagged all the men out?"

"No, that was Williamson. Anson calls him the best player in baseball, but everyone knows that Anson can't mean that because he really considers himself the best player in baseball. It looks like they're calling the game after five innings, but that still makes it an official game."

The guide knew all of these words except for innings, but he had no idea what they meant taken together. He did notice the players packing up their equipment, so he understood that matters were being drawn to a close.

"Perhaps now we can discuss my fee."

While the guide was informing K. C. that his services would cost a shilling, similar scenes were happening around the field. It seemed that the natives who were watching the game expected to be paid baksheesh for doing so. Unlike K. C. who handed over the requested coin, Spalding refused to give in because paying the spectators would have gone against his most deeply held principle.

When the natives were finally persuaded that their efforts had been in vain, the players were left almost alone. A contest to hit the Sphinx in the eye with a baseball was arranged, and unlike the pre-game pyramid toss, this time Fogarty succeeded in conking the old statue with an arching throw.

"Aren't we in danger of offending someone's religion," Ward suggested to Anson.

"No more than we would have been in Utah if anyone had seen it when we broke off a piece from Brigham Young's tomb. Besides, these people are Mohammedans, and they don't care about the old Egyptian religion. Let's race to the top of the big pyramid."

Ward wasn't sure that was a good idea.

"Are you sure that's legal? They must have some sort of an antiquity commission."

"Johnny, you don't want to race to the top of that overgrown triangle for the same reason you won't play me in billiards. You're afraid that I'll win."

No more mature than the others, Ward lined up for the race up the slopes of the Great Pyramid. Contrary to Anson's prediction, the nimble Ward was the first to the peak, followed by Crane, Anson and Pfeffer. Spalding's 62-year old mother was not far behind, just as eager to play a child's game as the men had been.

From the top of the pyramid, looking down on the Sphinx, Ward addressed Anson.

"I have a riddle for you, Adrian. What stands on ten toes when he's young, two flat feet when he's middle-aged, and one rump when he's old."

"I don't know."

"A ballplayer. A rookie is always on his toes. A veteran gets lazier, Then he's on the bench."

"Why is that funny?"

"You know what the Sphinx asked Oedipus. What walks on four legs then two legs then three? A human. First a baby, then a grown man, then an old man with a cane."

"I heard that one too. Why was that funny?"

14

The Mansion
49 Park Avenue, New York
February, 1889

Her honest accountant Bernie was the only person with whom Helen had ever discussed money frankly, so when she thought about selling the mansion, she consulted with him.

"Am I doing the right thing?"

"Helen, I'm an accountant. Black ink is good and red ink is bad. Income is good and expenditure is bad. Of course selling the house is a good idea according to that reasoning, but you can certainly afford to keep it. You don't need Mr. Ward's signature to sell an asset of Dauvray Productions, but are you sure he'll approve of your decision?"

"Mr. Ward sees the house the same way you do—an enormous expense to keep up, and he'd rather live in a hotel anyway. And now that her divorce has gone through, Clara might be getting married again. I'd like to buy out her share of the company and be done with it. I'm not sure if I'm through with acting, but I know that I don't want to be bothered with producing anymore."

"The newspapers say that Mr. Ward doesn't want you to be on stage. Is that true?"

"They make my husband seem like an anti-suffrage reactionary, but I think it's more that he's afraid I'll lose money. Selling the house will make him more comfortable. He says that owning a double mansion in New York means that you're involved in a confidence game, and we should stop being suckers and start cashing out. He also seems to think that we can live comfortably on his $4000 a year salary."

"So he still has no idea how rich you are. Well, as always, Helen, you're selling at the right time. A double mansion in the heart of New York complete with a modern stable is a millionaire's dream home. It may even command a premium because it belonged to a celebrated Broadway actress and her almost equally famous ballplayer husband. But you could afford to keep the house for sentimental reasons if you wanted to."

"Bernie, for me that is full of memories from 1887, and that's a year I am trying to forget."

Helen walked through her house, one room at a time, planning the advertisement while fighting the memories:

Music Room. 26' by 15', stage large enough to accommodate a small orchestra.

The music room. Here she had had her first seizure, convinced that she was going to die or had done so already. Back then her plays were all drawing packed houses, she was just becoming a baseball crankette, and she was beginning to enjoy summers in Saratoga Springs, but none of that mattered if she knew her brain could suddenly go out of control. Ward had been there and had been quietly understanding.

"My mother was a school teacher, so she taught herself not to be afraid of epilepsy. I got the right attitude from her. Stay calm and do what you can."

Still, there were no happy memories in the music room:

Lovely artist's studio 20' by 16', with large windows for northern light in the day and ample electronic lighting for the night. Bedroom with bath and dressing room attached.

Clara's room held not so many memories as imaginings. Even before the maid had written about Keefe, Helen had worried about how Clara was entertaining her gentlemen guests and how likely it was that Mr. Helms would find out.

Two bedrooms with attached bath, 20' by 15' each. Three guest bedrooms 10' by 12' each with washstands. Four servant rooms 8' by 12' with communal servants' bath.

Each of the upstairs bedrooms held a tender memory of love with John most of it between their secret marriage in August of '87 and their publicly announced marriage two months later. He had insisted on christening every bedroom in this fashion, saying that there was not much other reason to have so many rooms. These memories were not unhappy in themselves, but that they were only memories was sad.

Wide oak staircase with distinguished carvings, well-lit and eye-catching. The most striking feature of a magnificent house.

The staircase upset her the most, not for what she had seen, but for what she had heard. Here was where one of the maids said that Helen's brother Adolph had raped her. At first he said that she had made everything up, and then, after another maid had said what she had seen, Adolph said the sex had been agreed upon. What the truth was, Helen did not like to think about, but whatever had happened had happened on that stairway landing.

Paneled library, completely quiet with no windows on the street. Built-in shelves, sliding ladder for reaching top shelves.

The library was where Johnny had negotiated with the maid and her husband. After several days and five thousand dollars, Adolph had been kept out of jail, and he agreed to leave town. Clara had resented paying out the money and continued to feel that Ward had been insufficiently convinced of their brother's innocence. The library now held Johnny's law volumes, including a copy of the criminal code from each state his baseball team had visited, his own version of souvenir-hunting. Helen's books were mostly plays, some in French with handsome bindings, most in flimsy actor's copies. Johnny had his own collection of French books, mostly Alexandre Dumas père and Victor Hugo, all with English words written neatly above the French words he had looked up.

Ground floor office with street view.

The downstairs office was where she met with Bernie. Most of her memories here involved the struggle to divorce her unspeakable first husband and to keep her financial holdings away from him. Even after she had succeeded, his name had come up in the newspapers involving his schemes to defraud another woman. Bernie and she had been forced to revisit the whole scandal when the newspapers started asking around.

House wired for electric, light, telephone, gas heating and ovens. Modern plumbing throughout.

The telephone nook was where her mother had insisted on her immediate marriage when Clara mentioned that a newspaperman knew that Ward was spending the night there. Helen had truthfully pointed out that they were secretly married, but her mother insisted on a public ceremony the next day, one that she could attend herself just to be sure. The telephone had brought her very little happiness.

Modern kitchen with gas ranges and ovens. Sanitary sinks. Ventilation. Cold storage.

The kitchen had always been a burden. The previous owners had entertained lavishly, and Helen had kept their kitchen staff even though she and John rarely ate at home and then only the simplest of meals.

Modern stables with space for eight horses and two carriages. Direct access to Central Park.

The stables made her shudder with the fear of harm rather than harm itself. Johnny was such a poor rider that he was inclined to blame the horse for his own mistakes. With the stables right there, he sometimes rode through the park. If he continued to do so, he would inevitably have a serious accident. Selling the stables was something she had to do to protect John. She had even considered selling them separately, but it made more sense to include them with the house.

Downstairs master Bedroom 30' by 24' with attached bath and dressing room.

Tired from planning, Helen carried herself to the master bedroom, the worst memories of all. A man named Joseph Golding had rented the house across the street and spent most of the winter and spring of 1887 looking in her window. The police had arrested him, but he was soon out again, proclaiming his love for her and his intent to impress her with the fact that he had a job paying $3000 a year which he had quit to be near her. The more she thought about it, the more she realized that she had wanted to be married so that there would be a man in the house to drive this menace away.

She had made the house sound so good she almost wanted to buy it herself, but the memories were so painful that she would have been glad to give it away for nothing. John would be glad to get rid of it.

Back at the hotel in Cairo, Ward received a telegram from Helen telling him that she would be in Paris until the end of January meaning he had already missed a chance to join her there. He had been planning to bill and coo in French until he had won her back, and the thought of this still gave him momentary entertainment. But in his darker moments, he wondered who this Halévy was and asked himself if he should confront him when he reached Paris. But for the moment, he had to concern himself with the players' anger toward the Brush Plan.

15

A Fantasy Draft
Orient Hotel, Cairo
February 9, 1889

By the time the players arrived back at the hotel, they were all keen to have a meeting to discuss the Brush Classification Scheme they had seen in the American newspapers.

Classification	Maximum Salary
Class A	$2500
Class B	$2250
Class C	$2000
Class D	$1750
Class E	$1500

The classifications would be based on skill and sobriety. Each player was privately evaluating himself on both dimensions. Ward reserved a room in the hotel as discreetly as he could and called for an emergency meeting.

Organizing the White Stockings had been the Brotherhood's most significant National League challenge because in Chicago the newspapers had been creating an anti-union atmosphere, ever since the Haymarket bombing a few years before. But now, every player on the tour except Anson had joined the Brotherhood, and some players were paying back dues with up-to-date IOU's. Even Anson was offended at the idea that the best players would be limited to $2500 annually, not that he thought it would ever affect him personally. There was something in the Brush plan to offend everyone, from capped salaries for the A Class stars to park sweeping duty for the .220 hitters in Class E. In addition to those who had been active members for some time, new members like emerging star Jimmy Ryan were speaking out about the new salary limits. Ed Williamson had been skeptical of the union before, but he was quick to join when he heard about the proposal to base the classifications at least partly on sobriety.

Fury dominated the early stages of the meeting as the players read and re-read the newspaper accounts of the scheme. Two basic themes emerged when the players reacted.

1. It was a low and sneaky trick on Spalding's part to have the owners announce this while the players were scattered and Ward was out of the country
2. There had been agreements last year as to players' contracts and now the owners were ignoring their agreements before a full year had elapsed. Players from the disbanded Detroit team were being assigned against their will. So now the reserve clause bound the player for life even after that team had ceased to exist.

"The bastards waited until Johnny was nowhere near a telegraph, and then they did this," Hanlon began.

Pfeffer continued.

"Fines. I could wind up owing them for errors, especially with Spalding and Anson picking the official scorer."

Crane looked up from feeding his pet monkey. The long trip into the desert had sobered him up, and he was speaking clearly and intelligently, at least to the extent that a man hiding a monkey in a hotel could be said to do so.

"And we have to play unannounced specially scheduled games and don't see any of the money," he said. "Not our Giants, but that's what they did to St. Louis in the middle of the World Series. And when we left, it didn't look like the Browns were going to see any share of the gate for that exhibition with Brooklyn in the middle of the World Series. They weren't even sure if they'd get paid for the Series itself. Maybe we can get Comiskey to come over to our new league."

This was the first open mention of having the players start their own league, and at the time no one thought to challenge such a radical change in strategy. Instead, the others joined in.

"The club should have to pay for the uniforms. Mine gets all dirty from sliding and those blood stains don't come out sometimes," was Fogarty's contribution, bringing up everyday problems.

"If the players own the clubs, what difference does it make who pays for cleaning the uniforms," asked Hanlon who had thought the idea through a bit more than the others.

Williamson had another problem.

"If they can fine you for taking a drink, what are they going to do? They can take your money from fines and use it to pay more Pinkertons so that they can fine you some more?"

"There's more to this than your vanting to play drunk, Villiamson," growled Pfeffer, slipping into a German accent. The two had not gotten along since the time when a friend of Williamson's had been accused of being too much of a friend to Clarkson's wife and Clarkson was a friend of Pfeffer. "Ve should be more worried about whether they pay us ven ve're injured. I say that we start our own league on July 4. Ve can go on strike, and if they don't meet our demands, ve'll just start our own league. How about it, Johnny?"

"It's an idea, Fred, but it needs time to develop. And we have to have the best players from the American Association or the League will raid them and stay afloat."

"Without the owners we can make our own rules," said Hanlon who was already thinking of ways to slant any new rules toward his preferred roughhouse style of baseball.

"Invest in ourselves and be our own bosses," Tener suggested. "And maybe we could find our own backers. And we should be free to choose what city we want to play in. If they put me in the lowest classification and make me sweep the grandstand, I don't want it to be in Chicago. All those rotting German sausages make disgusting garbage, especially after that wedding ring of that butcher's murdered wife turned up in them."

Pfeffer brushed off the insult to his place of residence and its large German population. He had his own ideas.

"Ve're ready to make our own league. To make a baseball league, you need players, not money. Ve have all the players. The money vill follow. Ve just figure out who the best players are and make sure ve have them all. Ve could shtart by having each team pick its players. Jimmy Ryan is probably the best player in the league now, so whoever got first choice vould start with him."

"We should really just start with the teams that we have and adjust them," suggested Ryan, who nonetheless appreciated being designated the best. He turned to Tom Brown.

"Tom, what would Boston need to make a good nine in our new league. Mike Kelly's team will have to be the centerpiece when we start up on our own. He might be a drunk, but the cranks in Boston love him."

"That's because they're drunks too." Brown observed. "We could keep what we have if what I read about Brouthers coming to the club is true. I think we might use another pitcher, like Guy Hecker from Louisville so that Clarkson doesn't get too tired."

"Hecker's a member and wants to help us organize," Ward added. "Just for fun, I suppose we could all say what our club would do if we made our own league. How about the White Stockings, Fred?"

"Chicago vill need a manager and a first baseman. One who vould want to come to Chicago. That means Comiskey. And he could bring some of his Browns with him. Maybe Latham."

Williamson snarled.

"We don't need more infielders."

Ward looked at Healy. "What about Indianapolis?"

"The whole team needs to be replaced except Pebbly Jack Glasscock and me. They just don't draw enough cranks to pay the kind of salaries the other teams do. They have the same problem in Washington. Are you really going to be playing there, Johnny?"

"There's not a court in America that can make me go where I don't want to go. Washington's not much of a baseball town, and they don't have a very good club. When I see them, I want to yell, 'You're all muffins.'"

"The center fielder Hoy is pretty good," observed Hanlon.

"Yes," answered Ward. "But he's deaf, so I wouldn't be saying anything about him."

Crane spoke up. "If Johnny is going somewhere, and I'm staying in New York, we'll need a shortstop. Maybe we can get Glasscock if Indianapolis is disbanded."

Ward ignored the statement and looked at Hanlon.

"If they send you to Pittsburg, Ned, what will you need there?"

"Keep the pitcher Pud Galvin, and the young first baseman Jake Beckley and retrain the rest of them to play a new brand of baseball. I've been thinking it through for a while. More hit and run. More stealing bases."

"Nobody's mentioned the best hitter in the Association, the fellow they named the bat after, the Louisville Slugger. Who gets Pete Browning?" asked Tener.

"Nobody here from Cleveland? Let's pass him on to them," suggested Jimmy Manning, one of the few Association players on the tour. "Trying to get him to understand what you want him to do is impossible. He's as deaf as Hoy, but he won't admit it and doesn't know how to deal with it except by getting so drunk that nobody expects him to understand anything anyway."

"I'd rather have Big Davy Orr of all the hitters in the Association, even though he's a clumsy fielder," said Ward, who had been giving the matter some thought. How about Philadelphia, Jimmy?" Ward asked Fogarty.

"We'd like to add Jimmy Manning and Billy Earle," said Fogarty, diplomatically naming the two players on the tour who did not have a National League contract.

"Who should manage? Have you thought that through, Johnny?" Hanlon asked.

"Comiskey would be a good match for Chicago if we don't get Anson to go along. And I think you should manage Pittsburg, Ned. Fogarty, you're a leader. If Harry Wright doesn't join us, you'd be the best man for Philadelphia," Ward went on, as if building a new league in his head. Fogarty went along with the idea.

"Thank you, Johnny, and you should be managing New York instead of that oaf Ewing who leaves his mask out for people to trip on."

"I'd never say anything against Buck. Besides, didn't everyone say I'd be traded. Nobody's here from Cleveland, but Patsy Tebeau is a good Brotherhood man and he's ready to manage. Boston will probably wind up being managed by Kelly, if he wants it. Glasscock could manage Indianapolis if they keep their franchise.

"Who gets Tip O'Neill?" asked Crane, but the mood had changed.

"Who pays for the new ballparks, if we can't get the owners to sell us the old ones?" asked Tener who understood more about business than most of the players. But by this time, the players had discovered the end of the year batting averages for both the League and the Association. The statistical facts were incorporated into the discussion of who should play for which hypothetical manager on which hypothetical team, and this went on into the night and continued across the Mediterranean.

"The players can't be serious if they say they're starting their own league, Cap, no matter how angry they seemed."

"I'm pretty angry myself, Al. Last year I made $8,000 and now they're saying the top players will only make $2500."

"There's always profit-sharing. Don't worry. You know I'll always take care of you."

"I'm not the only one worrying. Nelly Williamson worries about Ed's future salary. Mrs. Anson has let me know that she does not want to try to live on $2500 a year, and I'm not going to ask her to."

"Tell the ladies they have nothing to worry about. They will enjoy continued prosperity, and when they reach Paris, I'll advise them to buy dresses at the very best shops. Mrs. Ward should be able to direct them. I know that my wife and mother will be on the boulevards looking for style."

"Not on $2500 a year. And it looks as though I'm not making any money on this tour, either."

"I am as shocked by the Brush plan as you are, but we both know that the best players will make side deals, like when they had the $3000 salary cap and Boston bought the rights for Kelly's picture for another $3000. But you'll agree that we can't go paying every duffer in the league $3000. And let's remember that we're on this tour is to promote the game. *Andamos a Napoli, poi Roma.* (We're going to Naples, then Rome.) See, I can speak Italian. We'll play in the Colosseum, then in Paris, then England, then maybe even Ireland."

"But what will happen when we get back to America? What if Ward and his rebels really try to start their own league?"

"From what I hear, and I think I hear it all, there was no talk about financing or building new teams. They just talked about who would be good on what team, like a bunch of cranks sitting around a hot stove back in Chicago."

16

Outdoor Exercise
Parc Aèrostatique, Paris
March 8, 1889

All Paris was welcoming the first fresh day of spring sunshine after weeks of cold, deep-soaking rain. Spalding had managed to secure a corner on a balloon launching field where the authorities had allowed him to lay out a diamond and surround it with improvised seating for five hundred at what translated to about a dollar a head. President Sadi Carnot had encouraged the event, but he was busy heading off a Boulangist coup, so he sent his regrets along with a proclamation recommending baseball to French youth as the kind of exercise which would prepare them for their military service.

Just across the Seine, the nearly completed Eiffel Tower was becoming a central part of the city's image. When first proposed, the tower had been denounced as impossible, dangerous, useless, ugly, expensive and American. Now replicas were being seen everywhere—on watch chains, dangling from feminine ears, and in confections the bakers had made from chocolate or marzipan. Ward gave a brief pre-game address in French. This served as a signal to the spectators that they were to cheer for the All-Americas and their handsome francophone captain. Spalding whispered to Anson as his manager prepared to take the field.

"There Ward goes again. Showing off like he did in Naples when he spoke Italian."

In Naples a foul ball had hit a *bambino*, and Spalding had attempted to pacify the crowed in Italian. Whatever he had said only enraged them more. Ward had only studied the language briefly, but he used a mixture of gestures and sufficient Italian to make himself understood well enough to prevent a Neapolitan *vendetta*. When Spalding had tried to schedule a game in the Colosseum, Ward had been the one to translate when the Italian authorities pointed out there was no floor in the ancient structure. To Spalding it seemed that Ward was siding with them.

Anson had an even darker view of Ward's motives.

"It's not just showing off. He's using his language to get the Frenchies to cheer for his team."

While in Paris, Cannonball Crane had discovered absinthe and believed in its special powers to remove inhibitions. His fast ball was traveling harder than ever, rising in on right-handed hitters, most of whom were content to strike out with their bones unbroken. The All-Americas were hitting the ball solidly, but third baseman Tom Burns was making one fine play after another. He had thrown out Ward on a bunt attempt and leaped in the air moving to his right to snag what should have been a line-drive double by Hanlon. In the top of the fourth, the All-Americas finally broke through. Crane, whose hitting had also improved inexplicably when he was under the influence, rapped a solid double and went to third on Hanlon's weak ball that floated through the sunny spring air like a butterfly before landing for a soft single. With runners on first and third, Hanlon stole second, and he followed Crane home on a single by Ward. The next inning an All-America basted a line drive between the outfielders. It skipped into the Seine for a home run.

K. C. found himself sitting next to three French adolescents who were cheering enthusiastically for the All-Americas, albeit with little understanding of the rules of the game. The boys had several sacks of baseball equipment, including a generous supply of National League quality Spalding $1 baseballs still in their red boxes and another sack of balls labeled Keefe and Becannon. Three Louisville sluggers made to Pete Browning's specifications gave off the smell of fresh ash. There were fingerless gloves for fielders and an overstuffed collection of rags that formed Jimmy Manning's new catcher's mitt, the one he had neglected to patent before heading overseas and which Spalding was now manufacturing. Another bag seemed to contain more catcher's equipment, a bird cage for the face and a breast protector.

Daniel, who spoke the best English, explained that his father knew Mrs. Ward, and now Mr. Ward was visiting with them while he was in Paris. Daniel seemed to know all of the government officials in attendance and was able to explain more about the politics of the Third Republic than K.C. would ever need to know. The tall athletic boy named Jacques was examining a pair of All America uniform pants with sliding pads and with a jock strap and protective cup sewn in. A third boy whom they called petit Marcel stared at the jock strap as he speculated on its use.

"It is to hold Jacques' enorme genitals."

Daniel said something to little Marcel in a tone which K.C. understood to contain a reprimand.

"Where did you get the uniform?" K. C. asked Daniel.

"Mr. Ward gave it to us. It was made for one of the players who did not appear for the tour."

"That must have been Mike Kelly. You must know his name. From the song, Slide, Kelly, Slide. The $10,000 beauty. That's why you have the sliding pads, to avoid bruises when you slide."

"What does slide wish to say?"

"That's when you throw yourself on the ground to avoid a tag."

"It must hurt a lot to be tagged if you would do that instead."

Back on the field, a play developed that gave the boys an illustration of why sliding pads were a good idea.

Williamson had spotted something in Crane's delivery that made him think he had a chance to steal second in spite of the slow, muddy base paths. He was one of the players who had disdained the sliding pads that Ward was trying to promote and who had been even more scornful when Jimmy Fogarty had suggested using a glove to protect the front hand on head first slides. Seeing that Ward had the ball waiting for him, Williamson attempted a wide sweeping hook slide only to encounter a jagged piece of rock sticking up through the mud. The sharp edge tore through Williamson's uniform pants and ripped a gash through his calf up to his knee where the cut felt even sharper as the rock tore tendons. Blood spurted in several directions, and bone appeared to be sticking out. Anson was the first to reach him, and he wrapped the rag they had been using to clean the bats around the wound, but even with the bleeding stopped, it was apparent that Williamson would not be able to finish the game. Ward agreed to allow a substitution. Anson moved Ryan in from center to play shortstop, sent Daly to center, called Mark Baldwin off the bench to play first and put himself behind the plate.

"Don't worry, Ed. Al will get you the best medical care available," Anson assured his teammate.

"And how did you boys get to know Johnny Ward again?"

Daniel answered.

"Mr. Ward's wife, Helen Dauvray, had done theater business with my father. We all met her when she visited Paris in January, and when Mr. Ward tried to find her, we met him, and now he is our friend, and he wants us to play baseball so he gives us these things."

Jacques broke in. "Mr. Ward thought his wife was having an amour with Daniel's father."

"Which is ridicule," said Daniel. "To my father, Miss Dauvray is an actrice. No more, no less.

"Une actrice charmante," commented Marcel.

"And when Mr. Ward saw Uncle Ludovic, he stopped being jealous because my uncle is an old man since a long time."

Jacques' mother was Daniel's father's cousin, but he called him uncle by courtesy.

"So, Mr. Ward stayed with us and became great friends with Jacques' step-father, M. Straus, who wants us boys to put our noses outdoors more," continued Daniel. "We are showing M. Ward Paris, and he is teaching us about baseball and baseball equipage."

"It must be a thrill for you all," K.C. said. "What other equipment is in the bag?"

"He gave us this big glove stuffed with rags and a piece of cork to protect our chest. And there is a mask like the one that hid Louis XIV's unfortunate twin brother."

Daniel pointed to Anson as the game resumed.

"Look, the red-faced man has finished his catcher's costume."

With Anson behind the plate, Ward instructed his players to steal bases whenever an opportunity presented itself. Before long Anson's hands were sore, and he was regretting his decision, but as a leader he had to show his men that he could endure hardship. Fogarty produced a run by stealing a base on one pitch, advancing on a groundout on the next, and scoring on a passed ball, sliding in ahead of the tag and placing his gloved hand on the nearest point of home plate.

The score was 3-1 going into the seventh, and both teams agreed to end the game after one more inning. Crane led off with another double, a ground ball that Daly caught up with before it went into the river. Hanlon singled him to third and then stole the second sack on an increasingly frustrated Anson. By the end of the inning, Ward's All-Americas were up 6-1, to the delight of those who had remained to watch the whole game. The bottom of the seventh wasn't much better for Chicago. Jimmy Ryan slapped a single, went to second on an out and scored on a solid single by Anson. However, the Chicago captain embarrassed himself by forgetting there was only one out and running on a fly ball to right fielder Tom Brown who caught the ball on the fly and ran over to tag first base before Anson could get back, thus ending the game on a rare unassisted double play by an outfielder.

Ward met the boys after the game. Daniel had made a list of prominent Parisian spectators which Ward used in a newspaper report he had agreed to write. Weather reports from England had resulted in the cancellation of the next few games, so Ward decided to stay a few extra days in Paris. If he couldn't be with Helen, at least he could be with her friends.

17

The Injury
March 1889
Paris

When Ward had gone to the Rue de Douaii, he had been re-directed to a double mansion on the Boulevard Haussmann, a street which ran through the center of all that was new and fashionable in Paris. Walking past the magnificent houses and the elegant shops, Ward had felt a growing sense of inferiority mixed with jealousy. However, upon reaching the residence and being shown in to meet his supposed rival, Ward's fears had evaporated. Ludovic Halévy seemed to be at least sixty, and he had his foot propped up on a pillow to relieve gout. He was surprisingly friendly.

"Your wife became friends with my cousin Geneviève who lives in the other half of this building. After the death of her husband, my friend and collaborator Georges Bizet. . ."

Here he interrupted himself to whistle a few familiar bars of Carmen.

". . . every man in Paris, myself included, wanted to marry his beautiful widow, my cousine, but Leo Straus was the most determined as well as the richest."

Mme Straus's salon attracted a mixture of writers, musicians, government officials and aristocrats carrying titles dating from as far back as Charlemagne or as recently as Napoleon III. Musical recitals or dramatic readings added tone to the proceedings, but gossip was the preferred activity, one for which Ward lacked both the background and the language skills to participate. There was, however, one way in which he won his hostess's warm appreciation. Most of the guests tended to ignore Leo Straus, whose Rothschild-derived wealth only partially compensated for his Jewish ancestry and Semitic appearance. Ward liked Straus immediately, probably because Straus spoke the best English Ward had encountered in France. Straus hoped Ward would help him in his endless quest to make his stepson Jacques and his cousin Daniel and their friends spend more time in outdoor exercise. Straus was also very re-assuring on the subject of Helen.

"You had not the slightest reason to be jealous of her. My wife's cousin Ludovic may have wanted her to invest in one of his plays, but sometimes he wants everyone he meets to put up money, but then he gets enough from somewhere, and then he forgets about money. Mostly he liked her because she listened to him when he complained about his gout. Mrs. Ward and her sister spent most of her time going around museums and concert halls and studios with my boys. You can't be jealous of them."

"Doesn't that one they call little Marcel send flowers to your wife?"

"By the wheelbarrow. But I couldn't be jealous of Marcel. Besides, it was your wife that he always used to sit next to at our soirées. It wouldn't surprise me if he didn't know your Helen better than anyone. Marcel has a knack for listening to women."

"Shouldn't that make him dangerous, even as young as he is?"

Straus laughed.

"I shouldn't tell you this story, but it's no secret. All the boys know about it. For a time Marcel's parents wouldn't let him leave the house, even to visit us. It seems that his father had walked in on him while he was practicing the solitary vice."

"You mean . . ."

"Yes. And that was why his parents wouldn't let him come to our house for a while."

"Probably because they guessed he was in love with your wife. Why would his father make such a scene over that? You overhear things like that all the time. That's why a ballplayer knocks before entering a room when he knows his roommate is in there alone."

"As men of the world, we understand such things, but Marcel's father is a public health doctor, and he has written on the physical and psychological dangers of the practice. So Dr. Proust did what any normal French father would do. He gave the boy ten francs and sent him to brothel."

"So that means that the boy has made love to a woman."

"No. It seems that Marcel paid his ten francs and was ready to go, if you know what I mean. Then he broke a chamber pot and became not so ready. They kept his ten francs and told him that if he came back, he'd have to pay another ten francs plus three more for the chamber pot."

"The poor boy."

The next afternoon Ward was showing the boys how to catch fly balls, but there was a brief rain shower. Jacques and Daniel disappeared, leaving Ward alone with Marcel to wait it out in the gazebo. Marcel's English was heavily accented and imperfect, but if he took his time, he could produce long complicated almost grammatically correct sentences.

"Your charming wife presented me with a copy of your very excellent book *Baseball* which I have comprehended more now that I have seen how you play because Maman could help me with the English but many of the words were strange to us both, like shortstop which is not in our Anglais-Français dictionary but it is what you are Mrs. Ward explained to me before she is gone back to New York."

Ward decided that Straus may have been right. Perhaps this boy could tell him something about Helen.

"Was she very angry that I did not meet her?"

"Her sister was enragé and called you names which I did not understand and which I did not want to ask Maman about, but Mme. Ward said it was her own fault that she left San Francisco. You should go to your wife and tell her that you appreciate her. She recites Racine so well, better than Sarah Bernhardt."

"I miss her so much. I can't tell you how often I think of her, picture her."

"The consolation for the pain of love is the image we carry of the beloved. An image we can call forth in our imagination."

"Or memory."

"I must imagine my memories. But they become so powerful that they overtake me, sometimes leaving a trail like the escargot secretes along his path."

Ward knew what kind of process led to such secretions. The boy must have been thinking of Mme. Straus at the awkward moment when his father walked in and caught him before his snail could start to secrete.

"I'm sure you will find a nice clean girl your own age and start making your own memories. And you should stay away from brothels. They're full of disease and lies and lies about disease."

"Do you have a favorite memory, a moment? An image you remember in lonely times?"

Ward could not believe that he was in the middle of a discussion of the most intimate details of a person's sex life, the relationship between mind and hand. For a second he thought of how he had remembered the swaying hips and exposed bosoms of the Hawaiian hula dancers, but he passed that over for a more persistent image.

"It was a night in Central Park with a lady wearing a corsage of lilies—cattleyas. The coach was a particularly luxurious well-appointed brougham with the fragrance of cedar wood and new leather. I pretended that I was adjusting the corsage, and I let my hand slip onto the very top of one of her breasts. I pretended that I had been clumsy, that it had been a mistake, but she took my hand and left it where it was. Remembering the touch of her hand on my hand gives me some consolation at lonely times.

Ward wondered if the boy's English was good enough to understand everything he had said, but he must have gotten the gist of it, because he sighed and observed, "We must all console ourselves during lonely times."

"Just remember to lock the door."

"One more thing, Mr. Ward. Your friend who was injured in the baseball game yesterday. My father says that Mr. Spalding picked the worst doctor in Paris, probably because he was also the most cheap. My father has recommended a doctor who has heard of Pasteur and understands the importance of hygiene. Here is his address."

Ward promised Marcel that he would return to America and begin to reconcile with Helen as soon as he could get a release from Spalding and arrange passage to New York. In the meantime, Marcel had asked Mme Straus to write a letter to Helen telling her how delighted everyone in Paris had been with M. Ward. She agreed to do so, but did not see the point.

"But Marcel, why must I write a letter like that?"

"Because the little American woman and her husband love each other."

"But why should she listen to me?"

"Because she wants to become a parisienne, and you are the most parisienne of all women."

"Always you proustify."

18

The Poem
Delmonico's, New York City and elsewhere
April 9, 1889 and days following

Spalding's returning tourists were honored by a lavish and well-publicized banquet held at America's most famous restaurant, Delmonico's. America's leading toastmaster, Chauncey de Pew officiated. America's favorite writer Mark Twain, who was finishing a book which included an attempt by a time-traveling Yankee to introduce baseball to King Arthur's knights, was also in attendance. New York City's Police Commissioner Theodore Roosevelt was among the rising young politicians elbowing each other in their eagerness to be identified with the increasingly popular sport. The gathering was taking on an almost official aspect, a national consecration. Spalding himself felt as Alexander might have if he had taken a trip back to Macedon to hear his countrymen praise his conquests. The international tour had spread the game while at the same time emphasizing that it was America's National Game.

"My friend Henry Chadwick claims baseball has an English origin. [Boos and catcalls] We know it's not just *an* American game; it's *the* American game."

The crowd began to chant "No Rounders," some directly into Chadwick's ears. This was followed by a series of toasts to Spalding and his players and the manly American game that they had shown the world.

While this was happening, two of Helen's Broadway friends, Digby Bell and DeWolf Hopper were waiting their turn to go on with a skit. Hopper stood over six and a half feet tall, and his friend Bell barely came up to his shoulder. Just seeing them walk onto the stage together was enough to start the audience to tittering. Both were rabid Giant fans, frequently arriving at the games in a hired Tally Ho coach, the kind that was driven by young millionaires who did it as a lark. The actors had been observing Helen and Ward with special interest.

"Helen looked as happy as she could be with Ward tonight," Bell remarked.

Hopper agreed.

"It looks as if we'll still be getting choice Giant tickets. When I heard that she had left the tour in San Francisco, I wouldn't have given two dollars Confederate for their chances."

"I thought it was over this winter when she came back from Europe complaining that Ward had failed to meet her."

"When I saw the mansion was up for sale, I figured she was cutting her losses with Ward and the theater business."

"When I heard that Ward was going to be sold to Washington, I remember thinking that Helen would never go to watch him play at Swampoodle Grounds or live in a house on Foggy Bottom. Why didn't that sale go through?"

Hopper had more inside information than his friend.

"Ward refused to be traded."

"Can they do that?"

"Ward can."

"Well I thought they were going to be divorced when that McDermott fellow started chasing Ward around complaining about finding Ward wrestling with his wife."

"That was just before they were married. About a week before."

Bell noticed the time was getting late.

"We don't have time for a full skit. Why don't you just recite the baseball poem you did at the baseball night at Wallack's Theater last year?"

"The outlook wasn't brilliant for the Mudville nine that day. . . ."

Helen admired the way Hopper could fill the room with his powerful baritone voice finding the music in the predominantly anapestic verse. The excitement built when he reached the point where there were runners on second and third and two out. Hopper made the audience hear the dull roar of the crowd, "rumbling through the valley and rattling in the dell." Then Hopper abruptly switched to a high-pitched and adoring female voice, shrieking excitedly, "For Casey, mighty Casey, was advancing to the bat."

Equally impressive to the actress was the way in which Hopper had orchestrated gestures to the point where the action started to take over. Hopper was sneering as he prolonged the word "sneeeeeeer," and Helen noticed how perfectly the portable new stage lights caught the expression. Just after Hopper delivered the first imaginary pitch, a new voice intruded as the umpire roared "Strike One," while lifting his right hand to signal a called strike. (This custom was said to have started when Hoy suggested that it would be of benefit to him personally and the fans who were far away.) When Hopper came to the line "Kill the umpire," Helen recognized an uncanny imitation of an ill-tempered crank who often used those exact words at the Polo Grounds.

Hopper pounded the plate with his imaginary bat after taking another strike, then switched to the pitcher's role, using a delivery that closely resembled Tim Keefe's. He then took a swing that might have been by King Kelly, and Hopper switched back to the real stars of the poem—the Mudville cranks.

"Oh somewhere in this favored land
the sun is shining bright,
Somewhere men are laughing,
and somewhere children shout,
But there is no joy in Mudville -
Mighty Casey has struck out."

"That was a powerful performance. I think our friend Mr. Hopper is on his way to being a star. It wouldn't surprise me to see him in a lead role soon," Helen commented.

"Timothy was the pitcher in that poem," Clara observed to her sister who was accompanying Ward as an ostensibly contented wife.

"But the poem comes out of California," Ward countered, always ready to contradict his sister-in-law.

"But Timothy's sisters say that the poem was written by Ernest Thayer, and he is from the Boston area, just like Timothy."

"Then it could have been about Clarkson. He's from there too," said Ward who never wanted Clara to get the last word.

Ward and Helen had reconciled rather easily. The sale of the mansion had taken away the pressure of living surrounded by servants and horses. Hotel living suited the couple, and separate hotels made it even better, with Ward staying at the Clarendon near Nick Engel's Home Plate Saloon while Helen had access to the shops and tearooms of the theater district from her suite at the Vendome. At night Ward would sometimes walk over to the Vendome where the hotel detective winked at him because he had been informed that, in spite of appearances, these were not extra-marital trysts. Before Ward had even arrived back in America, Helen had been softened by a letter from Mme. Straus that talked about how all of Paris had been impressed with her husband and that had urged her to bring him on the next visit. Ward had promised not to object to a future return to the stage and not to be jealous, promises that he knew were contradictory but which he would try to fulfill. Another thing he promised was that they would go to Paris together as soon as baseball season ended. Helen had told Ward about the letter from Mme. Straus and she was surprised to hear that he had also had a letter from one of their friends.

"That pale thin boy with bad asthma and slicked down hair wrote me a letter reminding me that I should be good to you because you're a better actress than Sarah Bernhardt."

"Little Marcel. How he does proustify."

"I learned that word too. It reminded me of O'Rourke. Long complicated sentences and generally flattering."

"That's it. So Marcel wrote to you just to say that I was beautiful?"

"He thanked me for the baseball equipment and said he was going to take it with him when he left for his military service in November."

"We'll have to go to Paris before then, before *l'Exposition Universelle* closes. Did he say anything else?"

"He said that Williamson is slow to recover from his injury. Ed would have been a lot worse if he hadn't switched to a doctor who was recommended by that boy's father. Spalding was having him treated by a quack. Your little friend might have saved his life."

"Did you save the letter?"

"Why?"

"His friends say he might be a great writer some day."

"Not with that penmanship. The only legible parts were where his mother had corrected his English. My publisher would never have accepted *Base Ball* if my handwriting had looked like that."

"They have machines for that now," said Helen, who was always aware of the coming technologies.

Keefe had been left to organize a pre-season Brotherhood meeting. Ward's contract with Spalding required his services through the month of April, so he had to tour for several more weeks, including a stop in Washington where the cranks let Johnny know what they thought of his refusal to play for them. Ward had arrived in time to preside, but the most conspicuous presence at the meeting was that of Mike Kelly, dressed in a pearl gray suit with a matching top hat, as befitted the $10,000 beauty. Kelly had arrived late, somewhat delayed by the new custom of cranks' soliciting his autograph, sometimes on the sheet music for the latest hit "Slide, Kelly, Slide," and other times on his supposed autobiography *Play Ball*.

"I think they ask me for my autograph because they want to see if I know how to write my name."

Kelly's main contribution to the proceedings was the promise that "The boys will stick together, and I will stick with the boys."

Ed Williamson had not yet returned to the States, and his injury was on everyone's mind. Injury pay was routine for some teams, like the Giants or Boston, but other owners reasoned that if a player could not put the uniform on, there was no point in paying him.

The one man all the others listened to was Jim White, also known as Deacon. White had been a star all the way back to the days of the National Association of

Professional Baseball Players, and he was possibly the most respected player in the game, partly because of his immense knowledge of baseball history backed up by his habit of saving every document or scorecard he had ever seen. People called him Deacon because of his profound Christian faith, something that found its expression in good-natured kindness.

White had hoped to start his own minor league team in Buffalo, but he was being told he had to report to Pittsburg. Worst of all, the Pittsburg franchise was paying a fee from which he was to receive nothing. White resented the idea that money was being paid for his services and none of it was going to him, and by now everyone knew his famous quote.

"No man's going to sell my carcass without my getting a share."

Spalding was still holding out the possibility that players could get a share of the money being paid for them and with sums like $10,000 being mentioned for a star, a share of one-third looked attractive. Some of the players were lured by the hypothetical money, each mentally calculating his worth, invariably rating himself higher than the others would. Those who remembered their fractions managed to estimate what a third would bring, and more than a few spoke in favor of pursuing this as a major item for negotiations. Dan Brouthers, usually silent enough that people listened when he talked, stood up and pleaded passionately.

"Let's set a structure that will give us all a fair salary and don't be fooled by promises to give you one-third of some price that the owners can always set among themselves. If they had to give us one-third of something, they'll figure out a way to make it one-third of nothing."

Ward had brought schedules for every team, including those in the American Association, and the players set about the task of picking the right date for their next meeting. After comparing train schedules and days off from play, there was only one day that made sense for a major meeting, and Ward announced the date dramatically.

"Le Quatorze Juillet." (The Fourteenth of July.) Bastille Day."

"What?" asked Kelly.

"The hundredth anniversary of the beginning of the French Revolution."

Part Two
Baseball's Greatest Season

19

The Song
St. George Grounds, Staten Island
April 29, 1889

The Giants were making their temporary headquarters on Staten Island, across the water from the Statue of Liberty, because New York City was extending 111th St. through the old Polo Grounds. The aldermen had refused to stop the project, and cynical newspapermen suggested that this was because Giants' owner John Day had not observed such traditional courtesies as handing out envelopes stuffed with cash. The state legislature, for whatever motives, voted to rescue the Giants by passing a bill blocking the street extension, but the governor had surprised everyone by exercising his veto, invoking the principle that the state should not interfere with internal city business. The Giants had planned to play in Jersey City, but it was soon apparent that they had to be closer to their fans, so they were trying to get the old New York Metropolitans' field back in shape. Matters had not been helped by a huge stage behind second base, left over from a theatrical production the year before.

In the bottom of the first, a ball bounded over the head of the Giants' center fielder Mike Slattery whose spikes had caught on an uneven part of the wooden stage. The groundskeeper had covered the wood with a thin cushion of mud, but even so the bounce was surprising. Fortunately for the Giants, it traveled at an angle and right fielder George Gore, always alert when he happened to be sober, was in position to field it and throw the Washington runner out at second. When the Giants came to bat in the top of the third, they loaded the bases, but the Statesmen's center fielder Hoy, clever enough to have switched to rubber-soled shoes, charged in hard and made a diving catch just as the ball was about to hit the hard surface. Because there were two umpires for this special occasion, Umpire McQuaid was in a perfect position to get the call right.

Hoy led off the fourth with a bunt between Crane and first baseman Roger Connor. Connor had hesitated and Crane had started after the ball far too late. Ward yelled across the infield to Connor.

"I think you had enough time to field that and get back to the bag, Roger."

Connor turned and looked to Ewing as if to remind Buck that it was the captain's job to criticize, not Ward's. Furthermore, Roger was now regarded as the second best player on the team next to Buck, so Ward was not following the protocol appropriate to their respective ranks. If anything, Crane should have been the one to hear a reprimand. The inning ended harmlessly when Hoy was forced out at second for the final out. As he left the field, he slipped a note into Ward's pocket, which Ward considered to be odd until he remembered that Hoy was deaf and reluctant to use his voice. Between innings, Ward pulled out the muddy missive.

Mr. Ward,

I wish to be associated with the Brotherhood in all ways. If we have a strike, I will strike. If we invest our own money, I have $500 savings.
William Hoy

In the bottom of the sixth, the Washington shortstop reached the initial sack on an error by second baseman Danny Richardson, proceeding all the way to third on a wild pitch while the catcher looked for the ball. Another wild pitch brought home the first run of the game.

K. C. had spent two hours getting to the game with the last leg of his trip a crowded ferry ride because the transit system was unprepared for an influx of 3000 cranks. Arriving at the ball grounds just before the first pitch, he found himself seated next to a young sport in a canary yellow plaid suit with a matching straw boater. Next to him, a young lady recorded each play on her scorecard with the attention to detail of an accountant and the painstaking calligraphy of a medieval monk. She called to the players, using their first names.

"Nice play Roger. Good throw, Johnny. Throw it past them, Cannonball."

Her escort applauded vigorously when Crane registered another strikeout. This gave K. C., who always liked to be rooting in the same direction as the fan next to him, a chance to address him.

"You're a Giant fan, I suppose."

"Most assuredly. All of us in the theater crowd have been Giant fans ever since Helen Dauvray started following them. She's been my favorite actress from the time she returned from France in triumph after appearing as Miss Maggie. But then Helen was in 'Mona' which we all adored. She was so good in 'One of Our Girls' that I even went out of town to see it in Boston and Philadelphia. 'Scrap of Paper' and 'Met by Chance' were exquisite too, no matter what the critics said. Then she took ill and retired to Saratoga Springs until she took up baseball and Mr. Ward. I suppose he is the most famous baseball player in the world, especially after the tour."

This put K.C. back on grounds he could understand.

"Johnny Ward is my favorite, but most people would say that Mike Kelly is more famous."

"'Slide, Kelly, Slide.' I know the song. Is that the one?"

The girl could not hold back a slightly disgusted look.

"That's him," K. C. assured the young dandy.

In the top of the seventh, Crane walked and stole second on the first pitch. He then scored on a double by Gore. In the eighth Ward tapped a weak ground ball which pitcher Hank O'Day fumbled, allowing Ward to reach first.

"If Crane can steal, so can I," Ward thought to himself.

Not only did he steal second, but he took third on a throwing error by Connie Mack, the gangly young catcher. Ward eventually came home to score the lead run. In the bottom of the eighth the visiting Statesmen got off to a good start when the Giant third baseman muffed a slow roller by Hoy. The diminutive center fielder kept distracting Crane by leading off the base and feinting as if he were going to steal. Unnerved, Crane walked two batters. When Captain Ewing, who was sitting out this game, started out to the mound, Cannonball waved him back with a snarl. He struck out the next two batters, but then a pop fly dropped in the outfield. Ward picked it up quickly enough so that only one run scored. This kept the score tied at 2-2.

And when the score was 2-2, the girl knew what to do. She sang a song encouraging all of the Giants by name, a clever anthem of her own design. After she finished, she sent her young man down to look for the vendor, which gave K.C. a chance to talk to this remarkable crankette with whom he seemed to share common interests.

"Your beau seems to know a lot about theater. Is he your intended?"

"Heavens no. I ain't about to marry him or anyone like him. When he asked me to walk out, he wanted to go to a show. I told him that Katie Casey was not about to go to any theater. If he wanted to take me out, he could take me out to the ball game. My mother said he should be glad that I was only costing him 50 cents plus a ferry ride instead of five dollars and a hansom cab. All he could talk about on the ferry was Helen Dauvray like she was the one playing shortstop. It'd be a cold day in hell before I'd ever marry somebody like him."

"So maybe you'd want to marry a ballplayer as Helen Dauvray did."

Katie interrupted the conversation briefly to criticize the umpire who had just called Danny Richardson out on strikes, but then she answered his question.

"From what I've heard, Johnny Ward's a better shortstop than a husband. No, I'd never marry a ballplayer," she said, crossing herself. "He'd always be out of town like a traveling salesman, and everyone knows drummers make the worst husbands. Or worse yet, he could be sold to another city and you'd have to fall in love with a new team. Or you might marry a good Irishman like Cornelius McGillicuddy and watch him start calling himself Connie Mack. No, I'd never marry a ballplayer. I'd prefer a loyal supporter because he'd know how to be faithful for better or for worse, in sickness and in health, in first place or in last."

"So you'd never want to marry a ballplayer."

"Not since I found out that Roger Connor was already married."

"Roger is a crackerjack. By the way, where did your friend go?"

"I just sent him to buy me some peanuts and popcorn snacks." She turned her attention back to the field where third baseman Whitney was coming to bat. "Come on, Ed, you can hit this O'Day fellow."

Whitney led off the ninth by hitting a ball that bounced over the fence for a home run. It could be seen rolling outside the park until it hit a pile of debris. One out later, Cannonball Crane assured his status as the day's hero by hitting a home run cleanly over the same fence, heading out into the Narrows and from there to the Atlantic Ocean.

Katie's escort returned with the aforementioned refreshments.

"We can beat the crowd on the ferry if we leave now. Your Giants are sure to win."

Katie was visibly shocked.

"I think I'll stay and root for the home team. I don't care if I ever get back."

K.C. had never enjoyed a day at the ball park more than this one. For the next twenty years he talked about Katie to anyone who sat next to him at a game. Since he rarely sat next to the same person twice, a great many people heard the story in detail. Eventually a pair of Tin Pan Alley songwriters who had never attended a ball game set the story to a catchy tune with snappy rhymes.

> Katie Casey was baseball mad
> Had the fever and had it bad
> Just to root for the home town crew
> Ev'ry sou
> Katie blew
> On a Saturday her young beau
> Called to see if she'd like to go
> To see a show, but Miss Kate said "No,
> I'll tell you what you can do:
>
> Take me out to the ball game
> Take me out with the crowd

Buy me some peanuts and Cracker Jack,
I don't care if I never get back.
Let me root, root, root for the home team,
If they don't win it's a shame,
For it's one, two, three strikes you're out
At the old ball game."

Katie Casey saw all the games
Knew all the players by their first names,
Told the umpire he was wrong,
All along,
Good and strong,
When the score was two to two
Katie Casey knew what to do,
Just to cheer up the boys she knew,
She made the gang sing this song.

It should have been an uneventful ninth, but Crane decided to complicate matters by avenging a slight by the left fielder who suggested that Crane was drunk. It took four pitches before Cannonball finally managed to hit the offending batter, but after that the Statesmen were retired easily. Ward felt a brisk sea breeze as he looked out over the ocean, and he was glad to be in New York with a settled contract. The Giants were going to repeat as world champions, his marriage was going to be at peace, and the Brotherhood would force the owners to deal with them fairly or the players would start their own league. In spite of the mud, spring was a time for hope. This was going to be baseball's greatest season.

20

The Holdout
New York
May, 1889

After publicly announcing that she was ready to return to the stage, Helen had quietly changed her mind. As soon as plans started to be made for a new play, she realized that her theatrical career had reached an *impasse*. The scripts she had been offered all seemed to feature a fresh-faced girl next door, loved by the hero and desired by the villain, but most of all, the darling of the audience. She wanted to do Racine or Corneille in French, or at least Molière if she must be a comedienne. Her mirror confirmed what the calendar had already told her—she had passed thirty and was starting to show her age. Worse than that, she was starting to lose the energy she had always taken for granted. But she was not going to give up the theater when pressured to do so. Helen was not about to let any man tell her what to do with her life, not after making all of her own decisions since she was ten years old passing for seven.

Ward's reasons for opposing her return to the stage were disappearing. With the sale of the Park Avenue double mansion, his financial concerns were reduced since he figured the proceeds from that sale could finance a few more flops before Helen had to start spending his money. Better still, her jewelry collection was now in a hotel safe, so he wouldn't have to worry about burglars any more. Most important, he was overcoming his jealousy after having made a fool of himself over it in Paris. M. Straus had assured him of Helen's fidelity while warning him.

"To have a beautiful wife is to have a wife that many men will fall in love with. To expect her not to enjoy that is to expect too much."

When Ward suggested that it was inappropriate for a wife to work, Helen found the most personal argument possible.

"You told me once that people back in Bellefonte thought that your mother shouldn't be an assistant principal because she was a woman. Were they right?"

Ward thought of himself as a suffragist, and he supported women's rights to property to the extent that he had made no claim on Helen's assets, whatever they were. With the $4000 annual salary he had just negotiated, they could both live well, especially now that they were not supporting a double mansion with its stables. And best of all, it seemed that Clara would soon be moving out.

Jim O'Rourke dropped by Keefe's hotel to give him some advice on holding out.

"Much as it would benefit us to have you return, you must not capitulate. Day knows he needs you, and the need becomes clearer each day. I would advise you not to sign until your remuneration reaches a satisfactory level, perhaps $5000 a year like Ewing. Day can afford it."

"Perhaps I'll sign for less if he agrees not to include a reserve clause. Ward says that's what holds us back."

"I support Johnny in his efforts, but I think he's wrong in this case. As long as the other owners collude to refuse to sign you, not having the reserve clause does not help. At one time, I agreed to a three year contract with no reserve clause, modestly assuming that someone would want to sign a .328 hitter, but with no offers forthcoming, I had to settle for the pittance Buffalo could afford to pay me. The other teams treated me like a pariah dog, even the ones in the Association that could have used proficient batsman."

Clara's divorce was final, but she was still living with Helen in the Vendome where they had taken a suite large enough to give her a well-lit studio. Keefe was still holding out for $4500 a year, giving the Giants a chance to see how they would do without their best pitcher. Clara had persuaded Keefe to pose for a statue while wearing the uniform which she had designed. New York was prominently lettered across the form-fitting shirt, but what caught the eye most was the bulge in the front of Keefe's pants. He was forced to hold his pitching pose indefinitely, rather like one of the lovers about to kiss on Keats's Grecian urn. Clara chipped away lovingly, displaying all of his long stringy manly muscles and then some. Competent judges had decided Clara lacked brilliance and originality, but Helen had paid for her sister to receive the best training available, and the lessons on anatomy had evidently been useful in completing this labor of love. After a long day of posing, Keefe was relieved when Clara released him.

"Being about to pitch is a good bit harder than pitching."

Ward had arrived to take Helen out for dinner only to find that she was out running errands. Clara was increasingly uncomfortable with Ward around, so she quickly excused herself, leaving the two ballplayers together. Ward giggled over the statue and the prominence it gave to Keefe's male member.

"Be glad there's a house detective, or she'd have you posing naked."

"We might be getting married if we can work everything out."

"Don't ever say I didn't warn you about that. But I'm glad to see you alone. I wanted to talk to someone about a letter I just received, and it looks as if we're going to be family in spite of my best advice."

There had been a time when Keefe and Ward had barely been speaking, but Brotherhood business had brought them closer together. When Ewing had replaced Ward as team captain a few years before, Ward had stopped telling Keefe how to pitch, and that had helped. Now they were good enough friends that Ward felt he could confide in Keefe, so he showed him the letter.

"Tell me what you think I should do about this."

Dear Mr. Ward,

Please do not turn me away, as I seek protection from my monster of a husband. George has become impossible to live with, and now I must seek my own career. People tell me that I would make an attractive actress. Now that your wife is returning to the stage, would you ask her to include me in her next theatrical production?

Your friend,
Jessie McDermott

After finishing the letter, Keefe took a minute to compose his thoughts so that he could phrase them diplomatically.

"Do you think I should tell Helen about it. That would show her that there was nothing to those rumors. I was as innocent as a newborn babe."

Keefe had happened to be listening when George McDermott had chased Ward around the Polo Grounds, accusing him, among other things, of burying his face in her décolletage. He couldn't hold back a comment.

"Show a newborn babe a tit, and he'll start sucking."

Ward realized that he had been caught in a lie or something like one, so he became a little more forthcoming.

"She was crying, and I was hugging her. Somehow, one of her bosoms started to pop out of her dress. I wanted to help her get it back in, but while it was out, I may have given it a little nuzzle. That's when her husband came in."

"Is she trying to blackmail you?"

"Oh no. She's an innocent young girl, barely eighteen. She would never think of doing something like that. She's just desperate because her husband abuses her. You saw him when he was angry."

"I heard that Jessie is kind of pretty."

"That's would be an understatement. She has high cheekbones, perfect features, deep soulful eyes, and a peaches and cream complexion. Her waist is so slender I can make a circle around it with my thumbs and forefingers, and her bosoms are so large and full and shapely that no man can turn his head way from them when she wears a low-cut dress, or even when she doesn't. She could be an artist's model or an actress. She's more beautiful than any woman on the stage today."

"Let me get this straight. You're saying this Jessie looks better than all of the other actresses. Is that what you plan to tell Helen?"

"Maybe not."

"And you want to introduce her to Helen even though her husband nearly got arrested complaining about you, and it was in all the papers."

"The only thing Helen said to me about that was that she believed I had done nothing wrong except by associating with a low Tammany type like George McDermott in the first place. Maybe she'd be sympathetic to a young wife trying to get away from him."

"I'm no expert on women, but it seems to me that introducing this lass to Helen would not be good idea. And you'd better stay away from Mrs. McDermott yourself, at least until she's fat, old and ugly."

This excellent advice found its mark, at least temporarily. Before the road trip to Philadelphia, Ward took his wife on another carriage ride, mentioning nothing about Jessie or Helen's theater career. She carried a bouquet of lilies, a clear signal in their private language that everything was going to be all right, at least for that evening.

The Strike
New York and elsewhere
April-May, 1889

Ward called a special meeting of the original Brotherhood members on the Giants: Keefe, Ewing, O'Rourke and Welch. As the players seemed to be moving toward a strike or establishing their own league, Ward worried about the owners' ability to find replacement players, so an opportunity to organize the American Association was welcome.

"I brought us together is to decide how much we want to extend our organization to include more Association members. We've all been following the troubles the Browns are having. I just got a letter from Arlie Latham. Let me read it to you."

Dear Johnny,

An injustice to one is an injustice to all. By now you have seen the newspapers and probably know something of what just happened in Kansas City, but let me tell you how it all came about. It started when Yank Robinson showed up in dirty pants. Now Yank gets fat sometimes and then skinny again, and this year he's in the skinny category. Now Herr Von der Ahe is always telling Yank to change his pants, especially on the day in question. So Yank had to send one of the boys from around the park to pick up his clean skinny pants, and when the kid got back, the old man at the gate wouldn't let him in. Yank saw what was happening and went down to explain things, but Von der Ahe heard them and he started cussing Yank, telling him that he was going to fine him $100. Yank said he wouldn't pay the fine, so the rest of us said we wouldn't go to Kansas City unless the German cancels the fine. Comiskey saw it all coming, and the boys at the pool hall tell me that he skipped placing his bets before he left for Kansas City, which told the boys something because he always bets big when we play muffins like the Cowboys. We all refused to get on the train until they lifted the fines. After the way he held up our share of the World Series money, it was like saying that we had thrown the series to you Giants, which you must know is not true, being that you Giants are an excellent nine. I do not know what people will say about the series in Kansas City. Anyway, the way our fellows stuck together shows that we can be union men too. And St. Louis isn't the only team in the Association ready to strike. Louisville players go on the road not sure that their train fare back will be paid. And some of the boys do not want to play in Philadelphia or Brooklyn because there is no protection from the cranks there becoming a mob, especially in Brooklyn where they regard the umpire as just another employee of the home team.

Yours truly,
Arlie Latham
The Freshest Man on Earth

After Ward had read the letter aloud, he summarized his reaction.

"Latham promised me he'd help organize in the Association. It seems that they can stick together to fight fines, and they want to join us."

"I'm not so sure we want any of the Browns, Johnny," said Roger Connor.

"Why not? We saw a lot of good players last fall."

"But they went to Kansas City and lost on purpose by big scores. 16-3, 16-9, 18-12. And those Kansas City Cowboys never score like that against a team that's trying. Von der Ahe and Comiskey all but accused them of hippodroming until they realized that if they kept saying that they'd have to suspend them, and they needed players like Latham, so they decided to say they were on the up and up. If Comiskey didn't bet on his own team, it means that he knew there was some dinky dink."

O'Rourke, whose career had been going on longer than the National League, spoke from experience.

"The old Association met its demise because some players like that accursed Englishman Dickie Higham were in the pay of gamblers. If we ever want to compete with the National League, we must take the most stringent precautions against the influence of gambling. The money bet on baseball will always exceed the money paid out in salaries, so some blackguard in a silk hat will always be there to tempt players who suffer from insufficient remuneration."

Ewing spoke next.

"Johnny, this Latham is the idiot who kept dancing around and singing to the fans and fainting when an umpire made a decision he didn't like."

"You should talk, Buck," Welch commented.

" I might disagree, but I don't try to get the cranks to start a riot. I wouldn't want someone like Latham representing us. We'll have enough players without him. We need players of high character."

"Jim White will be with us. That's enough high character for a whole league," Ward answered.

"I thought he was going to quit because they were sending him to Pittsburg," Connor said.

"No," said Ward. "He still wants to organize his own team in Buffalo. Maybe we'll let Jim White have a franchise in a new league. And Hoy passed me a note the other day saying that he would be 100% with us. And young Connie Mack too. We'll have every player worth having. And Pfeffer has brought along all of the White Stockings except Anson."

"Not having Anson in the league sounds good to me. We don't need no Baby, and I don't mean maybe." Welch said, looking up from his beer.

"And what about Williamson?" Ewing asked.

"He's still injured, but he'll be with us after the way Spalding has been treating him. No injury pay, and he had to pay his wife's ticket back from Europe," Ward added. "But if we're going to start our own league, there are a lot of traps to watch out for."

"So we're going to start our own league." Ewing commented as he stood up to leave. "I'll be with the boys when the time comes, but when did we decide to do that?"

"Spalding decided," said Ward tersely. "I plan one more meeting with him, but it looks as if he's stubborn about everything, and the rest of the owners will go along with him. All we will have to do is find a little capital and show that we want a clean league. No hippodroming or gambling, not even betting on your own team. And no booze on the field, not even beer. No Sunday baseball. And two umpires every game. Professionals."

"And will we have Negro players?" asked O'Rourke who had always been bothered by the color bar. "I think Latham was one of the Browns who refused to play against a team with Frank Grant."

"We'll settle that at a full meeting," Ward responded. "All the decisions will have to wait for July 14th which is the first time we have a general meeting. For now, let's get ready to play."

"So I hear that the players are still talking about starting their own league," said Spalding as he sat with Chadwick, baseball's house historian, statistician, arbiter of excellence and Spalding retainer.

"Not a one of them has the capability to manage a business, Al. They're bluffing."

"Ward has some brains. And O'Rourke is a lawyer too. They both signed contracts with no reserve clause."

"But we have Ward on record saying that the reserve clause is necessary for the game. I can show you the clippings from things he wrote himself. Besides, if he thinks he can sign anywhere he wants when his contract is over, we will just have to demonstrate to him that this is illegal, using his own words," Chadwick said as he leafed through his notes.

"I remember that article. We'll make a liar out of him if he opens his mouth. If Ward thinks there's room enough for three major leagues, he's delusional. There's already too much competition with the Association even though we're supposed to have an agreement with them. Have you seen the news from over there, Henry? They look about ready to fall apart with Comiskey losing control of St. Louis and Louisville all but bankrupt. How many teams in the Association could we move into the League?"

"Brooklyn," Chadwick answered without thinking. He had been a Brooklyn resident ever since he came over from England. He had made a career of writing about the Eckfords, the Atlantics, the Excelsiors, and now the Bridegrooms. "And St. Louis. Maybe Cincinnati could handle a franchise if they spent some money for new players."

"That's just the kind of bidding war we're trying to avoid. Didn't Boston just try to buy a pennant with Brouthers? If I had known what they were going to do, I would have never sold them Kelly and then Clarkson."

"You had to sell Kelly, Al. He was drunk one time too many, and he never bothered to hide it. What choice did you have? Besides, you got $10,000 for him. You had to do it."

"That doesn't mean I liked doing it. Things haven't been as much fun without Kel."

Anson entered the office without knocking. Spalding invited him into the conversation.

"What are you hearing about Johnny Ward's new league, Adrian?"

"Tener won't tell me anything, but a newspaperman told me that Ward is going to have a big meeting on Bass Steel Day, whatever that is."

Spalding managed not to laugh. Anson had not learned anything on his trip to France, no matter how much he talked about how he had been changed by the tour. What did they teach him during his year at Notre Dame? But Spalding knew that Anson would be his partner for as long as he could hit, and even at age 37 he wasn't slowing down. He had led the league in hitting the last two years, not entirely because of generous home town score keeping.

"Well whatever they do, Cap," said Spalding, employing the new nickname that the newspapers were starting to give Anson, "we'll be ready for them on July 14th or any other day."

The Hitter
St. George Grounds, Staten Island
May 23, 1889

New York trailed 7-1 in the fourth inning, largely as a result of infield errors and even clumsier misplays in the outfield, but now it was Chicago's turn to display defensive weakness. A soft pop fly landed between Anson and his pitcher Addison Gumbert and each glared at the other until the rookie pitcher remembered to say it was his fault. Another easy fly dropped among a deferential second baseman, a right fielder who had all been lamentably slow to respond, and Anson. From the grandstand near first base a booming voice had been trying to engage Anson in conversation, using his nickname.

"It's time to quit, Baby. My grandmother would have caught that one. Wait, that's not fair. You're a lot older than she is."

Ward batted next. He singled home a run and joined Anson down at first base, using the occasion to make the following remark.

"Keep it up, Adrian, and Spalding won't classify you as Class A player, and you won't be getting your $2500 a year. Maybe you'll be joining the Brotherhood after all."

Anson spat which he did for self-expression, not from necessity, because he was one of the minority of players who did not chew tobacco.

"We know what you're doing, Ward. Your bunch of socialists are going to ruin the game. We hang communists in Chicago."

"We're not communists, Adrian, although we do think the worker should have a say in his working conditions and a fair share of the money generated by his efforts. And if we were communists, I am sure your comrades would pay you in a manner commensurate with your skills, which are considerable."

"I'd rather depend on Al than trust my fellow players."

O'Rourke interrupted this discussion of labor relations by splashing a solid single into Lake Mutrie, the large body of water in center field. It had been named for Jim Mutrie, the jovial manager of the Giants whose job it was to greet the fans, and who left all the major game decisions to Captain Ewing. When most of the plank stage in center field had been removed, the resulting hole had filled up with water that refused to drain, forcing the outfielders to pick up soggy balls and fling them forward. A ground ball then hit one of the many infield rocks and bounced off Pfeffer's forehead for his third error of the game. Most baseball people would have judged it a hit, but the scorekeeper resented Pfeffer's efforts to encroach on the scorecard business. Jimmy Ryan was charged with an error when he hurried his throw to first on a dribbler by George Gore. Ryan, normally an outfielder, was playing shortstop in place of the injured Williamson, and he had not yet learned what a more experienced infielder would have known. When diminished by alcohol as he often was, Gore tended to stand at the plate a second or two, looking where he hit the ball, as if choosing whether to run. At the end of their half of the fourth, the Giants were only trailing 7-6.

K.C. was seated next to the deep bass voice that had been comparing Anson to his grandmother. When the Chicago team was at bat, Anson was in the coacher's box, swinging the oversize bat he always carried with him.

"Who you gonna hit with that wagon tongue?" the crank next to K.C. shouted, thus eliciting another piece of information.

"Anson says he brings the bat to the coacher's box in case he has to defend himself from a foul ball, but I think he carries it to add to the picture when he's kicking at the umpire."

K.C. was always glad to share his knowledge of the finer points of the game with other ball-goers. The rabid rooter next to him preferred to address his observations to the players who were within earshot.

"Anson, you stowed away with a delivery of Iowa hogs to Chicago and escaped the stock yards to become a ballplayer. Chicago was the only team desperate enough to hire a first baseman who couldn't catch a fly ball. You stink like a rump roast left in the sun for a month." Then, turning to K.C. he asked, "Doesn't he stink?"

"He has led the league in hitting four times including the last two years, but that was partly because the Chicago scorekeeper gave him a hit whenever there was a question."

The rabid crank did not respond directly, but he cupped his hands in a makeshift megaphone and used the new information immediately.

"We know all your hits came from a crooked scorekeeper, Baby."

Gumbert hit a long fly that bounced over the fence for a home run, bringing the score to 9-6. In the Giants half of the sixth, the Chicago left fielder stumbled under a fly ball and fell into a mud puddle near the aforementioned lake. Pfeffer extended the inning by throwing a little wide to first where the increasingly immobile Anson failed to come off the bag. The Giants' pitcher, Gil Hatfield, was on the receiving end of a base on balls, only fair because he had been walking Chicago players all day, even their weakest hitters. Gore laid an expertly placed sacrifice bunt, a maneuver he had practiced both drunk and sober. A single by Danny Richardson tied the score at 9-9. In the bottom of the inning, Chicago forged ahead again on a sacrifice by Anson. Ward led off the next inning with a single. This time he decided to discuss a less controversial topic—the pennant race. Boston had jumped out to an early lead, and both New York and Chicago were trailing.

"Well, Adrian, are your White Stockings going to catch Kel and the Beaneaters?" Ward asked with the friendly tone of a sufferer seeking sympathy from someone with the same disease.

"We're not the White Stockings any more. The newspapers are calling us Anson's Colts. And yes, we'll catch Boston. Clarkson can't pitch every day, and Kelly can't stay sober for a whole season."

Two more singles moved Ward around. Pfeffer nearly had his finger broken on a ball hit far to his right, but the unsympathetic scorekeeper charged still another error. Gore singled home another run, and another misjudged fly ball in left put the Giants ahead 12-10. In the next inning, Connor led off with a triple. Ewing laid down a bunt that caught Anson playing deep. Buck clapped his hands gleefully as he ran past the Chicago captain. In the next inning the Giants scored four more runs with a combination of walks and errors, bringing the Giants' lead to what seemed an insurmountable seven runs.

"Why can't the Giants hit like this every day?" the vocal crank inquired of K. C. whose baseball omniscience was becoming apparent."

"Gumbert's not one of Chicago's better pitchers, and for that matter the Giants are only pitching Hatfield because Keefe's still getting in shape after his holdout, and he can't go two days in a row yet."

"Anyway, this is my kind of ball game. This is like the old days with the Mutuals and the Eckfords before they ruined the game with those gloves. Seventeen runs. I'm getting my money's worth."

He then increased his volume and turned toward the field.

"You stink, Anson. You're rotten meat, like the whole city of Chicago. Your team is as bad as your city. Connor's a better first baseman."

K.C. knew that Anson had led the league in fielding percentage, (.986), but this was even more evidence of favorable score keeping.

"Connor's a better ballplayer."

K.C. agreed with this statement to some extent. Roger Connor was a powerful, consistent striker, and less of a defensive liability than the aging Anson. Connor was also a good base runner, the inventor of the pop-up slide, so K.C. was giving his mental assent to the loudmouth. But he could not agree with the next statement.

"And Connor's a better hitter."

Anson had ignored all the comments about his ancestry, his species, his odor, his city of residence, his fielding, his overall ability, and his team's play, but he could not accept this remark. As he left the field for what was probably going to be Chicago's last turn at bat, he turned his cold blue eyes in the direction of the offensive voice.

"Sir, no one, neither in this league nor the Association, is a better hitter than I. Recently I completed a world tour, and I didn't see any better hitters in Australia, Asia, Africa or Europe, either."

"Well, your boys are going to lose today," the rooter responded, pleased to have engaged Anson when Chicago was down 17-10.

In the Chicago ninth, the Giants pitcher finally started putting the ball over the plate. At first this seemed like a good idea, but it only made things worse. O'Rourke prevented a double by making an over the shoulder catch after a long run, showing that the orator was still spry at age 37. Connor fumbled a simple ground ball and Burns doubled. Two singles and a triple ate into the lead, and Ward helped the Chicago cause by tangling his spikes and tripping on an easy ground ball to his left.

"What's the score now? And who's this bum coming up to bat?" the loudmouth asked K.C., who as keeper of a scorecard was implicitly obligated to serve as a public information source.

"The Giants are still ahead, 17-14. Hugh Duffy is the batter."

"Duffy? He must be a duffer."

"Actually, he's one of the best young hitters in the league."

K.C. was hoping for a Giant victory, but as a self-styled baseball expert with a reputation to protect, he was almost glad to see Duffy confirm his opinion with a line drive to center, hit so sharply that Ward never had a chance to react. Anson came up next, in a position to tie the game with a long hit. Instead, as he backed away from an inside pitch, the ball hit his bat and rolled down toward first where Connor picked it up and stepped on the base to retire the Chicago captain.

"Dead ball," Anson shouted at Umpire McQuaid.

"It's only a dead ball if it hits your foot."

"Then it hit my foot."

Anson's usual carmine flesh turned a deeper shade of vermillion, and even his eyes seemed to fill with blood as he screamed at Umpire McQuaid.

"I didn't mean to hit the ball."

"You know that doesn't matter."

"These New York cranks didn't come out to see you umpire. You're calling the best hitter in baseball out over a technicality."

The argument went on for several minutes and would have gone longer, but with no home fans to support him, Anson eventually grew tired of kicking. A walk to Pfeffer and a double by Burns tied the score. By the time they retired the last batter in the ninth with the score tied 17-17, the Giant were relieved to have a chance in extra innings. Ewing threw down his catcher's mask in disgust and yelled loud enough for all in the vicinity of the infield to hear.

"Never mind. We are not done for yet."

"Yes you are," bellowed the vocal fellow. He seemed to have changed sides because he was now directing his denunciations at the home team. "That rank lot of muffins from the West have got you licked for sure. I'm ashamed to be a New York supporter."

In the tenth, the Giants went out weakly. In the visitors' half, the Chicago pitcher led off with a hit and Whitney made a wild throw past first, putting the winning run on third.

"You're losing because none of you can catch a ball or even pick it up when it stops rolling," screamed the rabid fan.

Jimmy Ryan ended the game with a long single to left allowing Gumbert to walk home while taunting the team that had scored 17 runs off him. The Chicago team assembled around Anson in joy.

"The umpire cheated us out of our best hitter in the ninth, and we still won" shouted Duffy as he hugged the man who had called Ryan and him worthless micks a few innings before. After the game, Anson stood surrounded by the New York press, all of them scribbling his words of wisdom as fast as they could.

"Some people think we're out of the race this year, but, mark you, we'll fool 'em. The old White Stockings are good finishers in the stretch, and some New York and Boston backers will realize that before the season's over. We've done it before, and we'll do it again, won't we boys?"

Anson strutted over to Ward and Ewing who were still both stunned.

"How long are you New Yorkers going to keep playing in this mudhole?" asked Anson.

"By the end of the year, we'll have a real ball park," Ewing said as he picked up his mask.

The best striker in baseball turned away from Ewing and looked directly at Ward.

"It's not as easy to build ball parks as you think, Ward. And it's even harder to build a whole league."

"How does he know about that?" Ward asked himself, wrongly suspecting Tener.

After Anson walked away, Ewing turned to Ward.

"I don't know what he's so proud about. He didn't have a hit or score a run all day. What did he do?"

"He led them. Our pitcher wore himself out pitching to Anson, so the rest of them could score eighteen runs."

The Jewels
New York
May, 1889

Helen was leaving for Paris, and her last step was to take an inventory of her jewelry in order to select some to take to Paris while leaving the rest in the hotel vault. Technically most of the jewels belonged to her theater production company, but she and her sister were the only stockholders and were therefore the owners of what the newspapers referred to as a $70,000 collection. This estimate was on the high side, but it never hurt to exaggerate the worth of your assets, especially if you planned to sell them some day. Helen felt she owned her jewels in four distinct ways.

First, as a woman. She knew how to use them. She knew which onyx earrings showed her black eyes to their best advantage, which necklace pointed suggestively to her décolletage in the most alluring manner, and which bracelets drew attention away from her plump forearms.

Second, as an actress. She knew how to select jewels for the effect they would have on an audience. A diamond tiara that flashed in the bright stage lighting made possible by Mr. Edison's newest inventions could be the key to a dramatic scene. Sometimes the jewelry fit the role, such as when it illustrated how Peg Woffington had risen in the world. Sometimes she just wore the jewelry even if it didn't fit the character because people came to see Helen Dauvray, the glamorous actress. On occasion, she dressed her supporting cast in her jewels, a pearl necklace to characterize a pompous dowager or a flashy ruby ring to indicate a girl led astray by a wealthy Lothario.

Third, as a businesswoman. She knew how to spot bargains at an estate sale or a bankruptcy auction, and she shopped without emotion. As much as she had delighted in buying jewels when she could first afford them, she had been even more pleased when she found she could sell them at a significant profit. Over the years, Helen had earned more money selling her jewels than she had spent buying them, and she still had an extensive collection of expertly cut diamonds with outstanding clarity, cornflower blue Kashmir sapphires, lustrous natural pearls, and garnets she had bought in Arizona for almost nothing. The color of her best pieces flashed from blue to reddish-purple. She particularly enjoyed jewels with interesting inclusions like tiger stripes. But most of all she collected amethysts, the birthstone for her Valentine's Day birthday.

Fourth, as an expert. She had her own loupe with a magnification of 20x which enabled her to spot the tiny flaws that reduced the price of an otherwise perfect gem. One of Clara's bohemian friends had even taught Helen to make a few simple rings and necklaces. Helen never became a skilled jeweler, but she had learned something from doing it.

One evening Clarkson invited her and John to dinner with him and Mrs Clarkson. Helen wore a modest but elegant pearl necklace. Clarkson worked in a family jewelry business, so he noticed the necklace and made a comment about it.
"You probably don't know anything about those pearls. Women never understand the jewelry they're wearing."

When John and Helen were alone together, Ward was curious.

"I was glad that you and Clarkson found something to talk about, I was afraid you would be bored with all the talk about baseball."

"If the talk had been about baseball, I wouldn't have been bored. All Mr. Clarkson wanted to talk about was your plans for the Brotherhood. I wouldn't trust him if I were you."

"You're just mad because he said women didn't know anything about jewelry. Why didn't you tell him that you have all those books and magazines about jewels?"

Helen didn't see any point in letting Clarkson know that she was an expert. Modesty was her basic learning tool, never trying to show off what she knew but always pushing to learn more. She had even learned something about the jewelry business by staying quiet while Mr. Clarkson talked about how his family bought pearls at a discount.

This was a pattern Helen had followed ever since she was Little Nell, too busy with her banjo to go to school, but always eager to learn. For example, when she was a nine year old with an aptitude for math, she discovered compound interest and put aside some money in high-yield bonds for her old age, which at that time she calculated as thirty. She went on to learn accounting and then how to invest in the stock market. When she heard about new discoveries in the Comstock Lode, she knew how to get her money down while the stock was still low. Then she shifted her money smoothly before silver prices went down. When Mr. Edison started electrifying the country, she took money out of cable car stock and put it into streetcars. She invested in his new stage lighting company before most of Wall Street considered it practical, and she shifted her money to Mr. Westinghouse's company when she understood the advantages of alternating current. When Johnny started wearing a jock strap with a protective cup and advocating such protection for others, she recognized the potential of this new business and quietly invested in the company holding the patent to manufacture them, planning to profit when the Spalding monopoly eventually absorbed the smaller company. She knew enough about men to understand their disproportionately protective attitude toward this part of their anatomy and the consequent eagerness with which they would embrace this innovation.

With less pragmatic motives but equally practical results, she had studied the arts. From an early age she took an interest in opera, although she recognized that her thin voice was pleasant enough for musical comedy, but not likely to hit the upper registers, nor was it powerful enough to be heard over a full orchestra. Her favorite operas were French, and that led her to go to France at age 14, already an independently wealthy young woman who wanted to learn more French. This was when she had first met M. Halévy. The story that she told the newspapers was that she had gone to France not knowing a word of the language, but by that she only meant that she didn't start learning to read and write the language until then. At a young age, even before she was Little Nell, she had had a French Canadian governess, and she was comfortable hearing and speaking the language before she had ever seen a French book.

Upon coming back to the United States, real estate law was another of her specialties, especially as it related to a married woman's ability to control her property. This had resulted in her obtaining a divorce from Mr. Tracy under Colorado law, far more favorable to a woman's independence.

When she started having seizures, she made it a point to learn everything she could about epilepsy medicine. At one time, she had collected books on motherhood, but after her health problems seemed to rule it out, she had put them aside.

One of her most successful learning projects had been baseball, beginning in 1886. She had taken up the game shortly before she met Ward. When they started seeing each other, she intensified her study. She applied herself to the sporting press and the statistical compilations found in the *Spalding Guide*. She read about the early days of baseball and discussed the game's past with veterans like Jim O'Rourke whom she had met before she met Ward. Another of her baseball teachers was Freddy Engel, the tavern owner's son who chased balls in the park. He had instructed her on the players and their relative merits, both professional and personal. Even the business aspect of baseball was of interest to her, and she had a better understanding of the expenses and opportunities of owning a baseball club than Ward ever would. For one thing, she understood what it took to build a ballpark, and she was following the political and economic efforts of the Giants to find a new home.

Modesty was the key to her learning, but self-promotion was the key to being a famous actress. Secrecy was the key to her business life, just as publicity was the key to her theatrical life. If her first husband had gotten an idea of her wealth, she would not have been rid of him so easily. Sometimes she wanted to let her accountant Bernie show Ward her entire balance sheet, especially when Johnny had been complaining about the Lyceum lease or the mansion's upkeep, but one divorce had taught her that keeping things to herself was best.

"This pile of jewels could build a fireproof ballpark," she said to herself as she packed up those headed for Paris before putting the rest in the hotel safe.

Although Ward had agreed to a trip to Paris in the off-season, it was clear that baseball wouldn't be finished before the Universal Exposition was closed, especially if the Giants were competing to retain the Dauvray Cup. When she had told Ward that she planned another trip to Paris, he had been gracious. He made plans to skip the Memorial Day doubleheader so that he could see off her ship to Liverpool, the first step of her journey to Paris. He knew that during the season he would be out of town half of the time and working on Brotherhood business the other half, so he was just as happy to have her away with their friends in Paris. More importantly, Clara was staying in New York, so no one would be poisoning Helen's mind against him. The year before he had worried about her seeing other men, especially actors, especially French-speaking actors, but now he had overcome these fears. His new fear was that she would spend too much time with Clara, so the sooner the sister was married to Keefe and off living in Cambridge, the better.

The Hazard
New York
June, 1889

"**S**tarting a revolution can be easy when the *ancien regime* cooperates by increasing its oppression," Ward thought as he worked out his plan for a new league. The owners were invoking the reserve clause to force players to accept salary cuts, thus breaking the only promise they had ever made to the Brotherhood. Spalding was still insisting that players from the disbanded Detroit team should report to the clubs they had been assigned to, including making Deacon White play in Pittsburg. Every player in the league was aware that Ed Williamson was not being paid by Chicago while he recovered from the injury suffered on the Spalding tour. National League players were already whispering about confronting the owners with a strike on the lucrative Fourth of July holiday, an action that Ward considered premature. "Gathering the *sans-culottes* outside the Bastille won't be difficult, although I might have a problem keeping them from storming it too early," Ward thought to himself, continuing his metaphor as he prepared for the July 14th Brotherhood meeting.

Ward was also keeping an eye on the chaos in the American Association. Organizing the players from the so-called Beer and Whiskey League was part of his plan, but the Association was continuing to disintegrate on its own. In Louisville the owner was said to be charging more in fines than he was paying out in salary. The team's best slugger, Pete Browning, had been fined for going into a batting slump. Players were suddenly released on the road without their train fare home. In Philadelphia Curt Welch had gotten in the habit of playing drunk every day, probably to dull the pain from being hit by pitches, something he did on purpose to get on base. On a particularly drunken and painful day, he had incited a riot by inviting fans on the field.

In Brooklyn there was little or no control of an unruly, snarling mob, especially for their Sunday games which the blue laws forced the Bridegrooms to play in New Jersey. The bitterness between St. Louis and Brooklyn had reached a level where the Browns, fearing for their safety, refused to play, accepting the forfeits. It was hard to see how the two teams could stay in the same league. The St. Louis papers were accusing Brooklyn of manipulating the umpires, a situation that was not helped when inactive Brooklyn players were pressed into umpiring home games. Brooklyn native Bob Ferguson had umpired several games between Brooklyn and St. Louis. The press from the Mound City accused him of favoring the City of Churches, charges which were, in the opinion of neutral observers, entirely without merit. St. Louis players were betting large sums on their games, and many of them were known to frequent the taverns and pool halls where scores were reported on the telegraph inning by inning.

Most frightening of all, the ball park in Brooklyn had burned down in the middle of the night, and many suspected that the gambling interests that ran the club were more interested in collecting on their bets than the safety of the fans. Except for the new park in Philadelphia, all the structures were made of wood. Helen had been horrified at the possibility that the next fire might happen in a crowded ball park and cause deaths from trampling or burning. The possibility had always been on her mind in the theater business. She had suggested that Ward consider sponsoring a ban on smoking in ball parks, a move that she said would bring in enough women to compensate for the heavy smokers who would stop coming. At first Ward thought this might be a good idea, but almost everyone he talked to about it scoffed at such a policy. "No real man wants to go an hour and a half without a cigar," was the popular opinion.

Ward knew that his new league could not be like the Association, nor could it be like the old National Association of Professional Base Ball Players. That league had been plagued by gambling scandals, and there was no central control, which gave Spalding a chance to claim that the National League had been formed to combat hippodroming and umpire fixing. Ward had acknowledged this by starting his manifesto with the words "Once the league stood for fair dealing . . . ." He was ready to recognize that some of the National League rules would still apply to the new Players League, as he was starting to call it in his own private thoughts.

No gambling would be the first rule. No bookmakers in the grandstand and no public betting. Players should not frequent gambling establishments or saloons known to be centers of betting. Structuring the players' pay so that it would depend more on team success than individual statistics would be a step toward assuring the public that all players would be playing to win at all times.

No drinking on the field would be another sensible rule. Spalding was wrong to think he could keep every player from drinking by assigning Pinkertons to each, but demanding that the players show up for work sober was not an unreasonable limitation on their freedoms, no matter what Mike Kelly or George Gore thought. Not selling alcohol in the stands was another policy that the League had enforced, and Ward preferred it to the Association's free flowing policy. He remembered the beer smell that permeated the ball park in St. Louis and considered it to be another obstacle to the goal of having more female spectators.

Charging 50 cents for admission was practical, and he intended to continue this policy at a minimum. Even the Association was starting to realize that a quarter was too cheap, and they would need to charge at the higher level if they were going to make enough to pay the salaries the players were demanding and to hire the security the parks needed to protect the players and spectators. Perhaps they could have special discounts for ladies and children. Helen would like that, and he thought about mentioning it in the next letter he sent her in Paris.

Putting the umpire in control of the game and of the crowd was something Ward wanted the new league to insist upon. There had been times when Ward himself had kicked, but he wanted to outlaw the endless arguments that sometimes resulted in games being called early because of darkness, often as part of a plan by the team that was ahead after the fifth or behind before it. Spectators should be kept from coming on the field to express their opinions, and managers, captains and coaches should be restrained in their arguments. Umpires should have the power to expel players from the game. That would put a stop to Comiskey's sarcasm, Kelly's standing on his hands and braying like a mule, Ewing's cursing, Browning's bellowing, Hanlon's nit-picking about the rules, Anson's whining, and Hoy's gesticulating. And there should be two umpires at every game, permanent well-paid league employees. That should eliminate players skipping third base and heading directly home or missing second on their way to third.

For the time being, Ward would meet with Spalding informally and privately while requesting a formal meeting with a players' committee that consisted of Brouthers, Hanlon and Ward. What Ward really wanted to do was to tour major league cities and convince other players of the wisdom of his course of action. This would mean cooling the hot heads who wanted to strike on July 4th and going through the motions of having a meeting with Spalding.

In Chicago, Spalding was also following the developments in the Association, but he was drawing different conclusions. The rumors about a strike or a new Brotherhood league had reached him, but he saw no reason to attach much importance to a business that had no capital behind it. Ward seemed to think there was room for three baseball leagues instead of two, while Spalding was planning to reduce the number to one. Monopoly was the only efficient model for a modern business, and Spalding was hoping to build a baseball trust just as he had established a sporting goods empire. Spalding opposed any and all anti-trust legislation, but if that pesky Senator Sherman ever succeeded in passing his anti-trust act, Spalding would make it his goal to get baseball exempted. As it was, the National Agreement with the American Association meant the two leagues were not bidding against each other for players, but they were still competing for paying customers. Spalding saw no reason for having two separate eight team leagues. For that matter, having all the clubs under one ownership would solve a lot of problems.

Ward had released a statement saying that if weak franchises like Washington and Indianapolis could not pay their players a fair wage, they should not have major league teams. That was why there were no longer teams in cities like Providence, Rhode Island or Troy, New York. Privately, Spalding agreed with this, but his answer was to lower the wages in general. The classification scheme was not working because the owners of wealthy franchises like New York and Boston refused to bring salaries under control, and even in Chicago Spalding was paying far more $3000+ salaries than he thought he should. Only weak franchises would impose the strict salary caps and that would weaken them even more.

Spalding still thought that the idea that the players could run their own franchises was laughable. The players would never be able to build their own ballparks, and the league would never rent them the existing structures. What worried Spalding more than a Brotherhood league was the possibility of an American Association franchise in Chicago. Von der Ahe and Comiskey both wanted to move the Browns to Chicago, and Spalding had sometimes acted as if this would be acceptable. At one time he had agreed to allow this at some unspecified date, but he would resist any attempt to make him honor his promise. There wasn't enough room for two major league teams in Chicago, no matter what Comiskey thought.

The best way to deal with Ward and his hotheads was to agree to a meeting to discuss their grievances and then to cancel that meeting. Spalding figured that if he postponed any meeting until the end of the season after all the players had scattered to their winter homes, he could avoid any unified action on their part. For now, his greatest worry would be helping Anson rebuild his young Colts so that they would resume their traditional position as the best team in the National League, which would always mean the best team in the world.

Real Estate
St. George Grounds, Staten Island
June 13, 1889

Buck Ewing hit a fly ball that looked to be a home run, but a strong wind caught it and dropped into the water below. Ewing rounded first and second at full speed and made it to third when he noticed the Philadelphia left fielder was having difficulty picking the ball out of Lake Mutrie. Ward smashed a daisy cutter just to the right of the second baseman who managed to field it, but who threw the ball away, allowing Ward to advance to second. After the last out, Ward heard someone say that the official scorer had ruled the play an error all the way.

"I had the throw to first beaten," thought Ward. "It should have been scored a hit. Maybe the official scorer, whoever that is, is against me too."

A few days before, one of the newspapers had carried a story stating that none of the Giants liked Ward. Anonymous quotes purporting to be from Giant players seemed to indicate that most of his teammates found him arrogant and self-centered. At first he considered that the story might have been part of his war with the National League, a response to the article he had just written about the reserve clause, an attempt to split the Brotherhood by creating problems in the inner circle, which had always been mostly players from the Giants. A similar story had appeared a few years before when there had been some grumbling by a few players who had preferred Ewing as captain, but Ward thought that all of that had cleared up after he had stepped aside to allow Buck to return as captain. But today he had to consider the possibility that his teammates were willing to tell the reporters that they disliked him.

Was it Keefe? Ward looked at his pitcher who was striking out one Philadelphia batter after another with a mixture of well-placed fast balls and confusing changes of speed, complemented by the occasional curve. With Keefe about to become Ward's brother-in-law, it amounted to having a hostile new family member if Sir Timothy was one of the ones criticizing him in the press. And Keefe was the secretary of the union, his alter ego. Did Keefe think Ward was moving too slowly on the new league? There had been some bad feelings a few years ago when Keefe failed to appreciate Ward's suggestions about how he should grip the ball for a curve, but lately Ward had left the big pitcher alone, and he had thought they were becoming closer friends in spite of the upcoming marriage to Clara.

Could it be Roger Connor? The first baseman had never appreciated Ward's suggestion that he should emulate Charlie Comiskey and stop hugging the initial sack. In his book *Base Ball*, Ward had criticized first basemen who played as if they were connected to the base by a lariat, and it was possible that Connor had read this and taken it personally. Even if dear old Roger hadn't read it himself, someone might have told him about it. In any case, if Connor didn't like him, that meant that second baseman Danny Richardson probably didn't either, because the two were inseparable, like Tim Keefe and Mickey Welch. Richardson was the only newcomer really accepted by the inner circle of players who had been on the old Troy club with Mutrie—Connor, Keefe, Ewing, and Welch.

Maybe the resentment came from the heavy drinkers, like Gore and more recently Crane. Ward's suggestion that players limit themselves to "wine with dinner and only if you're not fat," had been widely reported, and it was not impossible that some of the players would take it personally. Mickey Welch always had a beer in his hand, and he was probably the most popular player on the team. It couldn't be Mickey because it was hard to imagine "Smiling Mickey" saying anything bad about anyone. Ward also knew it couldn't be Silent Mike Tiernan because he wouldn't have been talking to a reporter, or anyone else for that matter, about his likes and dislikes.

Ward hoped it wasn't O'Rourke, the other lawyer on the team, his teammate in the old days at Providence. O'Rourke had been very cool to him around the time that George McDermott had chased him around the Polo Grounds, but after Ward and Helen were married and settled, O'Rourke had been an occasional guest at their home. He seemed to like Ward proportionately to how well he thought Helen was being treated, and things were going well between Ward and Helen, at least as long as she was in Paris.

Could it have been Ewing? No, not Ewing. Why would it be Buck? Two years before, Ward had stepped aside so that Ewing could resume his old role as team captain, and Ward had always deferred to him. Maybe Buck resented all the things

Ward had written against kicking at the umpire. Buck loved to complain. By the third inning, Ward was so distracted by his thoughts that he failed to pick up a slow grounder which was called a base hit.

"Maybe the scorekeeper doesn't have it in for me after all."

"Did you score that as a hit or an error," K.C. asked of a man with pearl cuff links showing under his gray business suit. sitting next to him. He had been taking notes on his scorecard, but as K.C. looked over his shoulder he could see that they had nothing to do with the game. Hearing no answer, K.C. supplied his own.

"I think the infield is too slow and it would have been a hit even if Ward hadn't muffed it. They shouldn't have to play ball on an ash heap like this. And they haven't been able to drain the outfield all season."

"Speaking of the field, what do you hear about plans for a new ball park? Will they ever be able to go back to Manhattan?"

Nothing pleased K.C. as much as having inside knowledge, the kind of information he had obtained by being willing to pay a nickel extra for each beer for the privilege of drinking with the Giants' personnel at Nick Engel's Home Plate Saloon. He had talked with John Day and his architect, and he had a good idea of what was happening.

"A fellow named Coogan wants to be mayor, so he wants to look good with the baseball cranks. He's offering a parcel of land around 155th St. in New York, so we won't have to take the ferry to come to ball games. They should start building any day now. Oh no! The Phillies are going to score two runs on that double. Harry Wright waved him home. He sure is a sharp manager."

"Who is Harry Wright?"

K.C. was stunned. How could any crank not know who Harry Wright was?

Between innings, Ward had approached Ewing indirectly. The same article that had said no one liked Ward had accused Ewing of missing a train because of immoral conduct, strongly implying that he had been visiting a brothel. All of the Giants knew that Ewing, far from frequenting floozies, had been visiting a seriously ill child at the request of the boy's family, but the newspapers went ahead with their innuendos.

"Buck, you can't let the papers tell lies about you."

"Johnny, I never believe anything I read in the newspapers except the score of the game," Buck answered. After a moment's hesitation, he added, "You know I'm a union man, Johnny. I was with the Brotherhood before the owners talked about the $2500 salary maximum, and I'll be with the boys until the end. Don't let them drive us apart."

This may have seemed like a non sequitur, but Ward understood it to refer to the reports about how everyone disliked him, and he took some consolation. Buck seemed to be telling him that the reports weren't true, just something the papers cooked up to answer Ward's magazine article about how unfairly the players were being treated. The game went on without any more scoring, and the Giants were due up for a last turn at bat when O'Rourke came over to Ward.

"Johnny, don't let the Lilliputians drag you down. Some may be jealous of the sublimely beautiful thespienne who shares your life or the elegant French garments you brought back from Paris in your matching luggage or your superb education at Columbia University, a law school almost as good as my alma mater Yale. Let's not worry about the newspapers, Johnny. The Phillies are ahead 2-1. We can't afford to lose a game and fall farther behind Boston, not after we've pitched and played so well."

"What a game," K.C. remarked to his new friend. He looked at his scorecard to confirm what he already knew. "Nine innings in the field without an error, and thirteen strikeouts for Keefe. I hope we can come back in our half of the ninth. Buck was smart to choose last bats."

"What makes you so interested in the game's outcome? Do you have a bet on the game?"

"I never bet. That's why my wife doesn't care when I go to as many games as I can, even out of town sometimes. That's why I can take the ferry here to Staten Island without hearing any complaints at home."

He refrained from adding that she had even allowed him to follow the players around the world because that would have seemed too much like boasting.

"So you're sure the Giants are moving to Coogan's Bluff this year?"

"You can take it to the bank. The transit connection at 155th and 8th Avenue is excellent, and Day is getting a good price on a piece of property 400' by 460', enough to build a nice ball park if you don't mind short outfield lines down left and right. The architect thinks the stands can be at least partially ready within four weeks or sooner. Look, Tiernan got a single. We still have a chance."

"How can the they be ready that quickly?"

"Day is willing to pay overtime so he can save the last half of the season. Playing out here in a park covered with seagull droppings is costing him money."

"I heard the players might go on strike on the 4th of July."

"Don't worry about a strike on the 4th. Ward has things under control."

"So Day will have a ball park in Manhattan within a month?"

"I'd bet on it if I were a betting man. Ewing just made a sacrifice. If Ward can get a hit, we'll have a tie game. He's up to bat now."

To K.C.'s astonishment, his interlocutor stood.

"I've had enough baseball for the day. It was nice talking with you."

As K.C. tried to make sense of this early exit, Ward slapped a hit past the first baseman, allowing the speedy young Tiernan to come home while Ward advanced to second because he noticed that the throw home was too high to be cut off. K.C. felt a need to tell someone how clever his favorite player had been, but his new friend had left in a hurry.

Ward had noticed that the pitcher wasn't paying any attention to him, so he promptly stole third. With one out, this would give him a chance to score on a sacrifice. Sliding in safely feet first, he dusted off his uniform, codpiece and all. Connor noticed that the second baseman was too deep for a throw to the plate, and he tapped the ball past the pitcher, allowing Ward to slide home with the game-winning run. The catcher had taken advantage of the occasion to bring his foot down on Ward's right arm, hoping to hold him off until he got the ball, but Ward was able to reach around and touch the plate with his left hand. Captain Ewing was the first to greet him at home base, followed by Keefe. In a few seconds, the whole team was congratulating him, knocking off his cap and tousling his sandy hair. His arm was aching, but this was no time to worry about something like that.

"This was the kind of game Chadwick loves," said Keefe. It should be good to read about in the Brooklyn papers tomorrow."

"Chadwick likes tight games, but there were too many strikeouts for his taste," Ewing observed to Keefe. "Besides, we don't need newspapers to tell us what's happening, do we Johnny?"

Ward felt the glow of his teammates' approval. He put aside all thoughts of the newspaper article and tried to ignore the soreness in his arm.

26

The Ball
New York and Paris
June 1889

A new machine had made it possible to wrap the yarn more tightly around a springy rubber center, giving extra distance for well-struck balls. Waterproofing the horsehide helped to combat the problem of the ball's becoming heavier as the game went on. Keefe and Becannon Ltd. was betting the company's future on its new baseball. Hopes of making money from uniforms had come to an end when the Giants uniform Clara had designed was pronounced indecent and another firm was given the contract. Now the best hope for their business was having their baseball accepted as the official ball of the new major league that the players were discussing. Keefe had designed the ball himself, leading to a question from his business partner, Buck Becannon, himself a former major league pitcher, albeit very briefly.

"Why would a pitcher be manufacturing such a lively ball?"

"I'm a hitter too, even if not a very good one. A lively ball makes a better game for the cranks. Besides, good pitching will still be important, maybe even more important when it comes to striking out batsmen eager for home runs."

Becannon was nervous about the prospects of a new league, which seemed to him a risky venture. It might just be a lot of hotheaded talk, and even if there was a new league, there was no guarantee that their firm would get the contract for the baseballs. Keefe seemed confident that the new league would start at least by next year, and he was sure that Ward would award them the contract. After all, they were going to be brothers-in-law as well as fellow union officers. One more thing bothered Becannon.

"Why did we ship a case of baseballs to that fellow in France?" Becannon asked.

"Ward asked me to do it, and I didn't want to tell him no. The boy is a friend of Ward and Helen's, and Ward wants to encourage baseball in France. That's what Spalding was doing when he toured the world, and I guess he knows something about selling sporting goods. We should be thinking internationally."

Becannon did not like the idea of sending free baseballs across the ocean, but he had a better idea about using samples to promote their business. There was no need to tell Keefe about it.

Keefe was more concerned with his family life than with either his business or his pitching. It was pretty well settled that he would marry Clara after she had agreed to take instruction in the Catholic faith. He sent a letter home about his intentions, and his sisters wrote back that they were happy for him and eager to meet their new sister. Unfortunately, they also reported the declining health of their favorite aunt, the one who had kept the family together while Keefe's father was being held in a Confederate prison camp.

Clara had begun to apply her substantial capacity for fault-finding to New York City itself. Her bohemian friends from the art world seemed shallow and predictable, always envious of each other's successes and patronizing toward Clara's work. Although at first Clara had been happy to give up her space in the double mansion, now she was growing tired of hotel life. A quiet existence in Cambridge seemed appealing, and not just because she loved Keefe. She saw her second marriage as a chance to step out of her sister's shadow, to end her association with Dauvray Productions and all of Helen's other dramas. Moving to Cambridge also meant she would be moving away from Helen and Ward and their disastrous marriage.

All Paris was celebrating the centennial of the fall of the Bastille. Legitimists, Orléanists, Bonapartists, socialists, and friends of the Republic put aside their differences and shared in a general sense that the world was paying homage to France. All the world shared in dancing, fireworks, musical celebrations, as well as cultural and industrial exhibits. The newspapers asked Parisians to put aside their natural and understandable contempt for foreigners in order to take in their pounds, dollars and roubles.

As soon as Helen was settled in the Hotel des Varennes, she called on M. Halévy to apologize both for her husband's jealousy and then for his subsequent lack of it. She brought a copy of the New York *Herald*, European edition for Daniel who gave her a copy of the newspaper *Le Figaro de la Tour*, published from M. Eiffel's now completed tower. Mme. Straus and Jacques invited Helen to ascend with them to the very top. Guy de Maupassant had exiled himself in protest at its ugliness, but most Parisians were accepting the tallest structure in the world as the symbol of their city.

Helen reciprocated by bringing Daniel, Jacques and their friend little Marcel to Buffalo Bill's Wild West in Neuilly. The show was selling out fifteen thousand seats, twice a day, every day. Parisians and tourists lined up to see re-enacted Indian fights, courageous French-Canadian trappers, and the sharpshooting of Annie Oakley. Helen had met Bill Cody during her days as Little Nell, and they had met again at parties in New York. She brought the boys backstage with her, where Bill introduced them to the chiefs and cowboys whose horsemanship was the most popular attraction in the city hosting the Universal Exposition. Cody was a gracious host, and the boys were the envy of their classmates at Lycée Condorcet.

Little Marcel, accompanied Helen on a trip to *Les Magasins du Louvre*, a fashionable department store. They followed that with a trip to the Louvre itself where Marcel played his favorite game, finding resemblances to people he knew in the paintings on display. The following is a translation of their conversation.

"Look at the servant in Anton Van Dyck's portrait of Charles I hunting. Doesn't he remind you of your husband's friend, Mr. Williamson?"

"A little. John says you saved Mr. Williamson's life."

"I only told my father, and he insisted on a change of doctors. The doctor Mr.

Spalding had chosen did not believe in Pasteur and took no steps to control infection. I am always eager to do things for your husband. I like him very much."

Little Marcel could talk for hours about theater, music, place-names and society gossip, but what she liked best about him was that he really seemed to have liked Johnny. They were even corresponding.

"Mr. Ward still sends me baseball gifts. He has given me all that I need to be a catcher if I can find seventeen other boys and a big field."

"He was trying to show you that he likes you too. What did you two find to talk about?"

"How much he loves you and how passionately he thinks about you."

When they stopped for tea, she found herself lingering over several cups, pouring herself out to this boy for no reason she could understand. She complained of the constant betrayals by her first husband. Within the limits of decency, she told of her other experiences with men, even being groped as a child star. Before she knew it, she was telling him about the first time Mr. Ward made love to her, his fumbling at her flowers during a carriage ride.

Petit Marcel found it fascinating to be hearing the same story from two different participants, and he couldn't help thinking as the novelist he wished to become. In those days, he still planned to write love stories with conventional happy endings and maybe even have such a story himself. Everyone who knew the boy agreed he had exceptional talent, but his instructors at the lycée always feared that he lacked the perseverance to stick to a long project.

"If I ever become a writer, I would like to describe a love like your husband has for you. You were all that he talked about with passion, except for baseball."

"Maybe that's all any American woman can ask, at least from April to October."

Having already discussed sex with this boy, Helen dared to venture into even more intimate and private territory. He had recently come into a small inheritance, which he was spending foolishly, leaving ridiculously large tips and buying expensive flowers for Mme. Straus and others.

"You need to put some of your money in steady bonds or a trustworthy bank. And you should put the rest in well-considered investments. If you want to be a writer, you might need the money to take you through hard times. Perhaps you could buy a building in an area of Paris about to become fashionable, or invest in something like telephones. People are sure to want more and more of them. Maybe your father could give you some ideas about investing in medical companies."

"Perhaps you could tell me how to invest in the theater."

"Don't do it. And don't send flowers to . . . actresses."

Marcel grew uncomfortable, and changed the subject.

"Mr. Ward just shipped me a box of baseballs that are manufactured by the man who is going to marry your sister Clara."

"Marcel, what are you going to do with a box of baseballs?"

"Each one will remind me of the shimmering spring day in March when the players of baseball strove to hit the ball across the river to M. Eiffel's tall steel tower that links our two countries as surely as the statue he helped build in the harbor of your home city, and more than the baseball game itself, I will remember how a handsome, manly American spoke so lovingly of the absent woman he loved, one whose beauty has electrified every stage in the United States more surely than Mr. Edison, and the intensity of his feelings for this woman, a love which would remind one of Lancelot's passion for Guinevere were it not that this licit love remains within the happy bounds of marriage."

"You're proustifying again, Marcel."

Ward received a letter from little Marcel thanking him for the baseballs. Between his tiny cramped handwriting and his questionable English, the letter was hard to understand, but he seemed to be telling him how much Helen loved him. (Ward, not Marcel). The farther apart Ward and Helen were from each other, the stronger their love, like those inverse functions he had learned about in math class at State College. It was easy to see her in French society and imagine himself in love with Ida Gibson's creation Helen Dauvray, now Helen Ward. (Ward hadn't learned that Ida Gibson was Helen's real name until their secret marriage in Massachusetts.) When they spoke French, they were in love. When they thought about France, they were in love. When one of them was in France, they were in love.

Perhaps he would learn to live with her in France from October to March with a few weeks out for barnstorming. Then, if she wanted to go back on stage, she could do it from April to September. If his sore arm didn't get better, he might have to forget about playing baseball, anyway.

One thing he was sure of. He loved Helen late at night, right before he went to sleep alone. He never thought of Jessie except when she was right in front of him, at which time it was hard for any man to ignore her. But Helen was still the woman he called the goddess, invoking her name and image whenever she was far away, and learning once again to use his left arm when his right one was sore, just as he had done years before while playing center field.

The Bat
Cleveland, Chicago, Louisville, Pittsburg, Indianapolis
June, 1889

Ward's right arm continued to hurt, diminishing his ability to throw and taking away his power at the bat. After a few games like that, Ewing excused Ward. The newspapers, always eager to assume the worst, accused the shortstop of malingering. When Ward took injury leave and stopped traveling with the club, rumors that he was neglecting the Giants for Brotherhood business found their way into print.

"Don't worry what the newspapers say, Johnny," Buck had assured him. And don't be afraid to use your time off to build the union. We all need it. Stars and duffers and everyone in between."

When rumors about a 4th of July strike had come to Spalding's attention, he had agreed to a meeting with Ward and a select committee of players to discuss their grievances. When his Pinkertons reported that there was no real plan for such a strike, Spalding decided that there was no pressing need for a meeting or even the pretense of a meeting. Ward himself was opposing any precipitous action according to what Spalding was hearing from Clarkson who had been keeping his former manager informed all along. There was some vague talk about the players' forming their own league, but here there was still little evidence of planning and none of money. Spalding informed Ward by telegram that they would not be meeting until after the season was completed, if then.

"Whatever problems the boys have will probably have worked themselves out by then," Spalding told the press. Off the record, he expressed the opinion that Ward was perfectly healthy and that he had invented the sore arm as an excuse to agitate. Nonetheless, Spalding remained confident that common sense and ironclad contracts would eventually prevail, no matter what Ward was planning to do.

Although he wanted to bring about a revolution, Ward was doing what he could to slow down its pace. In Cleveland, many of the players were ready to strike immediately without even waiting for July 4th or the Brotherhood meeting. Ward managed to convince Patsy Tebeau, the team leader, to wait so that all the players could act collectively. Ward then met with a wealthy streetcar line owner named Tom Johnson who saw ownership of a baseball team as a potential path into politics. After a brief meeting, Tom turned Ward over to his younger brother, Al, an enthusiastic twenty-four year old crank. Other young men dreamed of playing in the major leagues, but Al Johnson only dreamed of drinking with those who did. Ward soon discovered he could not match the youngster drink for drink, but they managed a conversation in spite of the ballplayer's staying sober.

"You're doing a great thing with this new league, Ward. An important thing. My brother and I want to be part of it."

"I'm sure your streetcars will benefit from a solid baseball club drawing large crowds."

"That's not it. I mean that the workers will see baseball players operating a cooperative, and every man in America will see that socialism works. It's the future. Baseball is America's National Game. Isn't that what Spalding says? And my brother and I want to put our capital behind you and baseball in Cleveland and socialism."

"We're not even sure we'll have a new league, but we'd be glad to have you working with us. We might decide something really radical at our Bastille Day meeting. Maybe we'll be the new Jacobins of baseball."

"I'd prefer you to be the Communards. That was the real revolution. 1871. Where are you going to bring the revolution next?"

I'm going to Louisville to meet with the team that has the most discontented players in the Association. The players aren't being paid, and some of them are released without train fare home.

"While you're there, tell Pete Browning that he and his Louisville Slugger bat will always be welcome in Cleveland. I'd love to sit down and get drunk with him. What a crackerjack he is! What stories he could tell!"

Ward had always heard that Browning was sullen, uncommunicative and violent when drinking, but he agreed to pass on Johnson's message.

The Louisville Colonels were hosting the St. Louis Browns, and this gave Ward a chance to meet with Charlie Comiskey, a potential manager for a Chicago franchise, assuming that Anson would not join the new league. Ward also met with Arlie Latham who claimed to be organizing for the Brotherhood in the Association, at least when he was not being suspended for suspicion of throwing games.

Ward's pursuit of managers took him next to Pittsburg to meet with his friend Ned Hanlon, the fellow who had urged him to sign with Providence years ago. Hanlon was not yet the manager of the Pittsburg team, but it was generally agreed that he would take over soon if they did not improve, and there was no sign of improvement. Hanlon was already preparing financing for a Players League team with some sausage makers who were interested in backing a franchise next year. However, Hanlon was still concerned with his team's performance in the current season.

"For now, we're a sad team, but a few more ballplayers, and we'll be fine. Will Jim White and Jack Rowe ever play with us? I still think we could win if we had them. Even if it was just for the rest of the season. And the union would look good too. We could look like we were giving in a little."

Spalding again had Pinkertons trailing Ward on and off. As far as he could see, Ward was not building a foundation for a new league. There were no meetings with bankers or businessmen or architects, just ballplayers talking to each other. And every sign seemed to be indicating that the ballplayers were ready to give in and accept management's conditions. Jim White and Jack Rowe were going to report to Pittsburg, a victory for the reserve clause.

From Pittsburg, Ward rejoined the Giants in Indianapolis. The Hoosiers were one of the National League's worst clubs and perhaps its weakest franchises. Pebbly Jack Glasscock might have been the only ballplayer worth having on the whole team. The hard-hitting shortstop, who got his nickname from the way he smoothed the infield, was furious about the way his owner applied the classification scheme to limit salaries, paying Glasscock significantly less than other .350 hitters.

"This town don't deserve no franchise, Johnny. Look around. There's no one in the park, and the owner ain't about to reach into his own pocket to pay a decent wage. If you do start a new league, I'm with you all the way, but don't come here. Maybe you could take this club and start a new franchise somewhere else."

Glasscock's remark about Indianapolis set Ward to thinking. Instead of replicating the National League with the same eight cities, he could give up the weak cities like Indianapolis and Washington. While persuading White and Rowe to sign with Pittsburg, Ward had promised to consider having a team in Buffalo, even though Brouthers had warned him that the city was too small to support a team and too cold for baseball. Perhaps Ward would want his own team in the new league, leaving New York to Buck and the other Giants. Helen would never want to leave New York except for Paris, but a franchise in Brooklyn would be close enough for her. Next year's revolution was taking shape.

For the time being, Ward concentrated on getting his arm back to full strength, waiting for Helen to return from Paris, and preparing the Brotherhood for action. At the same time, workmen were constructing a new Polo Grounds ballpark at 155th St. near 8th Avenue. Real estate near the ball park was already appreciating rapidly as the neighborhood prepared to be the new home of the New York Giants.

28

Beer
New Polo Grounds, New York
July 8, 1889

The inaugural game in the New Polo Grounds was interrupted with two out in the top of the first inning so that officers of the New York Stock Exchange could present Buck Ewing with a gold watch and matching chain. Buck held the gifts high in the air so that the spectators, many of whom were packed in rings around the outfield, could see the tribute. There were 10,000 crowded into a new ball park with 5000 seats. Ward, in the lineup for the first time since his arm injury, surveyed the ball park, parts of which were still being constructed as the game was being played. A few weeks ago this field had been nothing but hills and ditches, and now it was surrounded by a lower deck with another being built on top of it. To mark the occasion, there had been a pre-game ceremony with regimental bands' going oompah pah and politicians' making similar noises. Benjamin Harrison had sent his regrets, but the presence of so many stock brokers more than compensated for the absence of a mere president.

When play resumed Ewing hit a short pop fly to right field. Billy Sunday held back so that he could rush forward to catch the ball with a last-minute dive. As he trotted off the field, he tipped his hat to the grandstand and made an upward gesture as if giving credit to heaven.

Both teams posted goose eggs until the top of the third inning when Cannonball Crane led off with a single. Ward was the coacher at first base, and he suggested that Crane might remove the whiskey flask from his hip pocket in case he had to slide. The pitcher merely snarled something unintelligible back at him, so Ward let the matter drop. A passed ball sent Crane to second, but a base hit by Gore brought another hip flask down to first with Crane and his flask taking third. Mike Tiernan struck out silently and soberly, but Ewing sent a deep fly to center field where Nat Hanlon, the same man who had made the catch of the century in Denver, suddenly became a butterfingers and muffed a ball that a child of eight would have caught easily. To make matters worse for the Alleghenies, Jim White couldn't bend down far enough to catch Hanlon's throw to third, allowing the runners to move up. Connor drove in two runs with a single and Richardson's infield hit scored another run when shortstop Jack Rowe made an overthrow. O'Rourke hit the ball harder than any other Giant had all day, but right fielder Sunday made a miraculous catch, this time needing all the speed he could muster. Pittsburg's pitcher Pud Galvin retired Ward for the last out on a weak foul ball caught by the catcher, but the Giants led 4-0.

K.C. had not been able to elbow his way onto one of the first cable cars leaving 125th St., so he arrived too late to buy a ticket. He found a comfortable spot among the 5000 or so cranks watching the game from what was already becoming known as Dead Head Hill. Sitting on the grass meant his suit would probably need a steam cleaning, but the fifty cents he was saving on a ticket would cover the cost. A local beer garden on the hillside was selling tall glasses of foam with a little beer on the bottom for the unprecedented price of 10¢ each plus another dime for the glass if you hadn't happened to bring one from home. In spite of this, men and boys lined up to be robbed of their dimes, and the queue in front of the courtesy outhouse (customers only, which meant you had to be holding a glass that smelled of beer) was even longer. Those who had arrived earliest had seats on benches from which the game could be easily observed. K.C., who had been curious about having beer at the ball game in St. Louis, now decided to stand in the takeaway line, which was how he had found himself next to someone who did not share his admiration for Ward.

"Johnny Ward stinks. He was through last year, and now he can't get the ball out of the infield. We were better off without him."

"It is his first game back from injury," K.C. said defensively as he watched the barman draw him a golden amber from a tap marked Schaefer's. The opinionated crank continued to make unfavorable comparisons regarding Ward.

"With Buck hitting one 478 feet with the bases loaded the other day, you'd think that Ward would get the idea. And Connor hit one they're still talking about in Indianapolis. O'Rourke, as old as he is, hit one in Chicago that's still going. Now that all the players have gloves, the only way to be sure to get a hit is to whack it over the fence. The game is passing Ward by."

K.C. would normally have defended Ward and the concept of tight well-played games, but he was having trouble squinting at the action and guessing whether the last ground ball had been fielded by the second baseman or the shortstop, a matter that seemed to be of less concern to those around him than it was to K.C. Whenever the line for beer shortened, another wave of thirsty cranks headed down the hill, some not managing to keep their feet on the journey down. The line for the outhouse grew even longer than that for beer.

With a four run lead, Crane was letting his anger do the pitching. He resented that White and Rowe were playing for the opponent, and he blamed Ward for their presence. Why would a Giant go out of his way to help the other team? Maybe it was because he was friends with Hanlon, but that was no excuse. In the bottom of the third, Crane walked the first two batters and then faced Deacon White. Crane threw three fast balls aimed at the veteran's head before he finally hit him in the shoulder, making a gesture of triumph when White went down in pain.

Even the Giant players were embarrassed at what Crane had done because White was the most respected player in baseball. At one time he had been the best player in the league, and he was also appreciated for countless acts of generosity. Everybody was relieved when White got up and strolled down to first base where he said a pleasant hello to Connor. Rowe then hit a ground ball that Crane thought Ward should have had. In a voice loud enough to be heard in the ladies' pavilion, Crane let fly with an obscenity-laced tirade directed at his shortstop.

In the Pittsburg fourth, Billy Sunday came to bat with two out and no one on. Sunday had tried to give Crane one of Dwight Moody's pamphlets on the evils of drink, and the pitcher had reacted negatively. Once again, it took Crane four pitches before he plunked Sunday in the spine. After the third out, Ward brought up Crane's anger when he sat next to Ewing.

"Maybe we should take him out. He's too drunk to go on."

"Johnny, he's mean when he's drunk, and when he pitches mean he gets them out. You know that. Besides, I'm only allowed one substitute, and if I took out every player who was drunk, we wouldn't ever have nine and we'd have to forfeit every game. I will admit that I wish the boys would lay off the whiskey on these hot days. Beer is much more appropriate. But, it wasn't Crane's fault that Sunday wanted to pray over him, and he was just mad that Jim White was playing at all."

"You could ask him to stop cussing me out loud enough to be heard in the stands."

"Then he'd just cuss me, and there'd be two of us getting cussed, so the ladies would be twice as bothered. No, Johnny, let's just leave it alone."

The Giants scored another run in the fifth. Ward killed the inning by striking out on a weak swing at a pitch that should have been ball four. In the Giants eighth the home team benefitted from two more errors with hits by Ewing and Connor, bringing the score to 7-2.

In the Alleghenies' half of the eighth, Rowe led off with a solid single. Then a pop fly landed behind Ward who had turned the wrong way going back on the ball. The next hitter sent an easy double play ball to Ward who was embarrassed when it went through his legs. The next hitter cleared the bases with a long double bringing the score to 7-5. After retiring the side, Crane ran after Ward and seemed to be chasing him off the field.

"We're trying to catch Boston, and all you can do is help your friend by getting him players. And you gave in to Spalding, too."

Ward was too tired and too discouraged to try to explain to Crane that he had a complicated job heading off a premature strike. The issues were too complex to explain to Crane even when he was sober, but it would be impossible to instruct an intoxicated pitcher who had just watched Ward's error cost him three runs. O'Rourke stepped in before Crane had a chance to start punching.

"Listen, Crane. We wouldn't be winning were it not for the venerable Mr. White's numerous errors and misplays. Johnny wasn't doing them any favors. White is like Menelaus, a magnificent warrior in his day, but past his prime, not some young Achilles still ravaging the Trojan horde."

Crane had no idea what O'Rourke was talking about, but like a dog calmed by soothing words, he settled down and returned to his spot on the bench. Ewing was not happy to see how belligerent Crane was becoming, but Buck was the captain, and he was not about to let an ex-captain tell him what to do. Jim Mutrie stayed away from conflict, preferring to confine himself to walking among the fans, shouting "We Are the People" at the top of his lungs.

The endless cycle of waiting for beer and then waiting for the toilet was interfering with K. C.'s ability to follow the game. A boy of about eight was crying because he had tripped as he left the bar, spilling a bucket that he had presumably been bringing back to his father. This incident generated a beery mud puddle at the front of the line. K. C. gave up keeping score for the bottom of the ninth, deciding that he could figure out what happened from the box score in next week's New York *Clipper.*

Catcher Ewing calmed Pitcher Crane down as best he could before the ninth inning. Buck was not about to mar the memory of the day he got his gold watch with a defeat. Hanlon led off the Pittsburg inning with a short fly gathered in by O'Rourke. Then Sunday beat out a slow roller to shortstop, one that Crane seemed to think could have been played better by Ward whose weak throw had allowed the speedy evangelist/outfielder to reach first. The next batter stroked a single to left, and Jim White came to bat with two on and one out. Once the most feared hitter in the league, and still dangerous as recently as last year, the forty-one year old White was hoping to get on base for his business partner Jack Rowe, due up next. Ewing called for a high inside pitch to remind White of how much Cannonball Crane's fast ball could hurt. The next pitch was predictably outside, and White let it go by for ball two. Crane crossed Ewing by throwing a curve ball on the inside corner, and White pulled it solidly down the third base line. Whitney knocked it down, chased it into the outfield and managed to throw in time for a force at second. Danny Richardson pivoted successfully, and his throw beat White for an around the horn double play to end the game. White was showing his age and the damage to his knees done by a youth spent catching.

"We are the People," Jim Mutrie was shouting as he entered the beer garden, which had been emptying out and now was filling up again. "The next round is on me," Mutrie said, plunking down a dollar that would cover only a small portion of its cost, but who was counting? The Giant fans were satisfied with their new grounds, and K.C. regretted that he had drunk so much beer before a long ride home on the streetcars. And all that standing in line for the beer and for the bathroom had made it hard to keep track of what was going on in the game. Dead Head Hill was fun for a day, but for the rest of the season, he would be buying his tickets in advance.

29

The Statue
New York
July, 1889

Even though Helen was enjoying, Paris, she decided to leave shortly before the exact centennial of the fall of the Bastille. Because of the Exposition, Paris was even more crowded than usual, so Helen showed herself to be a true Parisienne by leaving the city when it was starting to come to a boil. Her ship arrived in New York while Johnny was playing ball, so she was alone with Clara at their hotel.

In the extra room that Clara used as a studio stood the now-completed life-sized statue of Tim Keefe, wearing the banned uniform. Clara had captured Keefe in motion, about to let go of one of his fastballs or one of the ingenious curves or changes of pace that used the same motion. It could be any pitch because the statue's stony expression gave no clue. Helen walked around looking for the indecency that had caused such a stir, and she found it in the most obvious place. The little codpiece in front of the uniform that had seemed so insignificant when Johnny had modeled the uniform, now made a significant bulge."

"It does emphasize the male member."

"We're alone, Helen. You can call it a cock."

An impressive and perhaps exaggerated protuberance made a shocking impression for an American statue. Clara had evidently gotten some ideas on her trip to all those sculptors' studios in France. It was also possible that she had gotten the idea more directly from nature. "Tomorrow, we're going to put in front of the Keefe and Becannon store."

"Maybe you should wait until you're married before you put this on Fifth Avenue. By the way, why didn't you answer my cables?"

"I didn't get them right away. I was out of town. While you were gone, Tim's favorite aunt died, and I went with him to Cambridge for the funeral."

"It must have been terrible. How did the family accept your traveling together?"

"That was the surprise. The parish priest said I wasn't really a divorcée because I had never been married in the Catholic Church, so I just agreed to mumble a few prayer words and everybody was happy. Oh, and I learned how to genuflect and to make the Sign of the Cross."

"How about his sisters?"

"They loved being related to the glamorous Helen Dauvray and they both had questions about you. Sometimes I think they thought that Tim was about to marry you."

"That couldn't have been pleasant."

"No, it was. They were impressed with me too. They saw the sketches of my statue of Tim, and they thought it was wonderful. All my friends in New York talk about my work as showing promise for the future, but Tim's sisters admired what I had already done. One of them said how brave you and I were to make it in a man's world, and the other said I was strong because I didn't depend on my wealthy sister. Tim had made me afraid of them. Sometimes I expected them to be snobbish and proper Bostonians, and other times I was afraid they would be shanty Irish just off the boat, but they're neither. They thought it was hilarious that the uniforms I designed were deemed indecent and the contract was canceled."

"How are John and Timothy getting along?"

"They had a fight when John falsely accused Tim of sneaking his baseballs into games, but that had happened while Tim had been home visiting his dying aunt. John had assumed that Tim had been the one who put Keefe and Becannon balls in the Spalding boxes, but it turned out to have been Buck Becannon's idea, and he got Ewing to go along with it. Tim's balls are livelier than the regulation ones, so there were lots of long home runs. Buck Ewing hit one 500 feet, they say. Buck substituted the ball in Indianapolis and Chicago, but he got the other team's captains to approve it."

"Glasscock and Anson. They're both hitters. The pitchers would have said no."

Without thinking, Ward had blown up at Keefe when he realized that the rabbit ball had been secretly used in National League games. Part of Ward's plan for the new league had included introducing the new ball with a consequent increase in batting averages and home runs. It was to have been his secret weapon in establishing the superiority of the new league. When Ward had confronted him about the weeks when long home runs were jumping off everyone's bat, Keefe had not bothered to defend himself. He had merely retreated to the company of his oldest friends, the players who had been with him on John Day's team back in Troy and later on the New York Metropolitans. Eventually Ward found that Keefe had been out of town when the balls had been switched. Buck Becannon had talked Buck Ewing into asking the other captains if they could use the new balls. Ward had started the argument without full possession of the facts, and he found himself in the uncomfortable position of owing an apology to a close associate.

"I was sorry to hear about your aunt's dying. I didn't realize you were out of town when the balls were switched. And now that you're going to marry her, I'm sorry about some of the things I've said about Clara."

"That's okay. You should hear what she says about you, and she doesn't apologize for it. I've talked to my business partner, and we won't let it happen again. The new balls won't be in play again until we have our own league next year."

Being in Paris had given Helen a deeper appreciation of her husband, partly because she had been in the company of people who talked favorably about him: M. and Mme. Straus, the Halévys, and, most of all, little Marcel. Helen had resumed talking about a return to the stage, and Ward was resigned to accept it when it came. However, the closer Helen came to starting a new production, the more dissatisfied she became. While feeling she had outgrown her role as sympathetic young love interest, she realized that no one was going to accept her as a Lady Macbeth or Medea. So she temporarily put aside her plans to return to the stage, and Ward said he wouldn't mind if she decided to return to it later. For the rest of that summer they were as close as a married couple living in two separate hotels not far from each other could be. And they both looked forward to spending most of the winter in Paris.

At Clara's insistence, the statue of Keefe was placed in front of the headquarters of Keefe and Becannon. If Becannon had wanted to object, he was in no position to do so after having embarrassed Keefe with the illegal substitution of their baseballs. The statue did expose him to some teasing, especially from Buck Ewing who considered it hilarious, but Keefe remembered that it had been sculpted by the woman he loved, and he interpreted it accordingly.

30

The Revolution
New York
July 14, 1889

"**H**ow did Boston do yesterday?" Ward asked O'Rourke who was meeting him by prearrangement at Helen's hotel in order to walk together to the Brotherhood meeting at the Fifth Avenue Hotel.

"The Beaneaters won, so we're .063 behind them. But didn't you read the newspapers today? You missed Al Spalding's fulminations about the multiple wrongs we players have inflicted on the impoverished owners by forcing them to pay wages far above those customary for carrying the hod, which is all he deems us worth, and then only if sober."

Ward had not read the day's newspapers. He hadn't even spoken English since the afternoon before. O'Rourke went on.

"The Boston board of directors just voted themselves $2500 a year for attending quarterly meetings where they complain that the boys on the field are an overpaid collection of intellectual inferiors who should be happy with any employment. And the principal owner has the temerity to imply that the players are not doing their best."

"That's why the Beaneaters are so enthusiastic about the new league. Even though they sit at the top of the current league, they want to start a new one. We're going to change the sport of baseball from a mere business to a game controlled by the players."

"We'll require more than ballplayers, Johnny. We're going to need civil engineers, lawyers, architects, crowd control experts and even politicians."

"That won't be a problem. We can be businessmen ourselves. And there are plenty of capitalists who would love to invest in our league, I'm hearing. And architects are easy enough to find. Look how quickly Day threw his ball park together."

"I wouldn't take that as a model. The new Polo Grounds is misshapen, extravagantly over what was a generous budget to start with and structurally unsound, at least in my opinion."

Ward had momentarily forgotten that O'Rourke was a certified civil engineer as well as a lawyer.

"But Day must have figured out how he could put up a park and make money this season."

"Johnny, the only money being made on this venture is by the real estate investors who anticipated a boom around the new park, and Day wasn't smart enough to see that coming or rich enough to take advantage if he had. Look, we're passing Keefe and Becannon where they make those wonderful baseballs. Will you look at that!"

O'Rourke was seeing the statue of Keefe for the first time. After a moment of staring at the conspicuous protuberance that seemed to be the statue's theme, O'Rourke made an observation.

"Well, your sister-in-law will have to marry Keefe now. Will that meet with your approval?"

"Tim and I had a long talk, and I apologized for thinking he was the one who put the Keefe and Becannon balls into play."

"I thought the new balls were excellent. How do you feel about having Keefe as a brother-in-law?"

"Any man who is taking my sister-in-law off my hands is doing me a favor. Naturally, I would have preferred if she had fallen in love with someone from Tierra del Fuego or a particularly remote part of Borneo, but if Tim wants marry Clara, it's fine with me."

As they arrived at the meeting room, they were greeted by a muscular man wearing a white shirt with silver buttons and the letter P. There was evidence of a barely concealed weapon. This puzzled O'Rourke.

"Johnny, I think Al sent a Pinkerton to intimidate us."

"I hired the Pinkerton, Jim. I did it to keep Spalding's spies out."

Ward called the meeting to order. Following previously established procedure, Keefe read the treasury report first.

"Our dues have never been so up to date. Last month we received $5 from every player in the league except Anson. We have also received dues from a number of players in the American Association thanks to the efforts of Brother Arlie Latham. We are accepting IOU's from the Louisville players who have not received their pay for some time. We have a specific complaint from Brother Pete Browning. . ."

Once again the meeting was interrupted by the arrival of the splendidly attired and equally well-oiled Mike Kelly. With his conspicuously tall stove pipe hat precariously balanced on the top of his head and a charcoal gray suit, he could have been mistaken for a judge, at least a Tammany Hall judge. The odor of alcohol was apparent but not overpowering.

"Was that a Pinkerton I saw on the way in, Johnny? I think he's one Al used to put on my trail when we came to New York."

"He's working for us now, Kel."

Ward did not like having his meeting interrupted, but exceptions had to be made for Mike Kelly. Who else had a song urging him to slide? Who else was stopped in the street by people who wanted him to sign his name? Who else bought the cranks a round of drinks instead of expecting the cranks to treat him? Who else could have commanded the unprecedented sale price of $10,000 a few years ago?

"You're all right, Mr. Pinkerton. Even if you are a spy for Spalding. I still love you. I still love Spalding. Tell Al I love him even if he treats us like cattle, but it's time we jump off the meat wagon."

Ward tried to call the meeting back to order, but Kelly had one more question.

"If we're a union, Johnny, why do we have Pinkertons?"

"To keep our business secret, Mike. And we're not exactly a union. We're a collection of businessmen united for our common good."

Kelly sat down in a chair vacated by a lesser catcher and smoothed out his vest. Ward switched to his most formal voice in an effort to recapture the tone he thought would be most efficient. He began as he always began.

"There was a time when the league stood for fair dealing, but now it seems to stand for nothing but dollars and cents."

By now everyone had heard Ward's speech, and no one wanted to listen to it again.

"So let's get more of the dollars for ourselves and leave them with the cents," Fogarty shouted, with less regard to order than Kelly. "We should get a share of the price when they sell us."

"We're going to need backers," said Hanlon. "We have a fellow in Cleveland and some butchers in Pittsburg. I don't know about New York."

"Maybe we can get Day to back one of the teams," Ewing suggested. "We are the people."

Ward picked up a set of notes he had brought.

"If we do start our own league, I would suggest that we all sign for three years at our present salary, and there won't be any selling of players. We should put the profits into a pool to be used to reward the teams that finish first, second, third and fourth."

At this point, the meeting veered toward anarchy. Some players took out pencils and calculated their annual salary times three. Nobody had any idea how to figure the profit-sharing or the bonus money, but everyone knew his own salary and almost all the players had planned to make more the next year. For example, Jake Beckley was a rising star currently making a paltry $1500 a year, and he spoke for several of the optimistic youngsters.

"Some of us are going to be a lot better in 1892 and some of us are going to be worse. You'll have to allow for that."

"Then you can earn the bonus money for finishing higher in the standings," Ward answered, but almost no one heard him above the general buzzing. Fogarty spoke again, and he was loud enough to be heard by all.

"What about those of us who are making less money this year than last? The one promise the league made to us was that they wouldn't use the reserve clause to cut salaries, and I'm not the only one who had that happen to him."

Each player had a suggestion, some general and some specific. Clarkson was writing everything down in a notebook. No one waited to be called on, so volume was the determinant of who held the floor. Dan Brouthers spoke next. Brouthers, who had been elected vice-president of the Brotherhood, always commanded respect.

"You can all take out your pencils and worry about who does this and who gets that, but we have to go beyond that. All modesty aside, with the year I'm having, I'm probably in line for the biggest raise in this room, but I'm going to sign because it's the right thing to do, and I'm not going to worry about a few dollars this way or that. And if the day comes when I'm not worth what I'm being paid, I'll take a sack of silver dollars back to Wappingers Falls and manage the family hotel. But we have to stick together if we're going to change this business. Right now they can sign a young boy for a $5 bonus and pay him whatever they want for the rest of his career."

This was the speech that Ward thought he was going to make himself, but he saw that it was time to call for action.

"Brother Brouthers has said it best. Now it's time for us to storm the Bastille."

The players burst into cheers loud enough to arouse Kelly who had calculated that three more years at $5000 a year would be fine. "What's this storming the Bastille?" he asked Hanlon.

"It's something to do with the French Revolution. It happened a hundred years ago today. It was in all the papers."

"Now I remember. The French Revolution. How did that turn out again?"

In Chicago, Spalding and Anson were having their own meeting.

"What do you hear about what the players are doing at their meeting in New York? I hear rumors that they're talking about forming a new league."

"They can talk all they want, Adrian, but it takes money and business sense to run a ball club. And if they have any business sense, they'll see that the players get all the money that comes in already, so they can't do any better under a cooperative arrangement. But that isn't what I want to talk about. I hear that there were several games in Indianapolis and even here in Chicago which used Keefe and Becannon balls instead of the regulation Spaldings. If we can get evidence that Keefe and Ward smuggled in illegal balls, we'll sue them. It violated my contract with the league."

Anson knew that Spalding would not be pleased with the facts, but it was not in his nature to lie or even to evade the truth.

"Buck Ewing came to me before the game and asked if it was all right to substitute the balls. It was while Keefe was out of town, and Ward was out with the sore arm. Buck showed me the balls in practice, and I agreed to try them. Becannon must have used the same trick with Glasscock in Indianapolis, but when Keefe and Ward got back, the Giants went back to the old balls. To be honest, I liked the Keefe balls. They made a nice sound when they hit the bat, and then they went quite a bit farther than expected. You should look into putting some more spring in your baseballs."

Spalding did not want to hear this. The money he made selling balls for a nickel depended on having the exclusive contract to supply the league balls for a dollar, but he wasn't about to discuss his sporting goods business with Anson.

"Just don't let it happen again."

"Al, you have my word it won't happen again. Now all I'm thinking about is beating out the Giants and the Beaneaters for first place."

31

The Most Valuable Player
National League Park, Cleveland
August 14, 1889

Buck Ewing connected squarely and sent a triple-bagger over the left fielder's head, driving in two runs before most of the fans were settled. The most enthusiastic Cleveland supporters were seated in the pavilion by first base, so they had to shout all the way across the diamond for Buck to hear their observations on his ancestry, his morals, and, worst of all, his origin in that inferior part of Ohio known as Cincinnati. When Umpire Powers called a two strike pitch to Connor a ball, the crowd shifted its attention toward him, deriding his personal hygiene, his ties with the gambling establishment and, most pointedly, his eyesight. Given what the fans considered a reprieve, Connor lifted a handsome fly ball to right field, deep enough to allow Ewing to conserve energy as he trotted home.

All that month, Ewing had been playing with a splendid rage, smashing home runs over fences that had previously never been topped and throwing out almost every runner who dared attempt to steal. Largely as a result of Captain Ewing's play and his leadership, the Giants had pulled to within .005 of the first place Boston Beaneaters, but Buck's success had not been achieved without controversy. His obscenity-laden tirade at an umpire in Washington had been heard in every corner of Swampoodle Grounds, resulting in a $25 fine. Players around the league had begun to resent how Buck left his mask on the path to home plate where runners about to score had to swerve to avoid it or risk tripping over it. One opponent had taken a bat to the mask and smashed the flimsy bird cage to pieces. Ewing had calmly walked to the bench and picked up a bigger mask with sharper edges.

In the bottom of the first, Ward, reduced to playing second base by a recurrence of his arm injury, dropped a foul pop fly, leading to two unearned runs for Cleveland. However, Mickey Welch then shut them down for the rest of the inning, allowing no more balls out of the infield.

The gentleman next to K. C. had cheered wildly when Ewing had hit his triple.

"Are you a Giants fan, too?" asked K.C. hopefully.

"More of a Cincinnati fan, and Buck is a home town favorite for us. Buck hits the ball farther and harder than anyone else, and he's the best at the most important defensive position. *Sporting Life* was right to vote him the best player in baseball. Buck hits better than .300 every year, and not just singles. He deserves to be first."

Of course, K.C. knew of the recent poll which had voted Ewing first ahead of Kelly with Anson third and Ward fourth, barely ahead of Connor. Nonetheless, he was not prepared to accept the collective judgment of the baseball world, perhaps out of a sense of loyalty to his favorite player. K.C. felt obliged to defend the proposition that Ward was still the best, or at least that his entire career made him the best baseballist in history, an opinion that K.C. would never abandon. The man from Cincinnati made some powerful points, but K.C. had his countering arguments ready.

"You have to include defense and base running when you rate a player. And shortstop is a more important position than catcher, now that a caught foul tip is only an out on strike three and the equipment lets everyone play close to the bat. Johnny is still the best shortstop in the league, and he always takes the extra base when the defense is napping."

"Without a catcher like Buck, Welch couldn't be throwing those low curves. He knows each batter's weakness and manages the game from behind the plate. I've been watching baseball since before the Cincinnati team became professional, and every top team starts with a great catcher. That's why Buck is the captain."

This brought up another topic about which K.C. had strong opinions, and arguing that Ward was the best choice for captain avoided the subject of batting averages and total bases.

"I have to disagree. I've followed the Giants for a long time, and I still think Johnny should be in charge. He knows more baseball than Ewing and Mutrie combined. He wrote the book."

"Being a captain isn't about knowing; it's about leading. And Buck is a leader. He talks to the other players in language they understand and kids them into playing their best. Yesterday he was yelling 'Hoe her down,' at them as they rounded the bases, and things like that make them play with more ginger. You notice that they won the league title last year with Buck as captain, and they never did that when Ward was captain."

"But leadership is about more than that. The captain shouldn't be the one who gets fined for cursing umpires."

"Cursing's part of the game. And Buck doesn't always curse. Sometimes he can be quite civil to the umpires. He likes to kid with them too."

By the fourth inning, a steady drizzle was interfering with everyone's vision, and flashes of lightning, quickly followed by rumbles of thunder, threatened even worse conditions soon to come. Spider Captain Patsy Tebeau, a tough third-baseman of French-German descent who had been given his moniker because he was accepted as an honorary Irishman, recognized that Mickey Welch was almost unhittable that day. He began to stall in the hopes that rain would wash out the game before the completion of the fifth inning made it official. In the Cleveland fourth, Loafer McAleer led off with a low line drive toward O'Rourke, a sly veteran not above trying to pretend a mere trap was a clean catch. Umpire Powers had to put himself in a position to see the ball bounce, so he ran out to the outfield with his back to the infield. McAleer, seeing this, skipped first and headed straight over the pitcher's mound to second base. When the ball was dead, Ewing removed his mask and argued cooly and respectfully, acting more like a lawyer than those members of the bar O'Rourke and Ward who were both jumping up and down with anger. Buck even showed Powers the path which McAleer had worn in the grass by going directly to second base. Persuaded by this visual evidence, Powers ruled McAleer out.

A dozen spectators invaded the field immediately, running directly toward the umpire. When others saw that there was no effort to stop the first wave, the diamond filled up with five hundred cranks, convinced that collective action could undo the perceived injustice. Among the weapons being brandished were sword canes, cudgels, brass knuckles, pistols, shotguns and one machete. The Giant players headed under the stands protected by the one policeman who had made himself visible. Then, armed with only a billy club, the courageous officer managed to bring the umpire to relative safety. The Cleveland players were mixing with the fans, encouraging their indignation. Tebeau was loudly proclaiming that under the latest rules Powers had no right to consult with anyone and change his decision. The fans continued to riot until a call went to the police, and even after their arrival, the field was cleared only gradually.

Under the stands, Ward was surprised to see Al Johnson, who had pulled out a flask to entertain the players as they took shelter. Ward turned down the offer of a swig.

"Thank you for talking to Pete Browning. We'll have him here in Cleveland next year, and I think we might have one of the strongest teams in the new league. We'll just need leadership. Do you think Patsy Tebeau would be a good player-manager?"

"I used to think so, but now I'd prefer someone who wasn't inciting a riot in hope of getting a rainout."

"I think it's a good strategy."

Powers was regaining control and had avoided a forfeit, not that any of the Cleveland mob would thank him. Forfeits were becoming common in the American Association, but National League ball-goers were supposed to be sober.

"The field's all eaten up now. It's in no condition to play," Tebeau continued, unwilling to go back out against Welch, who was throwing his best.

"Get back and play," answered Powers, still insecure in his police guard and wary about objects which could come flying out of the stands. About this he needn't have concerned himself because anyone with anything to throw had had already thrown it.

"That's what comes of kicking at umpires," K.C. observed. "I wish that he had just let Welch go ahead and pitch out of it. They can't touch him today."

"Buck wasn't kicking. He was just pointing out that the other team had cheated. Buck has the character to be a real leader, maybe president some day, after Harrison serves his two terms. Buck won't be thirty until later this year. And after he serves as president, Buck'll come back to Cincinnati and live among the people. Buck's a true son of the Queen City."

"Like the Roman it was named for."

"Exactly. And Buck's a stoic. Think of all the pain he plays with. It's only been the last couple of years that he started using a mitt to protect his hands. But he keeps going out there, shutting down the base stealers and catching the foul balls."

"He still shouldn't leave his mask where other players trip over it."

"Buck's just trying to slow them down so that they can't get a full head of steam when they bang into him at home plate. Self-defense."

The game went on without further rioting, but it became rainier and muddier every minute. Powers hesitated to call the game with a crowd that had already shown itself capable of violence and Cleveland only one run behind. The eighth started with Connor getting hit by a pitch. Ward fanned the air three times and walked humbly back to the bench. Then O'Rourke topped a ball toward third base and reached when Tebeau couldn't get a grip on the soggy Spalding ball to make a play. Connor noticed that third base was uncovered, so he hustled over there while the Spiders were still cursing their bad luck. A sacrifice fly put the Giants ahead 4-2. In the bottom of the eighth, Welch continued to retire Cleveland easily as the sky darkened and the rain increased.

New York scored two more times in the top of the ninth, even though by that time lightning was the only source of illumination. Even the most determined rioters were giving up and heading home. This encouraged the umpire to surround himself with police and announce the game was called on account of rain. He had just enough time to escape into a waiting carriage the Cleveland police had prudently provided for the occasion.

"The best player in baseball just won another one," the fellow from the Queen City gloated. "Ward's on the decline, so is Kelly, and Anson could never do anything but hit."

K.C. still refused to recognize the results of the poll that put Ewing as the best, but he couldn't very well argue for anyone over Ewing today.

K.C. wrote New York 6 Cleveland 2 at the top of his scorecard and didn't think to correct himself until he had gotten back to New York the next day and seen the score reported as 4-2. He had forgotten that the Giant runs in the ninth had been canceled when the game was called before the Spiders had a chance to bat. He found his scorecard, corrected it and put it back with all the other ones he had accumulated over the past year.

32

The Wedding
August 19, 1889
Worcester, Mass.

Tim Keefe had three tasks to take care of before he married Clara Gibson Helms. The first was the one he dreaded the most, notifying his best friend Mickey Welch that he would not be the best man at the ceremony. Welch had long urged Tim to marry and settle down, and now that it was happening, it would be a quiet wedding with no one present but family, which meant that Ward would be his best man.

"Don't worry about it at all, Tim," Mickey said with his characteristic smile.

"But I do. If I didn't have Ward as my best man, it might look as if I was one of the ones telling the newspapers we didn't like him, and after that fuss about the Keefe and Becannon baseballs it would really be hard for him to understand."

"Tim, I'm not one of those that don't like Johnny. I admire what he's done with the Brotherhood, and I've been with him from the start, just like you and Buck and the rest. And you know why I support him?"

"Why?"

"It's about family. We play baseball so we can provide for our family and put aside for when we're older and can't play ball or even work anymore. Family is the greatest thing, you'll be finding out."

"I already have a family. My sisters."

"Your own children, that's what I mean. And don't worry about not having me as your best man. When you and Mrs. Keefe are all settled, you can come visit me and the wife."

The next bit of business involved a private meeting with his sister-in-law to be.

"I thought we should talk about Clara's interest in Dauvray Productions. Clara will be moving to Cambridge, and we decided she should sell her theater stock back to you."

This was the moment that Helen had dreaded since she learned that Keefe had studied bookkeeping. Dauvray Productions owned most of her personal holdings, and technically Clara was entitled to about 25% of everything. Keefe presented her with two pieces of paper.

"I've been going over the figures you've given Clara, and as best I can make out, she's gotten back about ten times what she put into the business, and I can't figure out how that much profit came from so few successes, no offense to your art. I'm offering you what Clara and I agreed would be a fair price."

The bill of sale contained the amount of $1 (one dollar) and assigned all Clara's stock over to Helen.

"Mr. Keefe, I thought the man who could obtain a contract from John Day for $4500 a year could negotiate a better deal than that. Dauvray Productions is still valuable, whatever I decide about going back on the stage myself."

"I know that, but it's clear to me that you've used this company to subsidize your sister, and she won't need that any more. I make good money from baseball, as you seem to know, and my share of the sporting goods business should start paying me some real money next year when our baseballs become the league standard. Whatever Clara makes from statue-making she can keep for pin money, and we should be fine. When I'm through pitching, there's a lot of things I can do. Besides, I have a large house which is home to my two unmarried sisters, each beautiful enough to marry any man she wants and both sweet enough that I hope they stay home forever. Now, after you give me one dollar to give to your sister, as she has agreed which you can see from her signature, we're no longer in business, and we'll only be family."

The third thing Keefe had to do was to arrange the marriage itself and help his sisters prepare for Clara. One of his sisters had designed a studio for Clara, something that Tim and his friends would build when they had time. There was no obstacle to the marriage because the parish priest had baptized Clara as a Catholic. Both of Tim's sisters were thrilled to meet Helen and were an eager audience for any stories of the theater she chose to tell them, including racy anecdotes about Nat Goodwin and other members of Broadway's fast set.

Clara made a stunning bride, dressed in a simple blue dress appropriate for a second wedding and beaming one of her rare smiles. As she came down the aisle, one of the altar boys whispered to the other.

"Her sister's the famous actress, but this one is a lot prettier."

Keefe overheard the remark and added another dollar to the already generous tip each boy was already getting. During the nuptial Mass, the priest beamed his approval at Clara in a congratulatory manner as she successfully stood, sat and genuflected at the prescribed times without even having to look back to see what the others were doing. There was a brief sermon expressing the hope that the couple would have many children all of whom would be raised Catholic. For whatever reason, he seemed to give a wink at Clara when he said it. A year before Keefe would have been too nervous to ask a woman out to dinner, and now he was committing his life to one. However, he had no anxiety because both of his sisters had assured him that he was doing the right thing, and they were both a good deal smarter about women than he was, or Ward either, for that matter.

After the wedding, Clara had a chance to talk with Helen about her plans for the future.

"Are you going to let John stop you from returning to the stage?"

"I'll do what I want to do, and Johnny has too much sense to think he can order me to do things or not to do things. Besides, you're out of the business now."

"Have you heard that Johnny won't be with the Giants next year? When the new league starts, he'll be the captain of a different team, and Buck will take over New York, manager and captain both."

"Johnny said something about it, but it's not final yet. Do you know what cities are being considered?"

"New York, for one. But that will be Buck's team."

"Staying in New York would be fine. Why can't Buck move to some city like Cincinnati? That's where he's from."

"They're trying to keep things together, and Buck is the leader of the New York team. Besides, why would anyone want a team in Porkopolis? But they might put a new team in Brooklyn."

"With the new bridge, that's almost like being in New York. And real estate in Brooklyn will be on the rise, I know that."

"And there will be a team in Boston. Mostly the players they have now."

"I like the city well enough, but I wouldn't want Johnny on a team with them. Kelly was the drunken oaf who ruined my honeymoon by getting in the carriage with John and me, and I don't trust Clarkson."

"Tim feels the same way. He wouldn't want to play with Boston either, even though it's his home. How about Washington? Didn't they talk about Johnny playing there at the start of this season?"

"Mostly while he was on tour with Spalding. He wouldn't want to go there.

"What about Chicago?"

"That would be fine. They have great theaters, and they loved me there. It's a beautiful city by the lake."

"Philadelphia?"

"That's close enough to New York, I suppose."

"What if Johnny wanted you to go to Cleveland?"

"I'd ask for a separation."

"Pittsburg?"

"Divorce."

Later that day, Ward had occasion to discuss the meeting with Keefe and O'Rourke.

"I don't think we should have anything to do with that Welshman, Johnny," said Keefe. "He was terrible to play against last year in the World Series. Remember how he pretended to faint when the umpire made a call against him? And all that singing during the game. Plus he was the one that used to cheat so much as a coacher that they had to make a rule against running up the base line to confuse the outfielders. He's not the kind we want with us."

O'Rourke had graver concerns.

"No harm in a little deception running up the base line, but the man is worse than that. They say his divorce papers involved wife-beating, and he is a well-known habitué of the lower class of bordellos. And he didn't even deny that he had been hippodroming. He just said that he and Comiskey had worked it out. And for a third baseman, he's a coward. He ducks line drives. We don't need his sort of scoundrel, and if Comiskey is ready to let him back on the team, we don't need Comiskey either. We can't allow gamblers to infiltrate the game. Comiskey and his players wager excessively on their games, and it's going to get them in trouble. And Latham's ideas about selling beer and cigarettes are appalling."

"I'm not saying that we have to accept all his ideas, but the boys from St. Louis would give us a good start on a team in Chicago, and that would keep Spalding busy trying to save his own franchise. What's bad for Spalding is good for us. And Arlie seems to have done some of the organizing we need in the American Association. The cranks love him. They call him the freshest man in baseball. That hippodroming charge probably goes back to those games in Kansas City where they weren't doing their best to protest the way they were being treated, more of a labor action than a fix. Besides, if he had been throwing games, I'm sure Comiskey wouldn't be giving him a second chance."

34

Umpires
Polo Grounds, New York
August 30, 1889

Gore led off the bottom of the first with a ground ball that made Boston first baseman Brouthers range far to his right in order to flip it to the pitcher for the out. Because this was a crucial game between two teams competing for the pennant, the league had taken the exceptional step of providing two umpires. Umpire Powers had been in a position to make the correct call, as Ward, serving as first base coacher, could see easily. Nonetheless, Ewing spent eight minutes turning progressively redder, like a one-year old whose rattle had been taken abruptly.

"And this is why games are called because of darkness," Ward remarked to Hank O'Day, the pitcher whom New York had acquired the month before. Ward knew he'd get a sympathetic ear because O'Day had occasionally served as a substitute umpire over the last two years.

"Ewing's one of those managers who never thinks about darkness until the sun starts to go down, and then he measures it by whether they're ahead or behind."

Finally, Buck grew tired of his tirade, and the game was allowed to continue. Mike Tiernan hit a line drive just inside the right field line, cornered the bases sharply, and slid into third a half-second ahead of an accurate throw. Ewing saw that the shortstop was playing too deep to throw out Tiernan at the plate, so he directed a ground ball to the left side of the infield for a successful sacrifice. Connor followed with a triple, but he was left stranded when Ward flied out to center. Keefe kept the score at 1-0 going into the third, when Brouthers lifted an easy pop fly outside the first base line. Connor stumbled and dropped it, a move imitated by Mike Kelly from the coacher's box, as he addressed the crowd in a voice loud enough for all 6000 cranks to hear.

"If it'd been somethin' to eat, dear old Roger would have held on to it."

That batter was eventually retired, but the next one singled and took off for second on the first pitch. However, he was caught off first when Ward's old stallmate from their days sharing the pitching duties at Providence, Hoss Radbourn, hit a line drive back to Keefe. It should have been a double play, but Keefe threw wildly to first, allowing the runner to tag and go all the way to third. The next batter hit a high fly to Gore who seemed to lose the ball in the sun. When the ball found him, he dropped it, kicked it, and then took a while to figure out which way it had gone. Kelly was due up to bat next, and before he took his turn at bat he performed a pantomime of Gore's struggle, exactly imitating each of the outfielder's movements and adding a quick sip from an imaginary flask as if by way of explanation. Kelly eventually walked and gave the crowd a thrill with a steal of second, culminating in one of his many celebrated slides. A brave visitor from Boston sang a few lines from "Slide, Kelly, Slide," until he was discouraged by those seated near him.

K.C. found himself in the unusual position of sitting next to someone who knew more about the rules of baseball than he did. When Connor took a called third strike and the hometown supporters booed, the new friend turned to K.C. and said, "It went through the zone high enough. Just because the catcher had trouble catching it, doesn't make it a ball."

The stranger was effusive in his praise for the two umpire system, pointing out that on a close play at first like the one Ewing had been arguing about, having the umpire in close position helped make sure the call was right.

"I know," said K.C. "I was in Cleveland when McAleer skipped first base on his way to second, and there was nearly a riot when Powers finally called him out. But at least he got the call right."

"Begging your pardon, but Powers did not get the call right. If I understand it correctly, he initially ruled that McAleer was entitled to second base."

"Yes, but then Buck showed him where he had beaten a path straight down to second, and Powers realized he was wrong and changed his mind, which is what he should have done."

"That would have been what he should have done last year, but this year the rule changed. The umpire is not permitted to seek guidance from any outside parties. Even if McAleer did miss the base, Powers was wrong to listen to Buck's arguments. The principle that the decision of the umpire is final is more important than the principle that you should touch every base."

"You seem to have taken the umpire's side all the time today."

"That's because I've done some umpiring myself on the college level. We stick together. I always notice the umpire when I go to a game, or in this case, the two umpires."

"They say that what makes a good umpire is when nobody notices him."

"That usually means that all his calls were for the home team. If all the cranks were dispassionate and objective, they might be able to judge the umpire, but then they wouldn't be cranks. The best umpire in baseball is the one who has gotten the most unfavorable notice this year."

Ward reached first on a force-out, provoking still another delay, this time with the Bostons swarming over Umpire McQuaid who was taking his turn on the bases this inning. As team captain, Kelly trotted in from right field to join the argument.

"You must be thick with Queen Victoria if you can cheat an honest Irishman like myself," Kelly began, pretending not to realize that McQuaid was as Irish as he was. Kelly's Irish nationalism could be switched on and off as easily as one of Mr. Edison's new lights, his brogue adjusting accordingly. Before he returned to the outfield, Kelly walked over to Ward at first. Johnny suspected that Kelly might be concealing a ball pursuant to executing the hidden ball trick, but his concerns were groundless. Kelly just wanted to share a quick word.

"Johnny, the boys are with the new league. I'll be the captain and we won't need a manager. Brouthers, Clarkson, Hoss and all the rest will be with me. And we're going to win the pennant in the new league just like we're winning it in this league."

McQuaid prodded Kelly back into the outfield, and Ward came around on a sacrifice and a hit to put the Giants ahead 2-1. In the seventh, Tiernan hit a two run home run over Kelly's head. It was the kind of home run for which Kelly used to carry an extra ball so he could reach over the fence and fake a catch by presenting the spare ball. Having an extra umpire made this impossible. Ewing struck out, but a string of singles brought home three more runs, and with Keefe as sharp as he was, it seemed that a 7-1 lead should be more than sufficient. Boston was so discouraged that they even took advantage of this year's new rule that allowed them to bring in a substitute to replace Radbourn on the mound.

"You were going to say who you think is the best umpire in the league," K.C. said.

"The best umpire isn't in the league. He's in the Association. Bob Ferguson."

"The one who is having all those problems in Brooklyn? The one that St. Louis complains about so much?"

"Von der Ahe said he has poor judgment, bad eyesight and is generally incompetent. But the beer baron doesn't know what it takes to make a good umpire."

"Which is what?"

"Courage."

"I read that Ferguson made a wrong call that robbed Comiskey of a home run."

"Not a bit. The ball went over the fence foul, hit foul and spun fair. Comiskey saw that too, and unlike most ball players, he knows the rules, so he should have known better. He had been the beneficiary of the same call years before, so he knew the umpire was right."

"Maybe he forgot the rule."

"Charlie never forgets anything that has to do with baseball. In Cincinnati they had a riot because Bob Ferguson called the last out on a close double play, and he left the field under a shower of bottles."

"And you say that makes him a good umpire?"

"He could face that crowd and yell 'There are 10,000 of you and one of me, but I'm right, and you're not going to change my mind.' The other day, Arlie Latham was swinging and missing on purpose again, and Ferguson warned him to play ball. Scared him more than the gamblers did. Arlie got a hit."

K.C. usually forgot the names of umpires, but he remembered Ferguson as a manager of more teams than he could remember and a player who was known by the colorful nickname "Death to Flying Things" for his ability to catch and kill houseflies while he was on the bench."

"I remember when he was a player in the old National Association. Wasn't he the first one who was a switch hitter?"

"Yes. He turned around depending on whether there was a right-handed or a left-handed pitcher. He was the league president too. Johnny Ward only started batting left-handed because he thought he could get out of the way of the ball better."

"Ward and Lee Richmond used to always throw at each other. I remember hearing about that."

"Richmond was studying to be a doctor and Ward a lawyer. You would think they would have known better. An umpire with the authority of Ferguson wouldn't have let that happen."

"What do you mean by authority?"

"Once in the old days, Ferguson was umpiring and Nat Hicks was the catcher. There was a wild argument over whether Hicks had made a tag, and finally Hicks came after him with blood in his eyes. Then Bob did what all we umpires dream of. He picked up a bat and broke Hicks's arm. That's umpiring."

"But they say Ferguson favors Brooklyn because he grew up there."

"That's just silly. Living in Brooklyn doesn't make you like Brooklyn better."

Keefe kept the ball low, and the Boston batters were lucky if they saw it well enough to aim their swings high or low. Darkness was spreading over the field, and most of the Boston players were hurrying as if they still had a chance. Only Kelly had forgotten about winning and was enjoying himself by imitating each New York player in turn. When Ward came to bat, Kelly muttered a few words in what he imagined sounded like French. He imitated Keefe's slow windup and twisted his moustache in a way meant to mock Sir Timothy. Pretending to be O'Rourke, he used a bat for a cane to draw attention to the outfielder's advancing age. Finally, the umpires met at the plate and decided it was too dark to play any more, so New York won 7-2, bringing the Giants within two games of first place Boston. With the game over, Ward's thoughts turned to an optimistic future of baseball without the owners and a better marriage, one without an omnipresent sister-in-law.

35

Financing
New York
September, 1889

With Ward out of town on a road trip, Helen decided to visit her accountant Bernie, mostly to examine the balance sheet now that she was sole owner of Dauvray Productions. Bernie had always been uncomfortable with the way Helen had been subsidizing her sister, so he was relieved to hear that the arrangement had ended.

"This Keefe fellow must be a sharp bookkeeper. I did everything I could to make it seem as though Clara deserved the money she got. It seems he must be an honest person, too. You were worried about him for nothing."

"I was never worried about him, just Clara's first husband. Mr. Keefe's more than honest. My sister is getting ready to move out of the hotel and relocate in Cambridge with her husband and his sisters. How do things look for Dauvray Productions as of now?"

"As usual, Helen, I have more good news than bad. You could still use another run like you had with 'One of Our Girls,' but with the exception of 'Mona' none of your plays has actually lost money. You will be paying rent for the Lyceum Theater for a while, but some of that will come back to you, and you are subsidizing some young actors, which is what you want. The investment in Mr. Edison's theater lighting company seems quite profitable, and it more than balances out any losses for Dauvray Productions."

"I could tell that he had a good idea. My predecessor had the lights installed by Mr. Edison personally, and when I saw what he was doing, I picked up one of Mr. Bell's telephones and ordered the stock."

"Are you planning to buy more Edison stock?"

"No. It's my theater business that I want to talk about."

"'A Scrap of Paper' didn't make much money, but you held costs down, so you still turned a small profit, even after paying overly generous allowances to the actors after it closed."

"That's why people like to work for me."

"You spent too much on 'Met by Chance,' especially the money you paid Bronson Howard when you commissioned the piece."

"Well, we hardly paid him anything for 'One of Our Girls.'"

"Helen, it always amazes me that someone as fair as you are can make as much money as you do. You would have made more money on 'Masks and Faces,' if it hadn't been for . . ."

"Don't mention Rose Coghlan."

This was the actress who had opened as Peg Woffington in a rival production which cut the audiences for both. Worst of all, although the reviewers compared Helen's acting skills favorably to those of Miss Coghlan, some were unkind enough to remark that Rose was much younger and decidedly more beautiful.

"You still made over $4000 and if I know bookkeeping, she must have lost about the same amount. Her little stunt might drive her out of business. You were the one with the capital reserves to win a war. 'Mona' lost nearly $9000, but we used the theater to build goodwill with benefit performances, and you wisely cut back. We made enough on 'Walda Lamar' and 'The Love Chase' that we were still in the black for that year. Now that we don't have to pay what you used to call 'dividends' to Clara, we are well in the clear. Mr. Frohman has informed me that he will be operating the Lyceum at a profit, so he no longer needs to hold off on paying what he owes you. Although, as I always say, with your investment skills, any money you tie up in the theater is wasted, even when you do make a profit."

"Bernie, you never think of art. John's like that too."

"Your husband is worried because he has no idea how wealthy you really are. And I understand that you have a right to spend your money, and losing it on the theater, should that ever happen, would just be your way of doing what Carnegie does when he starts a library, or what Belmont does when he buys racing horses. But you almost never have losses anyway."

"I have one more investment I want you to check on, Bernie. Could you discreetly find out what it would cost to buy all eight National League baseball clubs and tell me if I can do it."

"Interesting. I'll find the prices as best I can, but I can tell you already, that if it's just money, the answer is yes, easily. You could raise over a million dollars without touching jewelry or stock. As I never get tired of telling you, Helen, you are a very rich woman."

Before Clara moved her things out of the hotel, she had one last thing to discuss with her sister. Keefe had accidentally said something about how Ward had ignored a plea from Jessie McDermott to ask Helen to help her start a theatrical career To Keefe, this seemed to be proof that Ward, whatever his past guilt, did not want to be associated with Jessie in the future. To Clara, it merely meant that Ward had been in contact with the woman and had obviously not told Helen anything about it.

"I don't want to be the one telling you this, but that woman has been in touch with him. Did he tell you?"

"No. Should he have?"

"The question should be will he be named as a correspondent. I hear her husband wants a divorce."

"I can't imagine there's any reason for John to be involved in any way."

"There was no reason for him to be involved in any way on her couch, but that didn't stop him."

"That was two years ago, and what happened isn't clear."

"We know what her husband saw happening. From what I hear, she is so pretty that when she walked past Nick Engel's place, they were talking about it a week later. She is so beautiful that coachmen fall off their perches leaning over to get a better look at her."

"Clara, that's something one of your beaux said about you once, and you're just re-applying it."

"You caught me. It's true that I'm not very original, but I hear she's tall, well-proportioned and has perfect, thick black hair. She's also unusually large in the areas where men most prefer a man to be large. I don't think you should trust your husband around beautiful young actresses.

"It so happens I do trust Johnny around beautiful young actresses. Stephanie Cowell has been interviewing me on a piece for *Cosmopolitan*, and I told her she could interview Johnny too. I think she wants to write about our marriage."

"Is she their war correspondent?"

"Johnny and I are at peace, right now."

"So you're going to follow him wherever the new league takes him. Tim says that Johnny probably won't be with New York next year, whatever they do."

Helen did not share her idea about buying the National League. She didn't want anyone to know she was thinking about it, and she was hoping she could do it in secret.

Johnny and Miss Cowell had been talking at cross-purposes for half an hour over a meal at Delmonico's paid for by *Cosmopolitan*. Helen had told him that Stephanie was more interested in their marriage than in baseball contracts, but Ward still hoped that the article would give him an opportunity to talk about the reserve clause and the importance of the new league, which was barely a secret now and would not be by the time the article appeared in the winter. But Miss Cowell kept asking questions like, "What do you think it would be like to catch a baseball while flying?" Or "How does being a baseball player resemble being a knight on quest?"

Ward tried to use this as a chance to argue against the reserve clause.

"Well, the knight should be free to pick what team he wants to slay dragons with and not let some owner order him around."

This didn't seem to fit her ideas, so he started talking about Helen and how much he loved her. Miss Cowell scratched away vigorously at her stenographic pad while he described his marriage in detail—omitting only that they lived in separate hotels, quarreled frequently and seemed to be teetering on the edge of divorce.

36

The Drunk
Cleveland and elsewhere
October, 1889

Al Johnson was deadly serious about committing his family's fortunes to a socialistic baseball league, but there was one thing he and his brother Tom needed to know before they made the final decision. Where would Mike Kelly be playing? The Johnsons were like many other cranks to whom the name Mike Kelly was synonymous with big league baseball. They would prefer it if Kelly were to play in Cleveland, but at least they wanted to be sure that the King would be part of the new league. They thought that they needed a commitment from Kelly to make the Players League a viable business proposition. For Al Johnson, this meant a night of drinking on the town, the only way for two manly men to get to know one another and to exchange promises.

Cleveland happened to be at the center of the National League pennant race, not because the hapless Spiders had a chance themselves, but because they were playing the two contenders for the 1889 banner. They would host Boston for a game before New York came in for the last series of the season. Johnson introduced himself to Kelly and found it surprisingly easy to persuade the ballplayer to tour Cleveland's extensive saloon district where they matched each other shot for shot. By three in the morning each was committed to Johnny Ward and the new league, as well as Irish independence and justice for the working man in America.

Ward had anticipated that it would be difficult to keep the new league secret, but even after news had leaked out all over the country, the National League owners still believed that the players were bluffing. Some of the players who had agreed to sign with the new league, like Ed Delahanty, were using the new league to get leverage for a contract with their old National League team.

Buck Ewing had suggested to the Giants owner John Day that Day might be one of the financial backers in the new league, and even after that, Day refused to believe that the players were serious about a new league. Some bakers from Brooklyn wanted to be backers, and it was decided that the City of Churches would be a better risk than staying in Indianapolis. It was beginning to seem that Ward would be the manager and part owner of a new team to be called the Brooklyn Wonders.

Being near New York would also give him access to national magazines, like the *Police Gazette* and *Cosmopolitan*, which was important because he was the spokesman for the new league. Ward still hoped that Miss Cowell's article would present his ideas about the future of baseball, even though she had yawned and put down her pencil every time he mentioned contracts. Ward would have to deal with the press while the players gathered the financing that would make their new venture possible. Keefe was already telling reporters that the league was ready to go, but Ward saw a need to keep things quiet until the end of the season. Ward did his best to continue lying, but he was not as skilled at it as the situation called for.

Albert Goodwill Spalding, on the other hand, was so skilled a liar that he had even managed to fool himself. First, he proclaimed that the reserve clause would force the players to play for their established teams, and he kept hiring and firing lawyers until he found one who agreed with his position. Chadwick helped him find more old articles that showed how Ward had thought the reserve clause was necessary to the game of baseball. Spalding knew that someone like Jim O'Rourke or Deacon White would bring up how Spalding had jumped his contract with Boston to join Chicago in 1876, but Spalding was confident that he could explain the difference to reporters or a court of law. Of course, if Ward found some socialist judge who would overturn the reserve clause, Spalding would have to prepare for a bidding war like in 1884 with the Union League. The current team owners would complain about any added expense, but eventually they would let Spalding manage their affairs. Ward's potential backers all seemed eager for a quick profit and were unlikely to sustain the expenses needed to build new ball parks and to develop new audiences. Spalding was aware of only one person of genuine wealth associated with the new league, and that was Helen Dauvray. How a modestly successful theatrical producer had assembled the fortune that she seemed to have was a mystery to him, but the Pinkertons assured him that she was one of the richest women in America. An even greater mystery was how Ward seemed to be relatively unaware of his wife's wealth. One of their agents wanted to press the matter.

"He's a ballplayer. We follow him on the road, and eventually we track him into a brothel and get her to sue for divorce. Or if that doesn't work, she's an actress, divorced once before. We could catch her with some actor, and get him suing for divorce. Then we wouldn't have to worry about her money."

For a minute, Spalding hesitated, seeing a simple solution to the problem. Then his conscience got the better of him. Could a good Christian man justify advancing himself by breaking up a marriage, even one between a self-inflated radical and an actress who seemed to have been dropped on her head and turned into a Frenchwoman? As he struggled with his conscience, he remembered that Ward had recently shown himself capable of hiring Pinkertons, and it wouldn't take them too long to discover an old girl friend in Rockford with whom he still spent time that his wife would be better off not knowing about.

"No. I wouldn't spy on a ballplayer except for his own good. I traveled around the world with Johnny Ward and through half of the country with his wife. I won't do things that way. Besides, even if they do get most of the players over there in their league, Anson and I can always rebuild. Ballplayers are everywhere you look, and it's the training that's important. We could make a club from nothing, if we had too. But we won't have to do anything. The players are too short-sighted, mistrustful and disorganized to start their own league."

O'Rourke was preparing legal arguments against the reserve clause and finding precedent everywhere. Helen had found an old theatrical case where a theater company had tried to enforce a contract with an actress and had been told that they had no right to reserve her services. Ward ignored his wife when she brought it up, but later she mentioned the case to O'Rourke, who looked it up and agreed with her. O'Rourke then made Ward consider that it really could be a precedent that could help them ignore the reserve clause that was in all their current contracts.

In the mean time, Boston was competing with New York for the National League pennant. Now the Giants were playing in games that would decide whether New York would return to the World's Championship Series to play either the Brooklyn Bridegrooms or the St. Louis Browns for the rights to the Dauvray Cup. Ward had agreed that young Al Johnson would be the principal backer of the Cleveland franchise, and had introduced Johnson to Kelly. Johnson was visiting taverns around the league in an effort to recruit more players.

Keefe stopped by Ward's hotel room before the game, making sure that he was up and ready. Keefe had read that day's newspaper.

"Did you hear what happened at the ball park here yesterday?"

"I heard that Cleveland beat New York, but I don't know much more."

"Our new friend Al Johnson and Mike Kelly went out the night before last to celebrate our new enterprise. You can read about the results in the paper."

"Just tell me what happened."

"Kel showed up too drunk to play, so he sat on the bench wearing a big overcoat. Boston was falling behind, and Kel started telling the boys, 'I'm the king, you never win without me.' Then in the sixth, one of the Beaneaters was out at the plate by ten feet or so, and McQuaid made the call. Kel got off the bench and said McQuaid had come west to rob them of the pennant and got ready to punch the umpire, but two policemen stopped him. They had to take Kel out of the park."

"So that's good news for us."

"If you're thinking as a New York player, yes. But we have a new business enterprise to promote, and one of our owners was tippling until 3 a.m. with one of our managers, who then made a public disgrace of himself. We might want to think about how we can handle it."

"There's nothing we can do. We need Kel to give the new league credibility, and the Johnsons are our source of money in Cleveland. Don't worry. It'll all work out. And it looks as if we're going to win the pennant after the best pennant race in history. And it will be the last National League pennant worth anything."

Part Three
Baseball's Greatest League

37

The Pitcher
National League Park, Cleveland
October 5, 1889

Mike Tiernan's line drive split the left and center fielders and bounced all the way to the fence. Tiernan touched the corner of each base with a crisp turn as he completed an inside the park home run, in spite of having to slow down at the end to avoid reaching home before Gore. The night before, Al Johnson had insisted on celebrating the imminent revolution with one of the players. Ward had turned him down, so Ewing then nominated Gore as the only player he thought capable of drinking with Johnson all night and playing the next day. At the end of the first inning, New York had a 2-0 lead in a game where a victory (or a Boston loss in Pittsburg) would decide the National League pennant and the right to defend the Dauvray Cup.

In talking with the Cleveland players before the game, Ward had learned that if the Spiders were to beat the Giants, Boston had promised them an honorarium. This seemed shameful to Ward, and he brought it to Ewing's attention, suggesting that they should file a complaint with the league office.

"We'd be on shaky ground if we complained, Johnny. Mutrie has offered the Pittsburg players money should they beat Boston, and he did it by telegram. Boston probably did it with a wink and a nod. Besides, why would I complain to the National League just when we're about to finish it as a major league organization? It doesn't make sense."

For the last few games, Ewing had put Ward third in the batting order, mostly because he knew it irritated Connor who considered a high place in the batting order to be his right, considering his high batting average and consistent power production. By putting Connor sixth in the order, Ewing knew he would be angry. By awarding his spot to Ward, the anger would be intensified.

"Come on, Roger. Show me I'm wrong," had been Buck's response to Connor's objections.

"We are the People," cried the young man sitting next to K.C.

"Are you a Giants fan?"

"I have become one because I believe the workers should control their own industry. I work in a shoe factory, and my comrades and I know more about how to make shoes than any investor. The ballplayers should know how to run their own business."

"I hear that they're looking for backing from capitalists."

"I hope not. They should work for themselves, a co-operative. That would be best."

"Do you come to a lot of Cleveland games?"

"No. Fifty cents is too much for a working man to pay. I used to go to games when I lived in Brooklyn and paid only a quarter. And I could go on Sunday and drink a beer with the game. This is my first game since I moved to Cleveland last month."

"So you've seen some Association ball this season. They're having a great pennant race over there too. Who's going to win—the Browns or the Bridegrooms?"

"The Bridegrooms are on their way up, and the Browns are headed down."

" I think the Giants can beat either of them."

"I hope so. I support the Giants because they are socialists, like me. I believe in the brotherhood of man, and they believe in the Brotherhood."

K C. considered any reason for supporting the Giants to be a valid reason, but he had not given much thought to the structure of the new league. What concerned him, when he did think about the uncertain future of baseball, was what kind of team would wind up playing in the New York area. But his most immediate thought was to find out what was happening in Pittsburg. If the Beaneaters won and the Giants lost, that meant that there would have to be a playoff. A young boy was being sent back and forth to a nearby tavern which was receiving the scores by wire every half-inning. K.C. turned to hear his announcement, as did the small group of Broadway characters that DeWolf Hopper had led to Cleveland.

"Pittsburg scored three in the first, and Pud Galvin is pitching."

K.C. felt confident because Galvin was the best pitcher Pittsburg had, one of the best in the league. Even though he had come all the way to Cleveland to see his Giants win, he would be happy enough if they became champions by default through a Boston defeat.

In the fourth inning, Connor was still angry with Ewing and Ward, Ewing for batting him sixth and Ward for all his suggestions about how a man should take care of himself. Sometimes he seemed to be hinting that Roger should cut back on beer, which made him feel that Ward was equating him with the old sots like Gore or young lushes like Crane. Ward also suggested that Roger should emulate O'Rourke by taking regular exercise. Worst of all, sometimes Ward gave Connor hints on what foods he should be eating to lose weight. Asparagus! Connor was still resenting this even as he delivered a sharp single to center. Ward, who was coaching first, passed along the sign for the hit and run that had come from Ewing. Roger took off for second, and O'Rourke hit a weak grounder to third instead of through the hole vacated by the second baseman. However, the old outfielder hustled down to first, forcing a quick throw from Tebeau which went over the first baseman's head, allowing Connor to go to third. Ed Whitney noticed that the center fielder had a weak arm and he managed to lift a lazy fly in that direction, giving Connor time to charge home, putting the Giants ahead 3-0.

Keefe had his fast ball working even better than usual, keeping the ball on the corners and relying on his change of speed only occasionally. Ewing's hands had healed up from their late season sores, so he was comfortable calling for mostly fastballs.

In the Spiders' fifth, the first hitter took a mighty swing and topped the ball to the third baseman for a lucky hit. After a walk put another runner on, Gore misplayed a fly ball into a double, letting two runs cross the plate. Keefe would have asked Ewing to take Gore out of the game, but Buck had named Crane as his substitute for the day, and that young man, having found the only place to get absinthe in Cleveland, was considerably drunker than Gore and hallucinating in the bargain. The ever-sober, always quiet Tiernan led off the Giants fifth with a walk. Ward followed him with a pop fly to the pitcher who got tangled in his own feet and dropped the ball. With most runners, he would have had time to throw to first for the out, but Ward always ran out everything he hit. Getting an out at second was impossible because Tiernan had been smart enough to go part of the way, enabling him to get down there before he could be forced out. Ewing hit a weak ground ball and Ward was out at second, Tiernan moving to third, setting the stage for a play the Giants had been practicing but had not used yet this season. Ewing set out to steal second. Tiernan delayed until it was clear that they were going to make a play on Ewing, and then broke for the plate. Ewing came to a complete stop, intentionally getting caught in a rundown while the second baseman held the ball, unsure what to do, so the run scored before the third out was made.

K.C. was prematurely rejoicing in the pennant. The boy had come back with the news that Clarkson and the Beaneaters were behind the Alleghenies 6-1. The Giants were probably going to be champions whether they won or lost.

"Why do you think the Bridegrooms will win?" K.C. asked the young socialist.

"You have to be careful of the Brooklyns at home, especially if they pick the umpire. The Association still has a week to play."

"If the Browns hadn't lost those three games to Kansas City in May, they'd be in first place now," K.C. reminded himself.

Connor came up again in the sixth, this time with his friend Richardson on first after a single. Richardson took a brief time to yell at Ward who had signaled him to stop at first.

"I could have had a double."

Connor singled his friend to third, where he was in a position to score on O'Rourke's sacrifice bunt, giving the Giants a 5-2 lead. Some of the players were hearing that Boston had lost, but the New Yorkers pressed on.

In the home half of the ninth, Richardson's error put a Spider on first, and Jay Faatz pulled the special trick that he had copied from Curt Welch, leaning into a pitch in order to get a free pass to first base. A deep fly to left seemed headed for extra bases, but O'Rourke turned and pushed his old legs to their limit, catching the ball just before he crashed into the fence that surrounded the outfield, but holding on to the ball. The runner on second had stayed close to the base, which enabled him to score on a rare two-base sacrifice fly, but it now seemed sure that the Giants would win what would probably be the last meaningful National League pennant.

"Runs that score before the tying run in the last inning are of little or no value," Ward observed in an effort to make Richardson feel better, but using that pedantic tone that always irritated the second baseman.

O'Rourke's catch proved to be all Keefe needed, and he easily retired the last two Spiders. When the last out was recorded, DeWolf Hopper led rousing cheer for the winners. Even though the Giants' last visit to Cleveland had resulted in a near riot, there had been no increase in security, so the cranks from New York were able to take the field for an impromptu celebration. Mutrie kept yelling, "We are the People," exuberant at his team's victory. For most of the Giants, it was anticlimactic because they had received the final score from Pittsburg and knew that the Boston loss had already made them champions. Gore was celebrating with the last dregs of the pint bottle that he had been sipping on throughout the game.

A special train carried the players back to New York where they were all met by enthusiastic cranks, all except for Ward who had gotten off the train in Pennsylvania to visit his ill brother. With all the secrecy about the new league, most of the writers assumed that he was lying, but he was telling the truth, just as Ewing had when he visited the sick child. But Ward could use the experience because he would have a lot more lies to contend with over the course of the next year.

38

The Owner
Broadway Theater, New York
October 20, 1889

Cranks flooded into the Broadway Theater, eager to pay $5 for admission and another 25¢ cents for each diluted beer. DeWolf Hopper had arranged for the use of the theater, and Nick Engel was providing the food and drink for free, so all the money collected went into a fund for the Giants. The cranks were happy to have a chance to meet the players, and a roomful of Broadway stars added to the glamor.

Helen and John were delaying their trip to Paris because of the World's Championship Series. It was to continue until one team had six victories, and so far the Brooklyn Bridegrooms were tied with the Giants at one game apiece. With uncertain weather and the possibility of a tie game being called because of darkness in these late October afternoons, there was no end in sight. Helen had already given up the idea that they could be in Paris for the end of the Exposition, and now John was saying that he would have to be at the Brotherhood meeting on November 4, which would delay their departure even more.

"You could have Timothy represent you at the meeting and keep in touch by transatlantic cable. That's how Mr. Bennett manages the New York *Herald*."

"He's just a boss. I'm a leader."

Apart from a disagreement about when they should go to Paris, Ward and Helen were getting along well. When Helen had asked John about Jessie, he had admitted what he had to admit and cursed Clara under his breath, correctly guessing that she had been the channel through which this information about the contact had flowed. When they did have disagreements about Jessie or anything else, Ward could always go back to his own hotel and wait until they had both decided to ignore the problem and continue as they were.

Similarly, Helen's relationship with her sister had improved as Clara shifted her life from the hotel in New York to a house in Cambridge. The last of her art supplies had been shipped, and Clara was now established as Mrs. Keefe of Cambridge, coming back to New York to accompany her husband to the benefit. The sisters were sincerely happy to see each other.

Helen and Clara walked around the floor and mixed with the crowd. Actors and actresses pursued Helen, wanting her to remember them for parts in future productions. Otherwise, the only topic of conversation was how the Giants were being cheated by the umpires. As Hopper prepared to perform his now obligatory recital of "Casey at the Bat," the sisters headed to their box where they could whisper to each other while the ballplayers made their speeches.

"Why do ballplayers need a benefit?" Clara began. "Tim says he feels embarrassed about getting a couple hundred dollars as a handout."

"You have an unusual husband, Clara. Not all the players make the kind of money our husbands do, and a couple of hundred dollars might be important to some of them, especially with the uncertainty about next year. John says that the money should go into a strike fund, but he gave up trying to convince the other Giants to contribute to it. Look, Mr. Mutrie is giving a speech. This should be amusing."

"WE ARE THE PEOPLE. CAN I HEAR YOU? WHO ARE THE PEOPLE?"

Clara turned to her sister.

"If John becomes a manager next year, will he wear a frock coat like that and greet the people when they come in the ballpark?"

"Johnny will still be playing shortstop, and he can't very well wear a frock coat out in the field."

"John could. He'd like something that would put him above the others. Hush, it's my husband Timothy's turn to speak."

Keefe presented a sober contrast to Mutrie.

"We celebrate our pennant today, and we will go on to win the Dauvray Cup. Next year, we'll be together again, and who knows what we will win. But we do know whatever we win, it will be fairer and better and more satisfying."

Helen looked at her sister.

"Aren't they still trying to keep the new league a secret? It seems that your husband has trouble keeping secrets."

"Not like yours, I'll admit that. Timothy can't lie very well—not at all really. You thought I only wanted him for a husband because he was so handsome, and maybe that was true, but every week my choice looks better and better. Here comes Mr. Tiernan. I wonder if he'll manage to say anything."

Silent Mike had passed an uncomfortable evening in the corner trying to avoid conversation about the new league. When he was called to the front, he managed to mumble a few words that sounded like thank you, and he introduced Roger Connor, who read from notes.

"We're all part of a team, and we all know how to do our jobs. We accept that Buck is our leader. He's the best of us, and we all know that if we listen to him, we'll do all right against Brooklyn this year and next year too."

Helen looked at Clara.

"Is that supposed to be a criticism of Johnny?"

"Probably. You know that Roger has never liked John."

"Why not?"

"You know why. He tells Roger how to play first base the same way he tells you how to be a wife. He used to tell Tim how to pitch. Quiet now. It's the drunks' turn. This should be fun," Clara observed uncharitably.

She had barely finished her sentence when the "We Are the People" banner came loose and crashed next to George Gore, who might have been seriously injured had the heavy pole fallen a foot to the left. Gore, however, went on to speak as if nothing had happened.

"I want to thank all the cranks who have been buying me drinks all night, and I want to thank them double because Nick Engel is giving us a percentage of each drink sold."

"Mr. Gore reminds me of Mr. Kelly," Helen observed.

"But without the charm. Here comes Tim's friend Smiling Mickey Welch. What will he have to say?"

Welch was flashing the smile that had become part of his name. Public speaking was easy for him after partaking of his favorite beverage, which, unlike Gore, he had been paying for, even buying the cranks a round or two.

"It's a swell (burp) bunch of fellows that won this pennant flag. And today we are here, with all this wonderful music and beer. Hey, that rhymed. Let me give you another recitation, this one in honor of Freddy Engel's father Nick who has brought us all together tonight.

The rarebit served at Nick Engel's place
Would please the taste of any man.
A mug of ale without a question
When drunk on top would aid digestion.

Welch concluded with a rich, reverberating final burp and a sheepish smile.

"So he's now part of your social set, Clara?"

"At least he's a cheerful drunk, not like that one down there."

It was Cannonball Crane's turn. He may or may not have been intoxicated, but he was angry either way.

"Last year when I arrived in New York, the city was covered with three feet of snow which no one knew how to get rid of and they were calling it the biggest disaster in history. Then this year, there came that flood in Johnstown. But neither of those things was as bad as what those Brooklyn-loving umps did to us the other day and plan to do again. Ferguson's been for Brooklyn all his life, and the other one, Gaffney, is even worse. Everybody knows that their owner Byrne is nothing but a crooked gambler and Chadwick and the newspapers cover up for him. We need to be sure that we have plenty of our own fans in Brooklyn to let the umpires know they won't get away with any funny business."

At this point, Ward popped into the box and greeted the two sisters.

"Crane made a drunken fool of himself again. I wish I had never taken him on the tour."

"Tim says he was such a nice boy before he started drinking, but he pitches better drunk," Clara added. "We should hush now because it's Mr. O'Rourke's turn, and he's always sober.

"From the beginnings of the National Association of Professional Baseball Players through the time when Al Spalding and the others defected to Chicago, there has never been a leader so skilled at keeping his underlings digitigrade as Buck Ewing."

"What on earth is he saying?" asked Helen who had asked Ward to translate O'Rourke's peculiar idiolect before.

"It's his way of saying that Buck keeps the boys on their toes."

"Mr. O'Rourke loves to proustify," Helen remarked.

"What does proustify mean?" Clara asked.

"To talk in long ornate sentences with complex words in a generally flattering manner, " Helen explained. "It's a word some French boys we know used to describe the way one of their friends talks."

"One of our friends," John corrected. "I just sent him a supply of sliding pads to sew into the uniforms. I know they'll want to use them because they saw what happened to Williamson."

Helen had little faith in Marcel's ability or inclination to promote baseball in France, but she was glad that John had liked him, and she looked forward to when they would all be together in Paris. Sometimes she wondered what they had found in common to talk about, but she supposed it was just some male activity she didn't know about. Ward got up to leave.

"O'Rourke will be finished in a few minutes, and I'll go on last. It should be Buck, but he hates speechifying as much as O'Rourke loves it."

Ewing spoke for a few seconds expressing gratitude that no one had been hurt when the banner came down, and he made way for Ward.

"We Giants have a tough fight ahead of us, but if you cranks come out and support us, we can go on to win another Dauvray Cup."

"How bland this is," thought Helen. "Johnny never says what he means in English."

That night Ward visited Helen in her hotel. He had some lilies sent to her room, and he performed the usual ritual of adjusting them. Helen smiled and used her sweetest voice.

"Nous irons à Paris, n'est-ce pas?" (We're going to Paris, right?)
"Bien sur." (Sure.)

Contracts
Oct. 24, 1889
Chicago and New York

Anson was rarely invited to visit Spalding's sporting goods office on Madison, so when the White Stockings' owner called him for a special meeting, he knew it must have something to do with those rumors about a new league. Normally Spalding would have been concentrating on preparing the Chicago team for the next season, but he knew now that he would be called upon to save the whole league, not just the Chicago franchise. With Ward and the players starting a new league, he had to gather the intelligence that he would need to formulate a plan.

"Which of the boys will sign with us next year,Cap? How about Duffy?"

"Not him. He says that I'm anti-Irish, me who put up with Mike Kelly all those years and wasn't the one who said get rid of him. And Williamson said he wasn't going to sign. And last year he was the one who came out the strongest against the Brotherhood."

"No loss. Williamson's not the player he used to be. It was a mistake to let him come back in August, especially after he told me he expected me to pay for the expensive French doctor Ward recommended. And he wanted me to pay his wife's passage back from Europe."

Spalding didn't mention that he hadn't paid for either. Anson went on.

"Well, Ed told me he's with the radicals. And so is Pfeffer, good riddance."

"How about Tener"

"Says he wants to play with Pittsburg, like it should be his choice. Why should you care about a muffin like him?"

"Tener never gives us any information, so I guess he was with Ward all along. I'm glad Clarkson keeps me informed. He's even invested in the Boston team, so he hears everything. I'd love to see Ward's face when he sees that Clarkson is staying in our league. So how many of the boys does that leave with us, Adrian?"

"Me. We don't need any of the rest of them. Ballplayers are as easy to find as apples in August. We'll scout the local leagues, send someone out to California maybe. And there are a lot of players wearing jockey silks over in the Association who are good enough to play fifty cent ball in real wool uniforms."

"You're forgetting that the Association is our partner. We have to respect their contracts, just like we're going to make the players respect ours," said Spalding, who was already planning to raid the Association to make up for his defecting players. If necessary, the National League might take in one or two of their better teams. Nobody thought Brooklyn and St. Louis could keep playing in the same league.

"You're forgetting that the Association says you promised they could put a team in Chicago. Are we going to let them? Von der Ahe and Comiskey would like that fine."

"I didn't say when they could put a team in Chicago. Maybe after we're all dead. For now we have to go to the courts to get them to uphold our player contracts. All our players signed a clause that reserves them for the next year."

"I say forget the courts. We go to the police and get them to break the players' skulls the way they did to the strikers at the reaper plant a few years back."

"An excellent idea, but we have to go to the court first to get the order to have the police break their heads. That's the law. Otherwise we'd have to hire Pinkertons. Don't worry. All those Brotherhood radicals will wind up playing for us, and at reduced wages to make up for our trouble."

"We should just let all those old war horses go and start training new colts."

"You might be right, but for now the Brotherhood does seem to have the best players like Kelly, Brouthers, Keefe, and Ward."

"Ward's not one of the best players. He's clever enough and can steal bases, but he's not a first class hitter. He didn't even hit .300 this year, I'll bet."

"Maybe you're right. The papers love John 'Much-Advertised' Ward. But whether he's one of the best players or not, Ward is their leader."

"So maybe the new league will speak French and have breaks for tea with doilies on the bases and no cigars in the stands."

"That reminds me. I just shipped eighteen sliding pads to some boy in France at Ward's request. I don't like doing it, but Ward does promote my products like the protective cup, and he says France might be a profitable market some day. I wish him luck with that. What do you hear about the other teams?"

"It's not just our boys that are deserting. Hanlon is taking out the whole Pittsburg team. The Beaneaters are all disgusted with their owners, and they'll all go over to the new league."

"Boston's NL team will have the best pitcher with Clarkson. He always stays in touch. Boston wouldn't have been in the pennant race without his pitching last year. And he told me that his wife doesn't want him to stay on a team led by Kelly. I must admit that Ward finally has me worried. He does seem to be getting most of the players into his new league."

"Don't worry, Al. They'll all be sick of Ward sooner or later. He's a communist who has the airs of a French aristocrat. How will he control that bunch of rowdy Irishmen? Remember in Naples how he showed you up when you were talking in Italian? He had to let everyone know that he could do it better than you did. He tells people what books they should read. Nobody likes him."

"Except the newspapers, Adrian. They love him."

"We can tell the newspapers what to think, and if we can't, we'll start our own newspaper."

"For now, we have to try to keep the Players League out of Chicago or at least see that they fail if they try. We have to keep them away from the real money on Prairie Avenue or Lake Shore Drive, the Fields, the Palmers, the meatpackers."

"We have to watch for their weakness and jump. If they play Sunday ball, we'll get the preachers after them. If they sell beer, we'll get the Anti-saloon League to break up their games. When somebody places a bet at one of their games, we'll have the police arrest their backers for bookmaking. If Ward brings in coons, we'll say that he's threatening the white race."

Spalding had some sobering ideas.

"If they do get the new league started, we might have to take some losses. We have to win the publicity war. We'll prove to the newspapers that the players are already making all the money that comes through the turnstiles. The owners are all going broke paying the high salaries to stars and even to muffins. We owners are operating more of a public service than a business. We're the ones who are in it for the good of the game, the national pastime."

Anson went on as if he hadn't heard anything.

"If they sign Kelly, we'll say they're all drunks. If Latham goes with them, we'll say they're all gamblers and crooks"

Spalding had to admit that Anson had the right idea. For now, they would sign whoever they could, maybe even paying a little more. It hurt Spalding to remember the times when there were two or three leagues bidding for players. In the mean time, Anson had calmed down and was looking through a newspaper on the desk.

"I was right. Ward only hit .299."

"Anson didn't lead the league in hitting this year," observed Frank Brunell, the Cleveland sportswriter Ward had hired to act as league secretary and take care of some business details. "He never forgave me for exposing his cozy arrangement with the official scorer in Chicago."

"We're here to talk business, not baseball, Frank. We have to finalize our clubs, arrange financing for the parks, and design a schedule. Our secrets are leaking out fast, but I want to have some surprises when we unveil the new league. For instance, I have decided that I will manage the Brooklyn team, and I plan to be one of the investors. Most of my players will come from the Indianapolis team that is disbanding, but apart from Glasscock, they don't have much talent."

"But he's a shortstop."

"One of us can move to second base. And Deacon White's Buffalo team will inherit the Washington players. Hoy and Mack are comers, both with enough brains to have money of their own to invest. Buck will keep the New York team the way it is."

"But without its star shortstop."

"That's why my Brooklyn team will beat Buck's Giants. Now you have me talking about baseball instead of business. Anyway, the other managers will be Fogarty from Philadelphia, Kelly from Boston, Hanlon from Pittsburg and I think Al Johnson wants Patsy Tebeau in Cleveland. And Rowe or White will find someone to manage Buffalo or one of them can do it."

"And who will replace Anson in Chicago?"

"We need a strong team there, so I'm talking with Charlie Comiskey about blending the Browns with the Chicago Nationals. They have plenty of players who are ready for fifty cent ball."

"That's what the Browns have been charging anyway. Is Comiskey going to bring Arlie Latham with him?"

"Probably. No one plays third base like Arlie."

"But you have to worry about gambling and rumors that Arlie threw games."

"If you mean that series in Kansas City, that was more of a labor action. And Arlie has been my best organizer in the American Association. We're going to get the best players from the Association too."

Brunell saw that the plan had already been made, so he went on to his next concern.

"And are you going to do something about the umpiring. Everybody knows the Giants are being robbed this series."

"We're going to use the double umpire system in each game and cut down on kicking and rowdiness. And we're going to hire the best umpires like Bob Ferguson and Honest John Gaffney."

"Didn't you punch Gaffney once?"

Brunell knew all the old stories.

"That was not on the field. It was in the hotel, and it was because he said my mother would be ashamed of me for the language that I had used that day. I knew he was right, and I lost my temper. He apologized when he realized my mother was dead. That was years ago, and I was very young. Anyway, I want to start by paying the umpires well, beating their salary in the Association."

"Won't having two umpires every game be too expensive?"

"Most of the problems have been that the umpires called the game or didn't call the game because of darkness. If both teams hadn't wasted time complaining about the umpiring, the games would have been finished. Having two umpires and giving them the authority to expel a player from the game will solve that. Between you and me, they were right to call the games. You can't play late afternoon ball in October. You know what Mrs. Ward said about the games?"

"A woman's insights?"

"She said we should have Mr. Edison build us some lights so that we can finish the games, and even play at night."

"Hard enough to keep ballplayers on the road sober for an afternoon game."

Ward didn't share the joke. Characterizing ballplayers as drunks was the kind of argument Spalding liked to make in order to assert control. Besides, even though Ward had frequently made similar remarks himself, he didn't feel someone who had never played the game was entitled to do so. Ward decided to change the subject by appealing to the side of Brunell that was still a crank and craved inside knowledge about the current World Championship Series.

"How about that game today?"

"I hear that you gave the boys a pep talk before the game, and they went out and played their best game yet.

"We're still down three games to two. We have to do something to protect the Dauvray Cup lest it fall into the hands of the Bridegrooms, and I won't have that. It would be like having another knight declare victory in the name of my own lady fair," Ward said, surprised to hear himself using the kind of language he had been hearing from Stephanie Cowell.

"I'm sorry I implied all the ballplayers were drunks."

"You are forgiven. I think we should head down to Nick Engel's Home Plate Saloon where I am sure you will find most of the Giants celebrating today's victory. You can have a mineral water or a fruit juice if you want. This might be my last chance to appear in New York as a hometown favorite rather than the leader of the soon-to-be hated Brooklyn Wonders."

40

The Hero
New Polo Grounds, New York
October 25, 1889

"The umpires have already stolen three games from us, but we still have a chance to even things out today."

Buck Ewing was making a point by delivering a pre-game address prior to game six of the World's Championship Series. Before the previous game, Ward had urged his teammates to quit complaining about the umpiring and to play their best. Buck suspected that Ward was once again usurping his role as captain, something he would not have to worry about next year when Ward would presumably have his own team in the new league somewhere else, probably in Brooklyn.

Gunner McGunnigle, the Bridegrooms manager was coaching at third base, conveying signals to his men with singular brio. Leaping, pirouetting, and hopping on one foot were all part of his special language, telling his runner when to steal or his batter when to bunt. Buck had decoded enough of this language to call for a fastball outside, enabling him to cut down the first would-be base embezzler. In the bottom of the inning, Ewing propelled a double-bagger off the left field fence, but he was left on base when Ward flied out to center.

K.C. was one of about 2500 cranks shivering in the damp, cold, intermittently rainy October afternoon, but today he was enjoying himself more than usual. Sitting next to him was a young boy who would have been regarded as a suspicious truant by most, but whom K.C. recognized as a baseball celebrity -- Freddy Engel, onetime Giant bat boy and son of the owner of the Home Plate Saloon. Few people were in a position to know more about the New York team.

"What do you think of the Bridegrooms' hoodoo?" K.C. asked by in order to begin a conversation with the young baseball expert. A puny monkey kept in a state of inebriation was serving as the good luck charm for the Brooklyn team.

"I don't pay much attention to mascots ever since the Giants let me go."

"And who was your favorite player when you were the Giants' mascot," K.C. felt he had to ask.

"Oh, Johnny Ward, for sure, and not just because he's a good tipper, which he is. But he was loyal to me when the rest of the boys dropped me for that Chicago hoodoo, Freddie Boldt. Mr. Ward wouldn't contribute to pay his way. My friends all say Ewing is the best player, but I think it's Ward. What do you think?"

K.C. responded like a Chautauqua lecturer asked to expound on his favorite subject.

"Ward's the best player I've ever seen, and I've been following baseball since I was your age, since before there was a National League. Not too long ago, Ward was the best pitcher in baseball."

"That was before my time. He never pitched very well for the Giants."

"He didn't come here until after he had hurt his arm sliding. When he was only seventeen he pitched for a local team in Janesville, and they beat the White Stockings."

"I never heard of Janesville."

"Nobody has. It's in Wisconsin. That's what makes it so great. Then in his first year as a pitcher with Providence in the National League, he would have led the league in earned run average if they had known how to calculate it back then. The next year, when he was 19, he won 47 games to lead the league, and he pitched the game that clinched the pennant. Then the next year Ward did something that only he and his rival Lee Richmond ever did. He retired all 27 batters without so much as a walk, a hit or an error. And that wasn't even his best game. That came two years later on August 17, 1882. You could look it up. He won an eighteen inning game 1-0. Hoss Radbourn finished it with a home run in the 18th.

After having had trouble getting the ball between the points in the first inning, O'Day decided to decided to throw it down the middle in the second. The first batter hit a sharp clipper to center, followed by Joe Visner's line drive single to left. O'Rourke made a strong throw which cut the lead runner down at third, and a relay to second almost caught Visner trying to take second. The Brooklyn catcher slid awkwardly, causing him to scream involuntarily.

"Mon épaule." (My shoulder)

Ward remembered that Visner was French-Canadian and Parisian Bob Carruthers and one-time French dental student Doc Bushong had both spent a good deal of time in Paris and all three spoke French more fluently than Ward. While McGunnigle was snapping Visner's shoulder back into place, Ward's thoughts drifted to forming a team in Brooklyn next year. With so many francophone teammates, maybe they could barnstorm in the south of France. Helen would like that. Ward was not aware that the Brooklyn owner had been anticipating the Players League by signing his star players to firm contracts. Ward's thoughts returned to the game, and he made a mental note of Visner's shoulder injury. Two solid hits followed, and the Bridegrooms led 1-0. Only a sliding catch by Mike Slattery playing in place of Gore prevented more from scoring.

K.C. remembered what his wife would ask about when she heard that he had met someone with inside knowledge about Ward.

"You must have met Mrs Ward, too."

"Sure. I knew Miss Dauvray and her sister before Ward did. After the Giants fired me as bat boy, they gave me a job chasing balls in the stands, so naturally I roamed around a lot. I can talk to people, high and low. It comes from my dad owning a tavern. So Miss Dauvray came to the games, and she was having an awful time."

"I know. I read the papers."

"Then you remember about the fellow who kept standing outside her house sending her notes, saying that he loved her and all. Then her health went bad. And the theater critics started saying mean things about her, or about the plays she was in. So she started relaxing at baseball games, sometimes with her sister and her brother, the one who had to leave town. Sometimes with her theater friends. So baseball was her new hobby. Then Mr. Ward spotted her, and he gave me a quarter and told me to take a note 'to the goddess.'"

"And she was glad to get it."

"Not at first. But then he wrote to her in French, like a secret code, not that he had any secrets from me. I talked him up to Miss Dauvray, how educated he was, how good a ballplayer. I even told her that he didn't drink or swear, but when she didn't seem to like that he didn't drink, I corrected myself and said that he enjoyed fine wine. I figured she could find out for herself that I lied about him not swearing. Oh, and the other lie I told her was that I had never carried notes from him to other women, but she was the only one that he had started it with. And I told her that he called her 'the goddess' and she liked that. But she liked even better that I said he was always nice to me."

"Did you lie to him about her."

"I told him that she was the nicest, sweetest lady I had ever met, but that was the truth. And the prettiest too, much prettier than her snippety sister. But I did say that she knew a lot about baseball which was a lie but which came true after I told it. At first she didn't know much, and what she did know came from actors and the papers, but I set her straight, showed her the *Spalding Guide*, and soon she knew way more than the average crank. Then her health got worse, and she started spending her time in Saratoga Springs. I wrote her letters telling her how good Ward and the boys were playing and how much he missed her. Then before I knew it, the season was over, and they were married. Look, Ward just stopped one in the hole."

Ward was starting a double play that ended the Brooklyn fourth, but the

Giants were having no luck against Parisian Bob. Meanwhile O'Day walked one of their weakest hitters and then paid no attention to his leadoff. When the runner stole second, Buck started barking at the base umpire when he should have been screaming at his pitcher. Ward knew that the two umpire system was proving itself, and the call had been correct, but once again he was not about to offer an opinion contrary to that of his team and the cranks. Mike Slattery made a running over the shoulder catch on which the runner took third. Then Slattery gave further evidence of the wisdom of Ewing's choice to play a sober center fielder by catching a short fly and making a perfect throw to Ewing, keeping the runner at third. The best play of the inning, however, was by old Jim O'Rourke who once again disappeared into the left field corner but was able to hold the ball up to show the hustling base umpire that he had caught it.

In the fifth, the Giants managed a single and a double after two were out, but O'Day flied out weakly to center. In Brooklyn sixth, two more deep flies were caught by agile outfielders, then O'Day gave up a walk, followed by a double. The inning ended with no scoring when he retired the sore-shouldered Visner on a weak ground ball. The Giants went out 1-2-3, and the Brooklyns finally did the same. Ward led off the seventh with a bunt attempt, but their third baseman must have read Ward's book because he was playing shallow and charged the ball well. He threw Ward out by a fraction of a step, at least according to the base umpire.

"Double the umpires, double the mistakes," observed Jim Mutrie who had been shivering on the corner of the bench.

Taking advantage of the informal manners of the ballpark, a stranger addressed K.C. and his young friend.

"Begging your pardon, sir, but I can't have you misleading youth. Ewing's the best player now, the best that ever was and ever will be. Ward couldn't even get a baby hit against a tired pitcher. Ewing would have smashed the pitch that Ward bunted over the fence.

"There's more to baseball than hitting a ball over the fence. Ward knows how to play. He runs the bases better than Ewing or anyone else. A few years ago, he stole over a hundred bases, more than anyone before or since. And he only steals when it can help the team and he's sure he can make it."

"I'm not saying he's not good, just that he isn't the best. He makes too many errors, and he makes too few long hits. And Buck plays all the time, even when he's hurt. Buck's tough."

"Johnny's tough too,' K.C. countered and turned to his young friend. "You can be proud of your favorite player, Freddy. When he hurt his right arm and couldn't pitch any more, he went out in the outfield and threw with his left until his right was better again. And when he was hurting from being hit by too many pitches batting right-handed, he turned around and batted left-handed, and that he kept doing even after his left side healed. Look, he's leading off the ninth, and we need one run to tie. Johnny'll come marching home for us, Freddy. Just you watch.

Ward noticed that the second baseman was playing too close to the bag, so he steered a ground ball single through the resulting hole. Everyone in the park knew that Ward would be trying to steal. The pitcher wouldn't allow him much of a lead, but Ward knew that Visner couldn't manage much of a throw to second either, so he stole on the first pitch. Connor was batting, and although he was the most powerful hitter on the team, he took another pitch to allow Ward steal third, making sure that he could score on any old kind of a hit. Connor grounded what would have been the final out to deep short, but the shortstop was too eager and fumbled the ball, allowing Ward to score the tying run.

"Johnny Ward! Johnny Ward! Johnny Ward!" screamed the cranks who punctuated their chant by throwing hats, umbrellas and canes on the field. Connor followed Ward's example and stole another base off the helpless Visner, but the score remained at 1-1 until the Giants batted in the bottom of the eleventh.

Sober Slattery singled to center. He stayed on first when Tiernan flied out, but he was able to advance to second on Ewing's groundout. This brought up Ward, and the crowd looked for their hero to end the game. There was some disappointment when Ward failed to connect squarely and sent a weak ground ball to the shortstop, who made a fine play, picking up the ball and throwing to first baseman Dave Foutz in one motion. Ward felt his foot hit the pillow just before the sound of the ball smacking against the first baseman's hand, so he knew he was safe. The umpire standing right there made the correct call, but Foutz instinctively turned to complain. While he was doing so, Ward stood on the base, combining with the umpire to block the first baseman's view of third base. Slattery had alertly turned without stopping and headed for the plate, scoring just ahead of the belated throw.

Leaving the Polo Grounds, K. C. looked for the fan who had been so dismissive of Ward's talents, but he had already left before K.C. could gloat. The cranks were still yelling, "Johnny Ward, Johnny Ward," as they streamed out onto 155th St. Carried away with the moment, K. C. made a pronouncement to his young friend.

"That was the best game I ever saw in my life."

Freddy felt a rush of optimism.

"It'll all work out. The Giants are going to beat the Bridegrooms, and the new league with the players in charge will be the best ever. And Mr. Ward and his wife will be happy forever. How could it not work out? If he can win that game, he can do anything."

41

The Fairy Tale
New York
November, 1889

Stephanie Cowell asked John and Helen for a joint interview as she put the finishing touches on her *Cosmopolitan* article. From the questions that she asked, it was hard to figure out what aspect of their lives would be featured. Ward had expected to be talking about the recent World Series which the Giants had won with three more consecutive victories after their 2-1 thriller. O'Rourke's rejuvenated play in the field had highlighted the fourth victory. In the next game, Ward had collected four hits for the first time in quite a while, leading the Giants to a 16-7 win. He would not have minded talking about that. The series ended with another game won by clever base running by Ward and Slattery. The Giants had retained possession of the Dauvray Cup, symbol of baseball's world championship, but that wasn't what Miss Cowell wanted to talk about. When John dropped hints about the structure of the new league, they fell to the floor unnoticed.

Nor did Miss Cowell want to talk about the theater. Helen had hoped to use the interview to make clear that her departure from the theater might only be temporary and to tell her admirers among the magazine's readers that they might see her again at some future time. Miss Cowell seemed to have even less interest in Helen's theater plans or lack thereof than she had in the future of baseball, preferring to ask more general questions.

"How does it feel to be America's most successful actress and married to the country's greatest baseball player? It's almost like a royal marriage. That's what our readers want to know more about."

By now Miss Cowell had figured out that Ward and Helen lived in separate hotels and that their marriage might not be quite so enviable as she had first thought. However, none of this knowledge would have the slightest influence on her story. Nor did any of the notes she had taken during their hours of interviews enter into the final article. She would not let facts get in the way of truth, and she decided that the best way to express truth was through fable.

Ward was trying to build a Players League team in Brooklyn. He needed at least one more strong bat, and he was considering Davy Orr from the American Association. Orr was grossly overweight and a liability in the field, but he was one of the best hitters in the game.

"Too bad I can't just use him at bat. With pitchers getting weaker and weaker as batsmen, maybe there should be a rule allowing someone to hit in their place and not play in the field. Maybe I could talk about that with the magazine reporter."

After the interview, Ward and Helen discussed their plans over a pleasant hotel dinner. Helen had given a great deal of thought to the finances of Ward's new league, and she wanted to share some of her ideas.

"Have you thought any more about playing games at night? They are making real progress with floodlights, and you wouldn't have to worry about stalling and having games called because of darkness. Besides, if you played at night, you could draw so many people who couldn't come otherwise. Workmen for fifty cents and the carriage trade for a dollar and a half."

"That's impossible. Baseball has to be played in the afternoon. It's the only time the light is right. In a few weeks we'll set the schedule, and then I'll send it to Spalding and the American Association so we can avoid conflicts."

"I wouldn't do that. If I were Spalding, I'd use the information to maximize conflicts and run you out of business."

"Why would he do that? Then everyone would lose money. Why would the owners of the other leagues go broke so that we would go broke?"

"When Rose Coghlan decided to stage almost the same play about Peg Woffington that I was putting on, we both lost money for a while, but I outlasted her. That's how trusts are built. The National League has more capital than you and more financiers willing to lose their money for a few seasons."

"Speaking of the league, how would you feel if we delayed our trip to Paris? Maybe we could go somewhere closer. If I went to Havana, we could make it a business trip, and I'd be close enough to stay in touch with the lawyers. Havana is a wonderful city, and you'll enjoy yourself there as much as you would in Paris. Besides, we can go to Paris later."

"But I don't want to see Havana. I want us to go to Paris so that the friends we made separately can see us together. Your lawyers can handle the lawsuits that Spalding is planning. There's no way he can hold you to service contract that lasts indefinitely. Any lawyer can handle it. Mr. O'Rourke could do just as well as you."

"I don't want to be across the ocean when they're making decisions on my league. And now you're telling me how to practice law. Which of us is a member of the New York bar, my dear? And I am still not sure how a theater case can be a precedent for a baseball contract."

Once again, Helen's mouth stood open in amazement at how little her husband understood about the law. Maybe Mr. O'Rourke was right about the inferiority of Columbia's law school.

"Does that mean that we're not going to Paris this fall?"

"Let's wait and see what happens after the Brotherhood meeting next week."

Stephanie Cowell knew it was her job to bring glamour to the lives of her readers, and this was the most glamorous couple she could imagine. The details of their married lives added nothing to the impression she was trying to convey. Ward's tiresome efforts to explain why overpaid baseballists were treated unfairly could be of interest to no one. Her editor informed her that the issue featuring Ward's article "Our National Game" had sold rather poorly, so she should avoid Brotherhood propaganda. Helen's theatrical career had been interrupted for several seasons now. There was not much point in discussing the career of an actress whom her readers were already beginning to forget. Stephanie had a sudden inspiration and wrote out a new title.

"The Enchanted Baseball: A Fairy Story of Modern Times."

42

The Constitution
Fifth Avenue Hotel, New York
November 4, 1889

"**T**here was a time when the League stood for integrity and fair dealing. Today it stands for dollars and cents," Ward began as he addressed the Brotherhood's general membership meeting.

Ward's speech was by now familiar to players who had been attending meetings or reading the newspapers. Some of the players fidgeted in their business suits, feeling not as free to scratch as they would have had they been in uniform. Others had dressed less formally, like workmen going to a union meeting. Everyone was eager to find out what club he'd be playing with and, even more important, what salary he could expect.

The meeting was being held to announce the new Players League's constitution to the assembled players and to the sporting world at large. Just as Ward started to outline the new contract provisions, he was interrupted by an entrance comparable to the appearance of British monarch in the House of Commons. Mike Kelly had arrived, wearing an oversized mink coat, open to reveal a well-tailored cream colored suit. A splash of color was added by a red boutonniere, matching shoes, and, it must be said, an equally red large bulbous nose.

"I hope I'm not interrupting anything, Johnny. Be sure to tell your lovely wife how good I look dressed up. She saw me looking like a bum a few years ago, but I'm stylish and sober now."

"I'll pass on a favorable review of your clothing, Kel, but I'll need more proof before I will be able to attest to you sobriety."

The meeting was supposed to be secret, but the presence of so many faces familiar from Old Gold cigarette cards and *Clipper* portraits had made the event public, and an adoring crowd had joined King Kelly's royal progress from hotel to tavern. Ward realized that he would not be able to keep anything secret any longer.

"First of all," he announced solemnly after he had control of the meeting again, "we're abolishing the reserve clause."

Everyone cheered this remark, especially the younger players who looked forward to selling their hitherto undervalued services in brisk bidding wars. Ward waited until the room had quieted down and then resumed.

"It has been decided that all players will have a three-year contract at their current salaries. Further . . ."

There were no more unanimous cheers. At this point, each player had an individual question.

"What if you had an especially good year and were due for a big raise?" asked Clarkson who had won 49 games while leading the league in earned run average the previous year.

"What if they used the reserve clause and cut your salary from 1888 to 1889 even after they had agreed not to do that?" asked Jimmy Ryan.

Ward had anticipated this second question, and it helped him avoid the first.

"Jimmy, we'll write your contract at the 1888 level. These are the shenanigans that led to the League cutting its own throat. The important thing to remember is not the salary, but the profit-sharing. We'll give prizes to the teams that finish high in the standings. After the backers take the first $10,000 in profits, we'll put the next $10,000 in a prize pool. We'll elect our own managers."

This was not quite true. No one had elected Ward to manage in Brooklyn where the club was still being assembled. Al Johnson had hired Tebeau after an all-night saloon interview. Philadelphia, New York and Pittsburg had elected Fogarty, Ewing and Hanlon respectively, and no one had challenged Kelly as manager of the Boston franchise. After a long discussion, the players seemed to accept the salary structure, although the younger stars like Jake Beckley were particularly unhappy. For that matter, almost every player looked forward to the coming season with optimism, so everyone feared he would be making a sacrifice in the years to come. Ward moved on to operational topics.

"We will not sell beer nor will we play on Sunday. We'll have enough legal problems without defying the Sabbath law in Brooklyn. We don't want the preachers working against us. Not if we're going to keep charging fifty cents. And we won't have franchises in Indianapolis and Washington. I'm forming a Brooklyn team with players from Indianapolis and some American Association players, The Washington players will team up with Jim White to start a player-owned franchise in Buffalo. Mack and Hoy have expressed interest in investing. We should have a good team out there in Western New York. And if we have to find more players, we'll know how go about it."

Ward didn't mention black players like George Stovey, but once the new league was on a sound footing, he might bring in one or two of those Negro players he saw in Florida. Or maybe he'd start with Cubans. During the winter, he might go down to Cuba and scout some stars down there. At some point, Ward envisioned expanding the league, adding teams across the country all the way to California, but for now that would be his secret.

Ed Williamson had the next question. He was one of the most popular players, one of the few stars with a reputation for modesty, even when he had led the league in home runs. He had been one of the first players to join the union and then one of the first to turn against it, but he was back in the fold now. The way he had been treated by Spalding over his injury gave him peculiar standing to ask his question.

"What about injury pay? Spalding told the papers he was still paying me, but I didn't see a dime until August and then he deducted my wife's passage back from Europe."

"A player injured in a game will be paid his full salary for the balance of the year."

This satisfied Williamson.

"We hear that Comiskey is bringing the Browns to Chicago. Will that mean that Chicago players will be out of jobs?" asked Tener.

"Maybe we can arrange for some of you to play on other clubs where there is a need, maybe Pittsburg. We want to have the strongest possible team in Chicago to give Spalding another headache. We'll all have to compete for jobs. The Indianapolis Hoosiers are going to be the core of my Brooklyn team. I'm not sure I can beat out Glasscock for shortstop, so I might wind up at second or in the outfield or out of a job."

Ward announced that Frank Brunell would be the secretary of the new league. Hiring baseball pioneer Harry Wright of the old Cincinnati Reds to replace Ward as league president was an idea some newspapers were putting forward. Others suggested that Bob Ferguson would be a good leader, but Ward thought it was more important to have him as an umpire. Ward wanted to help pick the rosters, manage the finances, oversee the schedules and supervise the court actions, all of which should leave him just enough time for scouting in Cuba and hunting in Florida, followed by spring training.

The rest of the meeting was turned over to Keefe, who gave a report on who was up to date on dues. Every player in the National League except for Anson was paid up. Latham had claimed he had made a list of Association players who were willing to play in the new league, but he never produced it. Committees were formed to revise the rules, including Ward's pet scheme to require two impartial umpires at each game. Hanlon gave a report on the progress in attaining financial backers for each team, but when he was asked, he confessed that he had very little idea of how much money they had or how much they were willing to lose. Ward was forced to realize that somehow Helen seemed to know more about the financial standing of these businessmen than any of the players did. She was also confident that the lawsuits being filed by National League owners were doomed to failure, another reason she resented his hesitation about going to Paris. She saw no reason for Ward to cancel their trip. Ward knew that Helen was not going to like it when he informed her of his decision to skip Paris in favor of Havana.

Spalding had begun his counterattack, and more than a few newspapers were ready to publicize his denunciations of avaricious players and faithless contract jumpers. Few journalists remembered and none reported on how Spalding himself had led the contract jumping from Boston to Chicago, the first National League champions. That was nearly 25 years ago, long before the memory of all the baseball writers except Chadwick, and he was on the payroll. By systematically understating profits and grossly exaggerating salaries, Spalding had been able to demonstrate that the players had been robbing the unfortunate owners for years, much as antebellum Southern apologists had contended that the slaves were the ones really profiting from the cotton trade. Ward, on the other hand, had been claiming that every team had made a fat profit, but his statistical techniques were almost as inaccurate in one direction as Spalding's were in the other. Their views on the legal situation were equally divergent, but here Ward was starting to rely on legal precedent, Spalding on baseball precedent.

Strengthening the National League to enable it to withstand the coming desertions would be Spalding's first step. Like Ward, Spalding recognized that Indianapolis and Washington were not major league cities, so he had decided to offer Brooklyn and Cincinnati of the American Association the chance to bring their franchises into the National League. The blood feud between St. Louis and Brooklyn had given Spalding and excuse for detaching Byrne and his Brooklyn Bridegrooms from the Association, and Cincinnati went along for the sake of balance. Spalding proposed that the Association should put a third team in Brooklyn, a team menacingly named the Gladiators. This would bring the number of teams competing for spectators in the City of Churches to three. Spalding's next move was to provide a loan to help New York sign Glasscock from the disbanding Indianapolis team so that he would not strengthen Ward's Brooklyn Wonders. Considering Ward's plan to merge the Browns with most of his Chicago players to make the Chicago Pirates, Spalding felt he needed to pin down his enemy in the same way.

"It's personal," Spalding explained to Anson. "The balls are mine. The gloves are mine. The best team is mine. The league is mine. The history of the game is mine. Even the name 'National Pastime' is mine. I'm not going to let Ward steal it from me. The newspapers are with me, except for a few like the *Sporting News*. When we finish crushing the players, we'll come back and crush those newspapers."

Ward threw himself into his work, denouncing traitors, revising rules and building a new Brooklyn team from the old Indianapolis nine. The National League sued Ewing and Ward, invoking the reserve clause, so Ward thought he had to stay and watch the outcomes. There would be time enough to make peace with Helen later. He hoped she wouldn't go through with a divorce while *Cosmopolitan* was writing an article about their fairy tale marriage. For now, Ward was a league president, a union leader, a manager, a lawyer, a scout, and either a shortstop or a second baseman, depending on what happened with Glasscock.

43

Cuba
February 1890
Parque Almendares, Havana
The Island

As a guest of Teodoro de Zaldo, the owner of the Almendares *Alacranes* (Scorpions), Ward was seated in the *glorieta,* enjoying fried fish and rum punch while listening to the band playing *danzón* music between innings. At the request of his host, Ward was wearing the blue colors of the Scorpions and their patroness *la Virgen de la Caridad del Cobre*. Pablo Ronquillo, the right fielder for the Havana *Rojos* (Reds) made a running backhanded catch near the foul line to stop a Scorpions rally. Surprisingly, the Almendares supporters rose to their feet cheering in appreciation. Ward had previously heard about the scathing denunciations and outright threats exchanged between supporters of opposing teams here in Havana, so this show of sportsmanship was unexpected. His host de Zaldo remarked, "That was a wonderful catch that little *postalista* made."

One of the terms Ward had picked up in Spanish was *postalista*, meaning a grandstander, a player who showed off, making a catch look harder than it was as if posing for picture on little postcards or cigarette cards, like Billy Sunday. Ward's Spanish was weak, but fortunately most of the baseball people he met spoke English, some having studied at Fordham and others having done business in New Orleans. Ward's original plan had been to bring a team down to challenge the Cubans, but all the Sundays in Havana were scheduled, and Ward's new Brooklyn team was still not ready for competition. Ward made the trip alone, scouting for *peloteros* (baseballists), especially *lanzadores* (pitchers). Miguel Prats, the pitcher for Havana, showed impressive speed and amazing *pointería*, another word Ward had picked up, this one meaning the ability to keep the ball over one of the corners of home plate, usually at the knees. Everyone said that Adolfo Luján was even better, if Ward had understood them correctly. Noticing that the band had both black and white musicians reminded Ward that he would have difficulty bringing players into the United States because the color bar might be stretched to exclude Cubans. Esteban Bellán had played in the U.S. in the 70's, but the color line had been hardening since then. There was even a racial bar down here. The best dark-skinned black players were playing for cotton mill teams and never made it to the big city.

Ward had heard Helen tell that woman from *Cosmopolitan* that he spoke five languages fluently. He hadn't bothered to contradict her exaggeration, but he hoped that no one down here would have read this claim. He realized the limitations of his Spanish because he had understood very little of what he had been hearing. For example, one young woman pointed to him and whispered to her friend "Está Algernon," and both giggled. He had no idea what that had meant.

In the *gradería* K.C. sat in less luxury than Ward was enjoying in the *glorieta* but with a better view of the field. By turning around, K.C. could see the *Calzada de Carlos III* in the fashionable *El Cerro* neighborhood. On his way to the game, he had seen children and adults scrambling up the laurel trees to get a free view of the game. The team owner had covered the trees with thorny vines, but the Cuban cranks were not so easily discouraged. K.C. was sitting next to a friendly cigar salesman who spoke excellent English and made frequent trips to New York where he did business with John Day. He tried to explain the structure of Cuban baseball to K.C.

"We have five teams that play each other, usually on Sunday. Almendares is our rival, but they have been weak since they disbanded after the riot of 1887. For now, Ernesto Sabourín has my Reds in first place. Look, another *escón* for Miguel."

K.C. had figured out that the word for skunk also meant a shutout inning, just as it did in English. His companion next addressed him in a hushed, almost conspiratorial tone.

"What I like about the Reds is that they defy the Spanish. The government wants us to go to the bullfights and cheer *olé* like in Madrid. I support Havana because I know that Sabourín gives part of the profits to José Martí and those who want to win our freedom from Spain."

Ward watched as his hosts fell hopelessly behind, waving their bats futilely as Prats struck out batter after batter. The Havana catcher, shaped like a box, blocked the plate as the Scorpions attempted to score their first run.

"That's Billy Tayor," de Zaldo explained. Havana likes to import their catchers from the mainland. Our Scorpions have fallen, but we have what we need to restore our former glory."

"What is that?"

"Money, just like in your country. Next year we'll sign a new team. What good is it to own a bank if I can't sign the best player in Cuba?"

"If you don't mind my asking, who would that be?"

"Antonio María García, a Matanzan who plays for Fe, for now."

"Is he the one they call *El Inglés*, the one who hit .448 last year?"

"Yes. And he will never leave Cuba, so I can tell you his name without any fear that you will lure him to Brooklyn."

"We'll need a first baseman if I can't sign Davy Orr, but I would never offer him a contract without your permission."

Ward was barely conscious that he had just implicitly recognized a reserve clause, but Spalding wasn't here to smirk at him.

K. C. had not expected to see such high quality baseball, even from the losing Scorpions. They couldn't solve Prats's pitching, but they played solid outfield defense and made three double plays, something that was a little easier with the Cuban rule that put a tenth man in short center field. In the *gradería*, conversation had turned to American baseball, and K.C. was explaining what he understood of Ward's new Players League. His Cuban friend was particularly interested in the New York teams because he knew both John Day, the owner of the National League Giants and the backer of the New York Players League team, Edward McAlpin. His opinion surprised K.C.

"Mr. Day is an honest man who wants to know that the cigars he buys are made by workers who are treated fairly, who have good ventilation and someone to read them fine literature while they work. Mr. McAlpin only cares about getting the lowest price. If I were a New York Giant, I would prefer to continue working for Mr. Day."

Before the discussion could go any farther, Almendares finally scored a run, and the other side of the ball park exploded in cheers. K. C. marked the event as best he could on his makeshift scorecard. His companion seemed happy even though his team had lost their shutout.

"Now that the Scorpions have a run, maybe there won't be a postgame riot. I'm afraid we're outnumbered, so I hope few more runs will improve their mood."

Ward was seeing three or four players who were good enough to play for a major league team. Maybe they could have a team in Cuba and American teams could come down on a steamer. There was enough talent down here to form a club and enough enthusiasm to support one. With the score 14-2, Ward was glad he had not brought down his Brooklyn Wonders to play the Reds. The Cubans looked efficient and crisp in the infield, and their hitters were hitting singles and doubles to all fields. American touring teams had been beaten by the Cubans before, and he didn't need his boys' confidence shaken before the season started. Nonetheless, de Zaldo talked about having a team come down the next winter. Ward had seen enough Cuban baseball that he set a condition.

"If we play you, you're either going to sit your tenth player down or give us an extra man. Our nations are baseball equals, so I am not giving your team any advantage."

"Fair enough."

Seeing the success of baseball in Cuba made Ward think about the progress of baseball in France. Perhaps he should have gone to Paris with his wife, but she had to understand there was so much to do if he was going to prepare his team to win the Dauvray Cup, assuming they could schedule a post-season tournament. Maybe he could arrange a playoff with the champion of what was left of the National League or a three-team round robin with the winner of the American Association invited. A surge of optimism made Ward think his team could win the cup, and he could win back the woman for whom it was named.

44

The Scandal
March 27, 1890 and days following
New York

Ward had hoped for a quick reconciliation with Helen after he returned from Havana, but he soon realized he would still have to wait for her forgiveness. This might take some time because his mail contained notification that she had filed for a legal separation. The marriage might not be over, but he felt as if there were two out and two strikes on him in the last inning. Before he had recovered from his sense of depression, he noticed a scented envelope with no return address.

> Dear Mr. Ward,
>
> My husband has become such a beast that I have been forced to establish a separate residence. This means that I will need legal advice and the support of my friends, of whom I have very few in New York. Perhaps you could be my lawyer. If you could meet me at Delmonico's on March 27 at 1:00 p. m., I would appreciate it greatly. If anything should prevent you from coming, please notify me at 5 East 41ˢᵗ st. Please extend my warmest wishes to your wife whose achievements as an actress and a producer fill me with admiration.
>
> Respectfully yours,
> Jessie McDermott

Ward decided that with Helen nowhere to be found and angry with him anyway, he had nothing to lose, so he decided to meet the young woman, tell her that he couldn't represent her and help her to find a suitable attorney. It bothered him that Jessie wanted to meet in such a public place, so near the theater district where Helen's friends might see them, but he took this as another proof of how innocent and naive Jessie was. Ward walked down Broadway looking over his shoulder, hoping not to see anyone from Helen's theater world when Jim Mutrie suddenly appeared, wearing a bright green suit and a neatly knotted blue tie with a freshly waxed moustache on top of an expansive smile—just as if he were greeting incoming cranks. Mutrie would be managing what was left of the Giants after most of them had defected to the New York Players League team and Ward was now a Brooklyn Wonder. It could have been an awkward moment, but Ward decided to use the old password.

"Who are the People?"

"We are the People," Mutrie roared back, and the two shared a laugh on Broadway before going their separate ways.

When Ward arrived at the restaurant, he was uncharacteristically early. Jessie walked in a few minutes later wearing a clinging blue silk , most striking for its daring neckline. All the men noticed her, and those who were escorting females had to struggle to hide their reaction. Some recognized Ward from his cigarette card or his picture in the New York *Clipper*. Most assumed that the beauty with him was his famous wife. Others knew that she wasn't and wondered who she might be, some with disapproval, others with envy, most with both. Contrary to Ward's expectations, Jessie seemed relaxed, composed, and almost cheerful. She ordered lobster, pointing out that it made her think of being back home in Maine. Throughout the dinner, she talked more about her future in the theater than her marriage and its dissolution. She accepted the business cards that Ward offered and, after glancing at her watch, went on to order cheesecake for dessert.

"One more favor, Mr. Ward. While I'm near my favorite milliner on Ladies' Row, I must stop in and buy a new hat. This one's blue feather is drooping, and I don't want to be seen in it, especially if I hope to make a good impression when I am meeting theater producers, which I hope will be soon."

Ward muttered something about how she would be sure to succeed in such an endeavor even hatless, but he agreed to accompany her to the shop, where she picked out a hat with a more erect collection of feathers, and they walked out of the shop at precisely 2:30. Before Ward's eyes could adjust to the spring sunlight, he heard George McDermott ranting and making use of ungentlemanly personal nouns of alternating gender. The epithets whore and blackguard were succeeded by bitch and whoremonger, leading to punches. McDermott landed a few glancing blows of the sort that could have been expected from a drunken office worker. Ward countered with short controlled jabs followed by an uppercut that landed McDermott on the pavement where he began to blubber. Jessie whispered to Ward that he should come to 41st St. and disappeared into a cab. Hoping no one had recognized him, Ward walked away rapidly, quickening his pace when he noticed a newspaper reporter interviewing those who had witnessed the fight.

An hour later, Ward knocked on the door of Jessie's apartment. He assured himself that his intentions were innocent—to comfort the nerves of the poor young victim and help her start a new life. That didn't mean he would ask for Helen's help.

Ward was optimistic about Helen's good nature, but not to the point of insanity. He heard Jessie's voice as he stood outside the open door.

"I'm still in the cabinet, but come in and wait for me. I hope you'll like my new hat."

Her tone was light and playful, as if no scene had occurred. She entered the room wearing her smart new blue-feathered hat, which might well have caught Ward's eye but for the absence of all other clothing. For a moment Ward stared at Jessie as if he were a camera taking a long exposure, then he undressed himself to join her. For a few brief spasmodic minutes, they had sex until she ordered him to pull out and finish his business in the style of Onan. Immediately after, she started putting herself back together, neglecting to bathe first as Helen would have. This reminded him that Helen had slipped his mind for the last few minutes.

"It's good that your baseball doesn't start for a few days. I need to go back to Maine and get my family's support."

"Your parents?"

"My aunt. My mother's dead and my father is in California chasing after a widow. But I want you to meet my aunt and my sister. And you're going to be separated anyway, just like me."

How did she know that? But Ward decided to agree to a trip to Maine. It might be a good idea to be out of town before tomorrow's papers came out.

When Helen returned to the city the next day, she was understandably embarrassed by the stories of the confrontation in the dailies, and she became even more furious when Ward failed to present himself to explain. Then anonymous letters began to drift in from Rockland, Maine, where more than one informant told her that Ward and Jessie were living in the same rooming house to the dismay of the entire town. One letter even described how one of Jessie's old sweethearts had confronted the couple. Helen saw a pattern.

"What a simpleton my husband is that he can't see that this girl is using him. I may take him back as a husband, but I'll never take him as a business partner. What was I thinking?"

Helen did not usually confide in Bernie about her personal life, but she did tell him about the possibility of a separation or a divorce. She also told him to forget the idea about buying the National League.

"I don't think anyone suspected that you were behind the offer. If you want my advice, I still think you should stay with Mr. Ward because it would be hard to find another husband who leaves your money alone."

Everyone was speaking in favor of Ward. Helen felt that she was surrounded by his advocates. Little Freddy Engel stopped by to praise Ward while blackening the character of Mr. and Mrs. McDermott.

"The husband is such a drunk they don't even want him working for the city any more. And I think the wife staged the whole thing outside the hat shop to set up Mr. Ward."

"You must not think the worst of people, Freddie," Helen responded, all the time thinking exactly the same thing herself and wondering how her husband could know so much less of life than a twelve year old boy.

Mr. and Mrs. O'Rourke came down from Connecticut, and Ward's old teammate put in a word for him, or rather several polysyllabic words. Even petit Marcel took time out from his military service to write about how she should forgive Ward for jealousies and indiscretions.

"In the presence of your beauty, many men would be enraptured, but your husband told me how the memory of your perfection, even in your absence, sustained him across the Pacific in his tiny stateroom where his imagination helped him recall the scent of cattleya lilies and the moments of your love."

Helen remembered telling little Marcel about that evening, but she was almost sure she had not mentioned what kind of flowers which led her to believe that Ward may have exposed more details, but that was what everyone did around the "porcelain psychologist."

Another indirect advocate for Ward was Dion Boucicault the French-Irish playwright and drama coach. He wrote Helen a note.

"The woman who made a scene with your husband wants to study drama with me. If you like, I will reject her out of hand, unless you think your marriage would be better served by having her in the theater where she is sure to meet men who can do many things for her. You are too good for Mr. Ward, but that would be true of any man."

Helen wrote back to Dion that of course he could accept Jessie as a student, but she was profoundly grateful that he asked.

"Bless his French-Irish heart. Maybe I'll commission a play for him some day."

Another of Ward's strong advocates was the *Cosmopolitan* writer Stephanie Cowell. Her piece turned out to be a strange account of a baseball game between Brooklyn and the New York Brobdinagians with a catcher named Duck Owing and pitcher called Timotheus. The main focus was on the character based on Ward.

"Algernon de Witt Caramel was a highly accomplished young gentleman. He conversed fluently in all the modern languages and had mastered Greek, Latin, and Hebrew. His voice was exquisite, pure tenor, and his paintings far excelled those of any living artist.

In appearance he was a veritable Adonis. He was, moreover, a graceful dancer, a fearless swimmer, a daring equestrian, a brilliant conversationalist, and was acknowledged to be, by all odds, the best-dressed man in town. These various and attractive attributes had placed him in a very prominent and enviable position, but he was yet to win another title that was to make him world famous. Who lives who has not heard of Algernon de Witt Caramel, the Champion Short-Stop of America."

The story couldn't have been sillier with Algernon chasing a ball by jumping over street cars and finally flying across the Atlantic. He briefly falls under the spell of a the evil Aldegonda, an eighteen year old princess. Had Stephanie known something about Jessie? Yet all of this seemed to make Johnny worth keeping, or at least too valuable to surrender to Jessie.

Even more convincing than all the pleadings for the defense was the chief advocate for the prosecution. Clara swooped down from Massachusetts calling for a divorce more than ever.

"You have proof of his adultery, so you can protect your property. If you don't act now, he might be more discreet the next time. You can't let him make a fool of you with this young beauty."

"I'm not exactly old myself."

"That's the spirit. You're young enough to start over. You don't want a husband who's jealous, arrogant, and openly adulterous."

Clara didn't say it, but her own marriage was happier than she could have imagined. She loved her husband, his sisters, most of his aunts, and the town of Cambridge. The one thing she wanted to make her happiness complete would be for her sister to leave her husband and move to Boston. At a minimum, Clara wanted Helen to promise that she would never forgive Ward under any circumstances. It was a promise Helen was tempted to make.

"And then she arranged for her old boy friend to find us together. She's been the main subject of the town gossip, for quite some time. I don't know if it's true, but they say she went away to have a baby when she was fifteen."

Ward was confessing his sin in what might be called manly fashion—one employed ever since Adam -- he was claiming he had been misled by a naked woman. He was telling the truth, but taking every occasion to blacken Jessie's name.

"And then, back in New York. She wanted to come to my hotel yesterday, but I insisted that she stay in her new apartment, and never bother me again. When I got to my hotel, Nat Goodwin knocked on my door. Now that I think about it, I think she wanted him to find us. She's planning her next conquest."

"Nat won't take much of her energy. He's chased after every actress in New York at one time or another. I hope for his sake that he doesn't catch this one."

"Peux-tu me pardonner?" (Can you forgive me?)

"Un peu. (A little) The separation will go through until you convince me that I can trust you to stay out of the newspapers for anything but baseball. And I'll go to Paris whenever I want, or California or the stage. But maybe I can learn to trust you again. So Vanessa might forgive her Algernon."

Ward wondered who Vanessa and Algeron were, but he was so happy to hear the word "forgive" that felt he could worry about what she meant later. Now with his marriage once again intact, he could concentrate on his new team and his new league. It was, after all, April.

Schedules
New York and Chicago
April, 1890

Some of the mystery surrounding this Algernon business cleared up when Ward finally purchased the latest *Cosmopolitan* and read "The Enchanted Baseball." Somehow between being in Cuba and then in Maine, he had missed the article, which was just as well because it might have been the worst thing he had ever read. He had to put it out of his mind as he prepared to meet with the executive board of the Players League to plan for their first season. Arriving only slightly late, Ward heard laughter mixed with nervous giggles. Ewing was reading aloud from a folded magazine.

> "And then far from left field he sends the magic ball swifter than thought into the ready hands of gallant Duck Owing."

Several of the players seemed to be following along from their own copies of the woman's magazine. There was a chorus of "Hello Algernon," when he walked up to his place at the front of the room.

"What makes everybody think I'm Algernon."

Keefe smiled.

"I liked the parts about the peerlessly beautiful Veronica Van Sittart, but I didn't see anything about her prettier sister Clara Van Sittart."

Even Ward's old friend Ned Hanlon had his copy underlined.

"This is my favorite part." He read aloud.

> "'Did it ever occur to you,' pursued the winsome fairy, 'that your unrivalled beauty and manifold accomplishments prove you to be something more than mortal?'
>
> The handsome Algernon acknowledged that he had frequently been impressed with such an idea."

"Now what I want to know, is was that an actual quote from the interview with this Cowell woman?"

"Enough already. We do have business to discuss," Ward said in one last effort to appear good-humored.

"Just one more Johnny," Hanlon asked until Ward relented and gave a favoring nod.

> "'As Caramel's earnings represent an income of several millions, the young couple are doing very nicely.'"

"That's something we can all agree on. Ballplayers making millions."

Ward use this as a transition.

"It might be silly, but all publicity is good publicity. We have to be ready to win our war with the League. Our first victories came in court when the judges ruled that Brother Ewing and I are free to play where we want. As to the traitors who signed with us and went back, we say good riddance Glasscock and Clarkson. And to one of our founding members, Mickey Welch."

Keefe looked the other way. Everyone knew that Keefe and Welch had been best friends for years. Ward went on.

"But we did win a lawsuit bring back a couple of young stars who signed with us first then tried to sign with the League. Jake Beckley and Ed Delahanty will be with us, as will some of the best players from the American Association like Davy Orr and Pete Browning and Brother Arlie Latham. Now most of you know that the League has stolen the Association's two best clubs—Brooklyn and Cincinnati. In spite of this, they will have a very low quality league. That brings us to the schedule. As some of you know, I sent Spalding a copy of our schedule as a courtesy so we could avoid conflicts. He proceeded to schedule a National League game in the same city as our

Players League game whenever it was possible. And he got the American Association to put a third team in Brooklyn to compete with my Wonders. Our parks are all ready to go except Chicago. Brother Ewing has used his carpentry skills to give personal assistance to our New York park."

Buck stood.

"We have good drainage in case this season has as much rain as last. And we have boxes for the carriage crowd. I'm pretty sure it won't fall down, and it looks better than the one the Giants will play in next door. We have our team flag and a pennant telling everyone that we were the Dauvray Cup champions last year. Of course, Day is planning to put up the same sign, but we have more of the boys than he has."

"Why would Buck know what Day was planning?" Ward thought in passing before he resumed addressing his group.

"Thank you, Duck. Er, Buck. And now Charlie Comiskey will tell us about his new team in Chicago. It's going to a blend of the best of Anson's Colts without Anson and the Browns without Van der Ahe."

Comiskey took the floor.

"They're calling us the Pirates, but I might just use the name White Stockings now that Spalding isn't going to use it any more. We're on our way to having a fine park in Chicago. There is a carpenter's strike about to happen, but we have a plan to start on time anyway. I'm betting we'll be in the park by opening day."

"How much are you betting on that?" Latham asked.

No one asked how Comiskey planned to circumvent the strike in Chicago, and soon everyone was engaged in a rather pointless discussion of which team was most likely to win the pennant. Most favored the New Yorkers to repeat or Boston to displace them, with or without Clarkson. Some even thought Comiskey's new blended team would be the best. Charlie made a confident announcement.

"I'll be betting on Chicago every game next year."

Spalding had called Anson and Chadwick together to listen to his complaints about the new league, the Chicago franchise in particular.

"Comiskey thinks he'll own this town because his father was a politician. I hope he has his own money invested because I'd like to see his face when nobody shows up to see his twenty-five cent team from St. Louis at fifty cent Chicago prices."

Anson corrected Spalding on this.

"You know St. Louis has been charging fifty cents for some seats. I'm sure we'll make a profit anyway."

"Cap, you take me too literally. And no one is making money this year. Our owners can afford to lose more money than theirs. That's why we're scheduling our games at the same time as Comiskey's. That Addison who's backing Comiskey will want out in the first month, and we'll inherit the park the Brotherhood is building with non-union labor."

"If we're going to be losing money, maybe we should have taken our share of that million dollars someone offered for all the clubs," Anson speculated.

"Just a trick, Adrian. There was no million dollars."

Spalding was absolutely sure that the million dollar offer had been sound because a Wall Street bank had guaranteed the availability of the funds, and he was almost sure that Mrs. Ward had been the source of the money. Rumors about Ward's trip to Maine had reached Spalding's ears, but he refused to spread them. Spalding didn't want to do anything that Ward would see as unforgivable. By now he saw that Ward and the players had a chance to win the war, and he intended to stay in baseball one way or the other. Perhaps he could still play. It was just a year ago that he had shown them he could still pitch in that game in Chicago before the tour. And in any case, any new league would still need to buy baseballs somewhere, especially after the dangers of Keefe and Becannon's rabbit ball became apparent.

Chadwick addressed himself to Spalding.

"Some of the papers are taking Ward's side. We need to develop our own newspaper that exposes them for the drunks, gamblers, communists, anarchists and overpaid has-beens they are."

Anson also had his thoughts on the situation.

"What will we do if they bring in darkies like Fleet Walker and George Stovey. I think that nigger lover Ward would like to do that," Anson offered. "We'll be the ones defending the white race, if he tries that. This is a war."

Spalding had long thought that he wouldn't mind signing Negroes himself, especially if he ever tried to develop a league in California. There was no point in telling Anson this, and there was no reason to concede ground in a war. Spalding liked the military metaphor.

"When he gave us the schedule, it was as if Lee had told Grant where he was going to attack. And Clarkson told me that they plan to assign the first $10,000 in profits to their backers and the next ten thousand to themselves. This means that no club will ever report a profit over $10,000 because what kind of an accountant would tell you to share money with the players? We're at war, Cap. We have to defend the League, defend Chicago, and defend baseball itself. We're paying already paying salaries double what we should, and we had to loan Day money so he could sign Glasscock away from Ward."

"Why would we loan Day money? Aren't we still competing with New York?"

Spalding ignored him and went on.

"We're not going to let Ward ruin the game. Not with his know-it-all book, his glamorous life and his perfect Italian. Has either of you seen the latest issue of *Cosmopolitan?*"

"What do you think?" Anson asked.

"Take my copy. Read the article 'The Enchanted Baseball.' It almost makes me wish we were playing Ward so we could kid him about it."

46

The Rivalry
Eastern Park, Brooklyn
April 30, 1890

Ward had consented to be awarded a wreath of flowers, just as he had twelve years before when the Providence management had persuaded then eighteen year old Ward that the ladies would love to see him covered with azaleas. Today he was dressed in a uniform designed to resemble a Wonder Bread wrapper. Helen had suggested that their bakers should pay for this privilege, but Ward told her it was just a courtesy and he wouldn't know what to charge anyway. The inaugural ceremony was so special that Helen made it a point to come. She was accompanied by Clara, and for the first time the sisters were cheering for different teams because Keefe was with the New York PL team. The presence of the Twenty-Third Regimental Band, playing Sousa's latest march *Semper Fi*, marked this inaugural game as the most officially recognized opening day in the metropolitan area. When all the flowers were gathered up, Ward stepped up into the left-handed batter's box, and the first major league game between Brooklyn and New York resumed in the second inning.

K.C. was talking to a weasel-faced man wearing a threadbare brown tweed suit that gave him the look of a government clerk. He had arrived a little late, and K. C. was catching him up on the new rules, the most fascinating topic imaginable for K. C., but less so for his companion.

"Yes," K. C. went on, "two umpires in every game. The pitcher's eighteen inches farther back, but from now on every good pitch that the batter doesn't swing at will be called a strike. And they won't let players drop the ball on purpose to start a double play with runners on first and second and less than two out. No more force off double plays. The game will be better with the players making the rules. I support Johnny Ward and his new way of doing business."

"Ward seems to be popular with the ladies," the weasel remarked while twirling his moustache and leering.

"He always has been."

"I wonder if that will be the case after tomorrow. When the news of a court hearing on a separation become public knowledge, I don't think respectable ladies will want much to do with Mr. Ward."

Ward enjoyed matching his team against the New York squad, even if he had been left with what the newspapers were calling "a job lot." Ward's Wonders had four rookies while Buck's Giants were almost the same team that had won the Dauvray Cup the year before. The only effective veteran batsman Ward had been able to sign was 250 pound Davy Orr who followed him in the batting order. Ward led off with a line drive single that dropped in front of the center fielder. While Ward was at first base, Roger Connor couldn't resist a comment.

"If you let me know that I was too fat and slow, what do you say to that ice wagon up at bat?"

"Not a word. You taught me my lesson. I just make sure that Davy has enough to eat before the games. And I noticed that you are playing farther away from the base now."

"Buck and I knew you were right, but we wouldn't give you the satisfaction of admitting it. Besides, in this new league, everything has to be the best. This is going to be baseball's greatest league."

Connor said this in such a good-natured way that Ward was forced to laugh too. The tension between them as teammates seemed to have disappeared. The conversation was brief because Ward stole second and came around to score on a deep hit to right which was only a single for Orr but which would have been a double had it been hit by any other player in the league.

In the field, Louis Bierbauer, another Association import, muffed an easy slow roller that cost a run. Ward walked over and consoled the young second baseman. If this had happened on the Giants the year before, Ewing and Mutrie would have taken turns bellowing at the youngster, and Ward might have joined them. But now he had new responsibilities, including the development of young players. He had been a captain before and even a manager briefly, but now he was also part owner and the league president. However, none of these titles gave him authority. To his young players, he was the baseball professor, the author of *Base Ball*. Each of them had been given a copy of the book that showed them how the game should be played. Not only was Ward showing up on time; he had even taken to coming to the park early.

On the next play, a fly ball to center that could have been caught by any of four players, the center fielder called loudly for the second baseman to take it, just as Ward's book had advised him to do. Ward was pleased with the way his less talented players had responded to instruction, and he had felt confident enough to challenge Ewing.

"My boys look a little rough now, Buck, but by the end of the year we'll finish ahead of you."

"Johnny, it's good to see you've kept your sense of humor."

K.C. found himself in the rare position of disliking the man sitting next to him. He seemed to be gloating about the marital misfortunes of other people. K.C. tried to discourage him.

"Everybody knows that Ward and his wife are separated, but I have it from the most informed source possible that there is every chance there will be a reconciliation soon. That's old news you're telling me."

Having seen Freddie Engel earlier that day, K.C. had every reason to believe that he was *au courant* (up-to-date) with the Ward/Dauvray situation.

"It's a different separation I mean. George McDermott's."

"Who is he, and what has that to do with Ward?"

"He's the man who more than once has caught Mr. Ward and his wife in improper conduct."

"That must be the drunk who attacked Ward on the street last month."

"George McDermott's no drunk. He's a respected civil servant and a loyal brave of St. Tammany."

"I heard he was some kind of Tammany Hall crook."

"Sure and the newspapers are always ready to blacken the name of those who help the immigrant and the working man. But tomorrow it will be Ward's name that they'll be blackening."

Brooklyn was staging a five run rally which had led to cheering of an unprecedented volume and duration. Even though the park was only half full and some of the crowd were New Yorkers who had crossed the bridge, the Brooklyn cranks were making so much noise that K.C. couldn't keep up with the conversation. He had been so absorbed in the discussion about Ward that he had even forgotten to mark his scorecard for a single, a double, a triple and another triple, this one by the pitcher. After the shouting settled down between innings, he was embarrassed to have to ask a young boy what had happened with each batter.

The hitting of Bierbauer and Scrappy Bill Joyce delighted Ward. Even his catcher had hit a triple. Five Brooklyn players dressed in uniforms featuring pictures of what seemed to be various colored balloons had crossed the plate.

"Don't be surprised if you're looking up at us in the standings at the end of the year," Ward shouted across the diamond to Ewing, as Brooklyn took the field ahead 6-2 in the fourth.

During the Wonders turn at bat in the seventh, Ward wasn't due up, so he sat with a friendly supporter in the first row of the stands. A boy came by to tell Ward that the Brooklyn National League team had won their competing home game. As his Brooklyn team was being retired easily, Ward had a friendly chat with the cranks.

"Brooklyn has Carruthers, Foutz and Oyster Burns," Ward said, shaking his head. "They were the best team in the Association last year, and they signed all their players before the Players League was ready to compete. Now they're the best team in the National League. They might be the only major league team left in the League, and they had to steal them from their so-called partners. And the Association put another team in Brooklyn, just to make it harder for us to succeed. Spalding is behind it all. There's the third out. I have to go back out in the field now and not let it bother me."

The weasel had been silent for a while, but he finally resumed the conversation.

"I see the New York pitcher is John Ewing. Any relation to Buck?"

"His brother."

"I suppose that's how he got the job."

"Oh no. John Ewing was one of those players who was cheated by Louisville in the Association, so the Players League made room for them. Like Van Haltern on Ward's team. The National League kept him from playing in the California League, and they blackballed him. What was that about Ward and tomorrow's papers?"

" Not that I was listening, but George McDermott was talking loud, the way any man might. He told the reporter that Ward and Mrs. McDermott had been living as man and wife in her home town in Maine, and that now he felt that Ward had finally succeeded in corrupting her chastity. He said that she showed Ward around as if he were her husband, making sure he met everyone in town, including her family and her former suitors.

Back on the field in the ninth, Ward was thinking about the day's poor attendance when he failed to get under a short pop fly, which bounced off his glove for an error, putting two men on base. Joyce, the young third baseman, came and put his arm around Ward just as Ward had done to Bierbauer. Umpire Gaffney called a line drive down the first base line fair, scoring two runs that the Brooklyn cranks thought should never have been allowed. Then Joyce made a spectacular play diving across the bag to catch a line drive and continuing there for a few seconds, looking like a loaf of bread squashed on the bottom of a grocery sack. Umpire Lynch ruled it a good catch. The Wonders got out of the inning with only two runs scoring, thus winning the first major league match between Brooklyn and New York. Even in victory, the Brooklyn faithful booed, cussed and threw objects at Gaffney while the Manhattanites present directed much the same attention in the direction of Umpire Lynch. The umpires had taken turns standing behind the plate, only fair considering the greater possibility of being hit with a thrown bottle from that position. As league president, Ward was satisfied with the umpires he had hired, but as the Brooklyn manager he had his doubts about Gaffney.

From now on, Ward would consider himself a resident of the City of Churches. He had invested in Brooklyn real estate, and he saw a future where he and Helen could retire from baseball and the theater and settle down and raise hunting dogs together, maybe out on Long Island. Someone had just told him that he was being named in court documents related to the McDermott divorce, but he knew that chapter of his life was over and couldn't hurt him. Helen had already forgiven him. And today Ward's Brooklyn Wonders from Brooklyn had defeated Ewing's Giants from New York in the first major league game between the two cities.

TheTabloid Story
New York and Paris
May, 1890

"**I** have nothing but the highest praise for Helen Dauvray and am extremely sorry that she was so unfortunate as to marry John M. Ward."

Clara had circled that quote by George McDermott from the New York *Times* which she brought over that morning. Helen had already read the article describing the court proceedings in which her husband was being named a correspondent in the McDermott divorce.

"Now you have the proof to institute your own divorce. John's adultery is already a matter of record."

"I will not give that woman the satisfaction of being named in public as the one who stole, or even borrowed, my husband. She wants my life, my career, my standing in the theater, and my business, as well as my husband. No, if there's going to be any adultery, I should be the one to do it. And I should do it in the most humiliating fashion possible. Johnny's always been jealous over nothing, so it's time to give him something to be jealous about. That Nat Goodwin has fancied me a long time, much as he does Jessie, so maybe I will concede him what he's been after for years. Then I could humiliate both Ward and Jessie at the same time. Or maybe somebody French. I'll give myself to M. Halévy to make up for John's insult of not being jealous of such an old man, if we can manage it without his gout flaring up. Or maybe I'll test John's liberal principles by bedding a Negro and finding out if what they say is true. Or maybe a cross-eyed man. It ruins Johnny's whole day if he sees one. Imagine how he'll feel in court when he sees his wife's lover staring at him from two directions. Or maybe one of the player who deserted to the National League. Mr. Clarkson seemed to admire more than my jewels. Or your husband's friend Mickey Welch who's always had a little different smile for me than for everyone else."

"Maybe we can find a cross-eyed Negro Frenchman who is playing in the National League."

"I have an even more humiliating idea. On the whole trip to California, Al Spalding was staring at my bosoms. I'll take him as a lover, and I'll make sure it's in the New York *Times*, just like the story today."

"So when do you tell your husband that there's going to be another divorce in the family?"

"Never."

"You won't divorce him, even now?"

" Especially now. I wouldn't dream of ending our marriage. I have too much to get back at him for. From now on, there'll be no more pretending the husband is in charge. I will go on the stage when I want, see whom I want, and travel to France when I want. Do you want to come with me?"

"I prefer returning to Cambridge. The people there are nicer than the ones in Paris."

"I'll go to Paris by myself then."

"To find a cross-eyed Negro French actor?"

"Who knows. I have some business to take care of. Maybe I'll put on some Racine or at least Molière."

"What are you going to tell John?"

"I'm thinking of being nice to him. That should confuse him."

Helen brought her anger under control before she saw John. At a minimum she would pretend to forgive him and see how that worked out. Financial considerations should have been her first concern, but they played very little part in her thinking. To the extent that she did worry about money, it was a fear that Johnny would not have enough money to live comfortably and keep hunting dogs after he was through playing baseball. She was fairly certain that he'd never make any money as a lawyer, so she wanted to make sure he kept the valuable properties in Colorado and Brooklyn acquired during the marriage. There was no need to leave him penniless.

Much to their surprise, John and Helen had a very pleasant evening together. Ward repeated his apologies for everything that happened. After he agreed that her theater career was her own business, she told him she was going to Paris. He said that was fine with him and asked her to check on the progress of baseball in France. She left him to worry about being a shortstop, a captain, a manager, a part owner, a league president, and the Brotherhood president.

In France, M. Halévy once again told her that the only way she could do anything on the French stage would be if she financed the production herself. For a while she even considered it. Selling off her French real estate would give her enough money to stage a production.

"Who knows? It might even make money," she told herself. But then the reality of producing a play set in. All of the headaches and inconveniences that she always encountered when producing a play in New York would be immeasurably magnified working in the unfamiliar theater world of Paris.

After a week in Paris, she was finally able to see the one person with whom she could talk about her husband. Petit Marcel was on furlough from his military service, and they were able to meet for a long museum walk and tea at the Ritz.

(The following discussion was in French, translated into English.)

"But John must have thought that I was a whore. That's why he looked for M. Halévy."

"But not at all. I understand jealousy. I am making a study of it, as a writer. There are two sorts. There is a man who is jealous because he suspects that his wife wrongs him with any man, no matter who."

"I don't think John feels that way."

"Certainly no. But there is also the man who thinks that his wife is so far above him that he has fear that someone better will steal her. He visited M. Halévy because he thought he was not worth you. Forgive him, s'il vous plait."

"Call me by the familiar, Marcel. You make me feel old."

"As you wish. Your husband knew that M. Halévy wrote the book for the opera Carmen by the father of my friend Jacques. He was jealous because someone very celebrated like that might steal away his treasured wife."

"And he ceased to be jealous when he saw that M. Halévy was an old man. That was not nice in any fashion for M. Halévy."

"Au contraire. For the next month, Daniel's father had something to talk about besides his gout. He told all Paris of how the American actress's husband accused him of the seduction. No, your husband does not take you to be a Messalina lying with senator and slave, but rather a Guinevere who wished to exchange Arthur for Lancelot."

"But still a whore."

"Not at all. Not in the French legends."

"You are a good advocate for my husband the advocate. You will do well on the faculty of law, Marcel. But why is it that you like my husband so much?"

"Because he has the good sense to know that he is not worthy of you. And because he likes M. Straus and M. Straus likes him."

"That is because M. Straus speaks good English."

Marcel switched to English.

"But he like me too, and I speak very bad the English. Maman always tells me." Then switching back to French, he continued.

"Also because M. Ward sends me gifts like clothes, baseballs, and clubs. Your husband did very bad with that little trollop, but he taught me one thing about baseball."

"What is it that that is?"

"You get three strikes before you are retired. The putain (whore) from Maine was one strike."

"So I must give him two more chances?"

"At least. The last one might be a foul ball. And the last chance must be in Paris. In accord?"

"Yes. I will give him more strikes. How is your baseball coming. We should speak English for that."

"Maman says I should not speak too much English with Americans."

"It would not be the first time you have done something your mother forbids, isn't that true? Besides, I'm an actress. If you want me to speak British, I can show your Maman that I can do that too. What are you doing with the baseball equipment?"

"Those beautiful All-American uniforms you designed are magnificent, especially the belt. I gave some to my friends and others to the officers. The Giant uniforms were more popular with the boys from the farms. Some of the Giant uniforms fit the big chaps with muscles, some nearly two meters tall. They liked being called Giants, especially with reference to the way the front of the uniform bulged."

"The idea of my sister. You should have seen the statue she made of her husband in that uniform. Obscene."

"One can imagine."

"But are you playing any baseball games?"

"Not yet. We throw the balls around. Some of the boys from Normandy use the bats for their games of *jeharque*. But most of us just throw the balls back and forth. I am not good at catching, so I usually wear the catcher's equipment. A paradox, no."

"I hope the other soldiers don't make fun of you."

"Not at all. I have never been happier. They know I try at the baseball and the shooting and the marching. They made me the company scribe. I was keeping all the records until they fired me for bad handwriting."

Helen was not surprised. Marcel had terrible, tiny cramped handwriting. It was as if the only area of his life in which he chose to economize was on paper.

"Johnny thought that you might write about baseball in France."

"I am not so talented that I can write about something that does not exist. I can only make stories out of things that I know."

"Will you make me a character?"

"If I do, you will be more interesting than Violet Veronica."

"So you have read 'The Enchanted Baseball' that I sent you. How did you like it?"

"We all thought it was frightful, but Maman said she was happy that the shortstop stayed with his first love, not the evil princess with the goggle eyes."

"Me too."

48

The Attendance
July 17, 1890 and days following
New York City

Colonel McAlpin, the New York backer who served as chair of the Players League Financial Committee reported on the condition of finances. There would be no bonuses for winning clubs, and there would certainly be no profits to share. There was a good chance that one or more of the clubs would fail to meet its payroll, and only the highly successful and well-financed Boston team had a hope of showing a profit. Except for Brooklyn, all of the Players League teams were inflating attendance figures, but even using the most optimistic numbers reported, it was clear to anyone with a rudimentary sense of accounting and arithmetic that the experiment was not working. National League attendance figures were lower although even more inflated.

Cracks in the players solidarity were starting to show. Dues were coming in late. Keefe had taken to calling Glasscock "the Judas goat" because he had led more than a few players back to the National League. Ward was hearing reports about secret meetings, and he wanted to discuss them with Keefe before he faced the New York press.

"Danny Richardson told me that Buck Ewing has been meeting in secret with John Day, and then Buck came and told me about it, probably after he figured out that I already knew. And he had been talking with Spalding too. Connor and Richardson think Ewing might be up to something."

"Buck goes back a long way with Day. Mickey and Roger and Buck and I were all together in Troy and then New York."

"How could I ever forget who went back to Troy? What puzzles me is why should Danny Richardson who never liked me be the one who is loyal enough to keep me informed? And should I still trust Buck?"

"If we can't trust Buck, we might have to admit that we're beaten. Anyway, he says that he only met with Spalding because Spalding told him that Mike Kelly had agreed to talk with him. And everybody knows what happened there."

"The newspapers say that Kelly was offered $10,000 a year for three years if he went back to the League."

"And he turned it down," Keefe said in Kelly's defense.

"After thinking it over for a day," Ward said with a slight scowl.

"Then he borrowed $500 from Al personally. But Kel stayed with the boys, and Buck will too."

Ward stopped himself before he mentioned Smiling Mickey Welch, Keefe's best friend and one of the founders of the Brotherhood, now pitching for John Day in the National League. He changed the subject to money.

"How do you think it would work if we decided to tax the players to build up a reserve fund for next year. Do you think we could hold back part of the salaries for an emergency fund?"

"Not possible. The younger players are already complaining about their salaries with no bonuses, especially the ones who are having good years and feel tied to a three year contract. I've even heard some of them call themselves "chattels," to quote an old article somewhere."

It wasn't the first time that Ward's own words had come back to haunt him.

"And Spalding has been signing young players to long term contracts," Keefe added.

"If Spalding's lawyers wrote the contracts, he'll find a way to break them when he wants to."

In addition to his other duties, Ward was the spokesman for the new league. When the newspaper boys asked him about the attendance, he sweated and stammered. Then he answered that he was sure all the teams were reporting accurately. Ward wanted to talk about how the game was being played on the field.

"The Players League is not only superior to the National League now; it is better than that league ever was. With the addition of stars like Pete Browning and my teammate Davy Orr, as well as most of the St. Louis Browns, we have taken the cream of the American Association. And having two impartial professional umpires every game has greatly reduced cheating and cut down on kicking."

But all the newspapermen wanted to talk about was attendance and money.

"Why is attendance so low in Philadelphia? Do you think they'll ever make money in Buffalo? We hear that some teams might not be able to meet their payrolls. Is that true?"

Al Spalding was much more comfortable with the press, partly because he had bought his own newspaper to get out his message, but he was winning the war in the wider press too. Some of the reporters might be union sympathizers, but the publishers of most major newspapers understood the importance of beating back the socialist tide. Stopping briefly in New York on a trip to England, Spalding dealt with the same questions that Ward had faced. The National League had been having even poorer attendance than the Players League, barely ahead of the Association. National League payrolls had gone up because of new expensive multi-year contracts, and even the rookies were aware that a bidding war was in progress. Spalding deflected attention by discussing the international game.

"We'll have a league in England within two years. Baseball is the Anglo-Saxon inheritance."

"Are you saying baseball was invented in England?" teased one of the reporters who knew of the supposed feud with Chadwick.

"Not at all. Just that the game has a special appeal for the English-speaking world. My business is already starting to take significant orders from our British branch."

Most of those orders were for infielders' gloves which were being used in cricket, but that wasn't something he was going to bring up himself.

What was worst of all for Spalding was that Comiskey's Chicago Pirates, now calling themselves by the discarded name "White Stockings," were outdrawing Anson's National League team, partly because of the novelty of their new park, and partly because they were a better team in a better league. Spalding was reduced to giving free passes, not just to aldermen and policemen, but to anyone who would take them. The stands would have been empty otherwise. But the newspapers allowed him to report attendance of 1824 when he had 18 on one side of the park and 24 on the other. After satisfying the press, Spalding had a brief meeting with Anson, in New York to play what was left of Day's Giants who were only operating through the grace of a loan from Spalding. As was often the case lately, Anson was so angry that he spat while he talked.

"Don't those newspaper boys know that Comiskey is nothing but a pool room hustler. How can he suspend a player like Latham for hippodroming and then have him back on the team? And Latham can only hit .250 even when he's trying. And why did we have to give money to Day? And now it looks as if Glasscock might win the batting title. Of course, if they counted walks as hits like in 1887, I'd be leading the league in hitting again."

Anson would have beaten Brouthers for the 1887 batting title except for the peculiar rule that counted walks as hits that year, and he had been loud in his protests. He took the opposite position now that he was the one who would have come out ahead. Spalding felt like pointing this out, but he had more immediate concerns.

"Well, we're beating them on the sporting pages, where it counts. Even if they have a newspaperman as secretary of their league."

"Ward just hired Brunell to make me angry."

Anson had never forgiven Brunell for publishing the story about how Anson had personally picked the Chicago official scorer, a man reluctant to call errors on Anson and equally hesitant to call errors on anyone attempting to field a ball Anson had hit. This had resulted in a new and less favorable scorekeeper being assigned to his games. Spalding didn't care about Anson's feud with Brunell which he considered a side issue existing only in Anson's imagination. Anson had not been happy when Spalding had loaned Day the money to keep Glasscock away from Brooklyn. It rather amused Spalding to think that Glasscock would probably win the National League batting title, knowing that the Brotherhood players called him "Judas Goat," and resented him more than any other National Leaguer.

"But we're the ones the newspapers are supporting. They recognize the players for what they are, communist plutocrats. None of them is worth what he's asking to be paid. Think what they'd be making if they had to do something else for a living. Mike Kelly can't even manage a saloon."

"Ward's a lawyer," Anson mentioned in an attempt to be fair.

"If Ward were any good as a lawyer, he wouldn't be wasting his time playing baseball. And he was careful to let other lawyers handle all those reserve clause cases."

"We should still appeal all of them. Make the players come back and play for us again. At whatever salary we tell them. Did you hear how Keefe injured his hand on a line drive from one of his own balls? I laughed so hard that I cried."

This was a separate front within the war between the leagues. Keefe's baseball was being used in the new league. Keefe and Becannon were also starting to compete for the larger national market in baseballs.

"And Ward claims that the ball is no more lively. They're all such terrible liars, Adrian. We have to expose them for what they are."

Now Spalding had been lying through his whole baseball career, starting with his ability to make a batter think he would be getting a fast ball when really a change of pace was coming, leaving the honest batter deceived and looking foolish. And he had gone on to build a career on lying.

Lied to his mother when he said that his new job in Rockford had nothing to do with baseball.

Lied to Boston when he said he wouldn't jump to Chicago in 1876.

Lied about who ran the National League when he was in control behind the scenes.

Lied to the press about profits and the percentage the players received.

Lied to his wife about the neighbor who was carrying his baby.

Lied to the neighbor about his sexual relations with his wife which were still warm and frequent.

Lied to the press about the Chicago National League team attendance.

Lied to the players when he told them all the long term contracts were unbreakable. (Some weren't)

Lied to the other owners when he told them all the long term contracts were breakable. (Some weren't.)

Lied to the American Association owners when he said that the League would honor their contracts, even as the League was already stealing players.

But the biggest lie of all was when he convinced the other owners that his principal goal was to see that everyone made money. Some of them suspected that his real interest was in keeping his sporting goods business profitable, but that was just another form of the same lie. No matter how cynical he had pretended to be, never in his life had he put money or family or truth ahead of baseball. From the moment he woke in the morning to the last second before falling asleep at night, all of his thinking concerned the peculiar geometry, sociology, economics, arithmetic and history of baseball. Spreading the gospel of baseball was more important than politics, profit, and religion. Baseball was the national pastime because he had made it so. Baseball was international because he was making it so. And baseball had been on a sound business footing thanks to him. He wasn't going to let Ward or anyone else wreck his game.

The Book
October 2, 1890
Olympic Park II, Buffalo

Ward moved a little closer to second base as he normally did for a left-handed hitter, so Hoy slapped a ground ball through the hole to his right The diminutive center fielder had previously noticed that Brooklyn's pitcher always took a long time getting the ball to the plate, and the catcher had a weak arm, so the next play was inevitable. Hoy stole second without even drawing a throw. As he had done once the year before, he passed a neatly folded note to Ward who stuffed it in his pocket and went back to his position. Connie Mack dribbled a grounder toward first base, but Orr couldn't bend down to make the play. The error seemed to upset the pitcher who walked the next two batters. Then third baseman Joyce fumbled what should have been a double play ball. Before the inning was over Buffalo was leading 3-0, and the visitors had not yet batted. On a cold day with an early winter wind blowing in, it was a very good start for a last place Buffalo team that would bring its dismal season to a close the next day. In April when Ward had shown Helen the schedule, she had said something about how cold it might be that time of year in Buffalo. Like Brouthers and O'Rourke, she had also warned him that Buffalo was not a major league city, but Jim White had persuaded him to take a chance.

Ward had every reason to be proud of his Brooklyn team composed of rookies and remnants. All that Brooklyn needed to assure a second place finish was to win one more game or for Buck Ewing's New York team to lose one, and Ward's Wonders would finish behind only Mike Kelly's Boston Reds, a team which had functioned smoothly and professionally all year under Kelly's surprisingly sober management. There was no shame in losing to Kelly's team because it was, in Ward's opinion, the best baseball team yet assembled, winning the championship of the best league ever organized. New rules, new ballparks and a new system of management had elevated the quality of play, and Ward was confident that next year would be even more successful. The relatively poor attendance and uncertain finances worried him, but he was sure that the baseball public would catch up with the league and start forking over more of their half dollars, maybe even dollars for reserved seats.

Ward led off the third with a bunt single. Van Haltern, shivering in the unfamiliar frigid weather, followed with a single to left. Ward headed for third and threw himself on the ground in a deceptive arc that constituted his version of the

Chicago slide, just as he had taught all his players to do, even Davy Orr. Ward felt his foot on the base a full beat before he felt the ball on his rump, clear evidence that he was safe, but he was called out. Last year he would have complained loud and clear, but earlier this year he had lost his temper over a decision by Bob Ferguson, and after the game the veteran umpire had told him, "When you're league president and can fire the umpires, it's not fair for you to do any kicking."

K.C. had looked forward to this final road trip and had bought his ticket by mail in advance, something that seemed foolish when he looked around and saw about eighty people in the stands trying to keep warm. He wasn't sure how many of them had paid, because when he had entered the park, there had been no one to take his ticket. By the time the clerk finally did show up, several people, who may or may not have been recipients of free passes, had walked past. For a while he had feared he would have no one with whom to share his opinions, but finally a young man came and sat within earshot.

"I'm from New York City. Are you from Buffalo?" K.C. asked.

"No, I"m from Columbus, Ohio."

Just then Hoy, who had been playing shallow, ran back almost to the center field fence to catch a Keefe and Becannon baseball propelled by a Pete Browning Louisville Slugger with all the force of Davy Orr's 250 pounds. Running back without glancing over his shoulder, Hoy caught the ball as he veered away from the fence to avoid damage to himself or the barrier. The few cranks in the stands were standing and pounding their hands together, so Hoy blushed as he raised his cap to acknowledge the applause he could see but not hear.

"Buffalo might have a bad team, but Dummy Hoy is the best outfielder in the league. He's great on the bases, walks and hits his way on as much as anyone, then figures out how to score. That's one smart dummy," K. C. finished, proud of his oxymoron.

"Then why do you call him 'Dummy?'"

"That's his name. That's what he tells people to call him."

"My father and mother don't call him that. His name is William. Or, if anything, his name is . . ."

Here the young man made a gesture with three fingers of his right hand formed into a W, touching the right side of his chin, followed by two fingers closed together touching the same place, WH in the manual alphabet placed at a common site for sign names.

"But I didn't mean anything wrong. I was saying nice things about him. He's the best center fielder in baseball."

"I'll tell him."

Getting Hoy's attention as he went off the field between innings was not difficult. The young man waved his hand up and down, and Hoy brightened. A rapid series of graceful hand motions and rapidly changing facial expressions took place, and Hoy and the young man were sharing a laugh.

"He says he's glad you think he's a good player, but he'd rather that you thought the Bisons were a good team. He's a part owner so he welcomes anyone who comes to the games from New York, and he hopes he'll see you again tomorrow."

Hoy turned to Mack and signed something to him.

"I've noticed the other players talk to Hoy with their hands," K.C. observed.

"He's good at teaching hearing people how to sign, and the ones who can't sign he teaches to fingerspell, if they can read.

A few innings later, Ward remembered Hoy's note and pulled it out.

Dear Mr. Ward:

Why have we allowed Buffalo to be the worst team? The new players have not helped. We are the only team in the league that started with a majority ownership by the players. Now most of the teams are owned by the players if you count back salaries owed as capital invested. You have some good ideas, and we all appreciate what you do, but you try to do too much. Shortstop, captain, manager, league president, newspaper interview, theater producer, lawyer, author. I think you should concentrate on what you do best.

In Brotherhood,
Dummy Hoy

Ward put the note aside. It was another version of the same old Buffalo complaints. "Why do we have the worst team in the worst city?" Sure, these Buffalo boys had given up 28 runs in a game, but he could see that they got a few more pitchers the next year. And Buffalo wasn't such a bad city. He used to enjoy coming here with Providence. For now, he just wanted to beat the Bisons, clinch second place, and head back to New York.

In the seventh, singles by McGeachy and Joyce and some clever base running brought home two runs. Brooklyn would have tied the game on a wild throw, but Hoy had been behind second base backing up the play. Still, Ward was encouraged as the score narrowed to 3-2.

K.C. was getting along well with his new friend in spite of their being for different teams. The young man's parents were graduates of the Ohio School of the Deaf where Hoy had been the valedictorian. That explained why the young man knew sign language. He had a question for K.C., an obviously well-informed baseball enthusiast.

"Why do you think Hoy is the best outfielder in the league?"

"Because he takes away more hits by playing shallow than any other outfielder. And he starts running at the crack of the bat, or when he sees the angle of the bat and the ball. His arm is not the strongest, but it's strong enough and he's always accurate and gets rid of the ball quickly. One inning this year he made three base runner kills at home plate. Nobody will ever do better than that, especially not Hoy because no one runs on him any more. And he's so smart. Sometimes he sneaks up on a runner on second base and makes a signal for a pickoff throw. I saw him embarrass Ward that way once. And Hoy's always on base with a walk or a hit, whatever the team needs. And when he's on base, he can steal if that's what it takes. Some day when all these players are old, someone will come along and talk to them about baseball in the old days, maybe write a book. And when he asks them about this era, the players will all tell him that Dummy Hoy is one of the best they played with, if not the best."

"I thought you agreed not to call him that."

"I won't. But that's what the players will call him. Look at that. It looks like Brooklyn will make a rally in the ninth."

K.C.'s mind was always called back to the present, the score, the count on the batter, the number out, and the league standings.

A crank who had just come back from a bar with a Western Union connection told Ward that Ewing's Giants had lost, so the Wonders would finish second. It would have meant a lot more if the league had generated the profits for the planned bonuses, but it was still satisfying to beat Buck Ewing and the New York team that had been eager to let him go. Now he'd take a train back to New York and see what he could work out with Helen. She had been planning a Broadway show and then canceled it. With the season coming to an end, Ward could concentrate on their marriage.

He was equally optimistic about the game after two quick hits in the bottom of the ninth. However, a line drive double play caught one of his careless youngsters off second base. The Wonders managed to make another hit, but a throw from Hoy cut down a runner at the plate. The fourth hit of the inning was on the infield, and the tying run advanced no farther than third. Ward struck out for the final out, and Brooklyn had lost. None of the players seemed happy, even when they were told they were in second place. No one protested when Ward announced that now that second place was guaranteed, he would be going back to New York.

K.C. and his left the park with the young man from Columbus and continued their conversation.

"There weren't a hundred fans in there. Can the league continue in Buffalo?" the young man wondered.

"It's not much better in New York or Brooklyn. There's too much baseball. Maybe the players can't run their own league."

"Mr. Hoy says the players have given too much to their new backers and have no control any more, even over their own money. He loves Jim White, but he thinks he was too old to be the star of a new ball club, and Jack Rowe the same. He thinks the players should really assume control.

"Does he share his opinions with Ward?"

"He tries, but he tells me Ward won't listen to him. Maybe it's because he's deaf."

"Maybe it's because Ward doesn't listen to anyone."

50

The Divorce
New York City and Cambridge
October, 1890

Helen made the announcement that she would not produce and star in "The Whirlwind" after all. Just as the newspapers had seen her return to the stage as a reason for the separation, they saw the cancellation as a sign that she had given in to her husband, but that wasn't true either. Shortly after casting for the play, Helen had begun to have second thoughts. Her physician cautioned her that there was no guarantee that her seizures wouldn't begin again and warned her not to place too much stress on herself. Bernie assured her that the show would be well financed without her, so she could withdraw without putting anyone out of work. Then she re-read the play and saw how much it was like ones she had done before.

With John's baseball season over, they began to see each other more frequently, and he was clearly hoping to revive the marriage. For a while, Helen was content to resume their marital relations disguised as extramarital relations, with John heading back to his own hotel at night. When John wanted to do something together to show that they were still a married couple, Helen suggested that they could visit Keefe and Clara in Cambridge, to which he hesitantly agreed.

Keefe's sisters were excited to see Helen again. When Clara had found out that Ward was coming with her, she wrote back, once again advocating a quick divorce, but she promised to be civil. At first everyone managed to remember that they were family, but when Ward was alone with his brother-in-law, he brought up that Keefe had gone to Mike Tiernan's wedding where he and Ewing had socialized with National Leaguers, especially Mickey Welch.

"How could you sit down with scabs like Tiernan and traitors like Welch, not to mention John Day?"

"Mickey explained to me that he had a chance to sign a three-year ironclad contract for the best salary of his life just as he felt his arm was starting to go dead. There was no way he could tell his wife that he was turning it down. I think I understand him better now that I've been a married man for a while. Besides, friends can't let one disagreement come between them," Keefe said, thinking of how Ward had acted when he thought Keefe had substituted his own baseballs for Spalding's. Ward didn't make the connection.

"I'm not sure I can ever forgive Mickey."

"He's my friend. You and I are family. After we have those peace talks between the leagues, we might all have to forgive each other."

At this point Clara entered the room, having heard only the end of the conversation.

"John Ward, you had better forgive other people's trespasses," she said, invoking the Our Father which she had recently learned in the Catholic version, "because you certainly have enough trespasses of your own to wish forgiven. You evidently trespassed all over the state of Maine."

Not much could be said after that. It was clear that Ward and Clara could never be in the same room again. There was nothing Keefe's cheerful sisters could do to lighten the atmosphere, and the visit ended with Ward's prompt return to Brooklyn where he said he would be working on preparing the Wonders for the next season. Helen stayed behind, thinking of how her physician had advised her to avoid stress.

Turning a separation into a New York divorce was a very complicated matter, especially when a person as wealthy as Helen was involved. The lawyer that Bernie found for Helen was ready to fight to protect her assets, but this proved easier than he had thought. Ward really seemed to have no idea how wealthy his wife was and had no interest in getting her money.

"I don't want a divorce, but if she does get one, I want to be sure that she's provided for. Do you think I should keep some of the property in case her theater company goes bankrupt?"

Helen's attorney had been given a confidential review of his client's finances, and he was surprised to see Ward really had no idea of his wife's wealth. It was more amazing that a law school graduate and member of the bar had so little understanding of what incorporation meant.

Ward's attorney seemed equally surprised when he found that Helen was making no demands on the ballplayer's assets and seemed willing to concede his exclusive ownership of valuable property recently acquired in Denver and Brooklyn. What the couple did fight over was Ward's adultery, not whatever he had done in the past, but what he would do in the future. Helen thought the least he could do was find some willing woman, not Jessie, and arrange to be caught by detectives. Ward refused to agree and suggested that Helen might just as easily find a willing partner herself and make him the injured party.

"I would, but I couldn't find a cross-eyed French-speaking Negro National Leaguer."

"Be serious, Helen," her attorney cautioned her, not having any idea what she was talking about.

"I am not about to have the newspapers brand me an adulteress. The public opinion of the morals of actresses is low enough already."

"The public doesn't have a very high opinion of the morals of baseballists either," Ward countered. "And there's no way you will catch me in adultery. I have a secret weapon."

Finally, both lawyers agreed that Ward and Helen were not getting along well enough to get a divorce. The meeting ended with no formal papers being filed. Ward left the meeting with a sense of optimism. For the time being, his marriage was intact. He had just finished a season where he hit .337, and he was looking forward to the next season, no matter what rumors he heard about desertions back to the National League.

Having her divorce delayed suited Helen. There were too many loose ends, and she was still not sure what she wanted. There was one thought that troubled her, and that was that Ward might still be carrying on an affair with that McDermott woman. Helen's policy of not allowing anyone to pronounce Jessie's name in front of her had limited the amount of information she could receive about her, but there was one place where she could ask about her. Dion Boucicault had died the month before, so Helen paid a condolence visit his daughter Nina, an aspiring actress in her early twenties.

"I loved your father's plays and always regretted that we never worked together. The play about the priest who worked with the deaf was my favorite."

"My father believed in deaf education

"And it works. The only one of the baseball players who had any sense of business was the deaf outfielder from Buffalo, William Hoy. I read the notes he gave Johnny. But what I appreciated the most about your father was that he asked my permission before he worked with Jessie McDermott."

"You should appreciate that. Father really wanted to work with her, but if you had said no, he would have sent her away. He changed her name to Maxine Elliott. She can't act, but she already has a speaking part in 'The Middleman.' 'What a charming collection of people a political candidate gathers around him in the course of his career, Mr. Chandler.'"

Helen knew what this meant to a young actress, and guessed why Nina had the line memorized.

"You tried out for the same part?"

"Yes, but I didn't have a chance. All the men swoon over Maxine's bosoms. I'm sorry. I didn't mean to say anything that bothered you."

"Not at all. If one has a husband who gives into temptation, one likes to know that at least the temptation was strong."

"You'll never have to worry about her having any interest in him from now on. Not unless he becomes a theatrical producer. Maxine doesn't waste her energy except on men who have a part for a woman with big bosoms. Or at least can write one in. I can only guess how she got the role in 'The Middleman,' but it would be a well-informed guess."

This last comment was delivered with a trace of Nina's father's Irish/French accent, and Helen felt a rush of warmth for the girl.

"You obviously don't like our friend Jessie/Maxine, and that's a point in your favor."

"And Miss Dauvray, one request please. If you know of any good parts for a woman with small bosoms, let me know."

As Helen left, she reflected.

"I do have connections in London and Paris as well as New York. If I can ever do a favor for that girl some day, I will."

After Helen accepted that Ward was no longer seeing Jessie, maybe it was possible to save her marriage. What had looked like strike three may have been a foul that the catcher could not catch. Perhaps she would give Ward one last chance in Paris.

When Ward got back to his hotel, he had a letter from Marcel. He politely thanked Ward for the uniforms and equipment, but the most interesting part of the letter concerned what Marcel had talked about with Helen.

"Remember, three strikes before you are out. Helen has been very enraged with you, but you have one chance to win her back. You must meet her in Paris. Walk her through the Jardin des Plantes. Dine at the Ritz. Shop for Fortuny gowns. Buy her red and white roses at Lachaume. Buy her lilies. Lots of lilies. If you think, why should I listen to a foolish young man, you would be right, but Mme Straus and my mother helped me with my list. They too want to see you reunited with your wife. We all hope to see both of you in Paris."

Ward crumpled up the letter as soon as he finished it.

"Everything will work out when we're in Paris. And I'll be back home in Brooklyn in time for next season.

51

The Wake
Nick Engel's Home Plate Saloon, New York City
January 16, 1891

An Irish-style wake was being held in honor of the death of the Players League, a death which had come about as a result of the peace talks between the three leagues. Jim O'Rourke had been out of town and avoiding the newspapers, so he had to catch up by arriving early and sharing one of Nick Engel's famous three-pound grilled steaks with Tim Keefe in a private room upstairs. O'Rourke tried to get an idea of what would happen to him and the Giants.

"Is it true that Day will once again be our employer?"

"We're back in the National League. There is no Players League."

"I know the final outcome, but I am impatient to hear an account of the events leading up to our surrender."

"Well, it started with the peace conference between the National League and the Players League, with the American Association joining in. Johnny called the conference, but he had to go out of town for his sick brother and a little bit of barnstorming, but it didn't matter because no players were allowed in the negotiations, even the ones who were part owners. Ewing and Day and Talcott had already decided that both New York teams would merge. That was supposedly before they knew what league they'd play in, but it was over. Even the Buffalo players were shut out, and they own a majority of the team. Our backers and the National League owners made deals together. The sausage makers in Pittsburg, the bakers in Brooklyn, and the fellow in Chicago all decided they didn't want to lose any more money."

"Did all of our backers join in this perfidious betrayal?"

"Prince in Boston never folded, and Al Johnson doubled down, buying a Cincinnati franchise to go along with his Cleveland team."

"Boston was the only team that made money last year because Mike Kelly stayed sober all year."

"I don't know about that. He's not sober tonight. You can hear him singing with the quartet. They left Al Johnson with two teams and no league to play in. But the other owners wanted to disband, and there was nothing we could do."

"How has Johnny taken it?"

"He doesn't want to talk about it. He's working out a contract to manage and play for Brooklyn in the National League next year. The Trolley Dodgers are going to fire Gunner Bill McGunnigle, even though they won the pennant two years in a row in different leagues. Ward will have to build a new team again, but they're paying him $7000 a year."

"He seemed almost cheerful when I came in."

"He's the one who organized this wake, so he feels he has to be a good host. He was bitter at first, but after some time passed, he decided he couldn't hate everybody, so he focused on a few like Glasscock for contract jumping or Buck Ewing for negotiating with Spalding during the season and promoting the New York merger. I'm the one who should be bitter. I have a warehouse full of Players League baseballs and a contract with a league that doesn't exist and a partner getting ready to sue me."

Spalding had not been invited to the celebration, but neither had he been excluded, so he and Anson decided to make a foray into the enemy camp. The presence of the two caused a momentary awkwardness, but Spalding understood enough of the group's psychology to make himself welcome.

"We're all together again, boys. Let me buy the next drink for everyone," he said, making it a magnificent gesture by tossing a ten dollar Liberty Head Gold Eagle to the barkeep. He then turned to face the players and their guests, "I want you to know that I have nothing but admiration for what you accomplished this year. The National League you return to will be stronger than ever with all the new stars we've been developing while you were gone. And I want us all to toast your leader, the incomparable Johnny Ward, a great player and a great student of the game as well as a leader of men. Here's to you, Johnny."

After the toast was offered and drunk, Anson and Spalding retreated into a small upstairs room, just as O'Rourke and Keefe were leaving. No smiles were exchanged, and all four men looked uncomfortable. As soon as they were outside the hearing of the others, a smirking Spalding addressed his manager.

"Listen to them singing out there, Adrian. 'My Good Old Friends Who Never Alter.' They're all happy that there's not going to be a blacklist, and they're ready to return for whatever we offer. Their backers were even more desperate. Addison traded me a new ball park for season tickets to our games. I asked him if he wanted me to assume his debts to Comiskey and the rest of the Chicago players, and he said he wasn't about to pay them, and he didn't see why I should."

"At least Comiskey will be out of Chicago for good now."

"And the beauty of it is that the league disbanded by itself. The butchers, the bakers, and the cigar makers all wanted out, and I named the terms. Ward and his boys will play for what we pay them."

"Speaking of Ward, we need a shortstop. Williamson's not worth taking back. He hasn't been himself since Paris."

"You're not telling me that you'd consider taking Ward, are you? We'll find all the shortstops we need. Those American Association contracts are easy to break, and we should be able to find someone who'd be less trouble than Ward. Besides, I hear he's going to manage Brooklyn."

"But you toasted him like you were friends again and said what a great job he had done."

"Because he didn't. It was you who made me see that, Adrian. If the players had had any other leader they would have won. John Day, Harry Wright, or even tactless Bob Ferguson—any of them would have been a better president. Or if they wanted a player to lead them, they would have been better off with O'Rourke or Ewing. Or me or you. For all his claims to act for everyone, he always stayed in a downtown hotel while the rest of the boys lived near the Polo Grounds."

Ward waited until Mike Kelly and his quartet had finished their rendition of "Slide, Kelly, Slide," with the eponymous Kelly adding a flourish by sliding over the sawdust on the barroom floor. Ward then proposed his own toast on the model of the traditional salute to a new French monarch.

"The League is dead. Long live the League."

Spalding and Anson stopped by Ward to say goodbye to their host. Spalding spoke first.

"When we get together next time, what stories we'll have to tell, Johnny. We still haven't had a chance to talk about our tour around the world. Maybe we both should write books about last season. You are the author of the greatest book yet written about baseball and will continue to be so until I publish my own."

"No rounders," said Anson, recognizing the point on which the two authors could agree.

"I'm not writing any books about last year," said Ward. "I just want to put it all behind us."

"That's what we all want."

"I don't want to express any opinions about the last year. I just want to go on to the next."

"That's the spirit."

The saloon emptied out as many of the players left with Mike Kelly for his new saloon, the 2 Kels. Ward stayed the latest because he considered himself to be the host, and he didn't have any place to go but his own empty hotel room. He was still there after almost everyone had left.

Nick Engel was supervising the cleaning crew, and Ward found himself alone with young Freddie who had been allowed to stay up late with his heroes in exchange for a promise not to drink any beer.

"So, are you fellows going to be all right now, Mr. Ward? Will you all get along? Will you come back to the Giants?"

"We'll all get along, but I'm not sure I'm going to be a Giant again. If I play in Brooklyn again next year, will you still be a Giant fan?"

"You're the one who stuck by me when they got rid of me as mascot. I'll stick by you and be a Brooklyn fan now."

"Loyalty is a good thing, Freddie. If we had more loyal Brotherhood members, our league would still be alive."

"So who do you blame?"

If a reporter had asked him that question, Ward would have evaded it. If a fellow player had asked, Ward would have answered diplomatically. But a young baseball fan deserved a better answer.

"At first I blamed the players who stayed with the National League."

"Like Mr. Welch."

"Sure. He was an original Brotherhood member, so that hurt more. Then I blamed the ones who signed with us then went back to the League, like Glasscock. Then I blamed the newspapers for turning on us and saying that we were communists. Then I blamed our backers for selling us out. But now I forgive everybody."

"Even Mr. Ewing?"

"Maybe not everybody. Buck was the one who started meeting with Spalding. I guess you never know who will be loyal. Anyway, before you knew it, we didn't have a league any more."

"So you blame Buck, mostly."

For a moment Ward thought it over. The only other person he could think of to blame for the league's failure was himself.

Maybe he should have listened to the newspapers when they said he should have named someone else league president to free up more of his own time.

Maybe he should have listened to Helen's accountant when he told him his backers were shady fast-buck artists who were woefully undercapitalized.

Maybe he should have listened to Hoy and Mack when they said that the players status as owners should be better defined.

Maybe he should have listened to Brouthers who warned him that Buffalo could not support major league baseball.

Maybe he should have listened to Brunell and the accountants who said he couldn't afford two well-paid umpires at every game.

Maybe he should have listened to Helen who had advised him not to share the schedule with Spalding.

Maybe he should have listened to Samuel Gompers when he said they shouldn't use scab labor to finish the park in Chicago.

Maybe he should have listened to O'Rourke who said they should sue the players who had signed Players League contracts and jumped back to the National League.

Maybe he should have listened when Richardson warned him that Ewing was meeting with the owners.

All of these doubts flashed through his mind in a few seconds.

"I don't blame anyone, and I forgive everyone, except maybe Buck. He was the one who was the best paid when we started, and it seems he'll be the best paid again."

"Is it always all about the money, like I hear my father say?"

"It's always about the money, but it's never all about the money. For me, money is only important if it lets me do what I want."

"And what would that be, Mr. Ward?"

"I'm going to sail to Paris and win my wife back. And I'll be back home in time to lead my new team to the National League championship. I have a good feeling about this season coming up in Brooklyn. Wait 'til next year."

Epilogue
Baseball's Greatest Museum

**The Manager
Abner Doubleday Field, Cooperstown
July 27, 1964**

George Altman's line drive cleared the right field fence, and many in the crowd of nearly 10,000 at Doubleday Field rose and cheered because there is always something exciting about a home run, even when the team hitting it is still behind 4-1, even when the teams playing are the two worst in the majors, even when the game doesn't count in the standings, and even when the fence is only, at most, 312 feet from home plate. Most of the fans had come in for the Hall of Fame induction ceremony the day before and had stayed for the annual Hall of Fame game in Cooperstown. None of the players was likely to be asked back as an inductee, but both of the managers were well-known. The Washington Senators were led by Gil Hodges, and the New York Mets were managed by Casey Stengel, once the winner of five consecutive world championships, who was now being heard to ask the question, "Can't anyone here play this game?" Challenged by the kind of sharp grounder to his right that had been making or breaking shortstops for over a hundred years, Washington's Ed Brinkman went deep in the hole and threw out Ron Hunt to end the inning.

Ken Courtney III had been looking forward to attending the induction ceremony ever since he heard that his favorite player, White Sox shortstop Luke Appling was being admitted. So was his late father's favorite pitcher, Red Faber of the 1917 champion White Sox. Then the old-timers committee had elected Tim Keefe and John Ward, two players from the days when his grandfather had lived in New York, and that had inspired him to look through the trunk in the attic where he found 17 scorecards, all but one containing the name of Ward. His wife had told him nobody would be interested in these old Harry Stevens scorecards with the same certainty she had shown in throwing out his baseball card collection. Much to her surprise, the people at the Hall of Fame had treated him like a V.I.P. Lee Allen, the Hall's historian, had arranged seats for him and his wife, and they found themselves seated with the special guests like Ken's favorite sportswriter, Warren Brown of *Chicago's American* who, along with Allen, had long advocated Ward's induction, and with a nephew of John Ward's widow. Keefe's family was represented by his two nieces, Paula and Ann. Paula had been conducting a long letter-writing campaign to keep her uncle in consideration for the Hall. The scorecards had generated a discussion of Spalding's

World Tour, the great season of 1889 and the rebellion that was called the Players League, much the same history that we have been reading about.

"What happened to Ward after the Players League farewell party? Did Brooklyn win any more pennants?" asked the nephew, a youngster who had been playing baseball too much to read books about it. Lee Allen had the records in his head.

"The next two years he managed at Brooklyn, and they weren't very good, but he got the best out of them. Then in 1893 he moved back to the Giants as manager. By that time he was playing second base and he hit .328."

"That was the year the mound went back and everyone's average went up," interrupted Courtney, who had an inherited tendency to show off his baseball knowledge.

Joe Cunningham drove a single through the hole vacated by the shortstop, a perfect hit and run, the play Ward had sometimes claimed to have invented. Don Blasingame slid into third where he was called safe. Stengel jumped off from the bench, as if suddenly awakened, and he went out to confront the third base umpire.

"You're standing right there and can't see what's right in front of you. In my day we were lucky if we had two umpires, and they still got the call right more often than you four."

"Take it easy, Mr. Stengel. It's too hot a day, and the game doesn't count in the standings."

"Did Ward have any more success as a manager?" the nephew asked Allen.

"Oh yes. In 1894, his second season in New York, his team finished second to the Baltimore Orioles who were managed by his old friend Ned Hanlon. The Orioles had John McGraw, and Ward had traded them Willie Keeler, and they were the first great team of the 60' 6" era. But in those days there was no opposing league because the National League had run the American Association out of business. So they had an end of the season series where the first place team played the second place team for the Temple Cup."

"Not the Dauvray Cup?" asked Mrs. Courtney who had focused on that part of Ward's life.

"No. From 1891-1893, Boston had won three pennants in a row, so they earned permanent possession. No one knows where the cup is now. Probably melted down for the silver. Ward's Giants beat Hanlon's Orioles in four straight games to win the Temple Cup for 1894, and Ward retired as a successful player and manager after that season. Look, Stengel's bringing in a pinch hitter. Does anyone know who the first pinch hitter was?" Allen asked.

"Smiling Mickey Welch," Courtney was proud to know.

"We knew him," Keefe's niece Ann broke in. "He was Uncle Timothy's best friend. He came by the house, and we used to visit him whenever we went to New York. He used to get us tickets because he worked for the Giants."

Ed Kranepool, the pinch hitter, took a long looping swing and struck out. In the bottom of the seventh, the Senators scored another run, and now the Mets were down 6-2 and Stengel appeared to be dozing off again on the bench.

"Is everyone enjoying this trip to the birthplace of baseball," asked Allen who did not forget that he was the host. Warren Brown and Ken both winced. Ken was the first to speak.

"Didn't that Doubleday myth get exploded about as soon as it started? Nobody believed that crazy old mining engineer with his original baseball. And anyway, Doubleday was at West Point in 1839 with no leave time to go back home. Spalding just wanted to prove that Chadwick was wrong about rounders."

Then Warren Brown, who had led the campaign to have Ward included in the Hall of Fame, added his observation.

"Ward was on the same side of the rounders argument as Spalding, although he knew that the term baseball went back to England."

"I saw the word base ball in Jane Austen ," Ann added, but no one paid attention.

"Look, Elliott just hit a home run," said Courtney who knew who the batter was because he had continued keeping score throughout the game.

After the home run, there was another hit, then a walk, then a second out when a hit followed the home run, then an out, then a walk, then a second out. No lead was safe in this small park, built on a tiny Works Progress Administration budget. Ron Hunt made a valiant effort to keep the game alive by being hit by a pitch, just as Curt Welch would have done nearly a century before, but he wound up striking out for the last out.

With the end of the game, Stengel walked over to Allen, whom he seemed to know well. The historian was happy to have a chance to add to the experience of his guests.

"May I introduce you to baseball's greatest manager?"

Without waiting to hear anyone's name, the Ol' Perfesser made his modest disclaimer.

"When my Yankees were fattening their paychecks every October some people were saying I was the greatest manager ever, but I remembered the names people had called me when I was losing in Brooklyn and Boston, but I must have a been different fellow then and even worse now, but a great manager is like that Huggins fellow that they inducted yesterday, who mostly just wrote down Ruth and then Gehrig, and then Joe McCarthy who did the same for a while then started writing down Dimaggio, so he was even greater for a while because what makes a manger great is not getting fired, so you might say that the greatest manager was the one who lasted fifty years, but he owned the team and he finished last a lot, which McGraw never did, so maybe he was a greater manager than Mack, but my old manager when I broke in with Brooklyn was Wilbert Robinson, and he was pretty good, but he and McGraw both said they learned their baseball from the old Orioles manager, Ned Hanlon, and they won a lot of championships between them playing the hit and run, spike and slash Orioles baseball, so I guess you could say that if I was a good manager, that would make Ned Hanlon the greatest. You could look it up."

53

The Fan
Shortstop Inn, Cooperstown
July 27, 1964

Without pausing long enough to take a breath, Stengel had continued his monologue as Lee Allen's party left Doubleday Field and headed toward the Shortstop Inn, a local restaurant known for excellent food and continuous baseball talk. In most places it would have been odd to see a man in his seventies in a sweat-drenched baseball uniform, but this was Cooperstown, so Allen even felt comfortable asking Stengel to join them for dinner in spite of how he was dressed.

"No, I have to go back to the hotel and change, but maybe I'll see you back there."

Mrs. Courtney had one request before he left.

"Could you sign an autograph for my husband? He's probably baseball's greatest fan."

Stengel, who had been ready to leave, turned back for a moment. Furrowing his brow, he hesitated to correct a lady, but his professorial instinct demanded it.

"With all due respect, ma'am, your husband can't be baseball's greatest fan because he's too young, which means he never saw Wagner or maybe even Ruth. To be a great fan, you have to be at least my age, and frankly most people my age are dead. You could look it up. Players get worse as they get older, and maybe managers too, but fans get better and better because they have more memories. Now the greatest fan I know is a little old lady who comes to Mets games and keeps score, cheering and observing from her own box. When she was a girl she saw Mathewson, and she knew who it was from reading his book before she came. They tell me she writes poetry."

"I too dislike it," said Ann, who had recognized Marianne Moore from the description and was reciting the first line of "Poetry," her best-known poem. Stengel now made an exit.

"How that man can proustify," Paula remarked to Ann.

The nephew perked up his ears.

"You use that word, too I thought that it was just our family. It means talking in long sentences and being overly polite, right? Aunt Catherine says it comes from the name of a boy Ward knew in France, the one he tried to get interested in baseball."

Paula knew much more of the story.

"He was one of France's most famous writers. Once a man from the University of Illinois came by our house looking for his letters to Aunt Helen, but we never found any. Some people say he wrote the greatest book ever."

"Nonsense," said Courtney III. The greatest book ever written was *The Chicago White Sox* by Warren Brown who is sitting next to me, but I would have said that even if he weren't right here."

"I guess it's all rather subjective," Ann said politely. "Our family used to use the word to describe Uncle Timothy's friend Jim O'Rourke. Anyway, Proust was one of the friends Helen and John made in Paris."

"So they did get back to Paris?" asked Mrs Courtney who wanted more love story and less literary discussion. "Did they get back together?"

Ward's nephew interrupted.

"Ward married my Aunt Catherine. They met on the golf course, and they were perfect for each other. They raised hunting dogs together on Long Island. She was a great golfer, and so was he. He was a member of the golf club at Augusta. He was on a golf vacation in Georgia when he died right after his 65th birthday. Today was the first I ever heard of this Helen Dauvray."

Lee Allen had something to add here.

"Your aunt wrote me a very nice letter that she sent along with several newspaper clippings. Mrs. Ward knew almost nothing about Ward's first marriage, except that he had been married to a woman named Ida Gibson whose stage name was Helen Dauvray and that he had mentioned her only once in the course of their marriage. I had been trying to find Ward's sister Clara until someone told me he never had a sister. Mrs. Ward said he was angry whenever he heard of someone named Clara."

"That must have been our Aunt Clara, Uncle Timothy's wife," Paula added. "She was Helen Dauvray's sister. I think we might be able to fill you in on the end of the story because Aunt Clara always kept up with the doings of her sister, and Maxine Elliott too for that matter. Our mother continued the scrapbook after Aunt Clara left Uncle Tim. We never found out why because he never talked about it."

"What happened when Ward met Helen went in Paris?" Mrs Courtney asked.

"Before the 1891 season, they went all around Europe together, especially Paris. They even made a trip to Malta. Then they came back to New York, and for a while they kept up their life as married people living apart. Aunt Clara was in New York often because Uncle Timothy was playing with the Giants, the team they named after him and his friends because they were so tall. But finally, Helen got tired of it and decided to go ahead with the New York divorce. That was in 1893."

"Who committed adultery?" asked Mr. Courtney, whose interest was now aroused.

"Ward. Two part-time private detectives followed Ward out of Nick Engel's place, and saw him meet a stout lady and they went to the United States Hotel and registered for a room. For two hours, they took turns looking through the transom. It was all in the papers."

"Was the woman Jessie?" asked Mrs. Courtney.

"No. The woman's name was never made public. We heard that she was a French tutor Ward had hired because he thought improving his French accent was the key to winning Helen back."

"Then it wasn't adultery at all," Ward's nephew said for the defense.

"Not until after a two hour lesson, but then the detectives saw the both of them strip to their skivvies." Ann said. "It must have been language tutoring of the sort Lord Byron recommended in *Don Juan*."

"Was Helen having Ward followed?" asked Mr. Courtney.

"No," Ann was quick to answer. "She refused to pay the detectives anything, just went ahead and subpoenaed them. Her lawyers won the case and made Ward pay for everything, including three years of Helen's hotel bills. But after the divorce, Helen made sure he got the money back, and he kept some property. Aunt Clara thought she gave away too much. Aunt Clara also said that Ward blamed her for the divorce because Ward always blamed someone else for his own troubles."

"Whatever became of Jessie McDermott?" asked Mr. Courtney. "Did Ward go back to her?"

"As far as we know, Ward never saw her again, but Helen did. The year after the divorce Helen was asked to perform in a benefit performance of 'The Prodigal

Daughter.' Jessie McDermott, now calling herself Maxine Elliott, was in the same cast. She had been building a successful career. After she had scandalized the town in Maine, she went out to California, but she came back and studied under Dion Boucicault, the one whose daughter Nina was the original Peter Pan in London. Boucicault died right after that. Aunt Clara said it was because he was sixty-eight years old and being with Jessie would have killed any old man. After that she found other producers willing to take a chance on her, and soon she had roles all over Broadway. Anyway, for five nights, Helen appeared with Maxine on stage, and Aunt Clara went every night. She said it was her sister's greatest performance."

"Did this Maxine have anything to do with the Maxine Elliott Theater?" asked Mrs. Courtney.

"Named after her. J. P. Morgan bought it for her for reasons we can only guess at. She had married Nat Goodwin, and they moved to England where she had dozens of lovers, including a former prime minister, a Rothschild, Lord Curzon, and maybe King Edward VII."

"Sounds like gossip to me," Ward's nephew ventured.

"I'm only counting some of the ones her husband mentioned in his autobiography. And now her niece has just published a book called *My Aunt Maxine* and listed all her lovers down to the tennis player she took up with in old age."

Ann reached in her oversize purse and took out a hardback book. On its dust jacket was a picture of a beautiful woman in a bored pose.

"Then she did have Helen's career in theater, after all," Mrs. Courtney added.

"And better. According to her niece she worked her way up the ladder by caring about nothing but costumes and how her hair looked. And she became a terrific snob. She had the Duke and Duchess of Windsor as house guests, and Winston Churchill too, at her house at Cap Antibes. She played cards with Noel Coward, Cole Porter and Elsa Maxwell. And after she quit acting, she devoted herself to eating. She weighed 230 lbs. by the time she died."

"So what became of Helen?" Mrs Courtney asked Ann, who seemed to know all the gossip.

"She stayed off the stage for a while, then went to Australia where she met Admiral Albert Winterhalter, and they were married and she didn't perform again until after he died in 1922, and that was only briefly. She was about 65, but no one ever knew her real age, not even Aunt Clara. Then Helen died shortly after her husband. I don't know who was her heir."

Courtney wanted to steer the conversation back to baseball.

"What did Ward do between the time he won the Temple Cup and when he died with his boots on? And what became of the players union? And what became of the old guys he played with?"

Allen had a response.

"Let's walk over to the Hall. I have a key, and you all might like a walk through the gallery of baseball's greatest museum at this time of night."

54

Baseball's Greatest Players
Hall of Fame Gallery, Cooperstown
July 27, 1964

"**A**unt Catherine says that Ward named the Polo Grounds after his hunting dog," the young man said.

Warren Brown knew the most about Ward's career, and he intervened here.

"That story isn't true because the name the Polo Grounds was used before Ward got to New York. Ward did like to make claims that can't always be substantiated. At various times he said he invented the pitcher's mound, the hit and run, and backing up bases for overthrows. But there were a lot of others claiming the same things. Anyway, he was almost elected president of the National League around 1910, then he became president of the Boston Braves. Later he became a part owner of a Federal League team, but mostly he just played golf. He became one of the top players in the United States."

Courtney had another question, this time for Allen.

"What about the issues he raised, like the reserve clause. Are the players today treated any better?"

"Oh my yes," answered Allen who drew his pay from organized baseball. "Some of the stars make $100,000 a year, and even the lowest paid gets $6000. The players today have nothing to complain about."

Courtney disagreed, having given the matter some thought.

"That minimum salary has stayed the same since 1948. The players today need a union. They never got rid of the reserve clause, and now the owners are talking about a player draft, so that a team can pick you when you're eighteen and pay you whatever they want for the rest of your career."

"Here we are at the Hall," Allen said. He had used his expense account to pay for the modestly priced dinner, so he felt he had a right to set the agenda, and he was not about to get into a discussion of players' rights. "Let's look at the plaques of the fellows we've been talking about. I'll tell you what I know, and if you have any questions, you can ask. The gallery has a special feel at night when there's no one here but us and the ghosts. I can tell you a few facts or a few stories about the members as we read their plaques."

Henry Chadwick

Baseball's preeminent pioneer writer for half a century. Inventor of the box score. Author of the first rule-book. In 1858 Chairman of Rules Committee in first nation-wide baseball organization.

"He was an Englishman and he loved to claim that baseball came from the English game rounders. This put him at odds with Mr. Spalding."

Warren Brown had to step in.

"Chadwick only defied Spalding on history. When it came to the Players League, Chadwick took the National League side. The one who gave the players a fair shake was J. G. Taylor Spink. The writers named their award after him, the one that they gave the late Hugh Fullerton yesterday. Fullerton was writer who started exposing the fix of the 1919 world series when Comiskey was trying to cover it up."

"Anyway," Allen continued, "Chadwick went on the tour with Ward and comes up a lot in our story, even if he wasn't a player. Here's another fellow who's better known for something other than his playing."

Connie Mack

A star catcher but famed more as manager of the Philadelphia Athletics since 1901. Winner of 9 pennants and 5 world championships. Received the Bok Award in Philadelphia for 1929.

"Mack was with Buffalo in the Players League, and he went on to own the Philadelphia Athletics, managing them for fifty years as Mr. Stengel said. You could look it up. I remember seeing him in his coat and tie on the bench."

Dan Brouthers

Hard-hitting first baseman of eight major league clubs. He was part of the original "Big Four" of Buffalo. Traded with other members of that combination to Detroit, he hit .419 as that city won its only National League Championship in 1887.

"What a hitter he was. He was one of the officers in the Brotherhood, and he was the best hitter on the best team in the Players League. He led the National League in hitting in 1889. But no one ever wrote a song about him, and hardly anyone knows how to pronounce his name. But they all remember the king."

Mike J. (King) Kelly

Colorful player and audacious base-runner. In 1887 for Boston he hit .394 and stole 84 bases. His sale for $10,000 was one of the biggest deals of baseball's early history.

"'Slide, Kelly, Slide' was one of the first phonograph records. He died at 36, the year after he quit playing. No one ever had a funeral like Mike's. Ward helped organize it and collected for the widow. All the players went over to the Two Kels after it was over."

James H. O'Rourke

"Orator Jim" played ball until he was past fifty, including twenty-one major league seasons. An outfielder and catcher for the Boston Red Stockings of 1873. He later wore the uniforms of the championship Providence team of 1879, Buffalo, New York, and Washington.

"Oh, we knew him, too " Ann almost squealed.

"He was the one we learned the word "proustify" about. Uncle Tim must have picked it up from Ward," Paula added.

Allen recovered the floor.

"That makes sense because Orator Jim O'Rourke was an attorney, like Ward. He was one of the best players in professional baseball from 1872 until just about when he died. After he was through in the majors, he played minor league ball in Connecticut. He was also the league commissioner. One time he swore at an umpire and stopped the game to fine himself $5. They brought him back for one game in the majors when he was fifty-four, and he got a hit. Let's move over to the class of 1939. You'll recognize some of the names there.

W. M. B. "Buck" Ewing

Greatest 19th Century catcher. Giant in stature and Giant captain of New York's first National League Champions 1888 and 1889. Was genius as field leader. Unsurpassed in throwing to bases. Great long-range hitter. National League career 1881-1899. Troy, New York Giants and Cleveland; Cincinnati manager.

"This was another teammate of Keefe and Ward. Some said he was the best player of his era back when catchers were the popular stars. He was captain of the Giants on and off during the time Ward was with them."

"Did Ward ever forgive him?" Courtney asked.

Warren Brown answered after Allen turned to him.

"When Ward became manager of New York in 1893, he traded him, but that was as a favor to Buck. Ward couldn't really hold a grudge."

"Except against Aunt Clara," Ann interposed.

"But Ward sent Ewing off wishing him well. He still blamed him for bringing the NL owners and PL backers together, but he managed to put it behind him. When Buck died young, Ward was there to help the widow with funeral expenses. He even liked his nemesis, this next fellow"

Adrian Constantine Anson
"Cap"

Greatest hitter and greatest National League player-manager of 19th Century. Started with Chicagos in National League's first year. Chicago manager from 1879-1897 winning 5 pennants. Was .300 class hitter 20 years, batting champion 4 times.

"This was another one who went on the tour with Ward. Cap was the best hitter of his era, and his era lasted a long time. He had more hits, more games played and a higher batting average than any other player in the 19th Century."

"Wasn't he the one who refused to play with Blacks and made baseball a segregated disgrace?" asked Courtney who was aware of the importance of civil rights.

Warren Brown knew the most about his fellow Chicagoan.

"He wasn't the only one. After he retired from baseball he might have had a change of heart because he began to umpire in the colored leagues in Chicago. And he had a career in politics."

"City Clerk," said Courtney, who followed such things. "When my grandfather moved to Chicago, he became a White Sox fan because he always associated Anson with the Cubs."

"Speaking of Chicago, this next plaque should be special to you."

Charles A. Comiskey
"The Old Roman"

Started 50 years of baseball as St. Louis Browns first-baseman in 1882 and was the first man at this position to play away from the bag for batters. As Browns' manager-captain-player won 4 straight American Association pennants, starting 1885. World Champions first two years. Owner and president Chicago White Sox 1900-1931.

"If you're White Sox fans, you know all about the founder."

"Just because you're a White Sox fan doesn't make you a fan of the cheapskate Comiskeys. My father always said he was in with Monte Tennes and other gamblers, and that he just pretended to be shocked over the World Series. When Joe Jackson tried to confess, Comiskey told him to shut up, and when he did confess in front of a grand jury, Comiskey had the transcript stolen. But my grandfather said he was a great first baseman."

Allen wanted to return to his tour.

And this next plaque is another baseball pioneer.

Albert Goodwill Spalding

Organizational genius of baseball's pioneer days. Star pitcher of Forest City Club in late 1860's, 4-year champion Bostons 1871-1875 and manager-pitcher of champion Chicagos in National League's first year. Chicago president for 10 years, organizer of baseball's first round-the-world tour in 1888.

"In the early days of baseball, he might have been the best hitter, and he was certainly the best pitcher. But he gave up playing and dedicated himself to the growth of the National League and the Chicago National League team. He made baseball world famous and the national pastime. Even today we call balls spaldeens, and in Cuba they use the word *espaldiños*. He also helped establish that baseball was invented by Abner Doubleday here in Cooperstown."

"Oh please," said Courtney. I bet that Spalding wanted to make it seem that baseball was invented by Doubleday because they were both theosophists."

Allen moved over to a blank space in the wall and picked up a facsimile of the plaques that would be there.

Timothy J. Keefe
1880-1893

Righthander who won 346 games for Troy, Mets, Giants, and Phils in only 14 seasons. His record streak of 19 straight triumphs paced Giants to Flag in 1888. One of first pitchers to use a change of pace delivery.

"Here is where we'll put your uncle's plaque. He may have been the best pitcher of his era, and if he wasn't, his friend Smiling Mickey Welch was."

Brown had a story to add.

"He was probably even a stronger union man than Ward. After he quit playing, he became an umpire, but after a few years he quit in the fifth inning of a game, fed up with the way players behaved. He seems to have had a good career after baseball in the real estate business."

Paula knew this first hand.

"He built a beautiful house in Cambridge that we still live in. Aunt Clara was always nice to everyone, and she and Uncle Tim seemed as about as happy as an old couple could be until she left. We never found out why. I don't know what Ward had against her."

"And now we come to him."

John Montgomery Ward
1878-1894

Pitching pioneer who won 158, lost 102 games in seven years. Pitched perfect game for Providence of N.L. in 1880. Turned to shortstop and made 2,151 hits. Managed New York and Brooklyn in N.L. President of Boston, N.L. 1911-1912. Played an important part in establishing modern organized baseball.

"Before he hurt his arm, he was one of the best pitchers in baseball, leading the league in earned run average one year and in wins the next. Then he was an outfielder who led the league in assists, and when his arm got a little better, he was the best shortstop in baseball. He still holds the record for the most stolen bases in a season, although they calculated that differently back then."

"And not a word about the Players League," Courtney noticed.

Ward's nephew had been examining a set of statistics that were on display.

"He led the league in pitching, like Sandy Koufax. And he seems to have had an outfield arm like Roberto Clemente. And he was the best fielding shortstop, like Luis Aparicio. And he stole more bases than Maury Wills."

"They'll all be here some day," said Allen, who expected to usher them in. "Who else do you think should be here, Mr. Brown? Now that Ward is in, who are we going to campaign for."

"I think the Hall should include Bob Ferguson. He was the first switch hitter, the president of the league that preceded the National League and the best and most courageous umpire of his day. He managed several of the other fellows we talked about today. Who do you think belongs, Mr. Allen?"

"My opinion has changed lately. There was a fellow around here writing a book after he had interviewed as many old timers from around 1900 as he could find. His son recorded them on a tape machine. *The Glory of Their Times.* I've read the manuscript, and the name that keeps coming up is Dummy Hoy. All the players respected him, He belongs here for a lot of reasons. What do you think, Mr. Courtney?"

Having his opinion solicited on an issue of this importance was the best moment of the best baseball vacation imaginable.

"I think Deacon Jim White belongs here. If you keep people out for bad character, they should get credit for good. And he was a good union man. 'Nobody should sell my carcass without me getting a share.'"

Allen was pleased.

"White collected papers about the early days of baseball and donated them to a baseball museum before there was a Hall of Fame. And he was probably the best player of the 1870's. There was a lot of criticism when he wasn't included in the first class and again when he wasn't in the first old-timers class. But now people seem to have forgotten about him."

By this time, they had walked back to the hotel and were seated on the swings on the front porch Ward's nephew had one more question.

"If Ward pitched like Koufax, threw like Clemente, stole bases like Wills and fielded like Aparicio, wouldn't that make him the greatest player ever?"

"Let's ask Mr. Stengel," said Mrs. Courtney who was the first to notice that Stengel had changed into a summer suit and was also sitting on the porch. "Mr. Stengel, these people want to know who was the greatest baseball player ever. Do you have any thoughts on who would help you win the most games? Who was the greatest player?"

"If you judge just by hitting, which most people do, then you'd have to say Cobb, but Joe Jackson was just as good a hitter as anyone who saw them both would tell you, and that Appling fellow they put in yesterday could hit foul balls until the pitcher's arm fell off, but Cobb ran the bases faster and smarter than Jackson, but you asked who would win a game, like for me it was Mr. Ford, so I might have to say Captain Mathewson who was also a good model for youth, but on a late afternoon with shadows, Walter Johnson's fastball was the best, and he never threw at night, God help the hitters, but maybe it was Cy Young that Mr. Ward traded for, you could look it up, but only after he had already won all his games, but you said best player, and that usually means someone whose name you write every day, like I did Mantle, but some said the colored fellow across town was even better because Mays could catch the ball like Speaker and hit it a lot farther, not just doubles, which is what people want, which would make that Negro League fellow Josh Gibson the best, and he was a good catcher too, but it is about hitting, and that fellow from Boston who wrote the book about hitting might have been the greatest, but the rules said between at bats you have to go out in the field, not catch fish or fly airplanes, but I never saw a better hitter than Williams who hit .400 long after they stopped hitting .400, you could look it up, but Arlie Latham was one of my coaches, and he went a lot farther back, and he said the best he ever saw was Dimaggio, but Latham wasn't afraid to lie, and Dimaggio was still around while a lot of the others were dead and could do nothing for Arlie, but Dimaggio might have been the best because he married the best-looking woman, but the best players are usually in the infield, so Gorgeous George Sisler might have been the best because he threw with his left hand which meant first base was all the infield he could play, but starting a team with a good left-handed throwing first baseman is something I always wanted to do, but Hornsby was an even better hitter and hit more home runs, but he couldn't catch a pop fly and was too stubborn to get out of the way and let someone else do it, and this Aaron fellow is as good from one year to the next as any I have ever seen, but he's not the best ever, not yet."

"Then who is?" asked Mrs. Courtney.

"Babe Ruth. Everyone knows that. Pitch, field until he got too fat, throw, run, hit, hit for power, talk to kids, and fill the stands. I'm afraid I have to be off to bed. It's been nice talking with you folks."

"How did you like your trip to the birthplace of baseball, Mr. Courtney?" Allen asked the fan who had donated all of his grandfather's score cards to the Hall.

"Well, we both know that Cooperstown is not where baseball was born, but as long as baseball lives, this museum will stay open. And if it ever closes, that will mean that baseball has come to Cooperstown to die."

List of Characters
(HOF indicates Hall of Fame)

Baseballists (team in 1889 and 1890)

Adrian Anson HOF: Chicago National League
Dan Brouthers HOF: Boston National League, Boston Players League
John Clarkson HOF: Boston National League
Charlie Comiskey HOF: St. Louis American Association, Chicago Players League
Roger Connor HOF: New York National League, New York Players League
Cannonball Crane: New York National League, New York Players League
Buck Ewing HOF: New York National League, New York Players League
Ned Hanlon HOF: Pittsburg National League, Pittsburg Players League
William Hoy: Washington National League, Buffalo Players League
Timothy Keefe HOF: New York National League, New York Players League
King Kelly HOF: Boston National League, Boston Players League
Arlie Latham: St. Louis American Association, Chicago Players League
Connie Mack HOF: Washington National League, Buffalo Players League
Jim O'Rourke HOF: New York National League, New York Players League
Fred Pfeffer: Chicago National League, Chicago Players League
John Ward HOF: New York National League, Brooklyn Players League
Mickey Welch HOF: New York National League
Deacon White: Pittsburg National League, Buffalo Players League
Ed Williamson: Chicago National League, Chicago Players League

Other Characters

Henry Chadwick HOF: Journalist, sometimes known as the father of baseball
Stephanie Cowell: *Cosmopolitan* writer
Helen Dauvray: Ward's wife, actress and producer
Clarence Duval: Chicago mascot on world tour
Freddy Engel: Giant batboy and son of tavern owner
Ludovic Halévy: friend of Helen's in Paris
Clara Helms: Helen's sister, eventually Keefe's wife
DeWolf Hopper: Broadway actor famed for reciting "Casey at the Bat"
George McDermott: irate husband
Jessie McDermott: aspiring actress involved with Ward, later known as Maxine Elliott
Marcel Proust: French friend of Helen and Ward, wants to be a writer
Albert Spalding HOF: baseball owner, businessman, former star, leader of the world tour

Fictional Characters

Knowledgeable Crank (K.C.)
Bernie, the honest accountant

Historical Note

By definition historical fiction blends fact and invention, so an author's note should help the reader distinguish history from fiction. Seen from another point of view, such a note gives the author a chance to confess.

With the exception of the game in Cuba, the baseball games occurring every third chapter are reported much as they happened, according to box scores and accounts of the games. Just as Harry Caray and Ronald Reagan began their careers reconstructing baseball games from bare facts, the author has added flourishes and imagined line drives or bloopers when a base hit was all that was attested. Needless to say, all conversations with Knowledgeable Crank are fictional, as are most of the people he talks with.

As to the personal lives of Ward, Helen. Keefe and Clara, I have followed the outline of their lives as led in the newspapers but taken liberties with the characterization and dialogue. Clara was widowed, not divorced, and she was rumored to have been involved with Keefe earlier than I indicated. The only connection between Helen and the friends I describe in Paris was Ludovic Halévy whose son and his circle was more or less as I described it. With the character of Clara, the only facts I worked around were that she was a sculptress, was divorced and then married Keefe within the time frame of the book, and she seems to have had a pronounced antipathy to Ward which was returned. As to Jessie McDermott, later known as Maxine Elliott, a great deal has been written, particularly her niece's biography mentioned in the text. Stephanie Cowell's fable about Ward and Helen did appear in *Cosmoplitan,* and the quotes are exact.

The events that led to the establishment and subsequent dissolution of the Players League are largely based on historical research although the characterizations of the players are mostly imagined and the dialogue is all invented except for Ward's "Once the league stood for fair dealing. . ."

Biographies

As you read these biographies, you will see the letters HOF after some of the individuals named. These stand for Hall of Fame and indicate that the person has been voted into it. The Hall of Fame in Cooperstown, New York did not open until 1939, but since then it has been an integral part of baseball at all levels. Virtually every amateur player fantasizes about a successful major league career ending in induction to the Hall. Speculation about who will be voted in is the most widely discussed topic in the game and figures in discussions about championships, player statistics, gambling and illegal steroid use. These biographies are numbered 1-54 and correspond to the featured character in each chapter.

1

John Montgomery Ward (HOF) was an outstanding pitcher for Providence at the age of 18, leading the league in earned run average in his first year. He later led the league in wins, winning percentage, shutouts, and strikeouts at various times. After hurting his arm, he became a star shortstop. He captained the All-Americas on Spalding's 1888-9 World Tour and demonstrated baseball in Australia, Egypt, Italy and France among other places. Ward was married to the Broadway actress and producer Helen Dauvray, the donor of the Dauvray Cup symbolic of the world's championship. His involvement with a young married woman, Jessie McDermott, who later became a Broadway star under the name Maxine Elliott, was the cause of some scandal during his playing days with the New York Giants. Ward earned a law degree from Columbia University while playing with New York Ward was the founder of the Brotherhood of Professional Base Ball Players (BPBBP), an early players' union which eventually broke away from the National League (NL) and in 1890 formed the Players League (PL). Ward went on to serve as a manager team president and a part owner after his playing career.

2

Timothy Keefe (HOF) was a standout pitcher through the 1880s. His nickname was Sir Timothy in tribute to his gentlemanly manner and handsome appearance. He served as secretary-treasurer of the BPBBP. During the 1889 season he married Helen Dauvray's sister Clara, a sculptor. Keefe partnered with Buck Becannon to form a sporting goods business which manufactured baseballs and uniforms. He studied bookkeeping and was a skilled carpenter who built his house in Cambridge, Mass. After his playing career was over, he became an umpire, but the consequent abuse caused him to retire in the middle of a game.

3

Albert Spalding (HOF) was the best pitcher at the time of the founding of the NL in 1876. He was also among the leading hitters. He became the owner of the Chicago White Stockings and the Spalding and Brothers Sporting goods company which manufactured the baseballs used in the National League as well as a variety of other sporting equipment. He organized and led a tour of the world in the 1888-9 off-season. He took the lead for NL owners in resisting the demands of the BPBBP and kept the league together after the desertion of most of the star players to the PL. He wrote *America's National Game* and was a leader in the movement to credit the invention of baseball to Abner Doubleday in spite of considerable evidence to the contrary. Later in life, he moved to California where he was an unsuccessful candidate for the U.S. Senate. He also became involved in the theosophist movement.

4

Edward "Dirty Ned" Hanlon (HOF) was an outstanding outfielder and a clever baseball strategist. He was a friend of Ward's from the early days of his career and was active in securing financing for the PL, particularly of the Pittsburg team which he managed. He went on to manage the famous Baltimore Orioles of the 1890s, noted for an aggressive brand of roughneck ball.

5

Mike "King" Kelly (HOF) was a flamboyant player who was probably the most popular player of his era, the subject of the song "Slide, Kelly, Slide." His propensity for stretching the rules led to changes in baseball practices. Some say that the customs of asking players for their autographs began with Kelly. His autobiography entitled *Play Ball* was the first by a baseball player. There is speculation that the book was ghostwritten or, at least co-authored by Jake Morse of the *Boston Herald*. Kelly had a reputation as a heavy drinker, one of the reasons that Spalding sold him to Boston for the unprecedented sum of $10,000, earning him the name of the $10,000 beauty. He was advertised as a participant in the Spalding tour, but he never showed up.

6

Jimmy Fogarty was a fine defensive outfielder known for his practical jokes and exuberant attitude. On the Spalding tour he was the leader of "The Order of the Howling Wolves." He was a native of California. Known as a cigarette fiend, he died of consumption in 1891.

7

Ulysses Frank Grant (HOF) was an African American infielder who played for Buffalo of the International League from 1886-8. Some considered him the best second baseman of his time and the best black player of the Nineteenth Century. Resented by his teammates and some of opposing players, he was frequently the victim of spiking, so much so that he was sometimes moved to the outfield. He went on to play for the Cuban Giants, the first great black club in baseball history. The Hall of Fame had intended to establish a separate wing for the Negro players who were active before the color bar, but an eloquent speech made by Ted Williams on the occasion of his induction put an end to this horrendous idea.

8

Adrian "Cap" Anson (HOF) was one of the leading hitters in the National Association (NA) and later of the NL when it was founded. He managed the Chicago White Stockings from 1879-1897. His refusal to play against Black players is said to have led to the color bar. His quote "Get that nigger off the field" in response to the presence of Fleet Walker is remembered as the moment that began the process of baseball segregation. After his playing career he was elected clerk of the city of Chicago.

9

Clarence Duval was the Chicago White Stockings' mascot during the 1888 season until he left to join a traveling show. He was an African-American of very short stature, considered to be a hoodoo, one whose job was to bring bad luck to the other team. Duval's path crossed the Spalding tourists, and he joined the trip around the world. He dressed in something like a drum major's uniform and performed "plantation dances," seen as related to the minstrel shows of the 19th Century.

10

John Tener was a pitcher for the White Stockings whom Spalding employed as a sort of a business manager on the world tour. Born in Ireland, his family moved to Pittsburg when he was nine. He played on the Pittsburg team of the PL. His playing career was not particularly distinguished. In 1908 he was elected to Congress where he organized the first Congressional Baseball Game between Democrats and Republicans, a tradition which continues to this day. He was later elected governor of Pennsylvania as a Republican. While he was governor, he was chosen as president of the NL and held both jobs for a while.

11

James "Buck" Becannon's playing career was brief and undistinguished. After working in Spalding's sporting goods company, he went into partnership with Tim Keefe who had been his teammate on the 1884 New York Metropolitans of the American Association. Keefe and Becannon manufactured uniforms and provided the baseballs which became the standard for the PL in 1890. In answer to charges that Ward had favored his brother-in-law and fellow union officer, it was asserted that the company had made the low bid. After the demise of the league, Becannon fell out with Keefe, and their partnership ended in lawsuits.

12

Henry Chadwick (HOF) was an English-born journalist who was recognized as the leading authority on baseball, having developed many of the statistical measurements such as batting averages and earned runs. As a historian of baseball's origins, he contended that the game was a descendant of the British game rounders which he had played in his youth. One of his pet ideas was that low-scoring games were aesthetically superior. As the editor of the annual *Spalding Guide*, he exerted an influence on how people thought about the game. During the year of the PL, he sided with Spalding and the National League, rather predictably since he was on Spalding's payroll.

13

Fred Pfeffer was one of the outstanding second basemen of his era. He was known as a fast runner and the winner of some long throw contests. Born in Louisville, Kentucky, Pfeffer lived in Chicago where he was part of that city's large German-American population. He wrote a book called *Scientific Baseball* and conducted what may have been the first baseball academy. After the founding of the PL, he worked with Ward to begin a business of selling scorecards.

14

John Brush was the owner of the Indianapolis franchise and the author of a player classification scheme designed to limit player salaries. He also advocated strong efforts to reduce the use of profanity by players. He later owned the Cincinnati Reds and the New York Giants.

15

Jimmy Ryan was one of the leading outfielders of the period, a rising star who had made an impression as one of the better players of the league almost immediately after he joined the Chicago NL team. In addition to being a fine center fielder, he was one of the strongest hitters in the league.

16

Ed "Cannobnball" Crane had a reputation as a total abstainer from alcohol when he came to the major leagues, but on the Spalding tour he began to drink and subsequently had troubles with alcohol which may have led to his suicide at an early age. He was discovered while playing professional baseball in Toronto and arrived in New York during a record snowstorm.

17

Ed Williamson was widely recognized as one of the top players of his time. His 27 home runs in 1884, aided by an extremely short fence in right field, stood as a record for a long time, although few people paid much attention to it back then. He never hit more than eight in any other season. He was unusually popular among the other players. He met his wife Nelly during a barnstorming trip to New Orleans. After his injury in Paris, he never recovered his skills, and he was soon out of the game. Billy Sunday used to point out in his sermons that Williamson had led a dissolute life, leading to his early death.

18

DeWolf Hopper was an independently wealthy young man who had become a fixture in the New York theater scene. He and his friend and partner Digby Bell were prominent New York Giant fans, sometimes arriving at games conspicuously in a Tally Ho coach. Hopper claimed to have recited "Casey at the Bat" over 10,000 times before his death in 1935, beginning with an 1888 performance of the poem at the Warrick Theater on a special baseball night attended by New York and Chicago players as well as General William Sherman. Hollywood gossip columnist Hedda Hopper was his fifth wife. Their son William DeWolf Hopper Jr. played Paul Drake on the Perry Mason television show.

19

Roger Connor (HOF), nicknamed "our dear Roger," hit more career home runs than any other Nineteenth Century player. His total of 139 home runs remained the highest until Babe Ruth surpassed it in 1921. Connor began his career as a left-handed throwing third baseman until Bob Ferguson switched him to first base where throwing left-handed conferred an advantage. He also switched to batting left-handed. He married early in his baseball career, and all reports indicate happily.

20

Jim O'Rourke (HOF) was known as the Orator because he was given to long erudite sentences made resplendent by his sesquipedalian vocabulary. He held a law degree from Yale and was also a licensed civil engineer. His career began in the National Association and continued into the 20th Century when he made a brief courtesy appearance with John McGraw's Giants. He served as president of the Connecticut League and played into his fifties. On one occasion he swore at an umpire and stopped the game in order to fine himself $5.

21

Yank Robinson struck out rarely and reached base often, statistics which were only publicized long after he had died young of consumption. Owner Chris Von der Ahe was in a constant battle with Robinson over a number of issues all of which resulted in fines. In 1889 many of the Browns refused to leave for a road trip until one of Yank's fines was rescinded.

22

Hugh Duffy (HOF) was a rising star with the Chicago team who went on to several successful seasons, including one in which he achieved the highest batting average for any full major league season (.440). Although invited to go on the Spalding tour, he stayed home in order to study.

23

John Clarkson (HOF) was one of the best pitchers for Chicago and later Boston. In 1889 he started 72 of Boston's 128 games, a heavy burden even in that era. Like Tim Keefe, he came from Cambridge, Mass., and both learned to pitch under the tutelage of Tommy Bond who in turn had learned the curve ball from Candy Cummings, sometimes called the inventor of that pitch. Clarkson's family owned a jewelry business in which he worked during the offseason. Many players suspected that Clarkson had been a spy for Spalding, signing with the PL and even investing in the Boston team before rejoining Boston in the NL. In subsequent years he was frequently called a traitor, but he always denied the charges. He died in an insane asylum in 1909.

24

Chris Von der Ahe owned the St. Louis Browns and was one of the founders of the American Association. He was a prominent tavern owner and contributed to that league's reputation as the "Beer and Whiskey League." Although he was generally believed to understand very little about baseball, he interfered in management decisions. Players, especially Arlie Latham, made fun of his strong German accent. In spite of his unprepossessing appearance, he was involved in several affairs and complicated divorces. Unsurprisingly, he died broke, dependent on the charity of Charlie Comiskey, his former captain.

25

Harry Wright (HOF) was the most successful manager during the early years of professional baseball. In 1869 he managed the Cincinnati Reds, generally recognized as the first professional baseball team. His Boston team won the National Association pennant from 1872-1876, and the National League pennants in 1877-8. He was a professional cricket player, like his father and his younger brother George. Wright was a respected figure throughout baseball.

26

Pebbly Jack Glasscock was a star shortstop who received his nickname from his habit of cleaning the area around his position in order to avoid bad hops. He managed the Indianapolis team for part of the 1889 season. After signing with the PL, he broke his contract and signed with the NL New York team, reportedly influencing others to do so. For this he was named the Judas Goat.

27

Pete Browning was one of the strongest hitters in the American Association. According to legend, the Hillerich and Bradsby Company designed a bat for him which was subsequently called the Louisville Slugger. Browning suffered from severe mastoiditis, a painful condition which impaired his hearing and may have caused his mood swings. The Louisville owner fined him for going into a hitting slump. While not in the Hall of Fame, he is featured prominently in the Louisville Slugger Museum.

28

Billy Sunday became the most famous evangelical preacher of his day, best remembered for the lyric "the town that Billy Sunday could not shut down." Like his first manager, Cap Anson, he was from Marshalltown, Iowa. For a time he was Anson's pet, but he was released to Pittsburg before the 1888 season. During his sermons, he liked to draw attention to how his teammates Mike Kelly and Ed Williamson died young after leading lives of dissipation.

29

William "Buck" Ewing (HOF) was regarded as the best player of his day because of his strong hitting and fine catching. He ranked first in an 1889 newspaper poll to vote for the best player of the time, and he was recently voted the best player of the 19th Century. He was captain of the Giants before Ward arrived in 1883, and after a time became captain again. Ewing went to the PL, but he was instrumental in negotiations leading to the league's collapse. He died young, and Ward was among those who helped the widow with funeral expenses.

30

Dan Brouthers (HOF) was a leading hitter of his era. His family managed a hotel in Wappingers Falls, NY. Brouthers, one of the highest paid players, sometimes insisted on receiving his salary in silver dollars. Brouthers was one of the "Big Four," who moved from Buffalo to Detroit, and when Detroit disbanded, he was assigned to Boston. He served as vice-president of the Brotherhood.

31

Oliver "Patsy" Tebeau was called Patsy as an indication of his status as an honorary Irishman, although he was of French-German descent. He acquired his nickname while working with Irishmen in the construction industry, and he even spoke with a slight brogue. He managed the Cleveland team in the PL and went on to manage the Cleveland team in the NL. It was during his tenure that the team acquired the nickname "Indians" in tribute to Louis Sockalexis, a Native American member of the team. He was known for an aggressive style and an abusive attitude toward umpires.

32

Smilin' Mickey Welch (HOF) partnered with his close friend Tim Keefe to form the best 1-2 pitching rotation in baseball for many years. Welch was known for his doggerel verse and a fondness for beer, not to be seen as alcoholism. He was reaching the end of a successful career when he chose to stay with the NL in preference to the Brotherhood of which he had been a founding member. He worked for the Giants for many years after his playing career, and he remained close to Keefe until Sir Timothy died.

33

Arlie Latham was a defensive star for the St. Louis Browns, given to antics on the field and outrageous behavior as a base coach. As a third baseman, he ducked when hard line drives came his way, something that came to be called an "Arlie Latham." Comiskey and Von der Ahe accused him of hippodroming (throwing games intentionally) and suspended him in 1889. During his suspension, he attended Browns games and conspicuously cheered for the other team. Although not a drinker, he frequented saloons where betting on ball games was common. He was a brothel habitué and a wife beater, according to his divorce records. In 1900 he was hired as a coach, perhaps to spy on another attempt at a players' union. He had a long career as a coach and remained a fan favorite.

34

Robert Ferguson was a pioneer of the early game, serving as playing president of the National Association, the first major league. He managed eight different major league teams, including the White Stockings in 1878, although Spalding said that Ferguson lacked tact. He had a reputation as a shrewd judge of talent. A lifelong resident of Brooklyn, he was one of the well-paid professional umpires in the American Association and later umpired in the Players League. His nickname "Death to Flying Things" came from his habit of catching and killing flies while sitting on the bench.

35

Connie Mack (HOF) (born Cornelius McGuillicuddy) was a catcher. As a teammate and friend of William Hoy, he learned sign language, and they were both part owners of the Buffalo PL team. Mack later founded the Philadelphia team in the AL, and he served as their manager for 50 years, a record unlikely to be broken. He was the owner of the team. His name lives on in Connie Mack baseball. His grandson of the same name served as a U.S. senator from Florida, and his son, Connie Mack IV is as of this writing a Congressman.

36

Ed Delahanty (HOF) was the best of five brothers who played in the major leagues. After signing with the PL, he attempted to return to the NL, but in his case Ward chose to sue and was successful. Delahanty played with the Cleveland club of the PL. Known to have problems with alcohol, he met a mysterious end. In 1902, he was put off a train for being drunk, and later his body was found at the base of Horseshoe Falls on the Canadian side of Niagra Falls.

37

James "Pud" Galvin (HOF) was one of the star pitchers of the era, known as the "little steam engine." One of the first pitchers to spit on his hand, he may have been a predecessor of subsequent spitballers. He also let it be known that he used the Brown Séquard elixir which contained monkey testosterone, a precursor of anabolic steroids. He died broke at age 45.

38

John Day was a cigar manufacturer who owned the New York Metropolitans of the AA and the New York team in the NL, using the first team to enhance the second. Relatively popular with his players, he had a reputation for fair dealing when they were injured. The attendance war of 1890 nearly bankrupted him, and only loans from Spalding enabled his team to finish the season. He died broke, showing that players weren't the ones to whom this happened.

39

Jim White was a steady hitter and a star catcher in the National Association and was the leader of the Boston team which won pennants in the early NL. In the opinion of some experts, he would have won the MVP many times had there been such a thing then, and it was thought that he would be among the inductees of the first Hall of Fame class along with Ruth, Cobb, Mathewson, Johnson and Wagner. He had the habit of saving newspaper clippings and other records of the early game. He was called Deacon because of his strong Christian faith. When Detroit's team folded, he was assigned to Pittsburg, but he refused to report because he and Jack Rowe wanted to start a Buffalo team in the International League. Ward persuaded him to report to Pittsburg in mid-season, and he and Rowe were given the Buffalo franchise in the PL.

40

Freddy Engel, the son of the owner of the Home Plate Saloon, was a mascot for the Giants until 1887 until he was supplanted. When the Giants left New York in 1957, he was interviewed by the *New York Times*, and he remembered his days carrying messages from John Ward to Helen Dauvray, both of whom he remembered fondly. He also recalled Mickey Welch, whose poems he provided for posterity.

41

Davy Orr was a 250 pound batsman known for hard hitting and poor fielding. At one time he broke a leg saving a woman from a robber. He was arrested when playing Sunday ball for Columbus of the AA. After the 1890 season he suffered a debilitating stroke. Ward later gave him a job with a Federal League team.

42

Jake Beckley (HOF) was a rising star who signed with the PL and then tried to go back to the NL. Ward sued to hold him to his PL contract. One of his peculiarities was holding his bat upside down while bunting. He played well on into the next century.

43

Esteban "Steve" Bellàn was the first Latin American in major league baseball, playing in the National Association from 1871-3. He studied at St. John's College (later called Fordham) in New York City. He was nicknamed the "Cuban Sylph" because of his graceful play. After he returned to Cuba, he was active in baseball in Havana. He is sometimes called the "Father of Cuban Baseball."

44

Jim "Truthful James" Mutrie was the manager of the New York Giants, a role that is similar to general manager today. He was an excellent cricket player, and a longtime resident of Staten Island. He managed the New York Mets of the AA before switching to the NL Giants and managed Keefe, Ewing and others on both teams. He was given his nickname by Henry Chadwick, who used the term sarcastically. Mutrie usually gave in to Captain Ewing when there was a difference of opinion. Mutrie continued to manage the NY team in the NL in 1890.

45

Charles Comiskey (HOF) was the first baseman and captain of the St. Louis Browns and then the Chicago team in the PL. He was the son of a Chicago alderman known as "Honest John." Charles Comiskey, "the Old Roman," is known as the founder and owner of the Chicago White Sox and the builder of "the Baseball Palace of the World," also known as Comiskey Park which was the home of Chicago's American League team from 1910-1990. Between the 1913 and 1914 seasons, Comiskey and John McGraw (HOF) led an around the world tour. Unfortunately he is best remembered as the owner of the Black Sox, the team known for the conspiracy on the part of some of the players to lose the 1919 World Series intentionally.

46

Louis Bierbauer was a journeyman second baseman who had played for Philadelphia of the AA before joining Ward's Brooklyn team in the PL. When the PL folded, Bierbauer was awarded to the Pittsburg team of the NL, a move which alienated the AA and won the Pittsburg team the name of Pirates which they retain to this day. This controversy contributed to the alienation of the AA and its merger into the NL in 1892 when four teams joined the NL and the rest were disbanded.

47

Robert "Parisian Bob" Caruthers was a star with St. Louis of the AA before being sold to Brooklyn. When his teammate Doc Bushong went to France to study dentistry, Caruthers went along and by all accounts enjoyed himself and came away fluent in French. Handsome and from a wealthy Chicago family, Caruthers was a standout on the mound and at bat.

48

Danny Richardson was a versatile player who settled down at second baseman for the Giants. A good friend of Roger Connor, he blended in with the group of players who had played for Mutrie at Troy and New York. Richardson reported to Ward on the dealings between Buck Ewing and John Day which undermined the PL.

49

William "Dummy" Hoy was a deaf outfielder known as one of the cleverest players in baseball, as might be expected of the valedictorian of the Ohio School for the Deaf. Trained as a shoemaker, he went on to a successful career playing in four major leagues. (NL, PL, AA, AL) Some claim that the use of umpire signs originated for Hoy's benefit, but others deny it. He features prominently in *The Glory of Their Times*, an oral history made up of interviews with players from the beginning of the 20th Century. Hoy lived to be 99, and he appeared at Opening Day ceremonies in Cincinnati in 1961.

50

Silent Mike Tiernan was a speedy outfielder overshadowed by the six Hall of Famer he played with on the Giants. He stayed with the NY NL team in 1890, one of the few Giants to do so. Originally Tiernan was signed as a left-handed pitcher, but he was weakened by illness and unable to pitch, so he turned to the outfield.

51

Nick Engel was the owner of Nick Engel's Home Plate Saloon, the unofficial home of the New York Giants. Grilling three pound steaks and insisting that they be eaten without benefit of silverware was one of his many eccentricities. The walls of his saloon were covered with pictures of baseball stars, and it has been called the first sports bar.

52

Charles "Casey" Stengel (HOF) was known for leading the NY Yankees to an as of yet unmatched five consecutive World Series victories. Later in his career he managed the expansion New York Mets. He was known for a convoluted use of speech, often assuming that his listeners could intuit facts that he never mentioned. You could look it up.

53

Marianne Moore was a celebrated American poet who wrote such poems as "Baseball and Writing" in addition to her frequently anthologized poem "Poetry." She was a lifelong baseball fan, as can be seen on her comment at one game. Some fellow poets took her to a baseball game, hoping to find an area in which she was not an expert. While observing the game, she asked if the pitcher was Christy Mathewson and being informed that he was, she said she had not seen him before but had read his book on pitching and commented on how well his practice matched his theory. She was frequently seen at Mets games.

54

George Herman "Babe" Ruth (HOF) was an outstanding major league player who, like Ward, started out as a pitcher and switched to being a player in the field, in his case the outfield. He was known for home runs, a prodigious appetite and patience with children. He was among the first five players inducted into the Hall of Fame.

Baseball Then and Now

In each chapter there are some differences between baseball in those times and current practice. The following section explains these differences, assuming little knowledge of baseball then or now. These comparisons between baseball rules, customs, and finances at the time of the setting of this book and in the current era (2012) are numbered 1-54 and correspond to each chapter.

1

THEN

When the baseball was hit into the grandstand, it still belonged to management, and efforts were made to retrieve it. The expectation was that the game could be played with one ball which gradually became softened and less resilient, which is why some captains wanted their team to bat first when given the choice.

NOW

Balls are changed frequently in the course of the game. Fans are encouraged to keep balls hit into the stands. Optimistic fans sometimes bring gloves in the hopes of catching a foul ball or a home run. Players sometimes toss the ball from the last out into the stands. Careless players like Milton Bradley occasionally throw the ball from the second out into the stands, resulting in considerable embarrassment. Balls representing some milestone of achievement such as a player's 500th career home run are marked and retrieved and sometimes sent to the Hall of Fame.

2

THEN

The World's Championship Series was a series arranged between the champion of the National League and the winner of the American Association. There was no set format, so the series had to be arranged each year between 1884 and 1891. In 1887, before she was married to John Ward, Helen Dauvray donated a cup said to have been produced by Tiffany's which was awarded to the winner of the series, with the provision that a team winning three straight series would take permanent possession. Gold medals were also awarded to the winners of the 1887 series. The Dauvray Cup seems to have disappeared, but a few of the gold medals still exist, and two of them are in the Hall of Fame. In 1888 it was agreed that the teams would play a ten game series with the winner being the first team to win six games, with an eleventh game to be scheduled if neither team had won six. Even after the winner's sixth victory, the series was to continue for ten games.

NOW

The pretentiously named World Series is a formal affair between the winners of the National League and the American League, played until one team has won four games. The winning team receives the Commissioner's Trophy, designed each year. The series has been played every year since 1903 with the exception of 1904 when John McGraw (HOF), manager of the National League champion Giants, refused to meet the upstart AL and 1994 when a players' strike had canceled the last part of the season.

3

THEN

Players traveled between games by rail, usually with Pullman cars. All NL teams used the Michigan Central which was owned by the New York Central to travel between Boston, New York City, Philadelphia, Washington D.C., Pittsburg, Cleveland, Indianapolis and Chicago.

NOW

Major league teams usually travel in chartered airliners. Some teams own their own planes. Teams are located throughout the United States from Seattle to Miami with one team in Toronto.

4

THEN

Three outs made up a half-inning and nine innings made a game unless interrupted by rain or darkness. Five balls were required for a walk, although this was changed to four before the 1889 season. Walking a player intentionally was rare and frowned upon by the fans.

NOW

There are still three outs in an inning and nine innings in a game unless shortened by rain. With the installation of lights in all parks, games are no longer called because of darkness. After four balls a player gets a walk, entitling him or her to first base. Walking a player on purpose is now rather common, either to set up a double play, avoid a strong hitter or to bring a weak hitter to the plate. This is now called an intentional base on balls, and it is still frowned upon by the fans who often boo, especially when a hometown favorite is avoided by this cowardly maneuver.

5

THEN

Players put on their uniform at home or at the hotel if they were on the road. Sometimes the trip to the ballpark was a ceremony designed to stimulate interest, especially before the first game of a road series or an exhibition game. Requesting a player's autograph was a new phenomenon.

NOW

The peculiar custom of begging for signatures has spread beyond baseball, and autograph seekers are a nuisance to a number of famous and not so famous people. Today baseball players arrive at the ball park in street clothes well before game time and dress in locker rooms. Signing autographs before games is considered a duty, usually assigned to a few players each game. The willingness to sign autographs is often used as a measure of a player's affability. Autographs are sometimes collected, bought and sold and a monetary value can be assigned to them. Players, particularly retired ones like Pete Rose (notice the lack of initials), participate in autograph shows where autographs are shamelessly sold for cash.

6

THEN

Owners professed to be greatly distressed by players' drinking, sometimes inserting sobriety clauses in contracts. Nonetheless, the rate of alcoholism seems to have been high, as it was in the society as a whole.

NOW

Although alcoholism is still a problem among players and the society at large, the rates seem to have gone down. Drinking only becomes a concern when drunkenness results in auto accidents or arrests, which are followed by public penitence and promises of rehabilitation.

7

THEN

From 1884 to 1947 major league baseball excluded players who were known to have any African ancestry. Cap Anson had been instrumental in formulating this unwritten but strict policy when he refused to play an exhibition game against the Toledo AA team on which Fleetwood Walker played. He was quoted as saying, "Get that nigger off the field."

NOW

In 1947 Jackie Robinson (HOF) was the first acknowledge Black player since 1884. He encountered considerable resistance, similar to what Frank Grant had faced in the International League. Major league baseball has claimed great credit for this breakthrough, but if the truth were to be told, they were well behind the times, especially considering none of the teams at that time was in the Old Confederacy. Discrimination against people of color is said to exist still, but it is in front offices and managerial positions rather than on the field, and efforts are being made to correct that. Programs like Reviving Baseball in Inner Cities are designed to address the falling, but still substantial, percentage of African-Americans in the major leagues.

8

THEN

No major league teams played in California which was beyond the reach of timely transportation. There was a flourishing California League with a quality of competition said to be higher than the minor leagues in the National Agreement.

NOW

In 1957 the Brooklyn Dodgers and the New York Giants moved to Los Angeles and San Francisco respectively. Today there are six major league teams on the West Coast with locations easily reached by jet. Because games there are played later due to time differences, there is said to be a publicity gap which causes West Coast players to be undervalued, but this is largely in the provincial minds of the East Coast media.

9

THEN

Teams employed "hoodoos," not so much to bring themselves good luck as to create bad luck for their opponents. The word can apply to a person or a thing which is believed to bring bad luck, but in a game where one team wins and the other loses, bringing bad luck to an opponent is the same as bringing good luck to the other team.

NOW

Many teams employ furry mascots like the Phillie Phanatic or the Pittsburgh Parrot. These are usually people wearing costumes designed to make them look like stuffed animals. They walk through the stands signing autographs and are available (at a charge) for children's parties. As of this writing, no mascot has been elected to the Hall of Fame, not even the San Diego Chicken.

10

THEN

Pitchers had recently been allowed to throw overhand, and batters were no longer allowed to request high or low pitches. Pitchers were not allowed to turn their backs to the batter and a running start was no longer permitted. The distance from which pitchers delivered the ball was being lengthened periodically in an effort to bring about more hitting.

NOW

Since 1893, pitchers have been restricted to a rubber 60' 6" from home plate.

They are required to keep a foot in contact with this rubber when releasing the ball with some allowances being made for the fact that this is almost impossible to do.

11

THEN

NL uniforms were drab and predictable. AA uniforms were made of silky fabric and were much more colorful. Uniforms did not contain names or numerals.

NOW

Today's uniforms still tend toward the drab in color and design with a few exceptions, most notably those of the Oakland A's who pioneered bright colors in the modern era. Teams have several uniform designs and sometimes wear "throwback" jerseys or other special outfits. This is because clubs have noticed that these can be sold for outrageous markups. Some teams put the player's name on his jersey, and all of them have numerals which identify the player. The classic vendor's cry, "you can't tell the player without a scorecard" is no longer true due to the oversized scoreboards which detail names and numerals and match them to a player's picture.

Uniforms from various teams and various eras may be seen in the Hall of Fame.

12

THEN

Baseball journalism is almost as old as baseball, and no one newspaperman was as important as English-born Brooklyn resident Henry Chadwick. (HOF) Newspapers carried accounts of every major league game, and some newspapers, like *The Clipper* and *The Sporting News* made baseball one of their most important features. Chadwick, sometimes known as the Father of Baseball, occupied a unique place in writing about the history of the game as well as its day to day development. He edited the annual *Spalding Guide*, a review of each season.

NOW

Newspapers still cover baseball in detail. Extensive statistical coverage has been a feature of daily newspapers for some time. Cable television brings the ESPN family of networks and the MLB network provides 24 hour coverage of the sport. No one journalist influences the game the way Chadwick did. There are other journalists in the Hall of Fame, but they are in a special wing for writers or broadcasters.

13

THEN

Scorecards were beginning to play a role in the game, and some fans used Chadwick's scoring system to keep a record of all occurrences in a game.

NOW

Scorecards are sold at every major league park, although some note that the custom of keeping score at a game is declining. Some of those who keep score do it in their own book because large electronic scoreboards take away the necessity of keeping a list of which numeral represents which player. Scorecards from important games may be seen in the Hall of Fame.

14

THEN

Some players, such as Buck Ewing, were making as much as $5000 a year. This was considerably more than players had made in the previous decade, probably because the AA had created more competition. Since 1883 the NL and the AA had a National Agreement to respect each other's contracts, so there were no bidding wars.

NOW

Even allowing for inflation, players today are paid considerably more. As of this writing, Alex Rodriguez makes over $30 million a year. The minimum in 2010 was $400,000, and the average salary is well over $3million a year. Salaries grew rapidly after court decisions in the 1970s allowed players to enter free agency. This was, in turn, a result of the players forming a strong union in the 1960s under the direction of Marvin Miller.

15

THEN

There was no draft of players; however, when a player signed with a team, the reserve clause could be renewed throughout his playing career, even if the team he was on disbanded. The reserve clause was strengthened by blacklisting.

NOW

Amateur baseball players throughout the United States are entered into a draft every June. After a team drafts and signs a player, he usually begins in the rookie leagues where wages are low, although some players receive large signing bonuses. The draft was designed to keep salaries low. Another kind of draft takes place in fantasy baseball leagues where fans with too much time on their hands select players in an effort to predict statistical outcomes.

16

THEN

Home runs were relatively rare and were often the result of swift base running. When there were fences, balls hit over them on the bounce or on the fly were usually home runs unless ground rules said differently. In some cases, a ball hit into a body of water or a group of spectators was a ground rule double.

NOW

Home runs are almost always the result of balls going over the fence, either directly or by bouncing off of Jose Canseco's head. Balls which bounce into the stands are now ruled to be doubles. Home runs are an important part of every team's offense, and hitters who hit the most home runs are often the most celebrated. Increases in home runs have been attributed to springier baseballs, improved strength and conditioning, use of performance-enhancing substances, smaller parks and poorer pitching.

17

THEN

Most teams refused to pay injured players, just as most employers refused to pay injured workers. A number of pieces of equipment to prevent injury were being developed, especially for catchers. These included padded mitts, breast protectors made of cork and masks referred to as bird cages. Sliding pads and sliding gloves were being used by some players. Fielders were beginning to wear fingerless gloves, and even pitchers were using gloves on the non-throwing hand. Some say Cannonball Crane was the first pitcher to do so. Although gloves improved fielding, some players still refused to wear them.

NOW

Catchers equipment has evolved to include shin guards, and the mask is now more of a helmet, protecting the back of the head. More importantly, batters wear helmets, reducing severe head injuries from pitched balls. Some batters wear shin guards to protect against balls fouled downwards and armor on their elbows to absorb the pain from being hit by pitches. Gloves have steadily increased in size and efficiency. Equipment from various eras may be seen in the Hall of Fame.

18

THEN

"Casey at the Bat" had been published the year before. In August of 1888 members of the White Stockings and the Giants attended a baseball night at Wallack's Theater for a musical entitled Prince Methusalem. General William Tecumseh Sherman was among those in attencance. In addition to altering lyrics to provide a baseball theme, DeWolf Hopper recited "Casey at the Bat" for the first of 10,000 times. Mike Kelly attempted to recite the poem for the Elks Club, but his memory failed him.

NOW

"Casey" remains one of America's best loved and most often recited poems.

The poem has been honored with a Disney cartoon, a postage stamp and a statue representing Casey at the Hall of Fame.

19
THEN

Occasional spontaneous singing was not unheard of at ballparks at this time. A fan like Katie Casey may well have composed a song to encourage her favorite players.

NOW

Today singing the chorus of "Take me Out to the Ballgame is common between halves of the seventh inning. The song was written in 1908 by two Tin Pan Alley composers who had never attended a baseball game. The hundredth anniversary of the song's composition was honored with an exhibition at the Hall of Fame. Singing the first verse of Francis Scott Key's "The Star-Spangled Banner" is obligatory before all games. Some listeners think its concluding words are "Play Ball."

20
THEN

Players sometimes held out for more money, but the agreement between leagues included the upper level minor leagues, and players were rarely successful holding out. Most players eventually accepted the salaries offered.

NOW

Players still hold out, but they are bound to a team for the first three years of major league service. Before the third year they are eligible for salary arbitration in which they propose a sum and the owners counter with one. An arbitration board chooses one or the other. Salaries awarded are a function of the salaries of comparable players, some of which have been decided by free agency. Few major league players complain of being under-compensated, and those who do receive little sympathy. One unfortunate side effect of this system is that salaries are based on flawed statistical measurements, often encouraging behavior contrary to a team's best interests.

21
THEN

Players were beginning to see a strike as a possible solution to their problems. The Browns reacted to unreasonable fines, and the Louisville Colonels complained of fines and missed paychecks. The Brotherhood was reluctant to call itself a union, but it was beginning to function as one.

NOW

Players belong to a union, and, as of this writing, they have struck eight times, the longest of which was in 1994-5. The strikes were hugely unpopular with the fans and the media, but the players won or retained significant concessions and advances.

22
THEN

Batting averages were widely reported, but they were somewhat confusing because newspapers carried different accounts of scorers' decisions. The official scorer was anonymous, often connected with the home team. Frank Brunell published an article accusing the Chicago scorekeeper of unduly favoring Anson. In 1887 walks were counted as hits, which meant that batting averages rose considerably that year. Subsequent generations have adjusted the averages from that year downward.

NOW

Official scorers are members of the Baseball Writers' Association of America, the same organization which votes for inclusion in the Hall of Fame. Their names are public. There are still accusations of favoritism toward the home team, but it is less blatant. Interestingly, whether an event is ruled a hit or an error has no influence on the outcome of the game. Such decisions may safely be ignored. Hugh Duffy hit .440 the year the mound was moved back to the present 60'6". Some recognize this as the highest batting average ever, but it is a record that is rarely discussed because of the refusal of most fans to recognize events happening before the arbitrarily chosen year of 1900.

23
THEN

Players, even catchers, usually played without any protection for their genital area, although this was starting to change.

NOW

Most players use some sort of protective cup enclosed in a jock strap. By extension, players in all sports are often called jocks, a common metonymy.

24
THEN

Smoking was permitted everywhere in the old wooden ballparks. Cigars were the most common form of smoking, although cigarettes were starting to become popular.

NOW

Most baseball stadiums either forbid smoking or confine it to a specific area. This reflects change in societal attitudes or new laws, not just a change in baseball.

25

THEN

Ball parks were built with funds provided by the baseball club. No one could imagine a state or municipality providing a venue for a private business.

NOW

Baseball stadiums are often built at state or local expense, sometimes under a threat that the team will re-locate, as was done on the South Side of Chicago where state funds built the current ball park. One reason for the building of new parks is the inclusion of sky boxes which enable teams to sell the worst seats to corporations and other entities with too much money. Some municipalities build stadiums in the hope of luring another city's franchise or an expansion team, as was done in Florida. Even when a team uses its own funds, as in New York, the government is expected to provide infrastructure. In Texas eminent domain was used to condemn extensive property for a baseball stadium in Arlington, a deal guided by co-owner George W. Bush, later elected president of the United States.

26

THEN

Baseballs weighed between 5 and 5 1/4 oz. with a diameter between 9 and 9 1/4 inches. A cork or rubber center was surrounded by string and covered with horsehide.

NOW

The dimensions have remained the same, but cowhide is now used. Some baseballs have become the object of cult worship and are sold at great expense. Baseballs from so-called historic events, such as a Hank Aaron's 715th home run, are displayed in the Hall of Fame.

27

THEN

As a marketing device, bats were beginning to be named after the player who used them. The bats were made of ash.

NOW

Some bats are still made of ash, but major league players are beginning to prefer maple, even though it shatters more easily creating a hazard for players and bystanders. Amateur baseball has begun to use aluminum bats which break much less, but which create a hazard for players because the ball comes off the bat more quickly. Unlike balls, there are substantial differences between bats. Many bats are now on display in the Hall of Fame.

28

THEN

The sale of beer or any alcoholic beverages was forbidden by NL rules. The AA permitted such sales which is why it was known as "The Beer and Whiskey League." A movement to prohibit the sale of all alcohol in the society at large was gaining strength.

NOW

Beer is sold at all major league parks, even in Toronto. Some teams have family areas where alcohol sales are prohibited, but all clubs depend on selling beer as part of their revenue stream. More importantly, radio and television income makes up a large share of team income, and beer advertising makes up a large share of this. Active players may not endorse a brand of beer, but retired players often peddle beer, especially Miller Lite.

29

THEN

Statues of players were rare, but St, Louis Browns owner Chris Von der Ahe had a statue of himself placed outside his ball park.

NOW

Many teams erect statues of former stars. For example, the Chicago Cubs have a statue of Ernie Banks (HOF) outside Wrigley Field.

30

THEN

Players were sold from team to team without their consent. Some of the players were beginning to demand a share of the money from such sales.

NOW

Players are still sometimes sold or traded between clubs without their consent. Some players have no-trade clauses in their contracts and such clauses become automatic for a player with ten years seniority in the majors and five years with the same team. Players often waive such clauses for financial considerations or because they want to be traded.

31

THEN

Few measures were taken for security. Owners expected local police to provide protection.

NOW

All teams employ professional security, usually provided by off-duty police. Field invasion is rare except for an occasional drunk or exhibitionist, and it is dealt with quickly. Forfeits due to riots are infrequent, except for Nickel Beer Night in Cleveland and Disco Demolition Night in Chicago.

32

THEN

No one was married at home plate, and to request such a thing would have been odd.

NOW

Fans occasionally are married in the ball park, but much more common is the custom of proposing through an announcement on the scoreboard. Jack proposes to Jill, and television cameras focus on Jill's gleeful acceptance. Presumably Jill is free to change her mind at a later date.

33

THEN

Players associated with gamblers openly. Pool halls or taverns where bets were taken were not off limits. Players and managers were known to bet on their own team.

NOW

Regulations against betting on baseball are strictly enforced. Players are not allowed to bet on their own team or any others. It is against the rules for active players to associate with known gamblers. This policy came when it was discovered that seven White Sox players had conspired with gamblers to throw games in the 1919 World Series. They were banned from baseball for life. (An eighth player was banned for having knowledge of the fix.) Joe Jackson, one of the best players of his era, is not in the Hall of Fame because of this. Team owner Charlie Comiskey also knew of the fix and chose to keep it secret. Pete Rose, the major leaguer with the most hits for a career, is not in the Hall of Fame because of betting on his own team and lying about it later. Some fans believe Jackson and Rose should be in the Hall of Fame. Others believe that Comiskey shouldn't be there.

34

THEN

There was only one umpire for each game except for special occasions such as the World's Championship Series or late-season games between pennant contenders.

The Players League required two umpires at each game. Projectiles were frequently thrown at umpires. There was a rule against arguing with umpires, but it was ignored.

NOW

There are four umpires at every major league game except when illness or injury occurs. For post-season games there are six umpires. Ball parks have banned glass bottles, making umpires somewhat safer. There is still a rule against arguing with umpires, and it is still ignored. As of this writing, umpires are allowed to use television replays on home run decisions, and some fans and announcers advocate extension of this to other plays. Presumably they feel that the games are not long enough.

35
THEN

Some owners were capitalists looking for a quick profit in a game that they did not understand, but others, like Spalding, were former players. Of the players mentioned in this book, Comiskey, Mack and McAleer went on to own major league teams in Chicago, Philadelphia and Boston respectively.

NOW

In spite of the small fortunes paid to players, none has gone on to own a franchise. Today teams are owned by extraordinarily rich individuals, groups of rich individuals or corporations. A player like Nolan Ryan may be the face of an ownership group, but the days of a player becoming an owner seem to be over.

36
THEN

Tragic early deaths from alcohol and other causes were relatively common among players. Crane, Kelly, Fogarty, Delahanty, and Williamson all died young, and at least some reports blamed alcoholism.

NOW

Players are less likely to die from excessive drinking, or, if they do, it is not reported as such.

37
THEN

Teams were just beginning to use pitching rotations consisting of between two and four starting pitchers. Because only one substitute was permitted per game, (starting in 1889) a pitcher who became ineffective traded places with a position player who finished the game.

NOW

Almost all teams rotate five starting pitchers who rarely finish the game. Relief pitchers come in at various points, usually beginning in the sixth inning unless the starter has been very ineffective. This might be related to the scoring rule that will not award a "win" to starters who pitch fewer than five innings. Relief pitchers are specialized, some being used to pitch to one left-handed batter. The task of finishing the game is customarily awarded to a pitcher designated as "the closer." Because Jerome Holtzman invented the statistic called the "save," such pitchers are valued more than others and tend to be jealous and protective of their role. When more than one pitcher is given such an opportunity, the situation is referred to, not without scorn, as "closer by committee." Holtzman eventually repented for having invented another category for players to fight about, but the damage had been done.

38
THEN

Owners sometimes threw benefits for players, inviting the cranks to supplement the players' salaries.

NOW

With the salaries players are currently paid, it is rare for such benefits to be held. Most extra fundraising events are given for the sake of club-sponsored charities such as the Jimmy Fund in Boston.

39
THEN

Multi-year contracts were rare before the PL began. During the 1890 season, the NL signed a number of players to long term contracts, and the PL gave three year contracts as a matter of policy.

NOW

Players sign contracts for as long as ten years. Clubs sometimes sign a player to a long-term contract just before he is eligible for free agency.

40
THEN

Young boys collected pictures of players, sometimes enclosed in cigarette packages. Larger cards, called cabinet cards, were awarded as an incentive to smoke more.

NOW

Trading cards continue to portray baseball players, although they are now in competition with other sports, movies, Pokemon and numerous other things. Bubble gum is the most common accompaniment. Adults are frequently the collectors of such cards, and their sale and re-sale has become an industry of sorts. Men of a certain generation regret that their mothers threw out collections which would now be valuable. Few realize that it was only throwing out most of these cards that made those that were left valuable.

41

THEN

Pitchers were still expected to do their share of hitting, but it was already becoming apparent that selecting players for their pitching ability made them less likely to be proficient hitters. The idea that pitchers should not have to bat was being floated. John McGraw, (HOF) a rookie in 1890, was one of the early advocates of such a system.

NOW

In the AL pitchers only bat in extremely rare circumstances. A designated hitter (DH) substitutes for the pitcher. In the NL the pitcher continues to bat unless a pinch hitter substitutes for him. Inter-league play makes the difference between the two rules a problem, which has been solved by following the rule of the home team's league. The principal advantage for AL fans is that they no longer have to see their pitcher walk the other team's pitcher. Most NL fans, such as the unbearably smug Cub fan George Will, believe passionately that their system is superior. Arguments about whether a DH should be included in the Hall of Fame are common.

42

THEN

The PL was attempting to base a larger share of player compensation on team success. This was based on the assumption that the team would make a profit after salaries and other expenses.

NOW

Although there is some bonus money based on participation in the World Series and finishing high in the standings, this has become a smaller share of total compensation, mostly because of the rapid growth of salaries. Salaries are based on seniority and admittedly flawed statistical measurements. Players are sometimes thought to have more incentive to increase their individual statistics than to have the team win.

43

THEN

Baseball was flourishing in Cuba, especially in the Havana area. Fans of different teams were enthusiastic and willing to pay to see their favorite stars. Cuban teams sometimes beat major leaguers who traveled to the island. Rules were slightly different, most notably the use of a tenth player. Although Cuban players were not kept out of major league baseball, only a few came to the U.S. before 1947.

NOW

Latinos make up an increasing proportion of major league players. The government of Cuba forbids its players to play in professional baseball leagues, but some players, such as Jose Contreras (El Titan de Bronce) have defected to the United States. Contreras received his nickname from Fidel Castro, who, contrary to widespread reports, was not a professional quality player. Cuban teams have won a number of international contests, and their teams have been competitive against professionals in the World Baseball Classic. The Dominican Republic has produced the most major league players per capita, especially from the town of San Pedro de Macoris.

44

THEN

Scandals involving players were covered gleefully by a segment of the popular press, but conventions of the day made such coverage somewhat circumspect. Extramarital affairs were rarely reported.

NOW

When Alex Rodriguez stepped out on his wife with a dancer, the tabloid press covered the situation extensively, and the mainstream newspapers, television networks and Internet sources ran pictures. Rodriguez's relationship with Madonna also attracted a good deal of attention. Occasionally a player's ex-wife like Cyndy Garvey might write a book detailing the player's adultery and other misconduct. As of this writing, there have been no reports of homosexual activity among current players, but this is probably a matter of time.

45

THEN

Schedules for the AA, NL and the PL were all set at 140 games, with each team playing each of its rivals 20 times. Teams played fewer games because of the difficulties in scheduling makeup games for contests canceled for rain or darkness. Championships were decided by the percentage of games won.

NOW

All teams in the NL and AL schedule 162 games, and canceled games are usually made up. When games affect the championship, they are always made up. AL teams play 18 interleague games, and NL teams play a maximum of 18. (There are 14 AL teams and 16 NL teams, both divided into three divisions.) All teams play 15-19 games against teams within their own division and 6-10 games with teams that are in the same league, but not their division.

46
THEN

Brooklyn and New York competed in a regular season major league game for the first time in 1890, and this became the most heated rivalry immediately. They were separate cities at the time.

NOW

The rivalry between the Dodgers and the Giants continued when the teams moved to Los Angeles and San Francisco, but now the most intense fan rivalry is said to be the one between the Boston Red Sox and the New York Yankees, whose territory overlap each other. Announcers sometimes call this the biggest rivalry in world sports. Presumably they have never attended a game between the Glasgow Rangers and Celtic.

47
THEN

Players were rarely reported to have had affairs with other players' wives, although some suspicion surrounded the relations of John Clarkson's wife.

NOW

There have been occasional incidents of players having conflict over affairs between teammates and the wives of teammates. The mostly widely reported concerned Mike Kekich and Fritz Peterson, friends and teammates who traded wives in the 1970's. Peterson is still married to Kekich's ex-wife as of this writing.

48
THEN

Attendance of 10,000 at a major league game was considered extraordinary. Exact figures were not always available and when available were not reliable, especially for the 1890 season.

NOW

As of 2010 some teams averaged over 46,000 paid admissions per game. The lowest average for any team was still over 17,000. Attendance is now reported on the basis of tickets sold, and it is generally considered to be accurate. In the past clubs were accused of reporting inflated attendance figures, but it is hard to imagine why a team would want to report more income than they have with current tax policy.

49

THEN

Ward's book *Base Ball* was prominent as an instruction manual and as a history of the game.

NOW

Many consider *The Glory of Their Times* to be the greatest book ever written about baseball, as well as a groundbreaking use of the technique of oral history, as acknowledged by Studs Terkel. It is really a book about old men looking back at their youth, and many of the players, particularly Sam Crawford, remember Dummy (sic) Hoy as one of the best of their era.

50

THEN

Divorce was rare but not unheard of in this era. Arlie Latham's divorce proceedings involved reports of wife-beating and brothel-based adultery. Grounds for divorce were very restricted.

NOW

Divorce is much more common in the society at large, and baseball players' marriages are even more likely to end in divorce, for whatever reasons. No fault divorce laws have made court proceedings less interesting, but details still reach the press.

51

THEN

The Home Plate Saloon has been called the nation's first sports bar. The walls were covered with pictures of players, particularly New York Giants. Players were known to mix with fans. Some bars were connected to the telegraph and reported inning to inning scores.

NOW

Today's sports bars feature televisions in every corner showing plays and replays from every angle. It is less common to see players mingling with fans in many of these venues.

52
THEN

Except in rare cases, managers were no longer active players by 1964. Every year two major league teams competed in an exhibition game known as the Hall of Fame game on Abner Doubleday field as part of the ceremonies during the week Hall of Famers were inducted.

NOW

As of this writing, there are no playing managers. The Hall of Fame game is no longer played because of a policy against major league exhibition games during the season.

53
THEN

The St. Louis term fan had long ago replaced crank as the most common word used for baseball enthusiasts. Most fans were men, and many wore coats and ties to games.

NOW

Coats and ties are rarely seen at games today. Fans often wear tee shirts or jerseys with the insignias of their favorite team, usually, although not always, the home team.

54
THEN

Players salaries ranged from a minimum of $6000 to approximately $100,000 for the best paid. Signing bonuses of $100,000 were not unheard of, but rules requiring such players to be on the active major league roster discouraged these. Owners were planning to institute a major league draft to guard against such extravagance. Increases in player compensation had roughly mirrored or fallen behind the rate of inflation, but the minimum had not been increased between 1948 and 1964.

Players of this era were said to be inferior to players from the Golden Age of Baseball in the 1920s and 1930s.

NOW

As of this writing, the minimum salary is over $400,000 per year. The player draft has not eliminated signing bonuses, which are sometimes in the millions for players projected to be stars. Other players sign for little or no bonus money and are paid very poorly in the minor leagues. It is not uncommon in the minor leagues to see millionaires outperformed by players making a few thousand a month or less.

Today's players, although admittedly bigger, faster and stronger, are considered inferior to stars from the 1960s. The players from the era in which the fan discovered baseball, whether the 1860s, the 1880s, the 1920s, the 1950s the 1990s or the 2000s, are always better than current players in the judgment of fans. This is not surprising, because it is a well-known fact that the fan's own level of skill in his youth increases as he or she ages.

www.ingramcontent.com/pod-product-compliance
Lightning Source LLC
Chambersburg PA
CBHW031053020726
47495CB00007B/1852